A FOREVER HOME AT HONEY BEE CROFT

JESSICA REDLAND

Boldwood

First published in Great Britain in 2025 by Boldwood Books Ltd.

Copyright © Jessica Redland, 2025

Cover Design by Lizzie Gardiner

Cover Images: Adobe Stock and Shutterstock

The moral right of Jessica Redland to be identified as the author of this work has been asserted in accordance with the Copyright, Designs and Patents Act 1988.

Every effort has been made to obtain the necessary permissions with reference to copyright material, both illustrative and quoted. We apologise for any omissions in this respect and will be pleased to make the appropriate acknowledgements in any future edition.

A CIP catalogue record for this book is available from the British Library.

Paperback ISBN 978-1-83518-300-7

Large Print ISBN 978-1-83518-301-4

Hardback ISBN 978-1-83518-299-4

Ebook ISBN 978-1-83518-302-1

Kindle ISBN 978-1-83518-303-8

Audio CD ISBN 978-1-83518-294-9

MP3 CD ISBN 978-1-83518-295-6

Digital audio download ISBN 978-1-83518-298-7

This book is printed on certified sustainable paper. Boldwood Books is dedicated to putting sustainability at the heart of our business. For more information please visit https://www.boldwoodbooks.com/about-us/sustainability/

Boldwood Books Ltd, 23 Bowerdean Street, London, SW6 3TN

www.boldwoodbooks.com

To Ashleigh Brooke, my very own little Swiftie. I say little but you're way taller than me (not difficult) and I can't believe that, by the time this book is published, you'll officially be an adult. Where have those eighteen years gone? With all my love, always xx

1

JOEL

'It's all yours,' Chris said, logging off the shared PC after our shift change handover. He stood up and pulled on his jacket. 'Any news about the job yet?'

I shook my head. 'Hoping no news doesn't mean bad news.'

'Got everything crossed for you. Have a good one.'

As he closed the door to the small office which the shift managers and engineering managers shared, I plonked myself down in the swivel chair he'd vacated and logged on for the last of three twelve-hour day shifts.

The wait for news was driving me mad and nobody seemed to know what the delay was – or they weren't telling me if they did. I was one of four shift managers at Claybridge Fresh Foods – a factory specialising in bacon and pork products on the outskirts of the North Yorkshire market town of Claybridge – and I'd been interviewed a few weeks back for the role of production manager.

Three years ago, I'd been interviewed for the same job and I don't think anyone in the history of being interviewed has ever made a bigger mess of the process. The outgoing production manager, Roger, had championed me at the application stage and

I'd put in stacks of preparation, determined not to let him down, but I'd let the pressure get to me. Leaving my notes at home on interview day had been a bad start and, even though my best mate Barney had managed to calm me down after I panic-called him, nobody could help me in the interview itself. Dry mouth, shaking hands, blank mind. I sat there looking at the thick script in front of each member of the interview panel thinking *Don't turn the page and ask me another question. We all know it's a definite no, so can one of you please show some mercy and end this torture?* But they continued to plough through the questions and I continued to stumble over my words, the facts and figures I'd so carefully prepared completely evading me.

'There'll be other opportunities,' our HR Director, Eloise, had said after confirming the only outcome possible – that I hadn't got the job.

I'd nodded and apologised for wasting her time.

'You didn't waste anyone's time, Joel,' she reassured me. 'You were a strong candidate and we were all rooting for you. What would you say to some coaching from me so you can perform at your best next time there's a vacancy?'

'The questions weren't the problem. It was the nerves.'

'I can coach you on that too.'

So she did, although neither of us expected the same role to come up so soon. Jeremy Dunn – the external candidate who'd secured the position – needed to relocate back down south due to a change in family circumstances. Thanks to a combination of Eloise's coaching and some amazing opportunities that Jeremy had given me during his tenure to further develop my skills, my interview this time couldn't have been more different. Calm, confident and articulate with stronger examples than before, I couldn't have performed better. I knew I was up against tough competition but the factory manager, Mack, had also championed me for the position, which had to stand for something.

If only they'd hurry up with their decision because I felt like my life was on hold until they did. It wasn't just about the promotion or the increased salary, although both would be nice. The reason I really wanted the job was so that I could spend more time with my eight-year-old daughter, Imogen.

I'd met her mum, Tilly, a decade ago when she'd temporarily joined the reception team at the factory. A couple of months later, we started seeing each other and were engaged within a year. We hadn't planned to start a family until after we were married so Imogen was a surprise, but an amazing one. We'd talked about expanding our family after the wedding, but then Tilly dropped her bombshell. One Saturday morning, exactly a fortnight before our wedding, she handed me a mug of tea, a plate of toast, and casually told me she was leaving. *I'm really sorry, Joel, but I can't do this. The whole marriage and kids thing isn't for me.* Despite us already having a two-year-old!

Turned out that marriage and kids *were* for her – just not with me. That night she went out with her friends *to celebrate being free* – her exact words to me later – and bumped into Greg, who'd been her boyfriend from age fourteen to sixteen. She'd spoken fondly of him when we'd been together but it was a shock to hear that he was *the one that got away* and that I'd never quite compared. He'd asked her out that night, proposed on their one-month anniversary and less than a year later, they said *I do*. Greg was divorced with a son two years older than Imogen and, over the next couple of years, two more children joined their blended family and I was left licking my wounds, wondering how I could have believed we were happy when clearly one of us wasn't.

You'd think I was the one who'd ripped Tilly's heart out from the way she'd treated me ever since. I often wondered what had happened to the kind-hearted, bubbly woman I'd fallen for because I struggled to recognise her in the woman constantly putting up barriers in my relationship with our daughter, the biggest one being my job. According to Tilly, my shifts were *disruptive to Imogen and to family life*, so she'd repeatedly pushed back against my requests to produce a formal schedule around them. I'd spent a small fortune on solicitor fees over the years – money that could have been put aside for Imogen's future – before I had to accept it was getting me nowhere. Every time my solicitor made contact with Tilly's, the response was a proposal for shared custody on set days each week, when Tilly knew full well that I was unable to commit to that due to a rotating shift pattern. I therefore only saw Imogen on an ad hoc basis, which broke my heart. That little girl was the best thing that had ever happened to me and I hated that some weeks could pass with me only seeing her for a few precious hours between school and bed or, even worse, not seeing her at all. Those weeks felt so bleak.

I could have applied for a court order, but I hadn't wanted to go down that route. Tilly and I had a just-about-tolerable relationship, so why escalate that into something hostile and risk dragging Imogen into it? And what would it do to her if she knew her parents were fighting over her in court?

If I landed the production manager job, I'd be working regular hours Monday to Friday. With the barrier of my shifts gone, Tilly would hopefully agree to a parent plan where I saw Imogen on regular days each week. I wasn't expecting her to spend half the week with me as I recognised that Imogen had friends who she'd want to play with and a couple of after-school clubs, but surely a couple of nights a week and every other weekend wasn't too much to ask.

But what if I didn't get the job? I'd spent the past few weeks imagining all the things Imogen and I could do together. I could teach her to cook, like my dad had taught me, I could take her to the riding lessons she longed for and to gymnastics. We could also enjoy just being together – how it *should* be. I *had* to get the job. Because we couldn't continue like this. This wasn't the kind of dad I wanted to be or that Imogen deserved.

* * *

'I still don't know how you can drink that.' I handed Sal – the engineering manager who worked the same shift as me – a mug of strong black tea four hours into our shift.

'And I don't know how you can drink that stuff,' she said, pulling a playful scowl at my coffee. 'Can't stand the smell or taste.'

The phone rang and she grabbed it. 'Managers' office... yeah, he's here.' She glanced up at me. 'Ten minutes? I'll tell him.'

I looked at her expectantly when she hung up.

'That was the new lass in HR. Can you go to Jeremy's office to see him and Eloise in ten minutes?' She grinned at me. 'About time too!'

I ran my hand across my chin, nerves tingling. 'This must be it!'

'Unless you've done something naughty that you haven't told me about,' she said, making me laugh. 'Look, whatever happens, you know you gave it your best shot and that we all believe in you.'

'Thanks, Sal. At least they've timed it on my last day on. Two days off to get my head together if it's bad news.'

'It won't be.' She held up both hands, fingers crossed.

Ten minutes later, I stood outside Jeremy's office and took a deep breath. The door was closed but I could see through the slanted blinds that Eloise was in there and they were sitting at the round table in the corner of the room engaged in what looked like a serious conversation. I took another deep breath and knocked.

When Eloise opened the door, my stomach lurched. She was usually all smiles, but she did not look happy today.

'Come in, Joel,' she said, indicating that I should join them at the table.

Jeremy looked up from a pile of papers and nodded his greeting to me. He was a great boss – really friendly and supportive – but he was one of those people who hardly ever smiled, so I couldn't read anything from his expression.

'We're sorry it's taken so long to come back to you,' Eloise said. 'We have some news, but I'm afraid it's not what you'll have been hoping for.'

My stomach sank. Clearly I hadn't got the job, which meant I wouldn't be free to spend more time with Imogen.

'There's been an unexpected development,' Jeremy said.

He and Eloise exchanged looks and he nodded.

'This is confidential at the moment,' Eloise told me. 'There'll be a formal announcement to all staff at one o'clock today, but Mack wanted you to know first out of courtesy and respect.'

'We've been taken over,' Jeremy said.

My mouth dropped open. I hadn't been expecting that. 'Who by?'

'Bramblecote Country Foods.'

Bramblecote had their origins in West Yorkshire but had embarked on a major expansion programme over the past decade, gobbling up smaller food manufacturers to increase their product range. I'd always assumed that Claybridge Fresh Foods would be too big for them but presumably their recent successful growth had provided the kind of capital they needed for a takeover bid.

'It came as a shock to us too,' Eloise said, as though reading my mind. 'We've been instructed to put a freeze on all recruitment – even internal moves – and have been advised that they're sending one of their production managers here a week on Monday to begin a handover with Jeremy. He'll be here for at least a year while they implement some changes, which means—'

'That there's going to be at least a year's hold on the position,' I finished. 'Or possibly no position at all.' Either way, I was stuffed. I felt as though I'd missed out on so much with Imogen already. No way could I wait another year.

'I'm so sorry, Joel,' Eloise said. 'This isn't the news either of us were wanting to give you today.'

'Are there going to be redundancies?' I asked.

'We don't know,' they said together.

'And what about the off-record answer?'

Jeremy shrugged. 'I've seen lots of takeovers and mergers in my time and all of them included redundancies.'

'Same here,' Eloise said. 'When or who is anyone's guess and let's be clear that it *is* only a guess at this point. Mack wanted to tell you himself, but he's been whisked away so he asked us to do it.'

It was good of Mack to ask them to give me the heads up. Everyone knew I'd applied for the job, and it would have been humiliating discovering that I hadn't got it at the same time as my peers and my team.

'I'm sure you have loads of questions,' Eloise continued, 'and I wish I could say we have answers but, right now, you know as much as Jeremy and me.'

Jeremy shuffling some papers was my cue to leave. I slowly pushed my chair back, feeling weary with disappointment.

'Thanks for your time,' I said instead, fighting to keep the frustration out of my voice. This was hardly their doing and I could imagine they were both feeling bad enough without me creating a fuss. 'I won't say anything to Sal about what's coming at one.'

Eloise fixed sad eyes on me and mouthed *thank you*.

I was about to pull the door open, but I dropped my hand to my side and faced them both. 'If Bramblecote hadn't come along, would I have got the job?'

'We thought you might ask that,' Jeremy said. 'Yes, you would. You were head and shoulders above the rest. I wish...' He sighed. 'I'm sorry, Joel.'

I thanked them again and left. Unable to face returning to the office and Sal's eager expression just yet, I headed through reception towards the exit. As soon as the second set of doors opened, the cold air wrapped round me and took my breath away. We were five days into March and, while the Midlands and south had been enjoying a recent warm spell, it was big-coat weather in the north.

The smoking shack was empty. It wouldn't give me much relief from the cold but it might keep the wind off me. Somebody had left an empty can of drink on the ground and I gave it an almighty kick, showering fizzy orange over my trousers and boots. Great!

With a heavy sigh, I plonked myself down on the plastic bench, arms folded tightly across my chest. I'd considered the worst-case scenario of the job going to a stronger external candidate, but I could never have anticipated this outcome. And to think I *would* have got the job too! So near and yet so very far.

Running my hands into my hair, I tipped my head back and stared at the cobwebs wafting from the ceiling, cursing under my breath. This was so unfair!

The only tiny positive here was that I hadn't said anything to Tilly about being interviewed. Or to Imogen. The only person whose hopes were dashed were mine. Again. And not only had I not secured a day job, I could be out of work altogether. My stomach churned at that thought. I'd started my first job aged twelve, pot washing in the restaurant owned by my dad and Uncle Alvin, and had worked ever since. The prospect of redundancy made me feel sick, as did the thought of Tilly's reaction.

I closed my eyes and fought hard to block out the voice of doom. There might not even be any redundancies and, if there were, they might not directly affect me, so there was no value in me getting worked up about it. Besides, there was a much bigger issue here – what was I going to do about Imogen? Taking over from Jeremy was meant to be the solution to spending more time with her and that had been taken from me. I needed to find a new solution, but what?

2

JOEL

The one o'clock announcement hadn't gone down well with my team or anyone else at Claybridge Fresh Foods. I spent the rest of the shift fielding questions and hated that I couldn't offer anything other than what Eloise and Jeremy had told me earlier – *you know as much as I do.*

Half an hour after the shift ended, my mood dipped even further as I pulled up to my house on the outskirts of Reddfield in East Yorkshire. Chez's rusting old banger was on the drive and there were lights on in the house which could only mean one thing – he'd broken up with Lorna yet again, he needed a place to stay and had moved himself back into my place without asking me if it was okay to do so.

There were fourteen and a half years between me and my nineteen-year-old brother Chester, although I sometimes felt more like a parent than a brother to him, giving him a place to stay, feeding him and occasionally lending him some cash to tide him over to payday – money which never got repaid.

Our parents had sold the family home and emigrated to Portugal a couple of months before Chez's seventeenth birthday, and he'd moved in with me at the time. Emigrating had always been their dream, but it had happened several years sooner than expected after Uncle Alvin collapsed at the restaurant – mild heart attack – and the brothers decided it was time to call it a day before Dad went the same way. The move had absolutely been the right thing for my parents as they'd both needed to slow down. The warmer climate was also so much kinder on Mum's arthritis.

Chez had struggled with depression since hitting his teens and our parents would never have left if they'd thought he was still in a bad place, but a combination of leaving education, securing an apprenticeship as a car mechanic and professional treatment had had a positive impact on him. I could clearly see how his CBT – cognitive behavioural therapy – had helped move his mindset away from always focusing on the negatives and going on a downward spiral every time depression took hold.

The thing that didn't help was Chez's relationship with Lorna. She'd been his on-off girlfriend since they were fifteen and, despite four years together, she still struggled with his depression. When it was heightened, she took it personally, thinking Chez was in a bad mood with her. Her hot temper and speak-now-think-later approach had led to the end more times than I could remember, but they always gravitated back to each other. I wished they wouldn't. I liked Lorna, but I worried for the toll that each break-up took on my brother and couldn't help thinking they might be better off calling it a day once and for all.

I parked in front of the house and switched off the engine, but I stayed where I was. After the day I'd had, all I really wanted to do was take a hot shower, crack open a beer, heat up a casserole and sink onto the sofa in front of a film. But now Chez was back, so I'd need to be strong for him while he offloaded and sound positive and upbeat while I heaped on the reassurance when, right now, I didn't feel any of those things.

In the porch, I picked up the post without glancing at it and stepped into the hall, cursing as I collided with several boxes dumped in the middle of the floor.

'Chez!' I called, keeping my tone light when I really wanted to shout at him for being so inconsiderate.

No answer. I picked my way through the bags and boxes and went into the lounge but there was no sign of him in there or the kitchen. Dumping the post on the kitchen worktop, I backtracked and stomped up the stairs towards the smallest bedroom which he used when he stayed with me. As I passed Imogen's bedroom, my ears pricked up at a low groan. Heart pounding, thinking Chez must be hurt or ill, I pushed open the door. But my brother was far from hurt and clearly he hadn't split up with Lorna. I dashed back onto the landing.

'You have thirty seconds to get dressed and out of my daughter's bedroom.' The volume and tone could have left them in no doubt about how disgusted I was with them.

Lorna squealed, Chez swore and I slammed the door and ran down the stairs, absolutely seething. Imogen's room? Imogen's bed? How could they? It was such a betrayal of trust.

My teeth ground as I unloaded the dishwasher with a lot of clattering of pots and slamming of cupboard doors. What a mug I was for staying in my car trying to push aside my crap day, preparing myself to be there for my brother and whatever had gone wrong for him, when all the while he was doing *that*!

'Lorna's gone,' Chez said, appearing in the kitchen doorway a little later wearing just his trunks and a T-shirt, his dark hair dishevelled.

'Good.'

'Sorry, bro.' But he didn't look sorry. He looked very pleased with himself, which inflamed me further.

'I hate it when you call me that,' I snapped, even though it didn't really bother me.

Chez held his hands up in a surrender position. 'Woah! Chill your beans.'

Being told to calm down had the opposite effect. 'You think this is funny?'

'I think your reaction's funny. Your face is nearly purple.'

'And you don't think that's justified? Using my bed would have been bad enough but using Imogen's? That's disgusting! Get upstairs, get her bed stripped and washed.'

'Oh, come on, Joel! We didn't even get to—'

'No details!' I shouted. 'Washing! Now!'

'You're not serious?'

'I'm *deadly* serious! She's staying tomorrow night so I want her bedding clean, dry and changed before then.'

'Jeez,' he muttered.

'And get your crap shifted out the hall too. I nearly broke my neck tripping over it.'

Without another word, Chez left and I swore under my breath. *Could have handled that a lot better.* But I'd been so mad at him for demonstrating such a lack of respect, especially when the bed in his room was made up. It was as though they'd been unable to contain themselves and had tumbled into the first bedroom they'd reached. Or they'd done it deliberately, thinking it would be a thrill. I hated that I'd yelled as there were better ways of expressing displeasure and that was the road I usually walked. If I hadn't had such a lousy day, I'd have been fuming and I'd have left Chez in no doubt as to how unimpressed I was, but I'd have delivered that message in a calm and considered way.

Chez reappeared with a bundle of bedding and shoved it in

the washing machine. I could feel his anger radiating towards me which was rich after what he'd done.

'Why are you here anyway?' I asked. 'I assumed you'd split up with Lorna but...' There was no need to finish that sentence.

He set the machine away and straightened up, glaring at me. 'Oh! So you're interested now?'

'Cut the sarcasm, Chez.'

He sighed. 'I've fallen out with Harry.'

I hadn't been expecting that. 'Why?'

'Because of Deana, the bi—'

'Chez!' I cried. 'Stop calling her that.'

'Well, she is.'

Shortly after Mum and Dad emigrated, Chez had decided he didn't want to live with me and moved in with his best mate. Harry's parents had bought the flat when he was young and rented it out, always intending for their son to move into it when he was ready to leave home. Chez paid him a nominal rent and they shared the bills. A year on, Lorna and Harry's girlfriend, Fern, had both moved in with the lads. I'd expected there to be tension but it worked surprisingly well, even when Chez and Lorna had one of their break-ups. Harry and Fern didn't take sides, and Chez and Lorna took it in turns to move out so it was all reasonably amicable. But then Harry and Fern split up last year and, over the summer, Harry's new girlfriend, Deana, who was four years older than the others, moved in. According to Chez, Deana was petty, unreasonable and completely took over, but Harry idolised her and went along with whatever she wanted. If that was true, I wasn't surprised it had caused tension between the lads, but I'd never thought it would lead to them actually falling out.

'I'm really sorry about you and Harry,' I said, my voice gentle, 'but that doesn't excuse what you did just now. You and Lorna were bang out of order.'

He at least had the decency to look shamefaced about it. 'Sorry. It won't happen again.'

'Damn right it won't.'

'So, erm... am I okay to stay here for a bit until Lorna and me find a place of our own?'

'You're looking for somewhere together?'

'Yeah.'

'Just the two of you?'

'Yeah.'

'And how will you afford the rent next time you split up?'

Chez glared at me, his jaw tight. 'Who says we're gonna split up?'

'You always do.'

'Thanks for the vote of confidence,' he muttered, shoving past me and storming upstairs.

I sank back against the worktop with a sigh. That hadn't gone well either, even if I'd only spoken the truth.

My eyes rested on the pile of post I'd dumped earlier and I flicked through it – pizza menu, credit card circular and... I ripped open the white linen envelope, removed the card and my heart sank as I scanned down the contents.

Save the Date
Nathan 'Snowy' Oakes & Zara Timmins
Saturday 16 October
Aversford Manor, East Yorkshire
Invitation to follow

I removed a spare pushpin from the cork noticeboard on the kitchen wall and stabbed it through the card, sighing as I pinned it alongside four other wedding invitations for this year and a save-the-date card for next. I hadn't been to a wedding in years and now I was going to six in the space of fourteen months. Six! It seemed like everyone I knew had met someone special and was settling down while I remained hopelessly single.

Zara was a good friend of mine but, if we hadn't both been so slow at acting on the attraction we felt towards each other when we first met, it might have become something more. Although even if it had, it probably wouldn't have lasted because I couldn't imagine anyone being more perfect for her than Snowy. Zara had once told me that she thought the pair of them had been destined to meet and, seeing them together over the past two years, I was inclined to agree. Was there someone out there who I was destined to meet? I hoped so. I was okay with being single most of the time but, on days like today, I missed returning home to a hug and some reassurance.

3

POPPY

I wasn't sure why I bothered setting an alarm anymore as I was always awake well before it sounded. That said, it served as a good reminder that I actually needed to rise and face the challenging day ahead when all I really wanted to do was hide under the duvet and wake up in the past where my daily 'challenges' were trivial.

My morning routine was always the same now – feeling the silence in the house screaming at me as I padded down the hallway to the bathroom. Glancing into my parents' empty bedroom and thinking how it would make more sense to have the larger room with the en suite, but knowing I'd never move in there. Remembering the happy days when the house was full of laughter, but recalling the tears more vividly. Some days those thoughts were fleeting, but sometimes they stopped me in my tracks. Like today. I sank back against the wall opposite their bedroom, my breath catching in my throat at the sight of the empty bed, an intense wave of loss pulling me down onto the carpet.

It had been five years since Mum died and eighteen months

since Dad moved into The Larks. During that time, I hadn't changed a single thing in the house despite me being the legal owner. I still expected to go downstairs and find them having breakfast together, a mug of coffee waiting for me. Would I ever get used to it being only me here?

I wrapped my arms round my legs for comfort and sat there for a while, trying to gather the strength to brave the day. Mum had a favourite quote from Eleanor Roosevelt, the first lady of the USA at the time Mum was born – *Do one thing every day that scares you.* She'd often said it to me when I was at school and afraid to step out of my comfort zone, and I'd found it opened doors and presented opportunities that would never have come my way if I hadn't faced my fears. It had become a mantra for a life well lived but it was now the soundtrack to my existence because getting up every day scared me. Visiting Dad at The Larks scared me. And knowing that, one day soon, I'd be the only remaining member of my small family absolutely terrified me.

* * *

As I left the house a little later, my next-door neighbour, Wilf, was returning from the village shop. He had his newspaper tucked under his arm and his Yorkshire terrier, Benji was trotting alongside him, his favourite soft toy pig wedged in his mouth.

'Morning, Wilf!' I called.

'Good morning, Poppy! Beautiful day.'

Our drives ran side by side, only separated by a low-barred wooden fence. Benji dropped his pig on Wilf's drive, scooted under the bottom bar and ran to me, tail wagging. He flopped onto his back, legs in the air, demanding a tummy rub.

'Hello, gorgeous,' I said, crouching down and stroking his soft belly. 'Who's a good boy?'

'I am!' Wilf joked. 'Although Benji says I'm stingy with the biscuits and he prefers his Aunt Poppy because she spoils him rotten.'

I couldn't help it. Benji was the most gorgeous, friendly and snuggly dog who'd had me under his spell from the moment Wilf's daughter turned up with him three years ago, shortly after Wilf's wife, Vera, passed away. A Yorkshire terrier like Benji was perfect for Wilf, not needing the same level of exercise that the large dogs had required in his former life as a police dog handler. Not that he'd have struggled with doing the exercise. At eighty-two years young, Wilf still regularly hiked for miles each week and was up early on weekday mornings to swim a mile at the local leisure centre. Benji stayed home and slept while Wilf went swimming but I often looked after him when Wilf went shopping or anywhere else dogs couldn't go. Most of the time, Benji would have been fine on his own in Wilf's house but, as I worked from home and enjoyed the company, Benji had become a regular visitor, bringing me so much comfort, just as he'd done for Wilf.

'Are you still okay to have Benji this afternoon?'

Wilf had plans to visit a friend who loved dogs but had allergies so Benji could only accompany him in the summer when it was warm enough for them to sit outside.

'Definitely.' I straightened up and Benji gave me a disappointed look before poddling back onto Wilf's drive to retrieve his pet pig. 'I'm off to the farm now and I'll visit Dad straight from there. Should be back by one at the latest, so any time after that.'

'Great. Give your dad my best.'

Wilf winced, presumably realising what he'd just said. I could absolutely do that, but it wouldn't mean anything to Dad anymore, so I smiled and nodded before getting into my van and pulling off the drive.

I glanced back at Dove Cottage with a heavy heart. Situated at the edge of the village of Winchcote, north-east of Cheltenham, it had been my childhood home. I'd loved growing up here and had missed the house and village so much when I went away to university and even more so when I married Phil eleven years ago and officially moved out. When we split up five years later and I moved back home, I was sad that my marriage had ended but happy to be back in my favourite place. If I'd needed to heal, Dove Cottage would have healed me, but Phil and I had parted amicably and remained good friends ever since.

But then Mum fell ill and the place I'd always thought of as my home, my sanctuary, my happy place, gradually became a place of sadness. The hurt over Mum's loss had run too deep for Dove Cottage to heal and now sometimes that beautiful house felt more like my prison than my home. I dined on my own off a tray in front of the television, watching programmes where people relocated for a new life in the country or overseas and I imagined doing the same. Where would I go? Anywhere but here. Except I couldn't leave Dad, so I couldn't leave the house and I couldn't move on.

* * *

I'd been a regular visitor to Saltersbeck Farm – a small dairy farm owned by Sharon and Ian Maynard – since the age of ten when I used to accompany my dad on weekends after he took over as the beekeeper. While he tended to the bees, I played on the farm with Sharon and Ian's sons, Phil and Bertie, who were a year older and a year younger than me respectively, or I spent time in the kitchen with Sharon baking cakes, biscuits and scones. Back then, I'd have laughed if someone had told me that, twenty-two years later, I'd be the beekeeper and one of my playmates would be my ex-husband.

The pretty cream farmhouse was set way back from the road, nestled in a low valley and surrounded by stunning countryside. I always felt at peace when it came into view. Away from traffic noise, the only sounds were the moos of the herd, the rustle of the crops swaying in the wind and birdsong. As I child, I'd appreciated the space to play but it was the tranquillity of the farm which captured my heart as an adult. Now, I needed my regular Friday visits as, no matter how stressed I was, I always felt the tension easing from my body as I drove along the farm track.

It had been a fortnight since I'd seen Sharon and Ian. Last weekend they'd been to East Yorkshire, staying in a holiday cottage owned by an old friend of theirs. It was rare I could stop and chat for long, but I hadn't appreciated how important even a five-minute catch-up was to me until I couldn't have one.

As I pulled into the yard, Ian was refuelling his quad bike and Sharon was pegging washing on the line but, as soon as I got out of the van, she abandoned the clothes to cross the yard, arms outstretched. I held on for longer than I normally would and was grateful to her for tightening her hold, evidently recognising that today was a tough day and I needed comfort.

'How are you holding up, honey?' Sharon asked when I finally released her, her soft grey eyes full of concern.

'Oh, you know.' I swallowed down the lump in my throat. 'Taking it a day at a time.'

'That's all you can do.'

There was a wooden bench nearby so we sat down on it.

'I had a bit of a moment this morning,' I admitted. 'Walked past their empty bedroom and *bam*! It still doesn't feel right being there without them.'

'That's understandable. So many memories for you there, good and bad. It's bound to take time.'

'How much time?' I shrugged. 'I've been thinking a lot about what Dad said before he moved into The Larks – that I mustn't stay at Dove Cottage out of misguided sentimentality and I should either rip everything out and make it mine or sell up and start afresh. I told him I loved the house and wouldn't be going anywhere, but now I'm starting to think he might be right. I know it's my home, but it doesn't feel like *my* home, if that makes any sense.'

'It does. Gutting it or moving are both major decisions. Is there one which—'

But she didn't get to finish the question as Ian joined us. I jumped up to hug him but he backed away, indicating some black mess down his overalls.

'As you can see, I lost a fight with the oil can so best not to hug you unless you want to be covered in it.'

'Quad bike playing up again?' I asked, sitting back down.

'It's on its last legs, but I'm determined it'll see me through to R-day.'

R-day was Ian's term for retirement day when he and Sharon would pass Saltersbeck Farm on to Bertie, who'd worked along-side his dad since he was a small boy. Phil had also helped out as a youngster but had never been interested in making a career of it, which had made for a straightforward transfer of ownership.

'R-day's getting so close,' I said to Ian.

'Aye. It'll be reet strange letting go after thirty-five years.'

The phrase made me smile. Despite living in Gloucestershire for most of their lives, the couple had never lost their Yorkshire accents, although Sharon's was much milder than Ian's.

'Taking it in stages'll make it easier,' Sharon said, smiling at her husband before turning her gaze to me. 'We've agreed that Ian'll gradually drop days until the end of the summer and then... drum roll... in mid-September we're off to Canada for a month.'

'A month? Wow! Big holiday.'

I was thrilled for them both as they so rarely got away. I wished I could pack my bags and escape somewhere for a month. A fortnight. A week. Heck, even a couple of days to switch off would be wonderful.

'We've never been away for that long,' Ian said, 'but we decided a big break would be best to give us a proper separation from the farm and Bertie a chance to make it his own.'

'I'm so glad you've booked a holiday. Can't think of anyone who deserves it more.'

Sharon raised her eyebrows at me. 'I can, and I'm looking right at her. You look shattered, honey. Are you sure you won't reconsider taking a break, even if only for a few days? I can visit your dad if that's what's stopping you. I popped in to see him yesterday, by the way. I must have just missed you.'

I had to ask, even though I knew what the answer would be. 'Did he recognise you?'

She slowly shook her head. 'We had a lovely chat about the birds, though.'

'That's what we usually talk about. If I hadn't already been an expert, I would be now.'

Sharon gave me a gentle smile. 'So, what about that break?'

'I can't. It's not just Dad. I've got the bees to see to, my clients, the garden...' I tailed off shrugging, aware that the reasons were valid, but my voice lacked conviction. I so badly needed a break. I'd been running on empty for several months, perhaps even years, and I wasn't sure how much more I could take. Moments like this morning had become far too frequent. It was as though my emotions had been captured in a reservoir across which I'd built a dam when Mum fell ill. Then, when Dad received his Alzheimer's diagnosis, a storm of tears had filled the reservoir and it was now so full that it was lapping against the edge of the dam. Every so often, the wind sent ripples across the water, spilling over that dam – a cascade of apprehension for the future, worry about Dad, anxiety that I had far too much on my plate and that something was going to have to give, and fear that the *something* might be me.

'I know you love coming here every week,' Sharon said, her voice gentle, 'but the bees don't need full weekly inspections until spring arrives and the garden won't need attention until then either. So the next fortnight is the perfect window of opportunity to get away.'

'And you could always get a gardener in,' Ian added. 'Can't Damon do it?'

'Damon only mows lawns. He's not safe around plants – can't tell a weed from a wisteria.'

Bertie drove into the yard on his quad bike and parked it beside Ian's. Their bearded collie Barnum jumped down from the back and ran over to us, tail wagging. I bent forward to stroke his head.

'Did you see the sunrise this morning?' Bertie asked as he joined us. 'I took this photo of the hives.'

He handed me his phone, showing the silhouetted hives backed by a stunning violet and gold sunrise and it instantly soothed me.

'That's beautiful. Can you send me it?'

'Already done it. Got to run. Catch you later.' He gave a low whistle to call Barnum and the pair of them raced towards the farmhouse.

'I'd best get to the bees and let you two get on,' I said.

'Think about taking that break,' Sharon said. 'And don't let the short notice put you off because I know for a fact that Mary's holiday cottage is available.'

I raised my eyebrows as I glanced from her to Ian. 'That's very convenient. Did you two plan this?'

She laughed. 'No. I wouldn't be that presumptuous. Mary's selling the house, but she wants to give it a lick of paint and do a few small repairs first, so it's available for friends and family until the decorators can fit her in. We loved it, didn't we, Ian? We think you will too.'

'It was great,' Ian agreed. 'We'd have been tempted to make it our home, but we don't want to be that far away, especially now.'

He put his arm around Sharon's shoulders and they exchanged smiles, making me wonder what was going on.

'Bertie and Cheryl are having a baby,' Sharon said, her voice full of excitement.

'Aw, that's fantastic news. Please tell them congratulations from me.'

A shadow fell over us and I glanced upwards. It was unseasonably warm this morning with a pale blue sky and gentle sunshine, but the forecast was for a temperature drop this afternoon with strong winds moving down from the north. The gathering clouds certainly supported that. Hive inspections were best avoided in cold, windy and wet weather. Bad weather could make the bees ill-tempered and there was also potential for harming the colony so I only ever did my checks when it was pleasant.

'Time to check on the bees before the weather turns,' I said, standing up.

'Promise me you'll consider taking a break before spring arrives,' Sharon said as she hugged me once more. 'It'll do you good.'

'I'll think about it.'

I returned to the van and set off along the track, deeper into the farm towards Honey Bee Croft – the name Mum had given to the field where the hives were kept. As I passed the adjacent wildflower meadow, Sharon's suggestion about taking a break nudged at me. I'd love that so much but where would I find the time to even squeeze in a weekend away? I ran through a list in my head of my many tasks for today and across the weekend, trying not to feel overwhelmed by how much work I had on. How much work I *always* seemed to have on.

I worked from home as a freelance accountant. I'd started out at a small company in Cheltenham but, after it was confirmed that Mum had a rapidly progressing type of motor neurone disease with short life expectancy, I made the decision to set up on my own so that I could be at home as Mum's condition deteriorated. Now, with Mum gone and Dad in a care home, I was struggling to find enough hours in the day to keep on top of my job, look after the house, see to the bees and visit Dad in The Larks, and it was only going to get worse. The approach of spring meant more time with the bees and, before I knew it, I'd have the garden at Dove Cottage to attend to. With a large lawn to the front, one five times the size out the back, shrubs, flower borders, planters and hanging baskets, keeping my dad's pride and joy in tiptop condition was no mean feat. Cutting the lawn had been Damon Speight's job so, in theory, that was one less task for me, but I'd prefer he didn't do it. He'd likely be in touch very soon, confirming the date for the first cut of the season. Could I tell him no? He wouldn't be happy, I'd feel bad about taking my business away from him and the last thing I needed was to add to my task list, but I couldn't be doing with a repeat of the back end of last year so maybe it was best to sever those ties.

A few months after I'd moved back home, Damon had turned up to mow the lawn for the first time that year. I'd recognised him from school and I knew our mums were friends – former nurses who'd worked on the same hospital ward together – so I'd said hello. If I was around any time he visited, I passed the time of day with him and he used to say *We should go out for a drink sometime and catch up properly.* I'd fobbed him off at first – *I'm just settling back in, I'm busy building my business, Mum's poorly and I don't like to leave her* – but he never stopped asking. Mum used to wind me up that he had a little crush on me but I laughed that off, telling her he barely knew me and he was just an old acquaintance curious to catch up on the years that had passed. Turned out she'd been right about him.

I parked by the entrance to Honey Bee Croft, opened the double doors at the back of the van and pulled on my protective clothing – a white all-in-one beesuit tucked into wellington boots and a pair of gloves – before picking up my smoker and the large cleaning caddy containing my tools, matches and some additional smoker fuel. I'd cleaned everything I needed before coming out this morning and had added fuel to my smoker – wood chips, broken pieces of pinecones and scraps of paper – saving me a couple of tasks on site, although I'd only need the smoker if I opened the hives, which was probably unnecessary today.

My winter visits were fairly quick, the purpose being to make sure the bees were safely overwintering. There were two main tasks. The first was hefting, which meant lifting the hive off the ground to check the weight. A heavy hive I could barely lift meant the supers – the boxes which housed the honey stores in frames – were full, giving the colony plenty of food for energy. If I could lift the hive easily, I'd need to feed the hive with sugar syrup.

The second task was to clear the hive entrances of any dead bees. Most people who were unfamiliar with beekeeping knew that hives had queens and worker bees but what they usually didn't realise was that there was a hierarchy of jobs for the worker bees which they gradually worked their way up with age, moving from hive to field. Although, as life expectancy was up to six weeks in a busy summer, it was a speedy progression through the ranks. One of the hive jobs was undertaker bee, responsible for removing dead larvae and bees to prevent disease. In the winter, when flying time was extremely limited, the undertaker bees might only travel as far as the hive entrance with the dead and the bodies could build up and cause blockages. A poke with a stick soon cleared it but it could lead to an encounter with an angry guard bee, hence the need for the beesuit.

When I'd completed my checks, I returned to the van, loaded up my equipment and removed my beesuit.

Mum had never joined us at the hives when we were working – hated being enclosed within a beesuit – but she sometimes accompanied us to Honey Bee Croft and sat on the wooden bench at the edge of the field. She often came on her own too, loving simply being at one with nature, taking in the spectacular views across the hives and surrounding fields. Whenever I looked at the bench, I pictured her there, smiling contentedly. When she died, we'd had a plaque made, playing with her name.

The bees gave her joy. She gave us joy. She was Joy

I returned to the field, ran my fingers over the plaque and whispered, 'Hi, Mum,' before sitting down and breathing in the fresh country air. In contrast to Dove Cottage, Honey Bee Croft only held happy memories for me, spanning back over twenty-two years.

Dad became a beekeeper by accident. Carter, an old friend of his, had kept ten hives at the farm and Dad, a retired journalist, was writing an article about beekeeping for a magazine. He visited the hives to find out more and take photos and, by the end of that session, he'd got what he needed for his article and he'd found himself a new hobby. He regularly helped out after that and, when Carter moved out of the area when I was ten, Dad took on full ownership. Over time he'd replaced the original hives and added another ten. He'd never been particularly interested in doing anything with the honey – it was the art of beekeeping he loved – so Mum had taken on that aspect, supplying jars of honey and delicious goodies baked with it to a local farm shop before passing that responsibility to me when she fell ill. Although I enjoyed the baking, my real passion had been using beeswax to create skincare products – something I'd been working on for a little over a year at that point. I'd imagined adding more hives and waving goodbye to accountancy as my business took off, but life had other plans for me and I'd needed to cast that dream aside.

Beekeeping had made my dad so happy and I loved how he'd shared that passion with Mum and me. My favourite photos back at Dove Cottage were one of Dad in his beesuit with a ten-year-old me beside him in a custom-made miniature version and another of us in our suits taken eight years ago when I was twenty-four. Back then, I'd been happily married, Mum was in good health and Dad's memory was intact. I was so glad I had those photographs because those happy days often felt like another life, so very long ago.

When Dad went into The Larks eighteen months ago, Ian and Sharon had been concerned that it might be too much for me to keep the hives running, but there was no way I could hang up my beesuit. It wasn't just because beekeeping held a strong connection to my dad. It was because I loved it as much as he had. I loved the bees and the incredible work they did, the sounds, the smells, being outdoors and doing my bit for the environment. And the truth was that I needed it. Without the bees to look after, my life was in danger of being nothing but a never-ending pattern of work, visit Dad, work some more, sleep, repeat. Tending to the hives was my escapism and this beautiful field peppered with wildflowers was my sanctuary. Without it, I feared I'd break.

4

JOEL

'You're early,' Tilly muttered as soon as she opened her front door on Saturday morning, her face bearing the withering scowl I swear she kept in a jar by the door just for me.

'Good morning to you too,' I declared brightly.

I had a full day and night to spend with Imogen and I refused to let yesterday's job news, Chez's bad attitude, a million weddings to attend without a plus one and Tilly's disdain for me spoil a single minute of it.

'The roads were clear,' I added, with a smile. 'No tractors this morning.'

Tilly pulled her long, thick navy cardigan across her body and glared at me. She looked even more shattered than usual with pale cheeks and dark shadows beneath her eyes. I wanted to ask if she was okay – a genuine question from a place of concern for someone I'd once loved – but the last few times I'd done that, I'd had my head bitten off. *Are you saying I look rough? Thanks a lot, Joel.*

When Tilly showed no sign of inviting me inside, I added, 'I can wait in the car if you prefer.'

'I suppose you'd better come in.'

She sighed heavily as she stepped back – a typical warm welcome from my ex.

'Imogen!' Tilly shouted up the stairs as she led me down the hall towards the lounge. 'Your dad's here.'

'Daddy!' Imogen cried, running down the stairs. She launched herself into my arms, wrapped her legs round my waist and buried her head into my chest – exactly what I needed after yesterday.

I kissed the top of her blonde hair. 'Are you excited about trying on your dress?'

She looked up at me, eyes shining. 'I can't wait! I've always wanted to be a bridesmaid.'

'You were my bridesmaid when I married Greg,' Tilly said, sounding and looking most put out.

'But I don't remember that, Mummy.'

'She was only three,' I said, and immediately wished I hadn't. If looks could kill.

I lowered Imogen to the floor. 'You go and finish getting ready, sweetie.'

'And put those tights and a dress on like I told you,' Tilly said. 'It'll be easier to try on your bridesmaid dress if you're wearing tights.'

There was nothing wrong with Imogen's T-shirt and leggings. They'd keep her warmer than tights and a dress and she could easily try the bridesmaid dress on over leggings, but I knew better than to go against Tilly's wishes.

Without a word, Tilly shoved past me and I regretted not doing as I usually did – parking round the corner and waiting, knowing how much she hated it when I was even one minute early for picking up Imogen.

Greg was on the sofa watching cartoons with the rest of the

family – his ten-year-old son Leighton from his first marriage, and the two kids he and Tilly had together, four-year-old Ezra and three-year-old Delphine. Every time I saw them all, I had a flashback to that Saturday morning when Tilly had pulled the rug from under me. *The whole marriage and kids thing isn't for me.* Yep, looked like it!

'All right, Greg?' I said, by way of greeting.

'All right,' he responded flatly without shifting his eyes from the television. Leighton looked up and smiled at me, offering his hand for a high five, but the two younger ones were mesmerised by their programme.

Greg didn't like me, but that was okay because I wasn't his number one fan either and I had far greater reason to dislike the man who'd married the woman I'd loved and got to live with my daughter.

Tilly swept some wooden building blocks and a couple of soft toys off an armchair onto the carpet and indicated wordlessly that I should sit. She sat down in an adjacent chair, and I braced myself for the usual barrage of instructions, as though I had no idea how to look after our daughter.

'Don't let her stay up too late,' she said. 'No more than one fizzy drink and make sure she eats some fruit. Check when she brushes her teeth because the dentist said she keeps missing the back ones.'

'You told me that the last few times. I'll make sure we don't upset the dentist.' As soon as the words were out, I realised I should have just nodded along.

'It's not about upsetting the dentist, Joel. It's about our daughter's teeth. Do you want her to have fillings before she's ten? Do you want her teeth pulled out because of decay?'

I could feel Greg's eyes on me now but I wouldn't give him the satisfaction of looking in his direction and seeing what I was sure would be a smug grin at me being dressed down.

'I'm sorry. Please go on,' I said, hoping I sounded sincere. Of course I didn't want any of that but Tilly was going over the top. We shared the same dentist, and I'd asked him about Imogen at my recent check-up. He'd assured me that she had great teeth and he hadn't been concerned that her brushing was ineffective. All he'd given was a gentle reminder to brush at the back which he gave to all children.

'Why are they getting married in March anyway?' Tilly asked. 'Imogen will freeze in a short-sleeved dress.'

I took it as a rhetorical question and ignored it. The date Barney and Amber had chosen for their wedding was none of Tilly's business and the weather comment was a daft one when the UK weather was so unpredictable that March could be warm and August freezing.

Barney, my best mate since senior school, ran Bumblebee Barn. The farm had been in his family for four generations and was a mixed operation with pigs, two breeds of sheep, goats, horses and hens as well as several crops. We'd both been unlucky in love throughout our twenties, although my problem was that I never seemed to meet anyone and his had been that he met lots of women – just not ones suited to a farming lifestyle. That all changed three years ago when his younger sister, Fizz, convinced him to try something radical and apply to a new reality TV show called *Love on the Farm*, aimed at helping single farmers find love. He'd been gobsmacked when he was selected as one of the featured farmers and, while he wasn't attracted to any of the three potential matches, he found love with the show's producer, Amber.

Amber had worked for many years as the producer on the

television show *Countryside Calendar* – a Sunday-night staple which focused on living and working in the countryside across the different seasons. After they got together, Amber sold her London flat and moved in with Barney but spent a lot of time travelling to film *Countryside Calendar* alongside her pet project, *The Wildlife Rescuers*. Showcasing a year in the life of several wildlife rescue centres, it mainly focused on Hedgehog Hollow Wildlife Rescue Centre, which one of Amber's best friends Samantha owned and where Fizz worked.

Although Amber loved her job, she found it increasingly difficult to be away from Barney, the farm and the friends she'd made in the area, so she decided to step away from TV production, filming her final ever episode of *Countryside Calendar* in Suffolk last summer. At the point she handed in her notice, Barney took her out for a meal, telling her it was to celebrate the end of her time as show producer but it was really so he could ask her to marry him.

They made such a great couple and I'd never seen my friend so happy. I got on brilliantly with Amber and felt just as welcome at the farm with her there as I'd always been, so I couldn't be more thrilled for them. But their wedding – and the five which would follow – did make me reflect on my own situation more than I cared to, with a tinge of sadness that it wasn't me. Would it ever be?

'Ready!' Imogen appeared and gave us a twirl in a pretty yellow and white dress which, despite being accompanied by thick white tights as instructed, struck me as more suitable for the height of summer than the first Saturday in March. Pretty ironic considering the comments Tilly had made about Imogen freezing in her bridesmaid dress at this time of year.

'Have you been to the toilet?' Tilly asked her.

Imogen shook her head. 'And I can't fit Cloud in my case.'

Cloud was Imogen's favourite soft toy – a round fluffy sheep – which she never slept without.

'Okay. You go to the toilet and I'll sort out Cloud.'

'Don't squash him!'

'I'll leave the zip slightly open so he can still breathe,' Tilly said, giving Imogen a reassuring smile. She might be hostile and snappy around me but there was no denying that Tilly was a devoted, caring mum. Just a shame she couldn't seem to see how much it hurt our daughter to have such limited contact with me. I had no comprehensive response to Imogen's frequently asked question – *Why can't I see you more often?* It was especially difficult when there was already a precedent set in their family – *Leighton spends half the week and every other weekend with his mum. Why don't we do that?* The answer I wanted to give – *Because your mum is being awkward* – would land me in deep water and I'd sworn I'd never badmouth Tilly in front of Imogen, so I simply hugged her, wiped her tears and assured her that, just because I didn't get to see her, it didn't mean I wasn't thinking about her and missing her every single day.

As Imogen ran out of the room, Tilly pushed herself up from her chair and my breath caught. I recognised that gait. She couldn't be pregnant again, surely? But her cardigan slipped to one side revealing a distinct baby bump. It seemed that the woman who didn't want children was pregnant with her fourth baby.

She must have noticed me staring as her cheeks flushed. 'I was going to tell you when you dropped her back.' Her voice was soft with a hint of an apology.

'Congratulations,' I said, my voice coming out a little husky. 'When's it due?'

'*They're* due on 20 July.'

'They? You're having twins?' Being halfway through a pregnancy with twins would explain why she looked so exhausted. She'd struggled with fatigue throughout the first and second trimester of all her pregnancies.

'Twin boys,' she said as she shuffled out of the room, clearly not interested in further conversation.

'Congratulations, Greg,' I said.

He grinned but he didn't look in my direction. I could imagine the words he wanted to say but had just about enough intellect to keep inside – *Look at me with my growing family. Bet you wish you could trade places.*

Thing is, I didn't wish that. Well, not completely. I didn't want to be with Tilly anymore and hadn't done for a long time. The way she'd ended things and the disdain with which she'd treated me over the years had erased any residual feelings of love for her. I would always care for her as the mother of my child, but I didn't particularly like her these days. And I wasn't as bothered about having a big family like I'd once planned. Imogen was an amazing little girl and I was so lucky to have her. Yes, it would be great to meet someone and have more children but, if Imogen was the only child I fathered, so be it. What I *did* envy about Greg's life – and the part I wished I could change – was all the time he got to spend with *my* daughter when I barely saw her.

My phone buzzed, taking my attention away from my moment of envy and giving me the ideal excuse to step out of the uncomfortable atmosphere and into the hall. I smiled at the WhatsApp message from Fizz.

FROM FIZZ

Hi you, Darcie wants to know if Imogen can come back to ours for cake and a milkshake after the dress fittings. I said I'd ask but warned her you might have other plans. I know your time together is precious

Even though Imogen loved spending time with me, I couldn't compete with an offer like that. The cake and milkshakes would be tempting but the biggest draw was time with thirteen-year-old Darcie. Despite the five-year age gap, the pair of them adored each other and were always begging to spend more time together. Darcie was the adopted daughter of Phoebe – Fizz's fiancée and Barney's future sister-in-law. Fizz had proposed to Phoebe at the start of the year on Phoebe's birthday. They'd been a couple for four years at that point and, although they hadn't wanted to wait for long to tie the knot, they'd been concerned about stealing Barney and Amber's thunder and said they'd wait until next year to get married. Barney and Amber had told them not to be so daft so they'd gone for May meaning the first two weddings this year were for the Kinsella siblings. After that it was my cousin's wedding in August, my mate Tim's in September, Zara's in October and my mate Levi's next May. If I did lose my job in the restructure, I'd have to hope I found another one quickly because six weddings and several more stag dos were going to set me back a small fortune.

TO FIZZ

I'm going to the farm while you're getting sorted but we've no specific plans after that

FROM FIZZ

Amber's coming back to ours too but Darcie's going out with friends mid-afternoon so how about Amber brings her back to the farm then?

TO FIZZ

Sounds good

'Why are you in the hall?' Tilly asked, pausing halfway down the stairs with Imogen's small purple suitcase in her hand.

I held up my phone as an explanation and took the first few steps, reaching for the case.

'I'm pregnant, not incapable,' she snapped, snatching it away.

I couldn't win with her, so I retreated and let her bring it down herself. Imogen appeared again, pulling on a thin white cardigan which she might as well not be wearing for all the warmth it would give her. Tilly placed the case by the door, removed Imogen's coat from the hooks at the bottom of the stairs and draped it over the case.

'I'll take these out to the car,' I said as the pair of them went into the lounge so Imogen could say goodbye. I'd spotted Imogen's favourite zipped hoodie hanging up so I sneakily grabbed that to give her something warmer to wear under her coat.

A few minutes later, Imogen was safely strapped into the back seat wearing her hoodie, having unsurprisingly announced that she was cold the moment we stepped outside the house.

'Joel!' Tilly called as I was about to close the door.

I stiffened. Was she going to lecture me for challenging her wardrobe choices?

'I'll be back in a minute,' I told Imogen. 'I'll see what Mummy wants.'

'Just making sure you're okay,' Tilly said when I joined her. 'About the babies, I mean. I didn't want you to find out like this.'

Her concern took me by surprise. Could she possibly think I still had feelings for her and would be hurt by her news?

'It's none of my business how many children you have,' I responded, keeping my tone nonchalant.

'I know, but...' The soft expression reminded me of the Tilly I used to know instead of the sparring partner she'd become.

'There is no *but*,' I said gently. 'If you're happy, then I'm happy for you.'

'I *am* happy. Shattered, but happy.'

'Then we're good. Congratulations, and I'll see you tomorrow.'

I turned to leave, but she called my name again.

'I'm sorry it didn't work out for you and Marley.'

'Marley? That ended over two years ago.'

'And I never said I was sorry at the time, but I was. I thought she was the one.'

That threw me too.

'So did I at first, but I've got form on that.' It didn't come out as flippantly as I meant it and I felt guilty when her shoulders slumped and tears pricked her eyes.

'I just want you to be happy,' she whispered.

She wasn't normally like this around me and it was unsettling. The unprecedented show of concern had to be down to pregnancy hormones.

'I'm fine, thanks. And don't worry about Imogen. I'll take good care of her, as always, and she'll have an amazing weekend.'

'I know. It's just that I miss her when she's with you.'

She missed her? Like I didn't? Frustration bubbling over, I couldn't bite my tongue any longer.

'Then put yourself in my shoes and imagine how I feel most days. You truly want me to be happy? Then let me see our daughter more often and stop using my shifts as an excuse.'

The softness had disappeared – probably thanks to my sharp tone – and was replaced by her familiar stony glare. 'You *know* it's difficult.'

'Only because you make it that way. I'll see you tomorrow.'

I dashed back to the car before she could respond, started the engine and drove away with Imogen waving frantically to her mum. God, that woman knew how to push all my buttons! She was sorry about Marley? Where on earth had that come from?

And why choose now as the moment to tell me that, two years after Marley had walked away? Better late than never I suppose, but I wished she hadn't said anything because now, as well as being frustrated with Tilly, I was thinking about Marley and how not wanting children had been the reason that relationship had ended too. Although, unlike Tilly, Marley hadn't gone on to have a brood with someone else.

Marley had been one of the three potential matches for Barney on *Love on the Farm* but, even if Amber hadn't been in the picture, nothing would have happened between them. Lack of chemistry aside, Marley had a serious pig phobia so could never have dated a pig farmer. After the production company pulled the plug on the show before filming finished, Barney stayed in touch with two of the contestants as friends – Marley and Tayla – and Marley and I got together not long after. Everything had been going really well between us until we approached Christmas that same year. Tilly had stunned me by saying that she thought we'd been together long enough for Marley to meet Imogen but Marley seemed hesitant to commit to anything. A couple of weeks into the New Year, Marley admitted that she'd never wanted her own children – something she'd never actually mentioned to me – but had now realised that she wasn't interested in children in her life in any capacity. Obviously, that meant no future for the pair of us, so I was back to licking my wounds and wondering whether I'd ever find what Barney and Amber had. Or Tilly and Greg, Fizz and Phoebe or the many other couples I knew who seemed to have cracked what I'd never managed – someone they loved who loved them and every part of their life in return. Even my other closest mates Tim and Levi – both of whom had never shown any interest in settling down – were getting married to partners they'd met after I'd split up with Marley.

Plenty of time for meeting someone. You're only thirty-four. Just because everyone else seems to be tying the knot, it doesn't mean it'll never happen for you. All in good time. Someone will come along eventually.

I hoped. But, knowing my luck, the next woman I fell for would just see me as a friend. They all did. It seemed to be the story of my life.

5

POPPY

On Saturday morning, I'd almost finished drying my hair after my shower when I spotted a voicemail notification on my phone. I recognised the number and my heart pounded as I dialled into the message.

'Morning, Poppy, it's Marnie Lloyd. Nothing to worry about. Your dad's absolutely fine but we had an incident last night. When you visit this morning, can we have a quick chat before you see him so I can tell you about it? No need to rush here. I promise it's nothing urgent. See you later.'

The manager of The Larks had a low, gentle, soothing voice which always made me feel calm and reassured. And she always spoke the truth so if she said I didn't need to rush in, she meant it, although I dreaded to think what the incident might have been. It could be connected to what Marnie referred to as *midnight meanderings* – Dad leaving his room in the early hours and wandering along the corridors. Initially he'd said he was looking for Mum but, more recently, it was his parents he was searching for. It broke my heart thinking of Dad being confused and upset when he couldn't find the people he loved, and each instance filled me with dread because the time-shifting further back into his memories meant the Alzheimer's was taking a stronger hold on his brain. Time-shifting. It sounded like an almost magical term conjuring up images of time-travelling heroes who'd find the serial killers before they struck. Sadly, real-life time-shifting was far from magical. It was heart-breaking.

I resumed drying my hair, a familiar knot of anxiety building in my stomach, my mind running through other possibilities. I had a stack of quick admin tasks I'd planned to do before heading out, but I wouldn't be able to fully concentrate on them until I knew what Marnie needed to talk to me about. I switched off the hairdryer, my hair still damp, pulled on a hoodie, grabbed my handbag and ran downstairs.

As I opened the front door, a figure lurched towards me and I leapt back with a squeal.

'Damon!' I clapped my hand to my pounding heart. 'What are you doing here?'

His hand was raised, as though poised to ring the bell, and he lowered it to his side. He was wearing his usual work uniform of a navy boiler suit, fleecy jacket, boots and a khaki beanie hat over his dark hair. He was so close that I could smell the stale sweat on his clothes and coffee on his breath.

'I'm booking in the first cuts of the year and I wanted to—'

'I can't today. I'm on my way out.' I already had my coat in my hands and shoved my arms into the sleeves to emphasise that.

'I'll come back later, then.'

I stepped outside but Damon, who had never been great at recognising personal space, stayed where he was on the doorstep.

'Do you mind...?' I asked, indicating with a nod of the head that I needed him to move. Most people would have stepped down from the doorstep to give me plenty of room, but not

Damon. He shuffled a few inches, and I held my breath as I brushed past him in my attempt to close and lock the door.

'I don't know when I'll be back,' I said, managing to sidestep him.

'This afternoon?' he persisted, following me towards my car parked on the drive.

'I've got a visitor.' It was the truth. He didn't need to know that my visitor was Benji the Yorkshire terrier again. 'I've got to go. Sorry.'

Even though it was the perfect opportunity to tell him that I didn't want him to return – especially since Troy Taylor who did several of the gardens in the village had confirmed that he could add me to his client list – I knew it wouldn't be a quick conversation. Damon wasn't going to accept a no and I really didn't have the time or energy to get into a debate about it.

'Are you going to see your dad? Is everything okay?'

I appreciated the concerned expression and the sympathy in Damon's voice, but I didn't want to get him involved. Not after last time.

'I won't know until I get there, but I need to go now.' I glanced towards his van parked across the bottom of the drive, blocking my exit. 'Can you move your van please?'

'Of course! Do you want me to come with you?'

'No, thank you. I just need you to move your van. I'm in a rush.'

'Okay. But if you need anything, give me a call.'

I nodded and got into my car but Damon showed no sign of leaving. I turned on the ignition before I put my seatbelt on in the hope that the car starting would speed him into action but he was standing halfway down the drive, watching me. I revved the engine as I pulled on my seatbelt. Surely that had to finally get him moving. No. I revved it again and released the handbrake, letting the car cruise forward a couple of feet. When he still didn't move, I wound down the window.

'Damon!' I called sharply. 'Stop messing about.'

He raised his hand, presumably in apology, and slowly sauntered down the drive, taking what felt like an eternity to pull his van back so I could exit the drive. I could feel his eyes on me but I didn't glance his way or raise my hand in thanks. After all, what was there to thank him for? He'd turned up unannounced and couldn't have made it much harder for me to leave, knowing that I was in a rush. What had got into him this morning? Any guilt I had about telling him I didn't require his services anymore had gone. I wouldn't take any pleasure in it but I would feel relieved about severing all ties.

Half an hour later, I pulled into the visitor car park at The Larks and hastened inside, my stomach still in knots. Marnie, a curvy brunette in her late forties, was talking to a woman in the foyer and nodded to acknowledge me. I waited nearby and caught enough of the conversation to glean that the woman was looking for a place for her mother. I recognised the shedload of guilt in her words and demeanour as I'd been the same and still felt that way eighteen months down the line, even though my logic-loving brain told me this was the best place for Dad. The woman took a brochure and, as she passed me, I gave her a weak smile and wished I could say something comforting, but were there really any suitable words of comfort for someone whose loved one had dementia?

'Poppy!' Marnie said, her smile as welcoming as ever as I joined her. 'Let's go through to my office, but do be assured that your lovely dad is safe and well.'

Safe? The staff here were amazing so I could easily believe that. Well? He'd never really be *well* again, but I knew it was just a turn of phrase and I did appreciate the attempt at reassurance.

Marnie's office was just behind the reception desk. The large room had several places to sit and she directed me towards the round table and chairs at the opposite end to her desk.

'I know you'll be anxious to see your dad so I won't keep you long, but I need to let you know that his midnight meanderings have escalated.'

'As in they're more frequent?' I asked.

She grimaced. 'As in he's also been going into other residents' rooms. Last night we were alerted to him trying to get into bed with one of our female residents.'

'Oh, my gosh! Are they both all right?'

'They were shaken but we were able to calm them and get them settled back to sleep.'

I ran my fingers into my hair and clasped my head between my hands, searching for something to say. The only words I could find were, 'I'm sorry.'

'Oh, goodness, there's nothing to be sorry about. I've seen everything over the years and this isn't the first time there's been a spot of bed-hopping. It's nothing sexual. With Alzheimer's, it's typically a combination of the person's confusion, disrupted sleep patterns and restlessness and, as you're aware, your dad is partic-ularly restless at the moment.'

I raised my head, nodding. Dad's restlessness had escalated as he'd progressed into later-stage dementia, always looking for someone or something. Even when he was sitting, his fingers would be restless, his eyes darting everywhere. For a man who'd always been so calm and restful, it was distressing to see.

'I'm not telling you this because it's a problem,' Marnie continued. 'As you'll remember when you first looked around, my promise to you was for honesty and transparency, so this is simply me being those things.'

I gave her a weak smile. 'Thank you. You're sure everyone's all right?'

'Everyone's just fine. I'd tell you if that wasn't the case. Do you have any questions for me?'

'What happens next? You won't lock him in his room, will you?' I couldn't bear the thought of my dad being trapped like that.

'Goodness, no! At night, we'll keep an even closer eye on the corridor where your dad is, but try not to worry. It's not the first time this has happened with our residents, and it certainly won't be the last. Belongings go walkies all the time too.'

I remembered her warning Dad and me about that when we looked around, suggesting that Dad didn't bring anything particularly valuable with him. Thefts were never intentional or malicious – just symptomatic of the confusion.

Moving to The Larks had been Dad's idea. During my teens, a neighbour and close friend of my parents had been diagnosed with vascular dementia. Dad had seen firsthand the toll caring for him took on his wife, who passed away herself shortly after him. At the time, Dad vehemently declared that he never wanted to put Mum or me through that if he went the same way.

None of us had noticed the dementia creeping up on Dad because we'd been so focused on filling Mum's time with holidays, trips and special moments before she was too ill to do little more than lie in a hospital bed with machines breathing for her, being fed through a tube. We'd put Dad's moments of forgetfulness down to stress but, a couple of weeks after Mum's funeral, Dad and I tore the house apart looking for his car keys. I found them inside the tub of butter in the fridge and called him through to the kitchen to show him. We laughed about it and then stared at each other, both recalling other incidents where objects had been found in unexpected places and the many occasions where he'd struggled to remember words or lost track of what he was saying. What if it wasn't just stress and old age? What if there was something more sinister going on?

Dad had been so brave that day, getting straight onto the phone to make a doctor's appointment, telling me everything would be okay even though we both knew it wouldn't be. He had dementia. We didn't need a formal diagnosis to confirm that. I'd tried to be strong too, telling him we'd tackle it together if the news was what we feared. But after we said goodnight at bedtime, I'd beaten my fists against my pillows, screaming silently with the injustice of it all. I'd just lost my wonderful mum and now this!

Shortly after we received the official diagnosis of Alzheimer's disease, Dad strongly reiterated his desire not to be a burden by presenting me with three care home brochures. The Larks was his favourite and he'd already made an appointment for a tour. He wasn't bothered what the rooms looked like – *it's just a place to sleep* – but the garden had been important to him. We stood on the lawn, surrounded by trees and birdfeeders and I saw that same look of serenity on his face that he had whenever he was in the garden at Dove Cottage. An ornithologist since childhood, he thought that watching the birds and hearing their song might soothe his increasingly confused mind. This was to be the place when the time came.

I'd held off as long as I could but, in the autumn the year before last, Dad went missing. I'd only nipped out to post a letter and when I got back, the front door was wide open and he was gone. I'd never known fear like it. It was dark and cold and he could be anywhere.

It was several hours later when a neighbour out walking her dog found him quite distressed sitting on a tree stump down a deserted lane and led him home. He had wandered off before but not that far or for that long and I had to accept that he was no longer safe to be left on his own.

Dad liked it in The Larks. The staff were kind and attentive and he'd been right about those birds soothing him. We both knew it was the best place for him, but it didn't make it any easier when I drove home without him that first night, when I opened the door to an empty house, when I walked past his bedroom and he wasn't there. And none of those things had got any easier since then. I feared they never would.

* * *

Dad was sitting in a high-backed chair in the residents' lounge watching the birds eating from the various feeders spread around the patio. He spent most of his time there or sitting in a chair in his bedroom looking out over the garden.

I watched him from a distance for a while. He looked every bit the immaculately groomed and well-dressed gentleman he'd always been – blazer worn over an open-collared shirt and chinos with his grey hair neatly cut – but I could also see that the blazer was too big and the shirt too loose. I knew that his trousers only stayed up with the help of a belt with extra holes punched into it. If I moved closer, I knew his eyes would be flicking back and forth – always searching – and there'd be lines of confusion etched across his forehead. His hands would be teasing the tassels and ribbons on the colourful fiddle cushion made by the kind members of a local charity.

'You okay?'

I looked into the concerned eyes of a care assistant I didn't recognise. They'd taken on a few new staff members recently.

'Just feeling a bit sad today. I sometimes need to gather my strength before I go and say hello.'

She glanced across at Dad. 'Is that your granddad by the window?'

'My dad.'

Her eyes widened and her cheeks flushed. 'I'm sorry. I just—'

'It's fine. I'm used to it. I had friends at school whose grand-parents were younger than my parents.' I didn't have the energy to tell her my story. Not today.

'He's a lovely man,' she said. 'I'll leave you to your thoughts, but let me know if you need anything.'

'Thank you.'

Dad had aged significantly since moving in. He looked his years now. Frail. Lost. Another reason for me to feel guilty. I had to keep reminding myself that he'd been blessed with a youthful appearance for most of his life and it was perhaps inevitable that it would catch up with him at some point, especially when he was only a day away from his ninetieth birthday.

Residents always got a cake on their birthday but a landmark birthday received extra-special attention. For Dad's, the staff had arranged a visit from Cuddles & Paws, a local charity that brought in animals – mainly guinea pigs, rabbits, cats and dogs – for the residents to pet. I'd visited once when they'd been here and it was incredible to see how engaged everyone became, talking about pets they'd had or had wanted and looking relaxed as they stroked the animals. I'd been so touched when Marnie told me she'd booked their next visit for Dad but, thinking about his birthday now, panic stabbed me. What if his ninetieth birthday was his last? The urge to rush up to him and bury myself in a hug was so strong that it took my breath away. I wrapped my arms across my body, blinking back the tears and trying to push down the lump in my throat.

I missed hugging Dad so much, but it was one of the many things this cruel disease had taken away from us, like being unable to call him Dad because it confused and upset him. The first visit when he hadn't recognised me at all would forever haunt me as the day I said goodbye to the man who wasn't connected to me by blood but who'd been the best dad I could ever have wished for.

I drew in several deep breaths and once I felt more in control of my emotions, I made my way over to the chair adjacent to Dad's.

'Good morning, Stanley!' I said, my voice bright. 'Do you mind if I sit here?'

Dad looked up with a smile and a nod before returning his gaze to the birds, his fingers twiddling a piece of blue satin ribbon on his cushion. That lack of recognition kicked me in the guts every time.

'Are you watching the birds?' I asked. 'My dad loved doing that.'

'I know all their names. My dad taught me.'

The proud tone of his voice made me smile but, seconds later, tears pricked my eyes as he twisted round, searching the room, and added, 'Not sure where he's gone. He asked me to wait here.'

'I'm sure he'll be back soon. How about you tell me the names of the birds in the meantime?'

And so my dad told me the names of the birds, just like he'd done when I was a child, and I encouraged him to tell me stories about twitching trips and birds he'd rescued. I didn't care that I'd heard them countless times before. All I wanted was to hear my dad's voice and be in the moment with him, even if he was talking about things from decades ago as though they'd only just happened.

Dad's voice became slower and his eyelids drooped heavily

until he drifted off to sleep. I stayed for another ten minutes, watching the steady rise and fall of his chest as he breathed, battling with my own fatigue. What I wouldn't do to be able to cuddle up to him and sleep too.

I yawned and rubbed my tired eyes. I needed some time away, but could I leave him? Having Sharon visit every day would be some comfort, but I hadn't missed a single day in eighteen months. Would I be able to break that pattern? Did I even want to?

Rising from my chair, I placed a light kiss on his cheek.

'See you tomorrow for your birthday, Dad,' I whispered.

* * *

Walking across the car park a little later, I was trying to keep the tears at bay while I hunted in my bag for my car keys.

'Everything okay with your dad?'

Startled, I squealed and dropped my keys on the ground.

'Damon! What are you doing here?'

'You looked upset earlier. I was worried about you.'

'So you followed me?' I snatched up my keys and stared at him defiantly, hating that he'd encroached on a private emotional moment.

'I didn't follow you. I knew you were coming here.'

'But I didn't ask you to come.'

'You looked upset,' he repeated as though that explained his presence.

'I wasn't upset. I was in a rush. I still am.'

'You look upset now.'

'What do you expect?' I waved my hand in the direction of the care home. 'My dad's in there and he has no idea who I am. Of course I'm upset!'

Cursing myself for saying too much, I set off towards my car, but Damon grabbed my arm, his fingers pressing into my skin.

'Let go!' I cried, snatching my arm from his grasp and rubbing it. I'd have a bruise there later. 'Why did you do that?'

'I want to talk to you, but you keep walking away.'

'Because I have a mountain of things to do in a short space of time and I want to crack on with them.'

'Can I take you for a coffee?'

I shook my head. 'Damon, please listen to me. I have a *lot* to do. I don't have time to stop and chat, so I definitely don't have time to go for a coffee. I'm sorry.'

'You never seem to have time for me anymore.' He stuck out his bottom lip like a petulant child. 'You used to chat to me but now you spend all your time working, or here, or at the farm with those stupid bees.'

Incensed, I glared at him. 'The bees aren't stupid.'

'Don't you care anymore?' he asked, ignoring my comment.

'About what?' Damon was trying my patience today. I had so much to do and he seemed to be everywhere, delaying me.

He looked bewildered. 'Me, of course! I thought we had a connection.'

I widened my eyes in disbelief. Seriously? This again?

'Our only connection is that we went to the same primary school. Nothing more.'

'You can't mean that. We went out.'

'That wasn't a date, Damon. You know it wasn't.'

'If you'd just let me take you out again, I could—'

I'd lost my patience now. How many times were we going to have the same conversation?

'Please stop!' I said firmly. 'We had one coffee, it was *not* a date and you know it so stop trying to turn it into something it wasn't.

Don't come here again. It's distressing enough without you turning up.'

'I *want* to be here. You don't have to go through this alone, Poppy.'

He took a couple of steps closer, his arms outstretched as though to hug me and I backed away, furious with him for overstepping.

'I *want* to go through this alone and this isn't about you. I don't care if you want to be here. This is *my* dad and *I* don't want you here. Do you understand?'

'But who else have you got?'

He'd said it gently and there was obvious concern in his expression, but those words! He might as well have punched me in the stomach. Those six words had tapped into my biggest fear for the future.

'I've got plenty of people,' I said, my tone sharp. 'Don't you worry about me.'

I dashed over to my car and started the ignition. Thankfully the car parked in front of me had gone, giving me the gift of a drive-through space. As I drove towards the exit, I stole a glance in the rearview mirror but Damon had gone. Thank goodness for that! Perhaps I'd finally got through to him.

I couldn't believe he was still banging on about our 'date'. It hadn't been a date at all. Last year, Dad had time-shifted more frequently and, when I arrived at The Larks one stormy October day, he'd shifted back to his days as a journalist and thought I was there to be interviewed for a job as a junior reporter. I wasn't sure I could blag my way through an interview so I told him I had a job already as a beekeeper. He'd stared at me for a moment and I held my breath. Any moment now, he'd realise who I was. Or even if he didn't know that, he'd remember that he'd been a beekeeper.

'A beekeeper?' He nodded and I was sure he was processing a memory, but my hopes slipped away. 'I've never met a beekeeper before. Is it dangerous?'

I stayed an hour while he quizzed me for an article he'd decided to write about beekeeping. It was a pleasure talking to him about my passion, telling him how much it had meant to me to learn it all from my dad, but it was heartbreaking too because there wasn't a single moment during our time together when he knew who I was. I'd known that day would come. I thought I'd prepared myself for it but nothing could truly prepare me for the moment I knew I'd lost my dad. The moment where his brain was so damaged by this horrific disease that the memories from the part of his life which we'd shared were gone. The moment where I effectively had no family left and was all alone in the world.

I was halfway home when I heard the first rumble of thunder and, by the time I made it back, a storm was raging outside but also within me and I desperately needed some release. Skidding to a halt on the drive, I slammed the door shut and sprinted along the pathway running down the side of the garage and into the back garden, seeking out memories of my green-fingered nature-loving dad chatting to the bees as he pruned the roses, laughing at the antics of the squirrels as they stole the nuts from the bird-feeders, beaming proudly at the beautiful garden he'd created.

The rain was so torrential that my hair was plastered to my face and my clothes were already clinging to me but I barely noticed as I stood on the grass and screamed. As the storm raged, I raged with it. With my fists clenched, I cursed and yelled and jumped up and down, stamping my feet, turning the lawn beneath me into a muddy mess. I hated this. I hated the injustice of it. I hated the cruelty to the dementia patients and everyone who cared about them. And I hated that my dad no longer knew who I was. And suddenly I had no voice left, no energy, no fire and I sank onto the grass, my tears lost in the rainwater on my face.

Damon found me and he helped me into the house, made me a hot drink while I dried off, and then he listened as I poured out everything I was thinking and feeling. It was cathartic to get it all out and I felt so much lighter. I asked if I could take him out for a coffee the following day to thank him for his kindness. We were only out for an hour and, as Damon wasn't the greatest conversationalist, there were several awkward silences. As we left the café, he told me he'd had a great time and asked me when I was free for our second date. I immediately corrected him – not a date, just a one-off coffee to say thanks for yesterday. Over the next few weeks, he messaged me every few days asking me out but then it fizzled out and I assumed he'd got the message. Apparently not.

6

JOEL

'All set?' I asked Imogen as I pulled into a space in the car park of Crafty Hollow – a creative studio in the grounds of Hedgehog Hollow run by Samantha's cousin Chloe and her auntie-in-law Lauren. They were both brilliant at sewing so would be undertaking any dress alterations this week.

She nodded, smiling.

'Off you go, then. I'll see you later.'

Her face fell. 'I want you to stay with me.'

'We talked about this before, sweetie. You'll all be getting changed so it's not right for me to be there, and I thought you didn't want me to see your dance until the wedding.'

Amber and the bridesmaids had been preparing something special for the guests and all Imogen had revealed was that it had been her idea, it involved a Taylor Swift track – unsurprising given my daughter was a major Swiftie – and they'd been practising it through a video link. This was the first time they'd been together as a group although there wouldn't be a full complement of bridesmaids as Amber's sister, Sophie and their brother's long-term partner, Tabs, had filming commitments out of the area so couldn't join them today.

'It *is* a secret, but I still want you there.'

'You can't keep it a secret if I'm there,' I said, gently. 'You'll be fine. You know everyone and you're going back to Darcie's afterwards.'

'But I've never been here before.'

I pointed to the entrance. 'It's just that door there.'

Her bottom lip started quivering and tears pooled in her eyes so I turned off the engine, surprised and alarmed by her reaction.

'How about I take you inside? I can't stay, though. You do understand why?'

She looked up at me with big sad eyes and nodded slowly, melting my heart. She'd never been a clingy toddler and starting at primary school hadn't fazed her either. She'd been praised by her teachers for her confidence and how great she was around new or shy children, making sure they were never left out. New places didn't normally bother her either, so I wasn't sure what had brought on this uncertainty and particularly the tears. I didn't like seeing her like this and it made me feel even more guilty that I wasn't always around for her. If something was bothering her, would she confide in me? I hoped so, but I couldn't be certain. It wasn't the time to quiz her now, but I'd see what I could find out over the weekend.

We exited the car, and she clung onto my hand as we headed towards the former stable block.

Samantha must have spotted us approaching as the door opened. 'Hello, you two. Come in!'

'Is everyone decent?' I asked.

She laughed. 'Aw, bless you, Joel. Yes, it's safe.'

As soon as we were inside, Imogen spotted Darcie at the other side of the room with Fizz and Phoebe, let go of my hand and was off like a shot.

'Bye, Imogen!' I called after her.

She turned and blew me a kiss before hurling herself at Darcie. They hugged and twirled round in a circle together. Fizz and Phoebe waved at me.

'She was adamant I had to come in with her, but I don't think I'm needed after all,' I said to Samantha, giving an exaggerated sigh.

'Those two are so adorable together,' she said, watching them. 'Amber and Zara are hanging up the dresses and Lauren and Chloe are making drinks. Do you want one?'

'I think I'll leave you to it.'

Even though Imogen seemed to have forgotten I was there, I joined her for a goodbye hug, before heading out to my car. She was back to being her usual sunshine self so hopefully that clingy moment had been nothing. I'd see how the rest of the weekend went before broaching it.

As I drove towards Bumblebee Barn, my thoughts turned to my job situation. I needed to do something about it. During my many battles with Tilly about working shifts, she'd suggested retraining for a job with regular hours and my challenge back had always been *retrain as what? Most of the jobs around here are in factories, meaning shift work.* But was that true or was I, like Tilly suggested, being *awkward and blinkered*? None of my friends worked in factories. Barney was a farmer, Fizz was a veterinary nurse, Phoebe an accountant, Zara an events planner and her fiancé Snowy was a former Olympic gymnast who now ran his own successful gymnastics club. Tim was a plumber and Levi managed a couple of branches of his family's estate agency. I shook my head. The only role that appealed among those was farming and I'd always loved helping Barney out, but he had enough staff already with Milo and Amber. I had nowhere near enough experience to secure a job on another farm and, if I did, it would be starting right at the bottom, probably on minimum wage. I couldn't afford to do that when I had a mortgage and bills to pay, child maintenance, and Chester to support.

* * *

Milo was in the farmyard at Bumblebee Barn hosing out a couple of buckets when I pulled in. He looked up but didn't smile or wave, although that was Milo all over – loved animals, couldn't stand people. He'd worked at Bumblebee Barn for thirteen years, starting with a part-time weekend job when he was fourteen, and I always found it strange I'd known him all that time except I barely knew him at all, and he certainly didn't know anything about me.

'All right, Milo?' I asked, crossing the farmyard to join him.

'I s'pose.'

'Is Barney around?'

'Top Pig.'

The fields at Bumblebee Barn were named according to where they were, what they contained, and sometimes both. Top Pig was the furthest away of three fields full of pigs. The sows in Top Pig had already produced a litter of piglets last month, the ones from Middle Pig had been moved inside ready for the piglets arriving, and the piglets of the sows in Bottom Pig weren't due until later this month or in early April so would be outside for a bit longer.

Bear and Harley, Barney's Border collie brother and sister, were lying down beside his quad bike parked by the entrance to Top Pig, and I could see Barney at the far end. The dogs stood up and weaved round my legs. I loved dogs and so did Imogen. She'd often asked if she could have a puppy or a kitten but it wasn't an option when I worked long shifts, so we had to get our animal fix at the farm. If I'd got the production manager's job, I was going to look into getting a pet – perhaps an adult rescue cat which was used to being on its own during the day. Another thing I wanted to do for my daughter but couldn't because I worked shifts. It was so frustrating.

Barney spotted me and waved me into the field.

'How are the piglets doing?' I asked when I joined him.

'All good so far. Most sows have had good litters. Not many losses.'

He talked me through numbers and progress as he finished his checks, and then we headed back to the farmhouse for a tea break.

'Are you okay?' Barney asked, handing me a mug of tea. 'You seem a bit quiet today.'

'Crap couple of days,' I admitted, sitting down at the kitchen table with him. I started by offloading about the job situation.

'Do you wish they hadn't told you you'd have got the job?' he asked.

'I'm not sure. It's a boost to know the coaching worked, but it's a case of *look what you could have won*.' I shrugged. 'I couldn't not ask. I'd have always wondered.'

'If there are redundancies, surely you're not at risk.'

'I'm probably most at risk. What's the biggest operating expense most companies have? Payroll. And what's the easiest way to cut that? Get rid of the managers who earn more and have better benefits packages.'

'But you're brilliant at your job.'

'Doesn't make any difference. I've been there the longest, I earn the most, I'm likely to be the first to go.'

'I hope not.'

'Me too. Could you imagine Tilly's reaction if I told her I'd lost my job? She'd use it against me.'

'If you did lose your job, what would you do?'

'Panic!' I raked my fingers through my hair. 'I was thinking about it on the way over and trying to imagine what I could do instead. I might have a word with Levi and see if his family would take me on.'

Barney's mouth dropped open and it was clear he had no idea how to react to that suggestion until he realised I was joking.

'You had me going there for a minute,' he said, smiling as he shook his head. 'I was trying to picture you in a suit every day, reeling off a sales patter.'

'I doubt I'd last a week. I'd be shockingly bad. I haven't got the gift of the gab like Levi.'

'But think how well you did in that interview after some coaching. If Levi took you under his wing...'

He couldn't even finish the sentence for both of us laughing. It was good that we could make a joke out of it but if push came to shove and I did find myself out of work, I might have to look into a career which was way out of my comfort zone just to bring in some money and provide for my daughter. I already felt like she missed out on so much because my shifts kept us apart, and I wasn't prepared for her to miss out financially too.

'In other shock news this week, Tilly's pregnant with twin boys.'

Barney's mouth dropped open once more. 'No way!'

'Found that out by accident this morning. I got over Tilly years ago so it shouldn't bother me but, weirdly, it has. What's that all about?'

'At a guess, it's probably because it's not you you're thinking about – it's Imogen. She's already got a half-brother, half-sister and stepbrother and now she's going to have another two half-brothers. That's a lot of siblings, four of them younger than her, so there's potential for her to feel left out.'

That made so much sense. 'She was clingy with me earlier and she's *never* clingy. I wonder if it's cos of the twins.'

Barney nodded. 'Could be. She'd probably benefit from lots of one-to-one attention from you right now but I'm guessing Tilly won't allow that. Unless...' He narrowed his eyes at me, looking thoughtful. 'Is she as knackered this time as she has been before?'

'Even more.'

'Could be your chance to ease that for her.'

He was smiling at me and, for the first time, I could see a positive in the situation. Greg worked full time and often brought work home with him so most of the childcare responsibilities fell on Tilly. The further into her pregnancy she got, the more exhausted she'd be and the harder it would be to run around after everyone. Tilly was awkward but she wasn't stupid and I could try to capitalise on her fatigue.

'And what about when the twins come along?' Barney added. 'Four kids aged four and under to deal with? She's gonna need help.'

Why hadn't I thought about that? Tilly's mum was local but they didn't get on, so Tilly wasn't going to want her help. Greg's parents lived in Norfolk so they weren't on hand and Tilly's friends all had young children of their own so she didn't have a support network. But she had me. Assuming I still had a job, I could book some leave and have Imogen stay with me for a week or two while Tilly settled into a routine with the twins. That would be amazing.

Feeling brighter, I managed to make light of Chez moving back home and what I'd found him and Lorna getting up to in Imogen's bedroom. Barney agreed with me that Chez had been bang out of order and thought I'd been very restrained in how I'd handled it, which made me feel a bit better about it. Chez had still been in bed when I left the house this morning and I knew he'd be on his best behaviour when I got home later with Imogen. He liked playing the part of the cool uncle and one of the things I admired most about him was how hard he pushed himself to act like nothing was wrong around Imogen when he was in the throes of depression. That had to be exhausting. I'd told him we could explain it to Imogen but he thought she was still too young to understand and we'd best give it a couple more years. I appreciated his thoughtfulness but I sometimes worried that it was less about Imogen being too young to understand and more about Chez being ashamed of having depression. It was a mental illness and absolutely nothing to be ashamed about, but some of the comments he made each time he split up with Lorna, taking all the blame for the break-up on himself, saying he was *no good* as boyfriend material did make me wonder. I'd tried to talk to him about it, but he'd walk off muttering that I wasn't his therapist, so I'd had to let it go and hope that he was being honest in his therapy sessions.

After we'd finished our drinks, Barney and I went back out onto the farm, returning to the farmhouse when Amber rang to say she was back with Imogen.

'How did your dress look?' I asked Imogen when we joined them in the kitchen where Amber was cutting up an apple into slices.

'It's really pretty.'

'And the routine?' I asked.

They exchanged looks and laughed.

'Bit rough around the edges and, of course, Sophie and Tabs weren't there,' Amber said, 'but we've still got a week to go. If it goes wrong on the day, it'll be part of the charm.'

'Amber says I can ride Munchie,' Imogen said.

Munchie was one of the farm's ponies and Imogen's favourite. Barney gave her a riding lesson most times she visited the farm. She'd been confident in the saddle from the very start and I wished I could sign her up for regular lessons at a riding school but Tilly had dismissed that idea immediately, being unwilling to take her and pick her up when I was on shifts – another reason for me wanting to keep more regular hours. I hated that my daughter needed to miss out on something she loved because of my job but, if I lost it, I'd have the time but not the money for lessons. Catch-22 situation!

'Only if it's okay with your dad,' Amber added. 'He might have other plans.'

'Can I, Daddy? Please?'

'It's fine by me.'

We gathered round the table with hot drinks while Imogen tucked into her apple.

'Are you excited about being our bridesmaid?' Barney asked Imogen.

'I am, but why aren't I one at Fizz and Phoebe's wedding? All the other bridesmaids at your wedding are and they've left me out. Don't they like me?'

I hadn't realised that was the case, but I wouldn't have expected them to include Imogen in the bridal party when she wasn't related to either of them.

'Of course they like you, sweetie!' I said. 'They *love* you.'

I was dithering about how to explain further but Amber thankfully dived in.

'Joel's right, they *do* love you. But when you get married, choosing bridesmaids can be a really difficult decision. You can't have every female guest as a bridesmaid so you need to narrow it down. Brides usually pick their best friends, their sisters if they have any and sometimes relatives who they're really close to. If they have a daughter already, they'll probably include them and if some of their other bridesmaids have young daughters, they might choose them too.'

I glanced at Imogen who was nodding, appearing to take it all in.

'When your Uncle Barney and I get married, I have eight bridesmaids which is quite a lot but every single one of them is really important to me. And you're not the only bridesmaid of mine not to be a bridesmaid for Fizz and Phoebe. Sophie and Tabs aren't either, but Fizz and Phoebe have some bridesmaids I don't have. There'll be lots of different things about all the weddings you've been invited to and you're a very lucky girl to be going to so many. I was way older than you before I ever went to a wedding.'

Imogen seemed placated and ate another slice of apple before frowning once more.

'Darcie's family's very different. Mine's different too but not like Darcie's. She doesn't have any step- or half-brothers or - sisters and she doesn't have a mummy. Well, she does, but she doesn't see her very often. She calls her Hayley which is her real name and I'm confused about that because she *is* Darcie's mummy but Greg *isn't* my daddy which is why I call him Greg, but he keeps telling me to call him Daddy.'

My stomach lurched. 'Can you repeat that, sweetie?'

'Greg wants me to call him Daddy but I told him I wouldn't because he's not my daddy. You are.'

'When was this?' I asked, clenching my fists.

'Last weekend. And he's said it lots of times before. He gets annoyed with me when I say no.'

I caught Amber's and Barney's eyes and they both looked as concerned as I felt.

'What do you mean when you say he gets annoyed?' I asked,

fighting to keep my tone casual so as not to alarm her. 'Does he shout at you?'

'No. Can we go to the stables now?'

'You'll need to get changed first but, before you do, it's important I know what you mean when you say Greg gets annoyed. What is it he says or does?'

Imogen shrugged. 'He walks off and doesn't speak to me until Mummy tells him off.'

'Does Mummy know he wants you to call him Daddy?'

Imogen shrugged once more.

'Has Mummy ever been there when he's asked you?'

She chewed on her lip, evidently thinking back, before shaking her head vigorously. For all her faults, I couldn't imagine Tilly encouraging our daughter to refer to anyone but me as Daddy. She'd actually raised the subject when she and Imogen moved in with Greg. *I know this can't be easy, but it's important you understand one thing. Greg might have taken your place in my life, but he'll never take your place in Imogen's. You are and always will be her dad. Greg knows and respects that. Leighton has always called his mum's new partner by his real name and that never changed when they got married. It'll be the same with Imogen and Greg.*

'Did I do something wrong?' Imogen asked.

'Definitely not. Greg is Greg and I'm Daddy and you were right to say no to him.'

There was an awkward silence, which I had no idea how to fill. I was seething and I feared that, if I spoke, something derogatory about Greg would spill out. How dare he ask my daughter to call him Daddy? Didn't he have enough kids of his own? Did he have to claim mine too? I glanced helplessly at Barney and Amber who both wore sympathetic expressions.

'Imogen,' Amber said, standing up. 'Why don't we let your

daddy and Uncle Barney clear away while we go upstairs and get you changed for your ride?'

I mouthed *thank you* to her as she took Imogen's hand and led her up to the spare bedroom where they kept the riding clothes and boots I'd bought.

'I'm so sorry,' Barney said when they were out of earshot.

I released a heavy sigh. 'Why would he do that?'

Barney shrugged. 'I don't like him any more than you do so I'm not defending him but, before you say anything to Tilly, bear in mind that you don't have the context. Greg *is* Daddy to the other three so it's possible Imogen questioned why they call him Daddy when she doesn't and he could have invited her to call him that if she wanted.'

I ran my fingers through my hair and exhaled once more. 'It's possible. But knowing Greg...' I was convinced that a lot of Tilly's hostility towards me was down to his influence.

'Yeah, you're probably right. I'd just advise against going in all guns blazing when you only have Imogen's side of the story, especially when she was a bit woolly on the details.'

'Fair enough. But if it turns out he's been telling her to call him Daddy and getting stroppy when she refuses...'

'If that's the case, you'll politely ask Tilly to have a word and you'll come over here, we'll race the quad bikes through the swamp and you can shout and swear until you've got it all off your chest.'

I smiled at him gratefully. 'You're on!'

The quad bikes were perfect for when it all got on top of me and I'd probably need to take Barney up on the offer after I raised the issue with Tilly. And if I discovered that she knew about it or, even worse, had been actively encouraging it, it would take a lot of racing through the mud to calm me down. She'd promised me I'd always be Daddy and I expected her to stand by that promise.

Mind you, she'd promised me she loved me and couldn't wait to marry me. Tilly didn't have great form for keeping her promises.

* * *

'She's looking great,' Amber said as we leaned against the paddock fence watching Imogen riding Munchie a little later. 'Has she said anything more about wanting lessons?'

'No. She seems to get that I can't take her each week because of work, and Tilly can't spend every evening ferrying them all around.'

'Any news on the promotion?'

I told Amber what I'd shared with Barney earlier and my worries about what an impending restructure could mean for me and Imogen.

'I'm so sorry, Joel. I know uncertainty can be frustrating but, in my experience, it's not worth wasting your energy on. You can't change or influence what's happening so best not to fret and just take it as it comes. If it's good news, great. If it's bad, then you can deal with it and we'll all be here to support you.'

'I appreciate that.'

An easy silence settled on us for several minutes as we watched Barney explaining something to Imogen and her nodding.

'Did you always want to work in a factory?' Amber asked when Imogen set off on Munchie again.

'Does anyone?' I said, laughing. 'I think it's one of those jobs you fall into rather than have as a career destination. I didn't know what I wanted to do after college so I took a summer contract at the factory to earn some money and hoped inspiration would strike. Sixteen years later...'

'What did you do at college? I don't think I've ever asked.'

'Catering and hospitality.'

'Oh! That would explain why you're such a good cook. You didn't want to pursue that?'

'I did originally, but it went a bit wrong. My dad and uncle used to have a restaurant and I had a part-time job there since I was twelve, starting on pot wash and working my way up to basic food prep. The plan was for me to work there full time after college and the long-term big plan was to take over when they retired. But in the summer between the two years at college, I worked there full time as a junior chef and it was a nightmare.'

I shuddered as I thought about it.

'Dad and Uncle Alvin had worked brilliantly together for years and they'd been fine with me working there part time but something switched when I stepped up as junior chef. Dad was really hard on me and I felt like I couldn't do anything right. He wasn't interested in hearing new ideas and shouted me down all the time. Uncle Alvin thought he was being unfair and called him out on it so they clashed and I hated being the cause of a rift, so I left to save the restaurant and my relationship with my family. I loved cooking – still do – but the experience completely put me off going down that route.'

'I'm so sorry, Joel. That's such a shame. Would you consider it now?'

I shook my head without hesitation. 'I'd enjoy the cooking and I'd particularly enjoy creating different dishes – experimenting was always what gave me a buzz – but I'd need to work evenings and weekends so I'd be in the same predicament I am now.'

'Good point. Anything else appeal? If you didn't need to worry about the money and you could work hours that suited Imogen, what would your dream job be?'

'I honestly don't know,' I said after pondering on it, 'but I'd love it to involve some time outdoors. After working half my life in the depths of a windowless factory, spending just a small part of every day in the fresh air – even in bad weather – would be an absolute dream.'

'Something will present itself,' Amber said, nudging her arm against mine. 'I think this is going to be your year, Joel Grainger.'

I wasn't sure I bought into the whole fate and destiny thing, but I would appreciate things going my way for once.

'You should do some manifesting,' Amber added.

I raised my eyebrows at her. 'Some what?'

'Manifesting. You must have heard of it. It's the idea that you can turn a goal into reality through positive belief.'

'You mean if I believe I can win the lottery, then I'll win it?'

She laughed. 'Maybe not that extreme but it's about having a positive mindset and being optimistic because, when you approach something with a negative outlook, it becomes an obstacle. When you applied for the production manager job first time around, did you believe you could get it?'

'Not a chance.'

'And that attitude contributed to your mind going blank in the interview which meant you didn't get the job which, in turn, confirmed your belief that you couldn't get it. But it was actually your negative mindset that stopped you getting the job and not any lack of ability because, if they didn't think you were capable, the outgoing manager wouldn't have championed you and you wouldn't have been shortlisted for interview.'

'That all makes sense.'

'Did you go into the interview this time around with that same *not a chance* mindset?'

'No. The HR Director's coaching helped me, and I genuinely believed I could get the job this time.'

'And you *did* get it. What happened next with the takeover was unexpected and out of your control but your behaviour in the interview got you what you wanted and the reason you behaved in that way was because you believed. So my advice is that you think about what you'd like your future to look like and start manifesting it.'

'How?'

'Think about it, focus on it, send those positive thoughts and wishes out to the universe and believe that what you want can happen. I've got a book about it that I can lend you if you like.'

I was about to say no but it struck me that doing so would be playing into the negative mindset.

'Okay. I'll have a read. Manifesting sounds a bit out there, but what you said about the different approaches to my interview does resonate so I accept there's something in it.'

Anything was worth a try as I definitely needed an injection of positivity about work. It might be fun to send my wishes out into the universe and manifest a positive outcome. Although if I was going to do that, I'd need to think about what those wishes really were. When Eloise and Jeremy said there could be redundancies, my first reaction was panic but could losing my job at the factory actually be a good thing? I'd get redundancy pay and I might even be able to negotiate a leaving date coinciding with the twins arriving and the start of the school summer holidays. I could take the pressure off Tilly by having Imogen stay with me for the summer, or at least part of it, which would give us valuable time together. I might even be able to convince her to let me take Imogen to Portugal to see my parents.

As I watched Imogen on Munchie, everything seemed so much brighter and the thought of losing my job wasn't quite so scary.

I glanced at Amber and she gave me an encouraging smile. 'It's going to be fine, Joel. I know it.'

She'd said *something will present itself* earlier. Maybe I didn't have to throw a wish into the universe to secure a particular job – just positive thoughts about finding the right role for me. I'd see what Amber's book said.

And while I was trying to manifest a positive outcome for work and more time with Imogen, maybe I could manifest one for my non-existent love life and break the curse of always being the friend, never the boyfriend. Before I met Marley, I'd tried a dating app and every single connection had friend zoned me, some after the first date, some before even getting that far. For those who did make it as far as a date, the evening always ended the same. I'd ask if they wanted to do it again and there'd be that familiar expression – the scrunch of the nose, the gentle smile, the tilt of the head – and those dreaded words. *Aw, I've had such a lovely evening, Joel. You're such a nice guy but I can't see us being more than friends.* I'd smile and nod in agreement, knowing that it wouldn't even be a friendship because they'd swipe left before they got home, the connection would be severed, and I'd never see them again. But thinking about what Amber had said about my interview earlier, could always being the friend actually be my fault? Did I turn up to dates expecting to be friend zoned and therefore put myself in that box before the date could? I strongly suspected I did. I was going to make sure I didn't leave without Amber's book and I knew what I'd be reading tonight after Imogen went to sleep. Chez's CBT was all about positive thoughts and it worked for him most of the time. Thinking positive thoughts and manifesting a happy future for Imogen and me – and hopefully somebody else – was going to be the way forward for me. No wallowing. No lamenting the past. Just looking forward to good times.

7

POPPY

I'd been awake for a couple of hours when my alarm sounded at half seven on Sunday morning. What a restless night. Damon's odd behaviour yesterday had unnerved me – especially him turning up at The Larks like that – and it had taken me way longer than usual to switch off. Once sleep finally came, it brought disturbing dreams. I was trying to visit Dad at The Larks but Marnie wouldn't let me in because his 'son' was already with him. When I finally managed to push past her and run to his room, Dad was lying in bed with Damon standing over him, a pillow in his hands. *You're mine, Poppy. No more distractions for you.* Marnie and her team had caught up with me and held me back as Damon lowered the pillow over Dad's face. I woke up screaming, heart pounding, tangled up in the duvet and hadn't been able to get back to sleep.

Even though I knew Dad wasn't in any danger, it didn't take a genius to work out that my feelings of discomfort around Damon had been projected into that dream.

Hearing a vehicle stopping outside, I peeled back the duvet

and crept to the window. Stomach churning, I pulled one of the curtains aside and parted the blinds, relief flowing through me that it was just Wilf's daughter dropping off a box of fresh eggs from her hens like she usually did on a Sunday morning.

I showered, dressed and made myself a coffee. I usually started the day with breakfast, but my stomach still felt in knots after my unsettled night. Every noise outside had me drawn to the windows, checking to make sure Damon wasn't there. I hated that he could make me feel this way.

Settling down at my desk for a morning of work, I checked my emails and responded to a couple of straightforward client queries about business expenses. Another client had a more complicated query about buying or renting office premises, but the figures he'd provided didn't ring true so I clicked onto a property website to do a bit of research which made me think again about moving. Before I knew it, I'd gone down a rabbit hole of recent sales prices on similar properties in Winchcote and the neighbouring villages as well as looking at houses for sale nearer The Larks. There were a couple of newbuild estates advertising two- and three-bedroom houses with a garage and small garden, but I closed the site down, shaking my head. If I did move, I didn't want to be surrounded by other houses. I wanted an edge-of-the-village location like Dove Cottage or even somewhere remote. I loved the peace and quiet at Saltersbeck Farm – a place I could relax, think, breathe. A place where I could just be.

I needed to focus back on my work so I made another coffee, closed all distracting tabs on my computer and cracked on with my tasks, only allowing myself a short break to heat up some soup for lunch.

Dad's birthday party was planned for 3 p.m. so I applied some light make-up and changed into a dress and boots. My naturally wavy dark hair had air-dried into soft waves, so all it needed was a quick comb and I was ready.

I cautiously opened the front door a little later but there was no sign of Damon. Maybe he'd got the message and I was building this up into something bigger than it was but, as I left the village, my stomach tightened. Damon knew it was Dad's birthday today. Might he turn up, despite my insistence that he didn't?

When I arrived at The Larks, I did a complete loop of the car park to make sure Damon's van wasn't there, relief flowing through me when it wasn't. I hated that I'd felt the need to do that because of him.

I grabbed the gift bag from the passenger footwell and hastened to the entrance. A teddy bear and a box of Dad's favourite childhood sweets – Jelly Babies – felt inadequate for such a milestone birthday but he didn't need anything and an extravagant gift from someone he didn't recognise would only cause upset and confusion.

Dad was at the far end of the residents' lounge wearing a pointed blue party hat and a large badge. There were blue and silver balloon bouquets either side of him and several gifts on a table. To the left side of the room beneath some *Happy Birthday* banners was a buffet of scones and cakes either side of a birthday cake. I paused, taking in Dad's name and one fat candle. Marnie had told me that, while they made a fuss of birthdays, they never showcased the age due to time-shifting. I understood and supported it, but choosing a generic card this year without the word 'Dad' on it and not even being able to replace that with an age one had hit hard. Much to the bewilderment of the sales assistant, I'd burst out crying at the till.

'Noting the lack of candles?' Marnie said, joining me. It was meant to be her weekend off but she'd told me she wouldn't miss

Dad's birthday celebration for the world, which I'd found touching.

I turned and smiled weakly at her. 'I know it's what's needed, but...'

'It doesn't sit right,' she filled in for me when I didn't finish the sentence.

She squeezed my hand. 'None of it's easy but try to enjoy the happy moments. Look at your dad right now. That hat. That smile. He might be confused about many things but he knows what his birthday means and who doesn't love a birthday?'

I watched him laughing as he pulled on a second party hat, making him look like he had horns. Seeing him so carefree like that lifted me. Marnie was right about there being happy moments within the sadness. I needed to take them in and remember that, at the end of the day, the man in the two hats was still my amazing dad and the sense of humour I'd always loved so much was still there.

'Happy birthday, Stanley,' I said, joining him a few minutes later and placing his gift bag on the table. 'Are you having a nice day?'

He smiled at me but there wasn't even a flicker of recognition. I sometimes wondered whether the sight of me might have triggered something if I'd been his or Mum's biological daughter and had inherited my looks from either of them. There might even have been a chance if I'd looked like my biological mother, Evie, but I apparently resembled my biological father and he'd never been in our lives. I didn't have any photos of him, although I had several of Evie and all I appeared to have inherited from her were my full lips.

'We've been to the zoo,' Dad said, smiling at me before rattling off a list of birthday presents he'd received including a train set. 'Mum's made me a cake.'

'How lucky are you? I bet it's really tasty.'

'Mum's cakes are delicious.'

I sat back in my chair and watched Dad opening his cards and gifts, my throat tightening with his cry of, 'My favourites!' when he unwrapped the box of Jelly Babies, and tears blurring my eyes when he unwrapped the teddy bear and cuddled it against his chest. I'd had it made from Mum's favourite bright red chenille throw and had sprayed it with her perfume. Dad sniffed it and made a comment that it smelled nice, but the fragrance didn't appear to trigger any memories. Probably just as well. It had been heartbreaking when he'd kept asking where she was and why she'd left him. Better now that he didn't remember her at all.

The team from Cuddles & Paws arrived and soon the residents were stroking the animals. The smile on Dad's face as he stroked the ears of a fluffy grey rabbit was a joy to behold. It was so much nicer seeing his fingers touching something alive rather than his fiddle cushion, especially as the rabbit was also holding his full attention. No more searching for something. Or at least for a short while.

Marnie approached me as the party began winding up. 'Do you need to rush home or have you got time for a chat?'

'Has he been wandering again?'

'No, nothing like that. There's just something I'd like to talk to you about without my work head on, so it would be good to go off-site if that's okay. The Farrier's Arms will be open.'

The Farrier's Arms was one of those newbuild pubs designed to look *olde worlde* but which fooled nobody. I'd heard that the food was decent but, as I had nobody to dine with, I'd never been.

'Fine by me. I'll just say goodbye to Dad.'

The teddy bear was sitting on the gift table. I picked it up and handed it to Dad, who smiled at me.

'Do you like your bear?'

'I love it.'

'Are you going to give it a name?'

He studied the bear for a while and shrugged. 'I'm not good at naming things, but maybe...' He tilted his head to one side. 'Poppy.'

My heart leapt. He recognised me! 'Yes?' I whispered.

'For the bear,' he clarified. 'It's the colour of poppies.'

I swallowed back the disappointment blocking my throat. Of course he hadn't recognised me. No miracles here.

'So it is,' I said, my voice a little strained. 'I'll tell you something funny. Poppy's my name too.'

'Is it?'

'Yes. I was called that because I was born on Remembrance Day – the eleventh day of the eleventh month.'

'Poppy,' he said, looking from the bear to me. His eyes locked with mine for a moment and I willed some sort of recognition. 'Do you...' He frowned and I wondered what he was trying to unlock. He leaned over to the table and picked up the open box of sweets. 'Do you want a Jelly Baby?'

Nothing more than wishful thinking on my part yet again. 'I'm all right, thank you. Full of birthday cake.'

'I don't know who gave me the bear,' he said, glancing round the room.

'It was from me.'

He knitted his brows. 'Why?'

'Because it's your birthday and birthday boys deserve nice gifts.' Because you're my dad. Because I love you. Because you're ninety today.

My spoken answer seemed to satisfy him as he smiled and thanked me, cuddling the bear closer to his heart.

'Would you mind if I took a photo of you with Poppy?' I asked.

Marnie appeared next to me as I took several photos. 'Stanley, why don't I take a photo of you with Poppy the bear *and* Poppy the person? Wouldn't that be good?'

Dad was happy to oblige and I crouched down beside him, smiling at the camera. It was so tricky to find reasons to take photos of Dad, never mind ones with the two of us, so I hoped it turned out well.

The last thing I wanted before I left was a hug and Marnie secured that for me too.

'What do you say to a thank you hug to Poppy for her lovely gift, Stanley?'

Stanley smiled and put his arms out. I knew I had to be brief, but I wanted to hold him tight and never let go. I wanted to tell him that I was his daughter and that the bear was made from his wife's throw. I wanted so badly for him to remember, but he was never going to. Dad was lost somewhere in time, his childhood mind trapped in an old man's body and one day, not far from now, he'd forget other things like how to swallow. It was all too cruel.

* * *

'How did you find today?' Marnie asked as we sat down in The Farrier's Arms with drinks a little later.

'Difficult. Every time I see him, there's so much circling round my head and I stupidly keep getting my hopes up that he'll recognise me.' I found myself welling up once again. 'I know it'll never happen now, but I suppose there's part of me still hoping for a miracle.'

'You're not alone there. It's such a tough thing to experience.'

We both took a sip on our drinks.

'You wanted to talk to me about something?' I prompted.

'Yes, but before I do, I don't think I ever told you what led me to do this job. My granddad died when I was eight and my grandma was so lost and lonely without him that she moved in with us. I was taking my GCSEs when she started showing signs of dementia. She had Alzheimer's like your dad and it was a rapid decline. By the time I finished college, she had no idea who any of us were and she wasn't safe on her own.'

'Sounds familiar,' I said.

'It broke our hearts admitting her into a home, but we thought it was the best place for her. She wasn't there long and, after she passed away, stories of neglect emerged. The things that went on...' She drew in a sharp breath, shaking her head, and I could imagine how painful it must be for her revisiting something so shocking.

'At that point, I vowed that I'd make a career out of supporting dementia patients and ensuring no vulnerable people ever went through what my grandma must have gone through.'

'I'm really sorry about your grandma. I find it so hard to believe that people can go into a caring profession and not care.' A shudder ran through me at the thought of Dad being mistreated.

'Same here but, sadly, it happens. Not at The Larks; every single member of staff cares deeply about all the residents and their families.'

'It shows.'

'Thank you. You're probably wondering why I'm telling you this. Having worked in dementia care for over thirty years and having lost a grandparent to Alzheimer's, I've got a wealth of knowledge about dementia not just from the perspective of the patients, but from the perspective of the families. I've seen everything from an angry child or partner practically slinging the patient in through the front door and never returning through to those who'd spend all day and night with their loved one if they could.'

She paused and gave me a gentle smile, as though acknowledging that I was one of the latter.

'We're all different and there's no right or wrong way to deal with the myriad of emotions that come with a dementia diagnosis or when a loved one moves into late-stage dementia. Feelings of grief and loss can kick in at any stage, they can come in waves, and different emotions will be stronger at different times. Do you mind me asking how you're feeling at the moment?'

The words *I'm fine* were on the tip of my tongue, but why lie to Marnie? She'd see right through it and I doubted she'd have asked the question if she didn't already know the answer.

My shoulders sagged. 'Honestly? I'm exhausted. I feel like I'm spinning plates and I don't have the energy to keep them all going and, pretty soon, they're going to fall off and smash.'

'And what happens to the plate spinner when that happens?' she asked gently.

'Broken too.'

She lightly placed her hand on my forearm – a sign of understanding and comfort which brought tears to my eyes.

'If you didn't visit your dad every day, what could you do instead?'

I removed a tissue from my bag and dabbed at my tears. 'I could slow down a bit. Relax. Go out.' A few more answers popped into my head, but they felt too personal to share. *Go on a date. Be a little less lonely.*

'So you'd get your life back? Because I get the impression it's been on hold since your mum fell ill.'

A sob caught in my throat and tears ran down my cheeks as I slowly nodded. Marnie had completely nailed it. I'd been so focused on my parents and my job that there'd been nothing left for me and now there was a very real danger of me having nothing left to give Dad because I was so weary of it all.

'You're no good to anyone if you're exhausted, Poppy,' Marnie said, her voice gentle, her eyes full of empathy. 'When was the last time you had a holiday, and I don't mean the bucket-list trips you did with your mum because they won't have been relaxing like a regular holiday?'

I wiped my cheeks as I considered it. 'It'll have been seven years ago, before Phil and I split up.'

Marnie released a low whistle. 'That's a long time without a proper break. So why don't you take one now? Find yourself a nice little holiday cottage somewhere by the sea or in the countryside and try to relax for a while. Recharge your batteries. Nobody would judge you for it.'

I sighed and nodded. 'A friend said pretty much the same thing to me on Friday.'

'And do you trust that person's opinion?'

'Very much. But if I did go away, what about Dad?'

'My team will look after him, he'll talk to the other residents, our volunteers will engage with him – all the things we do every day, whether a resident has a visitor or not. I know it hurts and I know it sounds harsh, but Stanley has no idea who you are anymore, he doesn't look forward to your visits, and he doesn't remember you from one visit to the next. He'd be none the wiser if you visited every other day, once a week, once a fortnight, or if you never visited again.'

'Oh, I couldn't do that.'

Marnie smiled. 'I know you couldn't, but it *is* an option and some do take it because visiting becomes too harrowing.'

I sipped on my drink, battling with my guilt. I wanted to get away. I *needed* to. But would I spend the whole time feeling guilty that I wasn't with Dad?

'I can see it written all over your face,' Marnie said. 'Guilt.'

'How did you...?'

'I've seen it countless times and I've felt it myself. Believe me when I say you've absolutely *nothing* to feel guilty about. I can say that to you a million times, but you're the only one who can give yourself permission to let go of the guilt. You're also the only one who can give yourself permission to take a break, but I really urge you to do it, and sooner rather than later, because this is gruelling and it's only going to get worse.'

I thought about Sharon's friend's holiday cottage in East Yorkshire. It sounded idyllic. 'I'm tempted. But what if—'

'If there's a *significant* change in Stanley's condition, I'd let you know.'

I noted the emphasis on the word *significant* and knew what that meant. Dad was deteriorating each day and she wouldn't want to call me back with each change.

'I'd like to sleep on it,' I said, 'but I'm thinking I probably will go.'

'That would be a good decision.'

* * *

I needed to work when I got home but I felt so drained that every task seemed to take twice as long as it should. My conversation with Marnie had moved on to the subject of burnout. I'd claimed that I might be shattered, but I was way off hitting burnout. She'd searched on her phone for a definition and signs of it – *physical, emotional and/or mental exhaustion as a result of feeling swamped, lacking motivation, reduced performance, feeling listless, anxiety, negative thoughts about self and others...* The list had gone on and, when she finished, she fixed a meaningful gaze on me. I had to concede that I'd either hit burnout or I was very close.

Marnie was right to have challenged me about the need to visit Dad every day. Sharon and Ian had done the same on several occasions. I hadn't wanted to worry them so had repeatedly assured them I was coping when, deep down, I knew I wasn't. Marnie had also been right to challenge me about feeling guilty for not visiting. My logical brain knew it was a natural reaction when facing grief and loss but, for me, the guilt cut so much deeper. My parents had sacrificed everything to raise a child in need when they'd never wanted to be parents in the first place. What sort of person would I be if I threw that back in their faces and abandoned them when they needed me? I'd cared for Mum until the end, and I'd do the same for Dad.

That evening, I went into Mum and Dad's bedroom to close the curtains. I was usually straight in and out but I found myself pausing and looking around. My eyes rested on a rose-gold photo frame on Mum's dressing table and I took it over to the bed, flicking on the bedside lamp as I sat down and read the embroidered words of Mum's favourite quote – *Do one thing every day that scares you.*

'To give us strength for what's coming,' she'd said, smiling at me as she passed her needle through the Aida stretched across an embroidery frame.

It had been a struggle but she'd been adamant she wanted to do it herself, even adding in flowers and bees to frame the words. When Mum was diagnosed with MND, our little family had faced things every day that scared us and I genuinely believe that the positivity that mindset brought – aided by that colourful embroidery sitting by her bed – had helped Mum face the end with strength and dignity. And now with Dad's Alzheimer's, every single visit scared me, but every moment I was away from him gave me the fear too. Fear of that phone call. Fear of the end. Fear of who I was when I had no family left. What if I did go away and that phone call came? But what if I didn't go and I made myself so ill that I couldn't be by his side at the end?

I switched the light off and took Mum's embroidery into my room, placing it by my bed. Going away on my own scared me, but burning out scared me even more. I'd make the phone call tomorrow, take that break, and come back with the energy and strength I was going to need to do for Dad what I'd done for Mum.

8

POPPY

I woke up on Monday morning to a message from Damon sent late the night before.

FROM DAMON

Hi Poppy, it's time to book in the first mow of the season. How about a week on Tuesday?

Hearing from him was not how I wanted to start the day and I instantly felt twitchy. I began typing but quickly deleted what I'd written, put my phone down with a sigh and headed for the bathroom. I'd respond later when my head wasn't so sleep-fuzzy and I could find the right words to tell him I didn't need him to cut the grass anymore without inviting a debate on the matter.

This morning, I'd been invited to a networking event. I hated things like that and would happily avoid them like the plague, but Mum's voice always came into my head with her favourite quote and I'd search for the positives. In this case, the woman running the group was a potential new client and she'd told me there might be others interested in my services. Even though I had more than enough work at the moment from my existing client base, things could suddenly change, so it made sense to keep my options open.

By the time I'd showered, applied my make-up and dressed in a smart trouser suit and blouse, another message had arrived.

FROM DAMON

It showed you typing but nothing came through.
Everything OK?

I sighed heavily. Damon was relentless and, if I didn't respond, he'd pester me all morning. I was just going to have to rip off the plaster.

TO DAMON

I'm really sorry but I won't be using your services this year. Wishing you all the best

Reading it back, I added a smiley face in the hope that it would soften the blow. Message sent, I turned my phone to silent, unable to face Damon messaging me back or, even worse, ringing me demanding to know why he couldn't mow my lawn/be my boyfriend/run off into the sunset with me.

I had forty minutes before I needed to leave the house, so I made a mug of tea and took it into my office, sipping it while I dealt with a few emails. I was resting my elbow on my desk as I went in for the last gulp and somehow my elbow slipped, spilling my drink. I looked down at my tea-soaked blouse in despair and raced across the landing to my bedroom to change.

I'd just pulled my jacket back on when the usually cheerful *ding-dong* of the doorbell sent a shiver of dread through me. Holding my breath, I peeked through the blinds to see if my suspicions were confirmed about who was at the door. At that moment, Damon looked up at the bedroom window and I released a nervous gasp as I ducked down. The doorbell rang again, and I remained frozen to the spot. How had it come to this? I was a thirty-two-year-old woman, for goodness' sake, not a teenager trying to hide from the village bullies.

'I know you're in there, Poppy,' Damon called through the letterbox. 'I only want to talk.'

I stayed where I was, heart pounding. The doorbell rang for a third time followed by several loud knocks.

'Please answer, Poppy. Don't I deserve a proper explanation?'

I couldn't be late to the networking event so, when the doorbell rang for a fourth time, I rose with a sigh and grabbed my bag from the office.

'I'm coming,' I shouted, stomping down the stairs. 'Give me a minute.'

I slipped on a pair of heeled boots, wrapped a scarf round my neck and pulled on my smart frock coat before grabbing my car keys. I'd speak to Damon, but no way was he coming inside.

I reluctantly stepped outside, closing the door behind me.

Damon smiled at me. 'You look beautiful.'

'I'm going out.'

His dazzling smile immediately switched off. 'On a date?'

'That's none of your business.'

'It is, isn't it? You're seeing someone else already! That's why you've done your hair and make-up. Who is he?'

'There is no he but, if there was, it would have nothing to do with you. We had a friendly chat over a coffee which I appreciated at the time – thank you very much – but that never made us an item.' It felt like I was trapped in time with the same conversation playing on a continuous loop.

'Is it Phil? Are you back together?'

'No! Where's this...?' I released an exasperated sigh. 'I don't have time for this. I've got a meeting.'

'Before you go, what's this all about?'

Damon thrust his phone at me, my response to his WhatsApp message showing on the screen and I winced. I probably should have explained why, but it was his fault I hadn't. If he hadn't chased me, I'd have had time to compose a proper response.

'It's nothing personal,' I said, gently. 'I just don't need you to mow the lawn anymore.'

'Nothing personal? I've mowed this lawn for the past ten years, long before you moved back home.'

'And you've done a great job, but I don't have time to look after the garden like Dad did, so I need someone to do that and it makes sense for that same person to mow the grass too.'

'Is it about the money? Because I can charge you less as long as you don't tell your neighbours.'

'It's not about the money, Damon. It's about time and how little of it I have.'

'I can look after your garden.'

'No, you can't. How many times have you told me you don't know the difference between a flower and a weed? My parents worked so hard on this garden, and I want their legacy to remain. I don't have the time or ability so I've taken on someone who does.'

'You've already done it? Without giving me a chance to pitch for the work first?'

'Damon! There was no work to pitch for. You and I both know you are *not* a gardener.' This was *exactly* what I'd wanted to avoid. I'd made a decision that I no longer required his services and I shouldn't have to debate it.

'You're saying I'm no good at my job.'

I couldn't bear people who didn't listen properly and who twisted words.

'What did I just say?' I demanded, a hard edge to my voice. 'That you've done a great job. Seriously, Damon, it's nothing to do with the quality of your work. It's about what I need which is an experienced, knowledgeable gardener to look after the whole thing and you're *not* that person. You *know* you're not.'

He stared at me and my stomach churned. His eyes were dark, almost black, and the look he was giving me right now made my skin crawl. Until now, I'd thought of him as a nuisance, but suddenly I found him quite creepy.

'It's Troy Taylor, isn't it?'

'I need to go.'

'Is it him you're meeting?'

I ignored him and strode towards the car, but he ran after me and grabbed my arm.

'Stop touching me!' I cried, yanking my arm away.

'What's going on?'

My heart leapt at the sight of Wilf striding towards our boundary fence. Benji shot past him, barking, and ducked beneath the fence.

'Damon was just leaving,' I called to Wilf.

'We haven't finished talking,' Damon said, his voice full of anger, his eyes flashing at me.

'Yes, we have. I need to be somewhere and you need to leave.'

When Damon showed no signs of moving, despite Benji jumping up at him and barking in his best attempt to intimidate, Wilf stepped over the low fence.

'Are you going to leave, son, or do I need to make a call?'

Although Damon had never cut Wilf's lawn, he knew that my neighbour was ex-police.

'I'm going,' he muttered, taking a couple of steps down the drive. He stared at me, a look of disgust on his face. 'I can't believe you'd choose Troy Taylor over me. You'll be sorry.'

'I don't see you leaving,' Wilf said, taking his phone out of his pocket.

Damon held his hands up in a surrender sign and backed down the drive, lip curled up.

'You'll be sorry,' he repeated.

'I hope that's not a threat,' Wilf called, holding his phone aloft.

'It's a fact,' Damon shouted, before turning and running down the last stretch of drive. His van wheels squealed as he shot away at speed.

'Are you all right?' Wilf asked.

'I think so.'

I felt pretty shaken and quite perplexed by the whole thing, my heart pounding, my throat dry. The repeated references to us dating had irritated rather than concerned me, but this was something else. I didn't like his recent behaviour at all. He was acting like a jealous boyfriend. Was I still seeing Phil? Was I meeting Troy Taylor? Where had that come from?

'You're sure?' Wilf asked.

I gave him what I hoped was a reassuring smile. 'Thanks for stepping in. He's not good at hearing the word no. I'm sorry, Wilf, but I need to shoot to a meeting.'

Wilf scooped Benji up and moved to one side. 'We won't keep you but if you fancy a coffee when you get back, we'll be here.'

I nodded, grateful for such a wonderful neighbour. I'd take him up on that offer of a drink when I got home so I could thank him properly and so I could steal some cuddles from Benji as I needed them more than ever right now.

As I pulled out of the village and drove towards Cheltenham for the networking meeting, the conversation with Damon played on a loop in my head. I'd never seen Damon get angry like that and it had been scary. What did he mean by saying I'd be sorry? Was that because he was bizarrely convinced that I was seeing Troy and a belief that he'd make a better boyfriend than Troy? I wished he'd stop obsessing about who I was dating. It really was none of his business. If he showed up again, I was going to have to take him to task on it and perhaps do what Wilf had done and threaten him with the police if he didn't leave me alone.

By the time I hit the outskirts of Cheltenham, I'd made a decision about going away. Sharon and Marnie both thought I needed to and they were right. Some space away from Damon would be beneficial to us both too. If Sharon's friend's cottage was free, there couldn't be a better time to go than this week while the bees didn't need attention, while I had no meetings, before Troy started on the garden and before I burned out completely. I'd have to work, but I'd have some time to relax and I needed that right now. I called Sharon and asked her if she could check whether her friend's cottage was still available this week or over the weekend.

A few minutes later, she rang back. 'Mary says it's free now and you can have it for up to eleven nights including tonight.'

'Wow! I won't be able to stay away quite that long, but that's great to know.'

'I'll send you her number. Let me know what dates you decide and if you need us to do anything with the bees.'

After the call disconnected, I felt more relaxed than I'd done in a long time. Whether the time away would recharge my batteries – especially when I'd have work to do – was anyone's guess but it was worth a try because, as Marnie had suggested, I was going to make myself ill if I continued like this. And if I was ill, what good was I to my dad, the bees or my clients?

* * *

The networking meeting was surprisingly enjoyable. I had positive conversations with a couple of attendees during the event and the host confirmed in our one-to-one afterwards that she wanted to join me as a client starting from the new tax year in April. It was all good, but it didn't fill me with excitement like it might have done in the past. I put that down to the altercation with Damon putting a dampener on things.

When I arrived back at Dove Cottage, Wilf was cleaning the woodwork on his bay window.

'Good meeting?' he asked me as Benji dropped his toy pig and dived through the fence for attention.

'Really good,' I said, picking Benji up and scratching his ears. 'Is that coffee still on offer?'

'It certainly is.'

'Let me change and make a few quick phone calls then I'll be over.'

'I'll pop the kettle on. Let yourself in.'

I put Benji down, but he followed me towards the house rather than returning to Wilf.

'He's been on edge all morning, watching out for you coming back,' Wilf called.

'Aw, Benji, are you protecting me? Come in with me while I get changed.'

I'd decided that, if I put my holiday off until later in the week, there was every chance I'd talk myself out of it so I needed to act now. I'd pack a case after lunch and drive up to East Yorkshire this afternoon, staying until Sunday to allow myself long enough for a proper break. By the time I'd factored in the travel, taking just a few days off probably wouldn't have much benefit.

Benji followed me upstairs and lay on my bed watching while I removed my suit and pulled on my jeans and a hoodie.

'That's better! I feel more like me now,' I told him as I hung the suit up in my wardrobe. 'I need to make a few calls and then we'll go to your house.'

I sat on the bed with Benji cuddled up beside me and rang Sharon again to tell her the news. She said she'd definitely visit Dad while I was away and report back, which was reassuring. Next I rang Marnie at The Larks who was delighted that I was taking her advice and looking after myself.

'Final call to Sharon's friend Mary,' I told Benji.

Before leaving Cheltenham, I'd seen a stack of messages and four missed calls from Damon, all of which I ignored. Just before I rang Mary, I noticed the missed calls tally had gone up to seven and shuddered as I pictured Damon's angry face earlier.

Mary Dodds sounded lovely over the phone. She had one of those warm voices where you could tell the person was smiling when they spoke. She said she'd leave the porch door unlocked and a key hidden under a plant pot inside, and would stop by tomorrow evening to say hello and see if I needed anything.

When Benji and I went next door, Wilf had the drinks ready and had even made us each a sandwich for lunch which was typically thoughtful of him. He asked me about my business meeting and about Dad's birthday as we ate but, when we'd finished, I figured it was time to address the elephant in the room.

'About earlier...' I began.

'I hope I didn't overstep. I heard raised voices and, when I saw who it was—'

'Your timing was perfect and I'm glad you stepped in. Damon's a bit too intense for me and I'm struggling to shake him off.'

'He's an ex-boyfriend?' Wilf was clearly trying to keep a poker face, but he didn't manage to keep the surprise out of his voice.

'No, but he does keep asking me out.'

I briefly outlined the moment with Dad last year which had led to me taking Damon out for a thank you coffee, his mistaken belief that it was a date, and his subsequent messages asking me out.

'The messages stopped over the winter so I thought – hoped – he'd given up, but it's like the first mow of the year has given him an excuse to kick it all off again. He even turned up at The Larks on Saturday, which wasn't on.'

'He followed you?'

'No, but he knew where I was heading and he was waiting for me outside. He said he was worried about me because I seemed upset when I left the house but whether I was or wasn't is none of his business. We're not a couple, we're not even friends, and it's not his job to be concerned about me. What you saw earlier was me telling him I didn't want him mowing the lawn anymore. Troy Taylor's going to do the whole garden for me.'

'Do you think Damon's got the message now?'

'I think so. But if he does turn up again, I won't be here. I'm going away for a week. Would you mind putting the bin out and keeping an eye on the post for me? And if Damon does return, feel free to tell him I've gone away – just not where.'

I told Wilf where I was going and he assured me Damon wouldn't find out from him if he did come sniffing around.

I said goodbye to Wilf and Benji shortly after and took my phone out of my pocket to make sure there'd been no calls from The Larks. Damon's missed calls were up to eleven and there were several more WhatsApp notifications. I glanced down the messages.

FROM DAMON

Can we talk?

FROM DAMON

Please, Poppy. I've done nothing wrong!

FROM DAMON

It's only because I care about you and I know
you feel the same way

FROM DAMON

How about dinner tonight? I'll pick you up at 7

FROM DAMON

Would 6.30 be better?

And so it went on. So much for him getting the message! I needed to get ready for my holiday and the notifications were distracting me, so I blocked Damon's number. I wasn't his client anymore and we weren't friends so there was no reason for him to be in touch.

I packed a case full of casual clothes, choosing my softest jumpers and loungewear for comfort, and placed all the paperwork I'd need in a crate with my laptop and stationery essentials. I'd work during the day but I'd need to ensure I took evenings off if I wanted to return refreshed. Sharon had told me that there were no streaming services on the television, but there was a DVD player. My parents had built up a large DVD collection so I scanned along the shelves and selected a few of my favourite films. As I reached the boxset for the TV series *Darrington Detects*, my breath caught and my chest tightened as a wave of grief crashed over me. Mum had always had a soft spot for Cole Crawford who played the eponymous Reverend Hugh Darrington, detective turned vicar in the 1960s-set Dorset-based series, and had watched everything he'd ever been in. She'd been ill when *Darrington Detects* started and only caught the first two seasons before she passed away, but she declared it his finest work to date and I had to agree. He'd played some amazing characters over the years, both heroes and villains, but there was something about this role that spoke to my soul. Each series had got better and better and it killed me that she wasn't around to watch them with me.

Don't cry! Think positive! I closed my eyes and focused on happy memories of settling down on the sofa with Mum to watch Cole Crawford, a large bowl of popcorn between us, laughing as we dipped our hands in at the same time. I missed that so much. I missed her so much.

Feeling calmer, I plucked the boxset from the shelf. Each episode was like a soothing hug and would be just what I needed while I was away. If I took another of Mum's favourite throws with me and her perfume, I could make some popcorn, snuggle under the throw, start from season one, and imagine she was right by my side.

9

JOEL

A car horn beeping outside pulled me from my sleep. I tapped my phone – 10.13 a.m. – and pushed the duvet aside. Time to get up and do some batch-cooking before I went into work for the first of three night shifts.

I usually went to bed late before starting on nights so that I'd rise later, but I'd felt shattered last night after a busy weekend and had gone to bed earlier than intended. I'd only just drifted off when Chez and Lorna arrived back from the pub with a takeaway. If them crashing through the door hadn't already woken me up, Chez shouting upstairs, 'Do you want any Indian?' certainly would have done. I'd shouted back, 'No, I'm in bed!' thinking they'd take that as a sign to hush things a little but, no, the TV had gone on at full volume. I've no idea what they were watching but it involved lots of car chases and shooting and I heard it all and felt every single vibration. I'd shoved back the duvet several times, planning to go downstairs and tell them to stop being so inconsiderate, but I was so riled up that I knew it wouldn't come out as a polite request and we'd end up arguing again, so I shoved in a pair of ear plugs instead.

It wasn't Chez's fault I was in a mood. Imogen's revelation that Greg wanted her to call him Daddy had preyed on my mind across the weekend so I'd asked Tilly if I could have a quick word when I dropped Imogen home. My request to talk outside clearly irritated her as she muttered several expletives under her breath as she stuffed her arms into her coat sleeves and stepped outside in her slippers, slamming the door behind her.

'What?' she demanded as she yanked up the zip. I hated it when she was hostile like that and had to bite back the impulse to snap at her in response.

'Imogen said something yesterday that I don't think she was meant to say and—'

'For Pete's sake. She told you about Scotland?'

My stomach lurched. 'No. What about Scotland?'

Tilly's cheeks flushed. 'That's probably where we'll go camping over Easter.'

She'd mentioned something about going away a while back but nothing had been confirmed, so I assumed they'd changed their minds.

'Fair enough. It wasn't that. It's about Greg...'

'What about him?' she asked, accompanied by a dirty glare.

'Erm, it's a bit awkward because I obviously wasn't there so I'm only going from what Imogen told me.'

Tilly planted her hands on her hips. 'Spit it out!'

'She said that Greg has asked her to call him Daddy.'

'He has not!'

She quite literally spat the words and I had to resist the urge to wipe my cheek.

'As I say, I'm only going from what Imogen said.'

'You planted the idea.'

'Oh, come on, Tilly! Why would I do that?'

'Because you don't like Greg. Because you're jealous of what we have and you want to cause trouble.'

I had no idea where that had come from – completely paranoid and unreasonable.

'I am *not* jealous and what I think of Greg has nothing to do with this. Our daughter confided in me about something that upset her and I thought you should know so you could nip it in the bud.'

'What if she wants to call Greg Daddy? Her brothers and sister do.'

I ignored the ridiculous comment about her siblings. Greg *was* their dad so of course they'd call him that!

'Believe me, she doesn't and before you accuse me of influencing her, that came direct from her. If she genuinely wanted to call Greg Daddy, I wouldn't like it but I'd respect her decision and I'd understand because I do get that he has a role in her life. But that's *not* what's happening here and I'd appreciate your support because you promised me this wouldn't happen.' My tone was sounding more forceful than I intended so I softened it as I added, 'If you don't want to speak to him about it, I'm happy to have that conversation.'

She lowered her eyes and kicked at a small white feather on the path. 'No, it's fine. I'll speak to him. I meant what I said back then.'

The fight was gone from her voice, so I decided to push it a little further. 'If he's doing it because he thinks he's more of a dad to her than I am, you know there's a solution to that.'

She sighed. 'It's too disruptive with your shifts. Why can't you understand that?'

'You're hurting our daughter by keeping her away from me. Why can't *you* understand that?' I kept my voice on the level, and she raised her eyes to meet mine. I'd hoped to see sadness or guilt but she still looked angry which was a joke. What did she have to be annoyed about? *I* was the one who had every right to be fuming about this.

'I'll speak to Greg,' she said, completely ignoring my challenge. 'Goodbye, Joel.'

'I haven't said goodbye to Imogen yet.'

'Tough!'

But Imogen came running out and hurled herself at me, thanking me for a fantastic weekend and telling me how she couldn't wait for Barney and Amber's wedding next weekend. I ignored Tilly staring at us, stony-faced, and focused on Imogen. I'd loved spending this weekend with her and couldn't wait to see her again for the wedding, but enough was enough. I was determined to find a way to see Imogen more which might mean leaving my job even if it was safe in the restructure and it might mean initiating court proceedings. I didn't want to but if that was the only way to see Imogen more, Tilly left me no choice.

* * *

I showered, dressed and went downstairs but, as soon as I opened the lounge door, I reeled back at the smell. I loved the spicy aromas of Indian food when I was tucking in, but plates of half-eaten food left to fester overnight weren't at all appealing.

'Chester!' I muttered under my breath, angrily gathering the abandoned plates and taking them into the kitchen where pretty much every surface was covered with foil containers, cardboard lids stuck facedown, blobs of sauce and chutney and broken poppadums.

I was loath to clear up after them, but I couldn't stand the smell and I needed the space to prepare my meals. After pushing the kitchen window open, I pulled up an uplifting playlist on my phone, hoping the music would lift me from my dark mood. Cooking would help. Even though I hadn't made a career of it, I still loved creating in the kitchen and found the whole process soothing.

I put the kettle on to boil then set about clearing away Chez and Lorna's mess. When I'd emptied the kitchen bin and taken it outside, I tossed a teabag into a mug and filled it with water. Opening the fridge, I grabbed the milk carton and released a frustrated groan. What sort of person finished the milk and put the empty carton back in the fridge? I ran my hands through my hair, taking several calming breaths. *Give me strength!*

I hated feeling like this – all tense and angry – when I was normally relaxed and easy going. Chez had stayed with me on many occasions and he'd always been messy but it had never got to me like it had this time. Although I hadn't had a pile of other worries to contend with at the same time before.

I tipped my black tea down the sink, tossed the teabag in the bin and poured a glass of water which would have to do for now. I'd make a start on the cooking and then nip to the shops.

By the time I'd made a chilli and spaghetti bolognaise, I was gasping for a cuppa. I left the food cooling on the hob and grabbed my car keys.

When I returned a little later with some milk, I tripped over Chez's work boots dumped in the middle of the hall.

Chez was in the kitchen, placing a pasta bowl down beside the sink. I glanced at the remnants of tomato sauce round the edges and flicked my eyes to the hob. He hadn't!

'Cracking scran,' he said, wiping his mouth with the back of his hand.

I stared at him, stunned. 'Have you just eaten all my chilli?'

'Not all of it.'

He might as well have done. The couple of spoonfuls left in the pan wouldn't even be enough for a starter portion.

'But that was for me for after my night shifts.'

'How was I supposed to know that?'

'You could have waited until I got back and asked.'

'I didn't know where you were or when you'd be back, and I was hungry. The food was there so I ate it. Get over it!'

His stroppy teenager attitude pushed me over the edge.

'You want to know where I was? At the shops because you'd used all the milk and put the empty carton back in the fridge. And now you've eaten what would have been three, maybe four meals for me, so I'm going to have to go back to the shops and buy some more ingredients. You're welcome to stay here, but would it kill you to be a bit less self-centred and a bit more considerate?'

'Less self-centred and more considerate?' He exaggeratedly clapped his hands as he added in a sarcastic tone, 'Ladies and gentlemen, may I proudly present my big brother, Saint Joel Grainger, who *always* thinks of others first and is *never* self-centred or inconsiderate.'

I reeled back, stunned at the accusation. 'When am I ever inconsiderate?'

'Erm, now!'

'You think this is inconsiderate? Me being annoyed that you've eaten the food I prepared for my night shifts?'

'No. What I think is inconsiderate is you having a go at me without pausing to question why I'm here in the middle of the day.'

It was a fair point. He only got a thirty-minute lunch break and that wasn't enough time to get to mine and back.

'So why are you here?' I asked.

He glared at me for a moment then barged past and left the kitchen.

'Because I've lost my job,' he shouted over his shoulder. 'The garage has gone bust. Nice of you to be so concerned.'

I winced and cursed myself. 'Chez! I'm sorry,' I called, racing after him.

He gave me another filthy look, snatched up his boots and stormed out the house with them, slamming the door behind him.

I sank down onto the stairs, feeling weary from yet another run-in with my brother. I shouldn't have jumped on him like that, although he shouldn't have helped himself to my food without asking. He'd be turning twenty in October and it was time I stopped making excuses for his behaviour. He was an adult and he had to take ownership for himself. My shoulders slumped and I shook my head. The food wasn't the issue here. Chez had lost the job he loved and that was going to wreak havoc with his mental health, especially when he must already be struggling after falling out with Harry.

'I hope you find another job quickly, Chez,' I murmured, heaving myself up and returning to the kitchen. With no income coming in, his plans to move in with Lorna would have to go on hold and he'd need to stay here indefinitely, which wasn't ideal with the way we were clashing at the moment, although at least it meant I could watch out for him. I really hoped depression didn't take hold or, if it did, Lorna didn't react in her usual way and dump him. I dreaded to think what no job, no best mate and no girlfriend would do to him. I couldn't bear the thought of my brother spiralling like that again and, with my own work worries and the ongoing issues with Tilly to contend with, would I have enough headspace to support Chez if he did? I'd have to somehow.

10

POPPY

I slept exceptionally well my first night in Whisperwood Farmhouse and woke up feeling more refreshed than I had in months, helped by a combination of fatigue after the long drive and an incredibly comfortable bed.

Mary had kindly left me some provisions including a fresh loaf of bread, some homemade soup, a home-baked apple pie and a pot of custard which saved me from going back out and hunting for a takeaway in the dark and rain. I'd had a lovely relaxing evening curled up on the comfy sofa under Mum's throw with a delicious meal and the first few episodes of *Darrington Detects*.

This morning it was clear and bright with no sign of rain so, after toasting some of Mary's bread for breakfast, I decided to take a walk before settling down to work. Stepping out of the front door, I breathed in deeply. There was something so delicious about the air after a downpour, so clean and fresh.

Whisperwood Farmhouse was lovely. The stone cottage was painted white with a slate roof, a sage-green door and matching window frames, and it oozed with character inside and out. A single-storey extension had been added to the side to create a large kitchen-diner with a cosy snug in what must have been the original kitchen and a double-storey extension had been added to the back to create a fourth double bedroom and extended lounge. There was a small lawn out the front with a picnic bench on it, enclosed by a stone wall and, out the back, was a larger lawn and further seating. There wasn't a garage but there was enough space to easily park three cars on the driveway.

I stepped back and snapped a few photos on my phone to show Dad. Even though he'd probably wonder why a 'stranger' was sharing her holiday snaps with him, I knew he'd love both the building and the beautiful setting, and it would give us something other than the birds to talk about. I paused, frowning as I scrolled through the photos. The man I'd known would have been interested but I wasn't so sure about the boy he'd become. Feeling sad about that, but determined to shake it off, I slipped my phone back in my pocket and set off walking along a narrow track, which ran round the back of the farmhouse and alongside the fields.

The farmhouse was surrounded by gently rolling fields. In the distance was another white house flanked by various outbuildings, which had to be Bumblebee Barn – the family farm which Mary's grandson ran. The nearest fields were arable and there appeared to mainly be crops on the far side of Bumblebee Barn, but there were animals in the fields in between. They were a bit far away for me to be sure but it looked like they had sheep and pigs.

My phone rang and I smiled at Phil's name on the screen with a FaceTime request.

'I hear you're finally taking a holiday,' he said after we'd exchanged greetings.

'Your mum told you?'

He nodded. 'She's been worried about you. We all have. And I bet you've got some work with you.'

I smiled at him. 'Guilty. I can't afford to take a week off, but I promise I *am* having some relaxation time. I watched TV last night and I'm out for a walk right now although I'm not sure whether I'll lose signal if I walk too far so I'd better stop here. It's very pretty.'

'Show me your view.'

I turned the phone round and panned 360 degrees.

'Very nice,' Phil said when I turned the phone back to me. 'Mum says you're staying till Sunday. Any chance you could make it Monday instead? I'm going to be in the area and I'm free on Sunday night if you fancy a catch-up. It's been too long.'

I hesitated. It was another day away from Dad, but Marnie's words came back to me. He would be none the wiser and I needed to accept that. And it would be so good to catch up with Phil in person.

'It *has* been too long,' I agreed, smiling at him. 'Mary's stopping by tonight so I'll check it's okay with her and let you know.'

'Brilliant. You stay out of mischief, and I'll hopefully see you on Sunday.'

I continued on my walk with a smile. It would be a lovely, unexpected gift to catch up with Phil while I was here.

Looking back, Phil and I had married too young, me being twenty-one and fresh from university, and Phil being a year older. Although both sets of parents had supported our marriage, Mum had urged us to wait a while, saying that the twenties was a decade in which people grew and changed and not necessarily in the same direction. Phil and I had appreciated the advice but were convinced that wouldn't be the case for us.

A couple of years into our marriage, I was blissfully happy. I loved my job, my beekeeping and living in a small house near my parents, and I was ready for the next stage in our relationship – starting a family. Phil was not so settled. He wanted to move from sound engineering into music production, was keen to relocate to London and wanted to wait until our thirties before we considered children. I agreed to put a pause on having a family – we needed to both be ready and fully committed to that – and was happy to support Phil's career plans, but I had zero interest in moving to London. So we spent a lot of time apart while he worked in London and travelled to Europe. That time apart took its toll on our relationship in a way that the time apart at university hadn't.

A fortnight before Christmas, after we'd been married a little over four years, Phil returned to the UK for a month and it was obvious to me over the next few days that something had shifted between us. It usually took a day or so to get used to being around each other once more, but this was different. I thought about what Mum had said about changing in our twenties, I thought about her favourite quote, and I knew what the scary thing was that I had to do that day.

It was one of the scariest conversations I'd ever had but also the best thing I could have done because Phil felt the same as me and we were able to navigate our concerns together and emerge unscathed as friends. We agreed to one last happy family Christmas before announcing our plans to divorce in the New Year.

Phil had since remarried. His wife, Reina, was Spanish and they'd met when he'd been producing an album in Ibiza on which she was a backing singer. He spent most of his time between London and Spain and I usually saw him and Reina at Saltersbeck Farm over Christmas. I adored her. Whenever I spent time with her, I felt like I'd been bathed in human sunshine. She and Phil were so well suited and it made me happy to know that he'd found someone who was part of his lifestyle, who loved moving around, who found bright lights and big cities exhilarating. She understood and supported my friendship with Phil and always encouraged us to meet up whenever he was in the UK.

I hadn't seen them last Christmas because their first child, Eliana, had been born in Spain just a few days earlier. The Maynards had gone over there for Christmas instead. I'd been invited to join them, but I'd gone to The Larks for Christmas Day with Dad.

Continuing on my walk, I spotted a quad bike travelling across one of Bumblebee Barn's fields. When I was little, Ian had often taken me out on his bike and it had been so much fun, bouncing over the tracks and fields, but I hadn't been on one for years. I wasn't sure I'd be brave enough to ride one now. I used to be carefree and daring but now I just craved a quiet, simple life with my bees. I wouldn't say no to finding love again, but now wasn't the time.

I rested against a metal barred gate, taking in the beautiful countryside surrounding me. My parents would have loved it here. I could just imagine Dad marching across the fields and asking the farmer if he'd like some beehives on his land. Picturing a field full of hives made me feel warm inside. Some might say that beekeeping was brave but bees weren't a threat if you had the right equipment and knew what you were doing which I absolutely did. Learning all about beekeeping from my dad had been the best thing I'd ever done with my life.

It was so tranquil here, just like at Honey Bee Croft, and I felt like I'd found somewhere I could finally relax and breathe. Extending my stay by another day would be an absolute pleasure.

* * *

At noon, I broke off from my work briefly to have the rest of the soup and bread which Mary had left for me. Mid-afternoon, I stopped again to go food shopping. There was a binder of information in the kitchen with details of local shops, eateries and places to visit, which I'd flicked through last night. I'd hoped to find a farm shop, but there didn't appear to be any in the area although there'd been details of a garden centre called Bloomsberry's which had a food section, so I'd decided to give that a try.

Bloomsberry's was on the outskirts of a pretty village called Cherry Brompton and it was huge. As I made my way through each section of the garden centre, I smiled thinking about how much my parents would have loved it. Dad had been the green-fingered one but they'd always shopped for plants together as Mum had a great eye for colour and what would work well together. Conscious I could easily lose an hour or two browsing – time I didn't have to spare – I tore myself away from the plants in search of food.

The produce section was packed with delicious-looking biscuits, cakes and chocolates and carried a wide range of locally made soft drinks and beers. There was a section for fresh bread, but it was obviously popular as there was nothing left. I popped a packet of cheese scones and a jar of chutney advertised as working well with them into a wicker basket, as well as a small packet of cherry tomatoes and some celery for my lunch tomorrow. Standing by an open fridge full of fresh ready meals, the basket on the floor by my side, I was trying to decide which I fancied for dinner tonight. They all sounded delicious. I reached out for one, then retracted my hand as I spotted another so I went for that, but changed my mind. Moments later, a man joined me so I moved aside to give him access to the fridge. He grabbed four meals and placed them in his basket and I admired his decisiveness as my eyes darted across all the tempting choices.

'Struggling to decide?' he asked.

I glanced up at him. He was tall – over six feet at a guess – and broad-shouldered like a rugby player. He was also incredibly attractive with short dirty-blond hair, a square jawline and a friendly smile, making my stomach do an unexpected loop-the-loop.

'Every time I think I've decided, I spot something else.'

'The smoked salmon and asparagus pasta's my personal favourite. The chicken teriyaki's really good too.' He tilted his basket and I laughed as he had two of each in there.

'Thanks for the recommendations.'

'Enjoy!' he said, with another smile before walking towards the tills.

I watched him for a moment, admiring those strong shoulders and imagining what it would be like to be hugged by someone with a physique like that. Must take all your worries away. Surprised at where my train of thought was heading, I turned back to the fridge and selected the two meals he'd recommended.

After adding a bottle of sparkling elderflower to my basket, I made my way towards the tills, pausing by a beautiful display of cut flowers. Mary was coming round tonight and I could give her a bouquet to thank her for letting me stay at such short notice and for charging me a ridiculously low amount which she claimed was because of the redecoration needed. Yes, there were some chips and scuffs but nothing I wouldn't expect from a holiday cottage, and it certainly didn't detract from the charm and comfort so there was no need for her to charge so little.

I studied the bouquets for a while and was drawn to a beautiful spring one bursting with yellow, purple and white flowers. There was only one left in the bucket and, as I wrapped my hands round it, so did somebody else from the other side and our fingers touched. We both let go and I looked up into the eyes of

Mr Rugby Physique from earlier, my stomach doing another backflip.

'Looks like we have the same taste in flowers as well as meals,' I said, laughing.

He had such a lovely smile, his eyes twinkling. 'You went for the salmon and the teriyaki?'

'I did. I'm putting the success of my next two evening meals in the hands of a stranger.'

He mock-grimaced. 'Risky! I'm sure you won't be disappointed, but you'd better take the flowers, just in case. I'll pick a different bunch.'

'You're sure?'

'They're not for anything special – just for a friend to say thanks for a favour.' He picked a bouquet of pinks and purples and held them up to me, as though seeking my approval.

'Good choice. If I was a friend who'd done you a favour, I'd be happy with them.'

We went to the tills and, as I was served, I was very aware of Mr Rugby Physique being served directly opposite me. We kept looking up and smiling at each other. He didn't have as much to buy as me so he left with another smile and a nod of his head and I felt strangely disappointed, which was crazy. What had I expected him to do? Suggest we go for a drink to compare opinions on the teriyaki? And what would I do if he had? He was obviously local and I lived nearly four hours away – absolute nonstarter. But, as I drove home, I couldn't help drifting into a little fantasy world where he'd been waiting for me in the car park and did ask if I fancied that drink. It would have been nice.

11

JOEL

With the flowers and ready meals on the back seat, I placed my keys in the ignition, but I didn't start the car. Glancing at the flowers in the rearview mirror, I muttered in a sarcastic voice, 'They're not for anything special – just for a friend to say thanks for a favour.'

I raked my hands through my hair, shaking my head. What the hell was that? My clumsy code for *They're not for my wife or girlfriend* in the hope that the woman in Bloomsberry's would respond with, *In that case, how about a drink?* As if something like that was ever going to happen. I'd come here to get a couple of fresh ready meals as I couldn't be bothered to remake the chilli Chez had eaten, and some flowers for Chloe to thank her for taking in Imogen's dress which I was collecting from Crafty Hollow shortly. I hadn't expected to meet someone. Not that you could call that little episode *meeting*.

A shaft of light from who knows where had been shining on her hair as I approached the fridge and I'd stopped, momentarily captivated. I'd been reading Amber's book on manifesting. I couldn't send out positive thoughts for the future until I was clear about what I wanted. That was straightforward for Imogen, but I was still struggling with the work thing. I knew what I *didn't* want – which was still helpful – but what I *did* want remained a mystery. As for meeting someone, I was more interested in personality and the type of relationship we had than appearance, but I thought it might be easier if I had a vague image in my mind. All I could think of was somebody who didn't remind me of Tilly or Marley. They were both blonde with blue eyes so a brunette with brown eyes would be great. Neither of them ever left the house without wearing make-up so perhaps someone who embraced the more natural look. I'd stood by my bedroom window, feeling like an idiot, as I channelled my positive thoughts into the universe. I believed in the power of positive thinking – my interview had been evidence of that – but I wasn't convinced by the whole manifesting malarky. And yet there she was – a naturally beautiful brunette with shoulder-length wavy hair, pink cheeks and full lips standing where I was heading with a shaft of light pointing her out. So did I say hello, introduce myself, flirt a little? Nope. I interrupted her thoughts, recommended some food and walked away. And then when our paths crossed again by the flowers... I tutted at myself. I was no good at this sort of stuff.

At that moment, she emerged from the garden centre and my heart leapt. Would it be weird to go up to her and ask her if she fancied going out for a drink at some point? What if she said no? What if she thought I was some creepy bloke who hung around garden centres trying to pick up women? What if...?

She pulled out of her parking space and left the car park and I exhaled loudly. There probably were blokes out there who could go up to a stranger in a shop and ask them out, but I wasn't one of them.

As I drove home to drop off the meals, I pushed thoughts of my missed opportunity out of my mind and focused on work instead. The first night shift back after the takeover announcement had been hard work and I'd found myself clock-watching, willing for 6 a.m. to arrive so I could go home. My team had wanted to know they had job security, but I had no reassurances I could give, and I hated that there'd been no more information. Telling them *you'll know as soon as I do* felt like a cop-out and provided little comfort. The problem with having no information was that it invited people to draw their own assumptions and those were invariably negative. Several of the production operatives had asked if they could put me down as a referee on any job applications and, when Sal and I broke for 'lunch', both tucking into portions of spaghetti bolognaise I'd brought in from home, she confessed that she'd spent the weekend sending her CV out.

'Before you know whether your job's even at risk?' I asked, surprised.

She put her fork down, her expression serious. 'I've been here less than two years, Joel, and I know how these things go. Last in, first out. If your role goes, you'll get a decent redundancy payout, but I'll get hardly anything. I'd rather jump ship and secure a new role before I'm pushed and forced to catch the others who are already swimming.'

It was a good analogy and, in her position, it did make sense. She asked about my plans and I admitted to going round in circles, desperate to keep my job one minute so I could financially support Imogen and my brother, and hoping to be made redundant the next so that my hand would be forced and I'd have to rethink my career, although I had no idea what that would look like.

'Something will turn up,' she said, echoing what Amber had said. 'Probably something you'd never have considered.' She sighed heavily as she gazed round the office. 'I'll miss this place and I'll miss working with you, but do you know what I'll miss the most?'

Her serious expression turned into a big smile as she scooped up some bolognaise. 'Your cooking. If I ever win the lottery, I'm going to employ you as my personal chef.'

It lightened the mood and we drifted off into an *if I won the lottery* fantasy discussion, our suggestions becoming steadily more ludicrous. While it didn't help with my decision-making, it did help with the positivity and I left the shift convinced that being made redundant, while scary, might be the best thing that could happen to me.

When I arrived home, I braced myself for walking into a mess, but the house was surprisingly tidy. Chez must have taken on board what I'd said as he'd even loaded the dishwasher. Things were looking up.

* * *

Ready meals dropped off, I headed over to Crafty Hollow for Imogen's dress. When Chloe had messaged to say I could either collect it this week or Samantha could take it to Fennington Hall – the grand hotel on the outskirts of York where Barney and Amber were getting married – I was going to ask Samantha to take it, but I imagined Tilly's voice in my head, demanding to know why she hadn't seen Imogen in the dress first, so I arranged to pick it up instead.

Chloe seemed really touched when I gave her the flowers, but it was the least I could do when she'd refused to charge me for the alterations. I'd carefully timed arriving at Tilly's so that Imogen would be home from school but they wouldn't be eating their tea yet. Surely Tilly wouldn't object to me saying a quick hello to Imogen before I went to work.

Imogen answered the door in her school uniform and her face lit up. 'Daddy!'

'I've brought your dress,' I said, holding the dress carrier and a bag up in front of me. 'I've got your shoes and a headband too.'

Tilly appeared behind Imogen, scowling at me. 'What are you doing here?'

'Imogen's bridesmaid dress was ready, and I thought you might like to see her in it before the wedding.'

Her expression softened. 'I would. Thank you.'

'Are you coming in, Daddy?'

I looked down at Imogen and shook my head. 'Sorry, sweetie, but I need to get ready for work. I've got time for a hug, though.'

She squeezed me tightly and kissed me on the cheek. I hated always having to say goodbye to her, knowing it would be days before I saw her again.

'Right, let's get this door closed,' Tilly said when Imogen released me. 'We're letting all the heat out.'

'But I want to wave Daddy off.'

'It's too cold. Wave from your bedroom window if you must.'

Imogen raced upstairs and I returned to my car, waving as I started the engine. I was about to pull away when the front door opened and Tilly emerged, pulling on her coat. Surely she wasn't going to have a go at me for turning up announced?

I wound my window down and looked up at her expectantly.

'I spoke to Greg about the Daddy thing and it's all a misunderstanding. Imogen had asked him whether the twins would call him Daddy and she seemed put out that she was the only one of the kids who wouldn't call him that. He said he wouldn't mind if she ever wanted to call him Daddy but there was no pressure.'

That wasn't how Imogen had told the story, but I knew better than to suggest Greg was a liar.

'Fair enough. As long as that's the end of it.'

'It is. Greg and Imogen are fine, and it won't crop up again. Thanks for having a word.'

She turned as though to go, but paused.

'Something else?' I prompted when she didn't speak.

'Yes, it's... erm... Are you going to lose your job?'

I tensed. 'Why would you ask that?'

'Greg knows someone who works at your place. He said there was a big announcement about a takeover and that there'll be redundancies.'

'Yes to the takeover, but there's been no announcement about redundancies.'

'But there will be some?'

'Nobody knows. It's all speculation.'

'But speculation comes from somewhere, so that must mean—'

'Speculation is speculation,' I said, determined not to give her any ammunition against me. 'It comes when nobody knows so they start making guesses and sometimes those guesses seem plausible enough to get presented as the truth.'

'So you're not about to lose your job?'

'Hopefully not, but no job is ever safe. If there are redundancies and I'm one of them, you don't need to worry. I won't be looking for a child maintenance reduction.'

'You think I only care about the money?' She sounded hurt at the suggestion.

'Can you blame me?' I didn't need to clarify that she'd continually fought me for payment increases over and above what would be considered reasonable. She'd know exactly what I meant.

Tilly folded her arms and bit her lip – her telltale sign that she knew she was in the wrong and was squirming about it.

'Whatever happens, Imogen won't be left without,' I said, my voice softer. 'I'll let you know if I hear anything. See you on Saturday.'

Tilly didn't say anything, but she stepped away from the car which I took as a sign that I was free to go. I suppose it was naïve of me to think that news of the takeover wouldn't reach her.

As I drove away, I hoped she didn't get to hear that I'd missed out on a promotion as I really didn't want her to know that. Or did I? Maybe it would be good for her to know that I'd been trying for years to secure that promotion so that I could spend more time with our daughter. What if part of her awkwardness was a misguided belief that I didn't care that much because, if I did care, I'd have done something about it? What if she thought that me no longer chasing her via my solicitor was further evidence of that uninterest? Tilly's mind worked in mysterious ways and, ridiculous as all that sounded to my logical brain, I wouldn't put it past her to connect the dots in that way. Well, I'd prove her wrong. If my job was at risk, I'd take the cheque and run. If it wasn't, I'd still leave. Amber and Sal both believed something would present itself, but I couldn't sit around waiting for that to happen. I'd trawl the online job boards, look at the local college prospectus and ask around as there had to be stacks of opportunities out there that I'd never have thought of myself. And after what had happened earlier in the garden centre – even though I'd messed it up – it couldn't hurt to engage in a little more manifesting. Things were going to change and *I* was going to make that happen.

12

POPPY

Mr Rugby Physique had been right about the chicken teriyaki. I'd had it for dinner in front of an episode of *Darrington Detects* and it had been delicious. I'd just finished eating when a text arrived.

FROM WILF

Hope you're enjoying your break so far. No sign of Damon but Benji's been a great guard dog

He'd accompanied the message with a gorgeous photo of Benji sitting on my doorstep, his pig beside him, his nose in the air as though sniffing out the enemy, which really tickled me. I replied with my thanks.

When the episode ended, I stopped the DVD, took my plate into the kitchen and flicked the kettle on. Mary had said she'd stop by to say hello and, just as the kettle finished boiling, a car pulled onto the drive and an elderly lady got out.

'Do you want to come in for a drink?' I asked after we'd greeted each other at the door.

'Only if I'm not disturbing your evening.'

'I'm not doing anything special – just relaxing in front of the telly. And I've just boiled the kettle.'

Mary requested tea and went through to the lounge while I made the drinks. When I returned with two mugs, she was standing by the coffee table with the DVD boxset in her hand.

'You like *Darrington Detects*?' she asked, smiling warmly at me before placing the case back on the table and joining me on the sofa.

'I *love* it. My mum has always been a huge fan of Cole Crawford and she got me hooked, but this is my favourite series. I can't tell you how many times I've watched each episode.'

'It's a great series,' she agreed. 'I've got the boxset too and I always watch an episode when I'm at a loose end or need cheering up. Cole's such a good actor and a lovely man too.'

'He seems to be.'

Sometimes when I'd spent the day on my own, I got the verbals around the first person I saw and this was one of those occasions. I couldn't seem to stop talking about how exceptionally talented both Mum and I thought Cole Crawford was, how much we loathed his villains and fell in love with his heroes, what a gift for accents he had, and how well he came across in interviews.

'I can't believe I just spilled all that out,' I said, when I paused for breath and my brain caught up with my mouth. 'I probably sound like an infatuated teenager or the head of his fan club.'

Mary laughed. 'It's fine. He's a very special man. The first time I met him, I was so starstruck. I'd never met a celebrity before, but he's so genuinely warm and friendly that you soon forget he's famous.'

My mouth dropped open. 'You *know* Cole Crawford?'

'I know the whole family. Cole's daughter Amber is marrying

my grandson Barney on Saturday. It's going to be a wonderful wedding.'

I listened, enraptured, as Mary explained how Barney and Amber had met and how highly she rated each member of Amber's family. I was dying to ask her more about the wedding and whether there'd be other celebrities on the guest list, but she glanced at the wall clock and stopped mid-sentence.

'Goodness me, how have I been here an hour already? I must get back to my dog.'

'What do you have?'

'A Border collie called Raven and she's gorgeous. She's mum to Barney's two, Bear and Harley.'

She tapped her phone and showed me a few pictures of Raven who was indeed an extremely attractive dog.

'Before I go, is everything okay and do you need anything – more towels, directions, advice?'

'Everything's great and thanks so much for the food you left. That was very kind of you.'

'It was nothing. I knew you'd had a long drive and I wanted to make sure you had something to eat if you hadn't had a chance to stop on the way.'

'I really appreciated it. And I do have a question. Could I stay one more night and leave on Monday morning? And would it be okay for a friend to stay with me on Sunday night? It's Phil Maynard – Sharon and Ian's son.' There was no need to add *my ex-husband*. If she knew the Maynards well, she'd already know that.

'You can have as many people stay as you have room for, but thank you for asking. I appreciate good manners. Call or text me if you want to extend your stay any further. It's free until next Friday.'

Mary pushed herself up and I followed her into the hall but

asked her to wait a moment while I nipped into the kitchen to retrieve the flowers.

'What are these for?' she asked, looking surprised.

'To say thanks again for letting me stay here. It's a beautiful house and the timing couldn't have been more ideal.'

She breathed in the scent and smiled. 'They're beautiful. That's lovely of you.' Reaching the front door, she paused with her hand on the handle. 'Do you have any plans for Saturday night?'

'Same thing I'll be doing every night this week – watching *Darrington Detects*.'

'Would you like to meet Cole in real life? You could come along to the evening do and I can introduce you.'

I clapped my hands to my cheeks, my heart pounding. I wanted to scream *yes* but it seemed a heck of a liberty. It wasn't like I was a friend of Mary's – I was merely a tenant at her cottage, and she'd only stopped by to check I'd settled in all right.

'I'd love to meet him, but I can't crash a family wedding like that.'

'You wouldn't be crashing. You'd be my guest. Bring your mum too, if you like.'

My stomach lurched. When I'd mentioned Mum, I hadn't used the past tense so Mary couldn't have known.

'She'd have loved it, but she passed away.'

'Oh, Poppy, I'm sorry to hear that. Was this recent?'

'Five years ago, although it doesn't feel anywhere near that long.' Tears pricked my eyes and I heard the catch in my voice. 'Sometimes I go to tell her something and it hits me like a wave that she's not there.'

'I know what you mean. I lost my husband, Frank, three years ago and the number of times I make a cup of tea for him or lay his place setting...' She tailed off, her eyes clouding with tears.

'I'm so sorry. I wish I could say the pain goes away. Time makes it a little less raw, though.'

She nodded. 'We were married for fifty-five years, together for fifty-six. It's been tough, but I'm fortunate to have a lovely family close by and Raven has been such a comfort.'

'Animals are such a gift at a time like that. My parents had been married for sixty-three years when Mum died, and my dad really struggled. I wondered about a cat or dog to give him something to focus on but ruled it out as he was more into wildlife than pets. Just as well as he started going downhill pretty quickly not long after.'

'You've lost your dad too?' she asked gently.

'Not physically, but he has late-stage Alzheimer's and no idea who I am anymore.'

'Oh, love, that must be difficult.'

'It's heartbreaking. He's been in a care home for eighteen months and this is the first time I've allowed myself to take a break. I wasn't going to but Sharon and Marnie – the manager where he stays – were both adamant that I needed it and, now that I'm here, I can definitely see it was the right thing to do.'

'But you're spending the time working?' she asked.

'I have to. I've got my own business so I need to keep on top of things.' I laughed lightly. 'I appreciate that probably doesn't sound much like a break but believe me, it is when I'm usually balancing my days with work, visits to Dad and seeing to the bees.'

'The bees?'

'I'm a beekeeper. Dad took over from a friend when I was young, and I took over from him a few years ago.'

'Sounds like an incredibly busy life you lead. I'm glad I could provide somewhere for you to slow down, if only for a week. I'll have a word with Barney and Amber about the evening do and ask one of them to drop off an invitation for you.'

'It seems really cheeky when they've never met me.'

'Believe me, they won't mind at all. A few guests can't make it so I know there's the capacity. I'll ask about a plus one in case Phil can come a day early and join you. Right! I really am going now.'

She pushed open the door and stepped outside, waving as she headed back to her car. What a lovely woman and what an unexpected turn in the conversation. I still felt a bit weird about turning up at a wedding for people I didn't know but, if Amber or Barney did drop an invitation off, I was definitely going to accept. Mum would have loved this opportunity and I was going to make the most of it for her and for me. If there was any way Phil could change his travel plans and be my plus one, that would be a lot less awkward, especially when he was used to being around celebrities and had a natural gift for chatting to anyone.

Closing the door when Mary pulled away, I settled on the sofa and messaged Phil.

TO PHIL

> Mary says it's no problem you staying on Sunday night but is there any chance you could be free on Saturday night as well or instead? Her grandson is getting married on Saturday to Cole Crawford's daughter! She's invited me – and you if you're free – to the evening do. I can't confirm it's definite until I actually get the invite but thought I'd sound you out just in case

FROM PHIL

Celebrity wedding! How exciting! I'm flying over to the UK on Friday and can probably adjust my Saturday plans to join you for that. Let me know when it's official and I'll see what I can do

I started another episode of *Darrington Detects*, scarcely able to believe that I might get to meet the man himself at the weekend. What perfect timing my stay had turned out to be.

13

POPPY

I was immersed in my work at the dining table the following morning when a message came through from Wilf.

FROM WILF

Hope you're having a good break. Got back from the shops earlier to find Damon on your drive peering through your window. Told him to clear off but he demanded to know where you were. I told him you were on holiday but not where. Might have emphasised my police connections. Don't think he'll be back. Benji sends a high paw your way

He'd accompanied his message with a pawprint emoji which would normally have made me smile, but my stomach was churning at the thought of Damon loitering around the house. I'd just have to hope that my absence, Wilf's refusal to give him any more information and the threat of speaking to one of his former colleagues would be enough to drive home the message that I didn't want him in my life. And if it didn't, maybe I would need to involve the police myself. I didn't want to go down that road but, if he wouldn't leave me alone, I might have no choice.

TO WILF

> Sending a high paw back to Benji and thanks to both of you for guarding my house. Fingers crossed he'll stay away from now on. Having a lovely break – just what I needed

I returned to my work, only to be interrupted by a knock at the door half an hour later. As soon as I opened it, I recognised my visitor and was momentarily starstruck. Amber Crawford was tall with long auburn hair hanging in gentle waves from beneath a forest-green beanie hat. She looked more like her mum – the TV presenter Jules Crawford – than her dad.

'You must be Poppy,' she said, smiling at me. 'I'm Amber. Am I disturbing your work?'

'No. I was just about to make a coffee,' I said, finding my voice. 'Would you like one?'

'I'd love one. White, no sugar, please.'

I felt ridiculously self-conscious. Mary would have told Amber that I loved her dad's work and I hoped she didn't think I was some sort of obsessed fan stalking him.

'Do you want to go through to the lounge and I'll be through with the drinks in a minute?' I asked, immediately regretting it as the *Darrington Detects* boxset was still on the coffee table. Although maybe that wasn't so bad. If Mary had told her about our full conversation, she'd know it had been triggered by her spotting the boxset.

'Mary says you're here on a working holiday,' Amber said when I handed over her drink a little later.

'Yes. I haven't had a holiday for years and this was a last-minute thing. I'm a beekeeping accountant and, while the bees have stayed at home, the balance sheets have come with me.' I was very aware of my rapid speech, but my heart was pounding. Although Amber wasn't on television like her family, she'd produced several programmes I watched, and I was having a serious fangirl moment.

'A beekeeping accountant?' she said, sounding intrigued. 'Not an obvious combination.'

I explained how I'd got into beekeeping and how there'd been a limited window to get away before the hives needed a lot more attention.

'What do you do with what you produce?' she asked.

'I sell the honey to a local farm shop but that's about it. There's so much more I'd love to do but I just don't have the time. Several years back, I was experimenting with products using beeswax and even had a company name and branding but my mum received a terminal illness diagnosis so I put it all on hold. After we lost her, Dad got a dementia diagnosis and time has never been on my side since.'

'I'm so sorry to hear about your parents.'

'Thank you. Dad's still with us but he doesn't recognise me, which is hard, and another reason I needed some time away.'

'You certainly chose a beautiful place to stay.'

I nodded with enthusiasm. 'I've never been to this area before, but I love it. I've had a walk along the path each morning and it's so peaceful looking across your farm. You're very lucky to live here.'

'I count my blessings every day. I visited loads of farms while filming *Countryside Calendar* and it was my dream to live on one eventually, and then I met Barney and my dream came true. Speaking of which...'

She reached inside her coat and removed a thick cream envelope which she passed to me.

I stared at the envelope, but I didn't take it.

'You don't have to invite me to your... Don't feel any pressure... Mary spotted the DVDs and she... I'm not a crazed fan... It's your day and...'

Amber laughed lightly and placed the envelope on my knee. 'I don't think you're a crazed fan, Mary's not the sort of person to pressure someone into anything, and it would be a pleasure to invite you and your friend to the evening do, or just you if your friend can't come.'

'Are you absolutely sure?'

'I'm sure. You're a guest on our farm and you're welcome as a guest on Saturday. One of us will make sure you get an introduction to my dad.'

My hand fluttered to my throat. 'I'm already nervous at the thought.'

'Don't be. My dad's lovely and he's really normal and down to earth. He finds the fame thing hilarious. My whole family do. Everyone's grounded, but I do understand the starstruck thing. Over the years, I've got to know loads of celebs through my work and my family, but sometimes I'll see someone at an awards ceremony who I've not met before and I swear my legs turn to jelly. It's ridiculous! They're just people but there's me having palpitations and getting all tongue-tied.'

'I feel a bit better about it now, knowing it happens to you too.'

'Not just me. It's happened to my mum, dad, brother and sister. They can all share a few tales of when they've been fangirls or boys. You know Annabelle Coates?'

I nodded. Who didn't? Annabelle Coates was acting royalty. Now in her early sixties, she'd had an award-winning career spanning five decades and, as well as a successful and versatile television career, she'd starred in several major films.

'I'm a huge fan of her work and when someone introduced us, I was so overwhelmed that my mind went blank and do you know what I did?' Amber clapped her hands to her cheeks. 'I still cringe thinking about this. I asked her if she knew where the toilets were. As if that wasn't bad enough, I told her how I shouldn't drink champagne because it goes right through me and I spend half the night peeing. Who meets their hero and tells them about their bladder functions? Honestly!'

'What did she say?' I asked, tickled by the anecdote and feeling much more relaxed that Amber was so *normal*.

'She looked a little shocked, but she pointed me in the direction of the toilets and I scuttled off. I thought I'd have to spend the rest of my life hiding from her, but she sidled up to me later that evening and said, *I have the same problem with Prosecco, darling, which is why I only ever drink champers. With the Prosecco, I'm never off the potty!*'

'She didn't!'

'She absolutely did and it broke the ice. We're great friends now and she's coming to the wedding.'

My eyes widened. 'I'm even more nervous now.'

'Don't be. She's really approachable. There are some pretentious *do you know who I am?* types out there but they're not our sort of people. Everyone who's coming is genuine and lovely. You'll have a great time.'

I gasped as it suddenly struck me that I had nothing suitable to wear. I'd only brought casual clothes and loungewear with me. I knew the closest city was York, but I really didn't have time to make that trip. Reddfield – the nearest town – hadn't looked very big on the map so didn't necessarily have any clothes shops.

'Everything okay?' Amber asked, looking at me with concern.

'I'd love to come – thank you – but I've just realised I've got nothing with me to wear. Where are the nearest clothes shops?'

'I can lend you something if you like. You look about the same size as me.'

Scarcely able to believe this was happening, we exchanged sizes. At five foot eight, I was an inch shorter than Amber and we were the same dress size so borrowing something to wear was an option, but I had small feet for my height – only a size five compared to Amber's seven – so shoes weren't.

'Why don't you come over to the farm with me now?' she suggested. 'We can see if I have anything you like. I won't be offended if you don't share the same taste as me.'

'I'd love to, but are you sure? It's bad enough that I'm gate-crashing your wedding without stealing your clothes too.'

Amber laughed. 'It'll be my pleasure. I've got a wardrobe full of clothes bought for events and awards and I can't see myself wearing any of them again now that I've left that world behind.'

'You're not a TV producer anymore?'

'No. I used to love all the travel but, after I met Barney, it got progressively harder to be away from him, the farm and the friends I'd made here. I finished filming a docuseries last spring – *The Wildlife Rescuers* – and my final *Countryside Calendar* in the summer.'

'I hadn't realised. What are you doing now?'

'All sorts. Obviously, there's been the wedding to plan, but I'm a guest tutor on a media studies course at the local tech, I volunteer at Hedgehog Hollow – the rescue centre where most of *The Wildlife Rescuers* was filmed – and I help out at the farm. I loved being a producer, but I hadn't realised how shattered I was until I let it go. It's been so good having time to breathe again.'

'Sounds amazing.' And exactly what I'd come here for.

Amber finished her drink and stood up. 'I'm conscious you have work to do, so let's go to the farm now. We'll go in my car and I'll drop you off after as I've got a few errands to run.'

I grabbed my phone and jacket and followed Amber to her car.

'Tell me more about your beeswax products,' she said as we set off. 'What did you make?'

'It was a skincare range. I started off simple with lip balms and soap and moved on to face cream and body lotion, but there's so much potential if you have enough bees, the right equipment, and enough time and space to make it all. I loved experimenting.'

'What was your brand name?'

'Honey Bee Hugs.'

'Aw, that's so cute. We're about to convert one of the barns into a farm shop and that's exactly the sort of product we're hoping to stock. If you ever pick things up again, let me know. I couldn't promise anything because we ideally want to source our stock locally, but if there's nothing available locally then it's not out of the question to consider products from further afield.'

My heart leapt and I felt a fizz of excitement. I'd love to resurrect Honey Bee Hugs. To have a farm shop in a beautiful area like this stock my products would be such a dream. But my heart sank because the reality was that it *was* exactly that – a dream. I couldn't even think about it while Dad was ill and I was struggling to keep all those plates spinning.

'I don't know if I'll pick it up again. I love it so much, but...'

'But it's difficult to think about while your dad's ill?' she suggested when I tailed off. 'I can understand that. Here we are!'

She pulled off the main road by a white wooden sign with the name *Bumblebee Barn* on it and a round bumblebee on a lavender stem. The gently rising track was flanked by crops and then it dipped down to reveal the farmhouse and several outbuildings. A few hens were strutting across the farmyard and a grey and black tabby ran in front of the car and leapt onto the bonnet of a parked Land Rover.

'That's Radley,' Amber said. 'Pumpkin will be lurking nearby too. She's a ginger tabby.'

'Mary said you have a couple of Border collies too.'

'Yes, Bear and Harley are out with Barney. We've got horses and ponies, Herdwick and Swaledale sheep, pigs, goats, hens, rabbits, guinea pigs and tortoises.'

'That's a lot of animals.'

'The rabbits, guinea pigs and tortoises are fairly new – part of a petting farm experience which Barney's mum runs with my best friend, Zara. It's only open for school groups at the moment, but the hope is to expand it when the farm shop opens and we have more footfall.'

As I followed her into the farmhouse, pausing to give Radley a stroke on the way, I told her about visiting Saltersbeck Farm with Dad when I was young and how the hives were still kept there.

'Funnily enough, Barney and I were talking about beehives the other day. Neither of us have our sights set on becoming beekeepers – more than enough here to keep us busy – but we have some space and wondered if a local beekeeper might like to put some hives on it. Assuming it's suitable land, that is. Not sure what's needed.'

'I can take a look if you like – maybe one day later in the week if you have time.'

'That would be great. Saves us messing anybody about if the land isn't suitable. How about first thing tomorrow morning? I can show you the field, introduce you to Barney and give you a quick tour if you like.'

'Name the time and I'll be here.'

* * *

That night, I propped myself up in bed, gazing at the stunning dress Amber had not just loaned me for Saturday night but had actually given to me. I'd seen the designer label on it and protested that it was far too much, but she claimed it had been an impulse purchase which she'd never wear because the burnt-orange colour was too close a match to her hair and made her look wiped out. The lace-covered dress was one shouldered with a high leg slit and diamante detailing round the waist and had to be the most beautiful, elegant item of clothing I'd ever worn.

I felt a lot more comfortable about going to the wedding now that I'd spent time with Amber and would meet Barney in the morning. As I'd tried on dresses, she'd given me the lowdown on her wedding party. I'd done a double-take when she said she had eight bridesmaids. Imagine having that many family members and friends to ask. When I'd married Phil, my only bridesmaids had been Shauna and Jo – my best friends from school and university respectively – and neither of them were in my life anymore. Shauna had got together with Bertie at our wedding and, when their relationship ended badly a year later, she'd expected me to take her side and cut him out of my life. How was I supposed to do that when he was my long-term friend and my brother-in-law? So Shauna cut me out of her life instead. Without her friendship, Jo and I became even closer. We didn't see much of each other as she lived in Portsmouth but we spoke regularly. She was the first person I called when Mum got her MND diagnosis and she was so supportive as I cried down the phone, promising me she'd be there for me every step of the way. But she wasn't. She never returned my calls after that and eventually I stopped trying. Looking back, they'd both been very needy, expecting me to be there for them but not reciprocating that. True friendship had to be two-way – there for each other through the good times and the bad.

If I lived near Bumblebee Barn, I could imagine becoming friends with Amber and her being a proper friend. She was one of the most genuine people I'd ever met. I could imagine being the Bumblebee Barn beekeeper and spending my days making Honey Bee Hugs products. But I didn't live locally. My life was in Gloucestershire near Dad and to wish it was anything different was to wish for the one heartbreaking event which I knew was coming but was already dreading.

14

POPPY

I was up early the following morning to drive over to Bumblebee Barn, but I wasn't feeling particularly fresh after another nightmare involving Damon. In it, I'd accepted an invitation for coffee but, when I tried to leave, I couldn't because I was glued to the chair and the chair was bolted to the floor. I implored my fellow café-goers to help me but they were all shrouded in cloaks and, when they turned and lowered their hoods, they were all Damon. I woke up pouring with sweat and had to go downstairs to make a calming hot chocolate, just like Mum used to make for me when I was a child and had bad dreams.

I knew exactly why Damon had infiltrated my dreams – because Wilf had messaged last night to say Damon had been at Dove Cottage yet again because he'd thought Wilf was lying to him about me being on holiday. Wilf had assured me that he hadn't given Damon the slightest indication as to where I'd gone, refusing to even confirm whether it was in the UK or abroad.

On a more positive note, I'd had a message from Marnie assuring me that Dad was as well as could be expected and there'd been no recent *midnight meanderings*. She'd included a lovely candid photo of him in the residents' lounge watching the birds with Poppy the bear sitting on his knee on top of his fiddle cushion. My phone lockscreen photo was the one taken of us together at his ninetieth birthday and the wallpaper was the one of just him, but I changed it to the photo Marnie had just sent, loving how relaxed and content he looked. He wasn't the only one. It had been strange not seeing Dad this week, but I was conscious how much better I felt in myself for not going to The Larks every day, building up false hope that he'd know who I was and dealing with the disappointment when he didn't. When I returned to Winchcote, I would cut back on my visits. The guilt would nudge at me no matter what Marnie said, but it would be so much better for my mental health.

It was getting lighter as I drove the short distance to Bumblebee Barn. Amber was in the farmyard topping up the water bowls for the dogs and cats.

'Good morning!' she called as I opened the car door. 'Early enough for you?'

'It's fine. I'm usually up by six.'

Radley appeared from the barn and curled round my legs.

'He likes you,' she said as I bent down to stroke him, and he wiggled his head to give me better access to scratch his ears.

'It's mutual. I've never had a cat, but I've always loved them.'

Radley had such a handsome face and his grey and black tabby markings were just like on one of the cats Cuddles & Paws had taken to Dad's ninetieth. Animals were such great company and the thought fleetingly crossed my mind that maybe I should get a cat, but I swiftly dismissed it. I didn't have the time to settle it in.

'It's not light enough to see the field properly yet,' Amber said. 'How about a tour round the farmyard first?'

'Sounds good to me.'

'This is the garage,' Amber said, indicating the barn Radley had emerged from. 'We keep the quad bikes and main tractor in here and it's used as a workshop. The long building you can just see beyond that is Events Barn. It was a dairy shed back in the day but we don't have cows anymore. Barney's mum, Natasha, runs an events management business and Zara works for her. They keep the stock and equipment in there.'

I remembered the name from yesterday – Amber's best friend and chief bridesmaid on Saturday.

Amber led me in a diagonal line across the farmyard. There was another barn on the left which she told me they called 'garage two' as it held more farm vehicles and equipment. On the left beyond the farmhouse was a copse. A wide track circled round it before opening out onto a second large yard with buildings on three sides. Amber pointed to the first building on the left. 'This will be our farm shop. We've only just had permission to convert it into retail space and add a second floor. The initial idea is to have locally sourced food downstairs, including food from our farm, of course. Upstairs will be gifts – probably a combination of local crafts and popular brands, but Zara's still working on that. She'll eventually step away from the petting zoo and the events and take over as the farm shop manager. She's the most organised person I've ever met, so she'll have the place running like clockwork.'

'You're not going to be running the shop?'

Amber shook her head. 'No. I'm the project manager of the whole thing but I wanted to give Zara something to get her teeth into. Sourcing stock and merchandising excites her, but it does nothing for me. I'm better at the big picture vision stuff. I'm involved in all the key decisions about the non-farming activities, but I'm enjoying not having a clearly defined role. I'm a spare pair of hands for whoever needs it – usually the one who shouts the loudest.'

We crossed the yard and entered a stable block opposite the shop. The lights were already on inside and I counted four stalls on each side with horses looking out over six of them.

'Morning, Milo!' Amber called.

I hadn't noticed anyone in there but a dark-haired man, probably late twenties, poked his head over one of the stalls.

'This is Poppy. She's staying at Whisperwood this week.'

'Hi, Milo!'

Milo didn't meet my eyes, mumbled something indecipherable, and ducked back down again.

I glanced at Amber, surprised at the lack of greeting but she mouthed, *Nothing personal.*

'Do you like horses?' she asked.

'I like all animals, but I've never been around horses. Never ridden.'

She introduced me to all six, giving their names and whether they were owned by the farm or stabled there.

'Do you offer riding lessons?' I asked.

'No. Barney gives the odd lesson on Munchie to Imogen – his best mate Joel's daughter – but he doesn't have the time or interest to offer lessons. We both ride and so do his parents and sister but not as regularly as we'd like. If you stay again and fancy a go, you'd be very welcome.'

'I'd like that although, with Mary planning to sell up, staying at Whisperwood Farmhouse won't be an option.'

'Fair point, although my friend Samantha has holiday cottages at her place, Hedgehog Hollow. You could always stay there.'

I followed her back into the yard.

'While we're out of earshot, don't worry about Milo. He's brilliant at his job but he doesn't do people. As I said, it's nothing personal. He's a bit grumpy this week. We have a groom but she's off sick so it's fallen on Milo to see to the horses and, even though he loves all animals, pigs are his passion and he'd spend all his time with them if he could.'

It was fully light now and showing promise to be another beautiful if chilly day. We headed down a wide track to the left of the stables.

'This is the petting farm for our school visits,' Amber said. 'Natasha and Zara have been running them and we've had some great feedback so far. There's a lot more we can do, but it's a starting point.'

I took in the lawned area containing various wooden shelters, houses and runs in front of a wooden barn and smiled at the large sign – *Welcome to Cuddle Corner* – with some cute cartoon animals on it.

Amber hadn't said what the third building at the bottom of the U-shape was used for so I asked her about it as we walked back to the garage.

'We're not sure what to do with it at the moment. We wondered about a holiday cottage but the location isn't right. There's too much going on around it so I could just imagine all the complaints about noise. We could expand the shop into it, make it smaller units for local businesses, expand the school activities...' She shrugged. 'Lots of options but nothing that screams for immediate attention.'

Before long, I was on the back of a quad bike and heading up a gently sloping track between the farmhouse and fields. It was such a thrill to be on one again, the wind blowing my hair and cooling my cheeks. In the distance to my right, I could see Whisperwood Farmhouse. We passed pigs, goats and then sheep. Bumblebee Barn was stunning and I really couldn't have come to a better place. I wondered whether Sharon and Ian had suggested it because they knew that, as well as falling in love with the surroundings, this was a place where I'd be able to relax, switch off and find the person I used to be before illness dominated my life.

Another quad bike was parked by the gate of one of the fields containing Herdwick sheep and a dark-haired man was making his way towards us who Amber introduced as Barney.

'I'd normally shake your hand but best we don't today,' he said, laughing as he wiped his hands down his mucky boiler suit. 'This isn't mud.'

'What happened?' Amber asked.

'There was some string tangled round one of the Herdies and I thought I'd pinned her to remove it, but she dodged me and I landed somewhere bad. Typical day in the life of a farmer.'

'You've got a gorgeous farm,' I said, glancing around me at fields stretching out as far as the eye could see. 'These views!'

'Stunning, aren't they? I'm so lucky to have all this and even luckier to have someone to share it with now.'

Barney and Amber exchanged loving smiles, making my heart melt. It had been a long time since anybody had looked at me that way and I really missed that connection with somebody special.

'Are you sure you don't mind me joining you on Saturday night?' I asked, feeling like Barney should have a say. If he said the right words but didn't look convinced, I'd make my excuses later, but he smiled widely.

'It's our pleasure.'

Milo coming in over Barney's walkie-talkie prevented any

further chat. Amber kissed Barney goodbye over the gate and we clambered back onto the quad bike to go the short journey to the field they were thinking of for the beehives.

'I haven't done any research,' Amber said as she pushed open a barred gate into the chosen field, 'so I have no idea if this would be suitable.'

The field was lush pasture with a spattering of wildflowers bursting between the grass. Surrounded by trees on two sides, it had the perfect combination of direct sunlight but shady areas.

'Is that a pond?' I asked, noticing an area of water in the distance.

'Yes, a natural one. It gets bigger when it rains heavily, although it doesn't flood the whole field or anything like that. It doesn't dry up in the summer as there's a spring which feeds it. What do you think? Any good for hives?'

I turned in a circle, taking it all in, nodding slowly. I could picture the rows of hives, hear the buzz of the bees, smell the woodsmoke and the mesmerising mix of honey, beeswax, resins and pollen. I felt the same peace and contentment here as I did at Honey Bee Croft, happy memories flooding my mind of tending to the bees with Dad, always learning from him and feeding off his passion and enthusiasm. What I wouldn't do to be the beekeeper here!

'It's perfect, Amber. Any beekeeper who gets this as their apiary is very fortunate. It's accessible, away from people and animals, it has light, shade and water and it's not visible from the road so unlikely to attract vandals. Your beekeeper might want some sort of storage shed or container but it's not essential. I used to keep my stuff at Saltersbeck Farm but there was a break-in so I keep it in the van now.'

'Someone broke into your storage shed? Why?'

'For a laugh. It was kids being stupid.'

'I despair of people sometimes. Who breaks into a beekeeper's shed for a laugh? I hope you got your stuff back.'

'I did, but it was damaged, so I had to replace it anyway. Mindless.'

She tutted. 'When I was filming *Countryside Calendar*, we came across some awful cases of mindless behaviour, but for every instance there'd be several lovely examples of people caring for animals or neighbours which restored my faith in human beings.'

I smiled at her. 'Most of them are good. My next-door neighbour Wilf is amazing. He's in his eighties but he's always looking out for me. I look after his Yorkshire terrier, Benji, when he's going somewhere he can't take dogs but I'm pretty sure he brings him round more than he needs to because he knows it takes the edge off the loneliness.'

My voice cracked as I said the final word and I drew in a sharp breath. I'd only recently admitted to myself that I was lonely so what on earth had possessed me to blurt that out to someone I'd only just met? What must she think of me?

'Wilf sounds lovely and so does Benji,' Amber said, smiling at me gently. 'I'm sorry you're lonely. I know how that feels.'

'You do?'

'How about we go back to the house for a cuppa and we can talk about it?'

'You're sure you have time? I don't want to impose any more than I have already.'

'Right now, I have all the time in the world. Let's get back and pop the kettle on.'

* * *

Still stunned with myself for telling Amber I was lonely, flight mode kicked in when we made it back to the farmyard and I was so tempted to make an excuse and leave, but I could hear Mum's voice in my head – *Do one thing every day that scares you.* Talking about the loneliness which had plonked itself down beside me when Mum died, wrapped itself around my body when Dad moved into The Larks and squeezed tightly the day he no longer recognised me didn't just scare me. It terrified me but, as I followed Amber across the farmyard, my stomach churning as she made us both a mug of tea, I knew I was going to let her in. And that was also scary.

We sat down opposite each other at the large kitchen table and she fixed her eyes on mine. 'So, talk to me about your loneliness.'

And I did. Out it all came. How Dove Cottage had once been a place full of warmth and laughter, but all I felt now was sadness and loneliness. How my elderly neighbour's dog was the best company I had most weeks and how I lived for the days Wilf asked me to dog sit. How my two best friends had both ditched me and made me feel worthless. And how, weirdly, I hadn't felt lonely at Whisperwood Farmhouse despite being in a strange place on my own.

Amber told me about how she hadn't realised she was lonely until she met Barney and then she faced up to how she'd avoided returning to her London flat between filming because she'd known she'd be lonely there.

'I know you said you don't feel lonely at Whisperwood, but how about you meet a few more people? Some of my bridesmaids are coming round tonight to help me prepare the wedding favours over a couple of glasses of bubbly. It'll give you a chance to meet some of my friends which means you'll know more of us on Saturday and, to be honest, we need all the spare hands we can get. We've got a lot of favours to sort.'

I stared at Amber, feeling quite overcome with emotion. She'd invited me to her wedding, given me a dress, shown me round her farm and now she was inviting me to spend an evening with her friends. She had to be the kindest, friendliest person I'd ever met and I already felt sad at the thought of not seeing her again after the weekend.

Driving back to Whisperwood Farmhouse a little later, I felt as though I'd been enveloped in a fluffy blanket. I had no idea that people you'd only just met could be kinder and more thoughtful than those who you thought were your closest friends. In a couple of days, Amber had shown me more about what friendship looked like than Shauna and Jo had across all the years they'd been in my life.

Not long after I got back, Phil rang to confirm that he'd managed to shift things around and would be able to join me at the wedding. He couldn't stay late as he'd have a very early start the following morning, but was free to meet me at the hotel at four, giving us a few hours to catch up before the evening do started.

'I've also taken the liberty of booking you a room at Fennington Hall,' he said. 'It was the last one available so it's fairly basic, but it means you can relax and have a few drinks. And don't even think about asking me how much you owe me because this is my treat to you as an apology for not being around more when you've been going through so much.'

'Aw, Phil, I couldn't expect you to be. You don't live near me and you've got a new baby.'

'I know, but I could have called you more.'

'Ditto, but I always knew you were on the end of the phone if I needed you. Anyway, I'm really looking forward to seeing you.

There's a lot going on in my head at the moment and I'd love to hear your take on a few things.'

'Sounds intriguing. See you on Saturday.'

I put the phone down feeling a lot brighter for so many things – for talking to Amber about how I'd been feeling, for new friends to meet this evening, for seeing Phil on Saturday and for feeling more like me again with plans in the future that didn't have anything to do with any terminal illness diagnoses.

15

JOEL

The day of Barney and Amber's wedding had arrived and I couldn't be more ready to relax and celebrate with my friends on their special day. Well, as relaxed as a best man with a speech to make could be.

Chez and I had been like ships that passed in the night across the week. He'd still been asleep when I returned from each night shift and was gone when I rose that afternoon. I'd sent him several WhatsApp messages checking in with him but they'd all been viewed and ignored. When my brother took the grump with me, he did it big time.

In typical Chester style, the considerate start to the week had given way to mess. When I woke up on Thursday afternoon after my final night shift, I'd had to spend an hour cleaning up after him before going on a big shop because he'd eaten me out of house and home. He hadn't come home on Thursday night and I'd spent most of yesterday at Bumblebee Barn helping Barney get ahead with his work. Amber had gone to Fennington Hall for an extra night with her family and I'd stayed at the farm for a pre-wedding meal with Barney's family. By the time I got home, Chez was in bed where he'd still been this morning.

I hated that we hadn't spoken for days and, as he was coming to the wedding, I didn't want any tension between us so I made him a bacon butty for breakfast and knocked on his bedroom door.

'It's early! What do you want?' he called, his voice gruff, instantly putting me on edge.

'I've made you breakfast,' I responded, trying to sound cheerful, 'and I was hoping to talk before I leave for the wedding.'

'So you can give me another lecture?'

Tutting, I tried to open the door but there was something jamming it. 'What's wrong with the door?'

'I've got a chair against it.'

'Why?'

'To keep out unwelcome visitors.'

'And I'm one of them?' I asked, struggling to hide my frustration.

'Yes!'

'In my own home?'

There was a pause in which I hoped he was reflecting on the irony of him referring to me as an *unwelcome visitor*.

'Just go to the wedding and leave me alone.'

'Are you still coming?'

'I was planning to. Unless you don't want me there.'

'Of course I want you there! What I don't want is any hostility affecting Barney's big day.'

'I promise to be on my best behaviour. Now bugger off and let me sleep.'

I could stay and argue with him but he'd already dampened my spirits and I didn't want him to bring me down further. It would also make me late so I left him to it, took the butty back downstairs and had to hope he'd stand by his promise. Mum and Dad were guests too and had flown over last night. They were picking him up later in a hire car and I knew he was looking forward to seeing them so hopefully all would be well.

By the time I'd cleared up in the kitchen and placed my overnight bag and suit into the car boot, there was still no sign of Chez stirring, but I wasn't going to prompt him and risk another mouthful. I left the outer porch door unlocked and messaged Mum with the hiding place for the spare key, just in case, before setting off to pick up Imogen, hoping Tilly wasn't in a foul mood today.

* * *

Tilly was surprisingly pleasant. She issued her usual rules, of course, but wished us both a good time. Imogen chatted excitedly all the way and, once we'd checked in at Fennington Hall and dumped our bags, I took her to meet the other bridesmaids to get her hair done, returning to my room to run through my speech before getting changed.

Sometime later, I'd just fastened the top button on my tweed waistcoat when there was a knock on the door. Fizz, Phoebe and Darcie were in the corridor wearing their bridesmaid dresses with their hair styled and I could see Imogen hiding behind them, clearly wanting to do a grand reveal.

'Nice suit,' Fizz said, nodding appreciatively. 'Looking good, Mr Grainger.'

'Nice dress,' I said, in return. 'All of you look beautiful, but I don't suppose you've seen a little bridesmaid anywhere? Long blonde hair, brown eyes, about this height.' I put my hand against my chest, palm facing down, to indicate where Imogen came to.

'Presenting Miss Imogen Amelie Grainger,' Darcie said, as the three of them stepped aside.

I'd heard all about the dresses but I hadn't actually seen them until now. All the bridesmaids were wearing pale pink, pale green or cream full-length dresses but, as the youngest one, Imogen's was a little different. It was green, calf-length and the skirt part was covered in net embroidered with pink and cream flowers. She was wearing a floral headband and her hair had been curled into spirals.

'You look so pretty, sweetie,' I said, smiling at her before giving her a tentative hug, taking care not to rumple her dress or mess up her hair.

I took a couple of photos of Imogen to send to Tilly and a few of the four of them together before they headed off to meet up with Amber and the other bridesmaids. I had ten minutes until I needed to meet Barney and the groomsmen – Tim, Levi and Amber's brother, Brad – in the bar, which was just enough time to send Tilly the photos of Imogen, fasten my tie and read through my best man's speech for the millionth time. I wasn't a fan of public speaking but neither was Barney so we were having the speeches before the wedding breakfast, which was a relief. I'm not sure I'd have managed to eat my meal otherwise.

My phone beeped which would either be Tilly responding to the photos or one of the lads telling me they were already in the bar and demanding I join them.

FROM TILLY

Is our daughter wearing make-up?

I ground my teeth at the message and the two emojis accompanying it – the wow one and the angry face. Would it have killed her to say something nice? I switched my phone to silent, not even dignifying her message with a response. So what if Imogen was wearing a spot of make-up? I'd been asked permission and, seeing Imogen's face light up, I'd said it was fine as long as it wasn't caked on. Which it wasn't. Checking the rings were still safely tucked inside my waistcoat pocket, I fastened my tie.

When I made it down to the bar, Barney, Tim, Levi and Brad were already there, sitting at a table with Barney's dad Hadrian and Amber's dad Cole.

'What are you having?' Cole asked, standing up as I approached.

I was going to order a soft drink, but they all had pints and it would be rude to be the odd one out. I followed Cole to the bar so I could see what they had on tap.

'All set with the speech?' Cole asked once I'd placed my order.

'The speech is ready, but I'm not sure I am. I'm so nervous. Any tips?'

As a successful television actor, Cole oozed charisma and confidence. 'Believe it or not, I used to hate public speaking.'

'Seriously?'

'Absolutely. When I'm acting, I'm taking on a character but when I'm public speaking, I don't have a part to hide behind. I have to be me and I found it really hard at first, but another actor gave me some great advice – to treat it as a role where my character is a brilliant public speaker, confident, funny if needed, not fazed by the task, so that's what I did. Believe me, it works. So my advice is to think about the type of best man you want to be and act the hell out of it.'

He clapped me on the back, and I nodded gratefully. I used to enjoy drama at school and even had a speaking part in a school play once. Granted, it had only been two lines, but I'd turned in a strong performance, so I'd channel that moment. I didn't want to let Barney and Amber down, especially when Cole would deliver an outstanding father-of-the-bride speech and Barney, despite the nerves, would knock it out of the park too.

We returned to the group but only had time for the one drink before Tim, Levi and Brad went to welcome the guests.

'Nervous?' I asked Barney after we'd met with the celebrant and had a quick recap over what to expect.

'Yes, but not about marrying Amber. I still can't get over how many celebrities Amber and her family are friends with.'

I'd seen the guest list and it hadn't helped my speech-making nerves. The first time I'd been in a room with Amber's family – Christmas a couple of years ago – I'd been gobsmacked at all the name-dropping. Not in a pretentious way, mind. Amber's family were down to earth and easy to chat to but it just happened that they knew a hell of a lot of celebrities and many of them were coming to the wedding.

'I don't know if it helps but my mum said they might have jobs which make them recognisable but they're just regular people who have to use the toilet like the rest of us.'

Barney laughed. 'Your mum's brilliant. Speak of the devil...'

I followed his gaze over my shoulder and spotted my parents in the corridor where it appeared Mum had accosted Brad and was waving an autograph book in his direction. I should have known she'd do that. She loved all the soaps and *Londoners* – the long-running soap he'd been in since childhood – was her favourite. Emigrating to Portugal hadn't stopped her getting her regular fix.

'I'd better say hello and give Brad an escape route. Back in a minute. Oh! She's got her phone out. Selfie time!'

'Should I take a photo of you and Dad with Brad?' I asked, approaching them.

'Joel! Aw, don't you scrub up well, son.' Mum flung her arms round me and kissed my cheek, then rubbed it to remove her lipstick mark.

I hugged Dad too and Mum thrust her phone at me.

'Just Brad and me,' she said, winking at my dad.

'How about one with only you and then one with Dad too?' I suggested, catching Dad's disappointed expression. He claimed he couldn't stand the soaps but he never missed an episode. 'And then we can let Brad get back to ushering.'

'I don't mind,' Brad assured me with a winning smile. 'Although I will get a ribbing from Tim and Levi for not pulling my weight. Those two do go on!'

'They take their roles very seriously and they know that if they mess up at Barney's wedding, he can get payback at theirs.'

I took several photos and then Brad was permitted to return to his duties.

'Where's Chez?' I asked, hoping he hadn't pulled out.

'He's on the phone to Lorna,' Dad said.

'What sort of mood was he in?'

My parents looked at each other and shrugged.

'I'd suggest overly enthusiastic,' Mum said. 'He claimed he wasn't bothered about losing his job or falling out with Harry and we don't believe either of those things for a minute. At least things seem to be going well between him and Lorna just now. Let's hope it stays that way.'

I held up my crossed fingers but I wasn't convinced, especially when so much else was going wrong and it felt inevitable that depression would take a hold. I couldn't decide whether Chez and Lorna were wrong for each other or whether they were simply too young and immature to work through their issues. I feel so old for thinking that way, but I swear that every one of their bust-ups aged me half a decade. When it was good between Lorna and Chez, they made a great couple, but when it was bad, it was horrendous. How many times did a couple have to split up before they accepted that it was never going to work? Maybe being single was a better option.

'I need to get back to Barney,' I told my parents. 'I'll catch up with you both later and, Mum, no more fangirling over the celebs.'

'Me? I have no idea what you're talking about.' She gave me a mischievous grin as she wafted her face with her autograph book.

* * *

I found Barney and Amber's wedding ceremony unexpectedly emotional. Everything about it was so personal and so perfect for the couple. I'd never thought to ask about the music they'd chosen for Amber to walk down the aisle. For some reason, I'd assumed it would be something classical so when the opening orchestral melody to Elbow's 'One Day Like This' filled the room, I glanced at Barney in surprise.

'Is this...?'

He nodded. 'Tune!'

He wasn't wrong. I turned to see the smiles among the guests as they recognised what was playing. After the instrumental introduction, Imogen and Darcie appeared at the end of the aisle holding hands and that was the start for me. Proud dad moment! My baby girl looked so beautiful, grown up and not at all nervous despite roughly 160 pairs of eyes focused on her. She and Darcie beamed at each other and set off slowly towards the front. As the first verse played, they were followed by Fizz and Phoebe, Samantha and Tim, Tabs and Brad, Sophie and Levi. When the chorus kicked in, Zara as chief bridesmaid set off down the aisle and, as the track skipped to the outro, Amber appeared on her dad's arm. My breath caught. I knew she'd look good, but this was next level. I found it an odd tradition that the groom stayed facing forward until the bride arrived at the front as surely seeing her walking down the aisle was a special moment. And for a couple who weren't sticking with tradition for their day, why stick with that?

'You *have* to turn round,' I whispered to Barney. 'She's stunning!'

So he did turn and the expression on his face – so full of love for his bride – had me all dewy-eyed once more. Amber caught his eye and her smile widened even further. She reached us at the front, Cole kissed her on the cheek before taking his seat and Zara took her bouquet from her while Sophie and Tabs adjusted her train. This was it. My best mate for twenty-three years had met the woman of his dreams and was about to commit to her forever and I couldn't be happier for them.

Brad was invited up for a reading. I hadn't heard it before but I recognised parts of it – a mystery which Brad solved when he announced at the end, 'And if you're thinking that some of what I read sounds familiar, that's because it was a blatantly stolen mash-up of the words of Taylor Swift, Elton John, Ed Sheeran, Chris Martin and various other talented songwriters. You might have spotted some ABBA lyrics in there as well as a few lines from *Londoners*, *Darrington Detects* and *The Book Sleuths* – a few programmes with a strong family connection to the bride.'

With a wink, he took his place among the guests. It must have taken them ages to pull all that together but it was such a great personal touch. As were the vows which Barney and Amber had written themselves, which had me tearing up yet again – no idea where it was coming from as I wasn't usually one for getting emotional.

As they signed the register, 'Your Song' played – the version from the film *Moulin Rouge* sung by Ewan McGregor rather than the Elton John one, and Take That's 'Greatest Day' played as they walked out. I was meant to be walking beside Zara but Imogen rushed up to me and took my hand, demanding I twirl her. Zara laughed and hung back to walk alongside Darcie while Imogen twirled and danced her way down the aisle.

The hotel staff welcomed us with trays of drinks, but I only took a soft one, keen to have my wits about me while I delivered my speech. Mum and Dad appeared with big hugs for Imogen and a few tears on Mum's part. I knew that not getting to spend much time with Imogen troubled them, so I always made sure that, whenever she stayed with me, we had a video call with my parents. They'd been over to the UK several times and spent time with her then, but Tilly had never permitted me to take her to Portugal. She claimed it wasn't fair taking Imogen abroad when her siblings weren't getting the same opportunity. I thought that was spectacularly unfair. Why should Imogen miss out on the chance to travel? Why should I? And why should my parents miss out on time with their only grandchild? I hadn't pushed it massively so far because Imogen was still young and unlikely to remember holidays abroad, but I was determined to push it in the future. I was determined to push everything.

'Where's Chez?' I asked Dad.

'At the bar getting a pint. He didn't fancy champagne.'

I glanced towards the bar at the same time as Chester turned with his drink. His eyes caught mine and the look he gave me could have withered Amber's bridal bouquet. So much for his promise that there'd be no atmosphere. I was about to join him when the photographer called for the wedding party, so I took Imogen's hand and followed Barney and Amber outside. I'd have to catch Chez later and hope that, with a few drinks inside him, he'd be less hostile. We'd had our bad moments in the past but nothing like this, although he'd still had his job and his best mate before. Still, there was no need to take it all out on me. I hadn't caused either of those things. I was the one giving him a free roof over his head and feeding him. I didn't need a big thank you speech, but it would be nice if he could lean on the side of grateful rather than resentful.

16

POPPY

I set off for Fennington Hall straight after an early lunch. I'd got myself so worked up with nerves about meeting Cole Crawford and the rest of Amber's family that I'd been unable to concentrate on any work and, rather than pacing the farmhouse floor, decided that I might as well get checked into my room. I'd been on the venue's website and there appeared to be extensive gardens and grounds which I could explore to kill some time, or I could (try to) relax in my room and watch TV.

I arrived at half one and there were several guests milling around in the entrance foyer dressed in their wedding finery. I spotted Amber's close friend Samantha who I'd met at the farm on Thursday night, and she gave me a wave and beckoned me over. I'd loved hearing all about her rescue centre and wished I'd been staying longer so I could squeeze in a visit and perhaps even volunteer my assistance for a few hours.

'Lovely to see you again,' Samantha said, giving me a hug, which helped unknot my stomach a little.

'And you. You look amazing. I love the dress.'

The full-length gown was in a warm cream with chiffon

flutter sleeves and sparkles on the bodice. I'd been told on Thursday that all the bridesmaids were wearing the same style of dress but the colour theme for the wedding was 'sage and blush' with the bridesmaids either wearing sage green, blush or cream dresses. I could imagine the three colours looking stunning together.

Samantha introduced me to her husband, Josh, and their two children – four-year-old Thomas and three-year-old Lyra, who looked adorable in their smart outfits. They each had a soft toy pig with them, Lyra's dressed as a bride and Thomas's as a groom.

'Because Barney's a pig farmer,' Samantha explained.

'We've got hedgehogs ready for Fizz and Phoebe's wedding,' Josh added.

I crouched down in front of the children. 'Are your pigs getting married today?'

Thomas nodded, wide-eyed and Lyra giggled as she passed me her pig to admire.

'Such a beautiful pig bride,' I said, straightening out its dress before handing it back.

'I need to find the others,' Samantha said. 'I'll see you tonight. Have a good time with your friend this afternoon.'

'Thank you. Have a great wedding.'

Josh headed off with the children and I made my way to the reception desk to check in.

'The ceremony starts at two o'clock in the Magnolia Suite just down that corridor.' The receptionist – Blaine according to her name badge – pointed to my left.

'I'm actually an evening guest,' I said, pulling an apologetic expression. 'A very early one.'

She laughed lightly. 'I hear you. I'd rather be five hours early than five minutes late. The evening starts at seven in the Rowan Room which is in the other direction. Most of the guests will be gathering in the Juniper Lounge which is a huge bar running along the back of the hotel. The drinks reception will be in there after the ceremony but there's a quieter bar – the Sycamore Snug – which will probably be empty for a while if you want to get a drink now. The wedding party has taken over the whole hall so there won't be any non-wedding guests here today.'

'The Sycamore Snug sounds good to me.'

'There's also a roof terrace with lots of hidden seats if you want even more peace and quiet. It's a little complicated to find so just ask if you'd like directions to that later.'

I thanked Blaine for her help and took my key – an actual key rather than a keycard which instantly made me feel like I was staying somewhere very posh – and went off in search of my room on the second floor.

Phil said it had been the last room available and was basic, but if this was basic, the better rooms must be fit for royalty because I was seriously impressed. With high ceilings and ornate cornicing, it had pretty floral wallpaper, modern artwork and soft furnishings in a blend of rich peacock blue, light blue and pale gold. I ran my hand over the soft throw across the end of the king-sized bed. It was beautifully romantic, and I wished for a moment that I had someone to tumble onto that bed with at the end of the evening. My heart raced as I imagined bursting through the door in a passionate clinch, the door slamming behind us as I unbuttoned his shirt and he unzipped my dress. We'd stumble across the room, both of us lost in our kiss, shedding more clothes as we neared the bed and... Heat ran through my body as I thought about it and I shook my head. How odd that the *he* in my little fantasy had been Mr Rugby Physique. He'd popped into my mind a lot since my visit to Bloomsberry's which was so bizarre considering all we'd done was exchange a few words and several smiles. He really shouldn't be occupying any space in my head after such a meaningless interlude. Although, to me, it hadn't really been meaningless and that's probably why it had stayed with me. He'd made me smile, I'd felt noticed by a man for the first time in years and it had been a welcome boost to know that a stranger had found me attractive. Or at least I assumed he had or why would he have kept looking up and smiling like that?

I removed my gorgeous orange dress from the suit carrier Amber had loaned me. As I adjusted it on the hanger, an article I'd read in a magazine at The Larks a few weeks ago came back to my mind. It had been a commentary on the world of online dating and how it was still possible these days to meet *the one* in a more traditional way such as while in education, at work, in a pub or club, at the gym or at a wedding. I don't know why, but the wedding stats had stuck in my mind. A survey claimed that 15 per cent of the people asked had spent the night with someone they'd met at a wedding, 10 per cent were in or had been in a serious relationship with a guest they'd met there and 5 per cent had married someone they'd met at a wedding. So it *did* happen. Could it happen to me? I hung my dress up on the outside of the wardrobe shaking my head. No chance, especially when I'd be retreating to my room alone when Phil left.

Thinking about Phil, it made sense to let him know I'd arrived.

TO PHIL

> I know you'll be surprised to hear this, but I'm already here! So if you are able to get away any earlier, please do, otherwise I'll see you at 4 x

I'd just plonked my overnight bag onto the bed when a reply came through.

FROM PHIL

Absolute shocker!!! Wish I could get there early
but I might actually be late. I'm thinking 4.30 but
will keep you posted. What are you going to do?

TO PHIL

Toying with a walk but might hide in my room
which won't be a hardship as it's beautiful

FROM PHIL

Don't you dare! Get yourself down to the bar,
order a drink and do some celeb-spotting.
Seriously, Pops, how often do you get to mingle
with the stars? Put your big girl pants on and
seek out your favourite vicar. My challenge to
you is a selfie with him before I get there. Go!
Go! Go!

I shook my head, laughing. What was he like? Cole Crawford
would be needed for photographs immediately after the ceremony but perhaps I could do a walk-by selfie with him in the
background a little later.

My bedroom was at the back of the hall and I could see a
maze with a central fountain and a rose garden to the side of it. It
was too early for the roses to be in bloom but it still looked inviting. I'd go downstairs in a bit and tuck myself away somewhere to
do some discreet celeb-spotting when the ceremony finished.
After that, I'd grab my coat and take a wander round the
grounds.

A ping from my phone alerted me to another message from
Phil.

FROM PHIL

Let me guess. You're planning to hide in a dark
corner where no one can see you. PUT THAT
ORANGE DRESS ON AND SHINE!!!!

TO PHIL

You know me far too well!

I accompanied my message with a selfie of me in my casual clothes, shrugging.

FROM PHIL

Is that tomato soup on your T-shirt? Orange dress. Do it! Shooting into a meeting but I expect to see a selfie of you in your party dress when I come out. See you later. You can do this x

I looked down at my white T-shirt and tutted at the tomato soup slop. How hadn't I noticed that earlier? Luckily I'd had my coat on when I'd been talking to Samantha and Josh or they'd have seen me looking a mess. I could put my hoodie on but if I was hoping to blend into the background, jeans and a hoodie weren't the way forward – I'd stand out more as the only person not dressed up. I was going to have to put the dress on which meant I might as well refresh my make-up and tidy up my hair, not that it would take long. I never applied thick make-up and was blessed with hair that, once styled, tended to stay where it was.

When I was ready, I slipped my feet into the pair of sparkly strappy sandals Fizz had kindly loaned me. Unbeknown to me, Amber had messaged all the bridesmaids to ask if any of them were a size five shoe and could lend me some footwear for the wedding. Fizz had come up trumps with the footwear but Samantha had loaned me a necklace and earrings and Barney's mum Natasha had loaned me a clutch bag, so my ensemble was complete.

A little later, I walked into the Juniper Lounge which was deserted except for a young female bartender wiping down the bar. She smiled at me and asked what I'd like, so I ordered a Pimm's and lemonade. It was probably more of a summer's day drink but I wanted some alcohol to take the edge off being somewhere unfamiliar and it felt a little early to start on the wine.

'Too late for the wedding?' she asked as she prepared my drink.

'Erm, no... too early, actually. I'm here for the evening do.'

Her eyebrows quirked. 'You do realise it's only twenty past two?'

'Yeah, I know. I've always been overly punctual. I'm meeting a friend first but he's running late so I thought I'd grab a drink and catch sight of... erm...' Would she judge me if I said Cole Crawford? Probably. I was already judging myself.

'The newlyweds?' she suggested when I didn't finish my sentence. I nodded. 'So which side are you? Bride or groom?'

'Neither.'

Her eyebrows shot up once more and I couldn't muster the energy to attempt an explanation, especially when I was still questioning that moment of madness where I'd said yes to coming. Best to end the transaction and get out of there.

'It's complicated. I'm a family friend.' I gave my room number for the bill and grabbed my drink, slipping out into the hotel lobby. Sitting down on a high-backed chair which would give me a great view of the guests exiting the Magnolia Suite, I took a sip of my refreshing drink and commended myself on a good choice.

I sank a little further back into my chair, feeling very conspicuous and cursing myself for being so starstruck but, every time I considered backing out, I thought about Phil's encouraging messages and pictured my mum's face. She'd have loved to meet her idol and would have been tickled pink that I'd unexpectedly been presented with that opportunity so I wasn't just doing this for me – I was doing it for her.

When the door to the Magnolia Suite opened with a burst of music and chatter, butterflies swirled in my stomach. The photographer emerged first, followed a little later by Amber and Barney, huge smiles on their faces. What an attractive couple they made. Amber's lace wedding gown was stunning – a capped-sleeved sheath design which clung flatteringly to her hourglass figure before opening out into a fishtail with a train. A sheer panel on the back broke up the lace. Her auburn hair was worn up although, from a distance, I couldn't see whether it was a simple or elaborate style.

They headed towards the Juniper Lounge and the rest of the bridal party followed them. I spotted Samantha, Zara, Phoebe and Fizz. One of the bridesmaids wearing sage green had auburn hair so had to be Amber's sister Sophie. I recognised their brother, Brad, walking beside his onscreen wife in the soap *Londoners* and offscreen long-term partner, Tabatha Bellingham. Her character always dressed in dowdy clothes so it was lovely to see her resplendent in blush pink. The bridesmaid dresses were gorgeous, and I loved what the men were wearing too. Rather than morning suits, they looked much more countryside in green tweed waistcoats, chinos and brown shoes. Barney had a cream shirt on with a pink tie and the rest of his groomsmen were wearing sage-green shirts with dark green ties. As they walked away, I noticed that the back of Barney's waistcoat was also a different colour to the others. I liked that subtle touch.

At the back of the wedding party was a groomsman and a young girl in a green dress with a net skirt who I guessed must be Barney's best man, Joel, and his daughter, Imogen. Joel held Imogen's hand while she twirled in a circle, her dress fanning out around her, her blonde ringlets bouncing. Her happy smile was so captivating. Oh, to be that young again when the simple act of twirling in a pretty dress could bring such joy. I glanced up at Joel and my stomach did a loop-the-loop. It was Mr Rugby Physique!

I leaned forward, my heart racing, but it was definitely him and he looked even more attractive than he had when we'd met at the garden centre. This time, it wasn't just his looks that were drawing me in – it was that he was twirling too. He was dressed up at a celebrity-filled wedding in a posh venue and he was twirling and laughing with his daughter as though he didn't care who saw him. The phrase *dance like nobody's watching* sprang to mind and I couldn't take my eyes off the pair of them. I always admired adults who could be as uninhibited as young children, having fun and being completely in the moment. I wished I could be more like that. I sometimes felt that I lived up to the *boring accountant* stereotype but what was wrong with being straightforward, organised and reliable? I admired those who could throw caution to the wind and who either weren't bothered by what people thought of them or gave a good impression of being that way. They disappeared out of view, but I was already excited about our paths crossing later, being properly introduced, having a conversation about something other than the tastiest ready meals.

And then came the moment I'd been waiting for – the father of the bride emerged and I held my breath. Cole Crawford in the flesh looking taller and even more handsome in real life than on the screen. He certainly didn't look sixty-one, but neither did his wife, Jules. I was completely frozen to the spot and couldn't have moved even if I wanted to, not that I'd have dreamed of interrupting them. I couldn't even reach for my phone for a discreet selfie. Phil would be disappointed. My eyes burned and my throat was tight as I imagined Mum being here to share this with me. I couldn't wait to tell Dad. I blinked back tears as it struck me that it would mean nothing to him. Cole Crawford no longer existed in his world. I took a deep breath, determined to hold it together.

The rest of the guests filed out and it was like a photocall for *OK!* or *Hello* magazines. I spotted Annabelle Coates who Amber had been telling me about, looking fabulously showbiz in a floral frock coat and wide-brimmed feather-strewn hat. There were so many other celebrities that I felt quite overwhelmed, completely starstruck and very conscious that, even though I was hidden from view, it was somewhat cheeky of me to be here. No way could I take any photos.

It took quite some time for all the guests to file out of the Magnolia Suite and head into the bar for the drinks reception. Despite feeling like a gatecrasher, I was glad I'd come down. I'd imagined Mum sitting beside me giving me a running commentary about who they were dating, any awards they'd won recently and exciting future plans as well as sharing her observations about her favourite dresses, hats, shoes and handbags. One of the many things I'd loved about Mum was how, despite being celebrity-obsessed, she only focused on the positives and never gossiped. If she didn't like what someone was wearing, she wouldn't voice it. *If you can't say something nice, don't say anything at all.* If only more people were like that. I'd learned so much from Mum about looking on the bright side – from Dad too – and it angered me that they'd been taken away from me, both in such a cruel way. I was determined to do them proud and embrace life with positivity like they'd done.

I stayed where I was long after the guests had gone, thinking about Mum. For a woman who'd chosen not to have children because she didn't feel any draw towards being a mother, she'd been a natural. It would have been so easy for Mum and Dad to harbour some resentment at being tied to a family life they'd never planned or wanted but they'd both wholeheartedly embraced it. I didn't only think of them as my parents – they'd been my teachers and my friends, which made the void they'd left in my life so much deeper.

'Can I get you anything?'

I'd been so lost in my thoughts that I hadn't even noticed Blaine, the receptionist who'd checked me in, approaching.

I smiled up at her. 'I'm fine, thanks. Just lost in my memories. My mum was celebrity-obsessed. She'd have loved this.'

'My mum is too. She's a hairdresser and she claims the celebrity magazines are for the customers but they never make it into the salon until she's read them cover to cover.'

'She'd have got on well with my mum. I bought her a subscription to *OK!* and *Hello* every Christmas and every time I asked her if she'd prefer a surprise gift instead, she'd say, *Don't even think about cutting me off from my celeb fix.*'

'She sounds lovely,' Blaine said.

'She was.'

'You're very welcome to stay here and reminisce, but I wondered if you might like directions to that quieter bar I mentioned when you checked in.'

'That sounds great. Actually, you mentioned a terrace. I might like to check that out instead. I'm assuming you can see the grounds from there.'

'You can so you'll be able to watch the photos being taken out the back. I'd recommend you grab a coat. Bit cold up there.'

I retrieved my coat from my room and followed the directions Blaine had given me. There were several columns on the terrace, wrapped in solar-powered fairy lights. Wooden screens and planters divided the space into sections meaning guests sitting on the metal benches, chairs and tables could remain hidden from others. At the far end of the terrace, the view over the gardens was stunning.

Amber and Barney were having their photos taken on a wooden bridge over the lake. Once that was done, they continued onto a small island where there was a pagoda. It looked to be covered in flowers so had presumably been decorated especially for the wedding. Those photos would be so beautiful.

Sudden chatter and laughter drew my attention back to just beneath me where the rest of the wedding party had exited the building, evidently required for group photos. I spotted Cole and Jules Crawford walking with Natasha and another man who must be Barney's dad. I'd have expected Cole to keep my attention but someone else caught my eye and sent my stomach into another loop-the-loop – Joel. He and one of the ushers were walking either side of Imogen, picking her up and swinging her in the air and I was captivated watching him once more, my heart racing. It made no sense to me. In my whole life, I'd never been instantly attracted to a man like this. For me, attraction usually emerged from friendship. If we got on, had shared values and enjoyed being together, feelings of more than friendship might develop.

That's how it had worked with Phil and that's where I'd thought it was heading with one of my colleagues, Vince, after Phil and I split up. He'd been through a recent break-up and I genuinely thought we'd connected over a few nights of drinks after work and a couple of meals. When he invited me back to his place after the second meal, I agreed because we were in the middle of a really interesting conversation which I didn't want to end. Turned out that, in his mind, going back for coffee meant I wanted to jump into bed with him and he wasn't impressed when I turned him down, accusing me of being the most boring woman he'd ever met because apparently all I did was talk about work and my mum's health problems. I could have brushed aside the *boring* accusation but in the early stages of Dad's dementia, Bertie's wife, Cheryl, set me up on a blind date with a colleague of hers and I thought it had gone well but the feedback filtered back via her that he *hadn't found the conversation very stimulating.* Translation – he also thought I was boring. To be fair, I might have talked too much about Dad's diagnosis but it hadn't been the only topic of conversation. That was the last time I'd dated. If we had a proper conversation, would Joel come to the same conclusion about me?

I tried to focus on the bride and groom, but my attention was continually drawn back to Joel. All I knew about him was the brief summary Amber had given me when she told me who was in the wedding party. He was Barney's best friend since senior school, single, and dad to the youngest bridesmaid. I knew nothing else about him except his taste in ready meals, but I wanted to find out and the only way I'd be able to do that was to stay at the evening do by myself after Phil left and talk to him. Could I do that? I wasn't sure. Doing one scary thing today – being here – was already pretty overwhelming without throwing in a whole pile more.

* * *

By the time Phil arrived, the photos were complete, the guests had moved in for the wedding breakfast and I'd ditched my coat and made my way down to the Sycamore Snug for a drink.

'You look amazing,' Phil said as he kissed me on my cheek then stepped back to take in my outfit. 'I don't think I've ever seen you in this colour before. It really suits you. Reina said she'd love a photo of you. Do you mind?'

I posed for a photo which he sent and, moments later his phone rang with a FaceTime request from Reina.

'I don't want to see your face, Phil,' she said in her lilting Spanish accent. 'I want to see that beautiful girl. Poppy! *Hola!*'

Phil grinned as he handed me the phone.

'*Hola*, Reina.'

'Poppy, you look radiant! Give Phil the phone and give me a twirl. Yes! Stunning!'

I thanked Reina and sat back down. 'Is Eliana asleep?'

'She is but if you are quiet, I can show you. Ssh!'

Moments later, their gorgeous pudgy baby appeared on the screen, lying in her cot, her hand curled around a comforter.

'She's so beautiful,' I said when Reina announced she'd closed the nursery door and we could talk again. She thanked me and gave us an update on her day and then told us to enjoy our evening, blowing a kiss to each of us before disconnecting.

The smile on Phil's face and the sparkle in his eyes warmed my heart.

'You chose well second time around,' I said, smiling at him.

'I did. But I chose well first time around too. We just weren't meant to be forever but I like that we stayed good friends, that you're still part of my family and that my new family adore you.'

'Me too. How grown-up are we keeping it together like that?'

He laughed and clinked his glass against mine. 'To adulting.'

I had zero regrets about our relationship ending but equally had none about our marriage. It worked for many years and then it didn't and what we had now worked brilliantly too.

Phil cocked his head to one side, and I knew what was coming next – the question he always asked me when we had some time alone. 'Anyone special in your life?'

I shook my head. 'My time's divided between Dad, the bees and work so I barely ever meet anyone, not that I'd have time to see them even if I did. What I really need is a time machine so I can travel back a few years, meet someone special and get so settled in a relationship that he understands and accepts the me of today – the person who's usually too drained at the end of the day to do anything other than cuddle in front of the TV. Someone who understands that, although I have to prioritise other parts of my life over him, it doesn't mean I don't love him.'

'I wish I had that time machine for you. I'd send it into the future to find a cure for Alzheimer's and MND.'

I placed my hand over his and squeezed. 'If only you could.'

My parents had always treated Phil like a son, and they'd remained close to him after the divorce. He'd attended Mum's funeral and had visited Dad in The Larks on several occasions. The first time Dad didn't recognise him had hit him hard too.

'So, how has your week in Yorkshire been?' he asked.

'Exactly what I needed. I hoped to get caught up with work, but I've actually got ahead. I've accepted that it's okay not to visit Dad every day which is a massive breakthrough for me. And a couple of huge, unexpected bonuses are seeing you and meeting Cole Crawford later. Oh, and I've slept brilliantly most nights – must be all the fresh air I've been getting. Could have done without the nightmares about Damon, though.'

Phil already knew about the coffee I'd had with Damon last year and why I'd agreed to it, so I brought him up to speed on recent events. He was shocked to hear that Damon had turned up at The Larks and that he'd repeatedly turned up at Dove Cottage while I'd been away.

'I wish he'd leave me alone,' I finished. 'I can't face going back and having the same conversations with him over and over again.'

'You shouldn't have to. As it's not getting through to him, is it worth speaking to his mum?'

'I've thought about it, but how do I phrase it without sounding petty? *Your son keeps asking me out and won't take no for an answer. Can you have a word with him please?*'

'How about this? *Your son keeps turning up at my house without invite and now he's started turning up at my dad's care home. It's scaring me and, even though I've asked him on numerous occasions to stop, he refuses because he seems to believe we're meant to be together. I'd appreciate any help you can give in getting the message through to him that we're not.'*

It sounded pretty serious when he put it like that, but I couldn't deny that it was how I felt. Maybe I'd given Damon too much slack because I'd known him from school and our mums had been friends. Maybe it *was* more serious than I'd realised.

'I'll see how he is when I get home and, if he turns up again, I'll definitely go and see Jenny.'

Our conversation moved on to my thoughts around putting the house on the market. I'd thought a lot about it this week and had concluded it was the right thing to do. Dove Cottage deserved to be lived in by someone who loved it and that person was no longer me. While I had hundreds of happy memories from the past, the more recent memories weren't so happy and it was time to make a fresh start – somewhere with a smaller garden closer to The Larks for Dad and Saltersbeck Farm for the bees.

'I understand selling Dove Cottage,' Phil said, 'but I'm not convinced buying somewhere near The Larks is the best idea. You've said yourself that breaking the habit of visiting your dad every day has been liberating and I'm worried that, if you move closer, you'll find yourself falling back into the daily visiting pattern. And when the worst happens and your dad's no longer with us, where does that leave you? Tied to somewhere you don't need to be anymore. I know renting can seem like wasted money, especially when selling Dove Cottage will give you the funds to buy your own place outright, but renting gives you the flexibility to do what you want – put your stuff in storage and travel for a while, move somewhere different or just take some time to decide what you want from life. Maybe that will still be a beekeeping accountant in Gloucestershire but maybe it'll be a beekeeper only in Devon, Pembrokeshire, Lancashire or—'

'East Yorkshire,' I said, without even pausing to think about it.

Phil raised an eyebrow at me. 'Where you're staying has really captured your heart, then?'

'It's beautiful. I love the house, the countryside, the farm next door, the people. Amber says they're thinking of getting hives on their farm and she showed me where. It's perfect, Phil. I imagined I was their beekeeper, selling the honey and my Honey Bee Hugs range in the shop they're setting up and...' I tailed off, rolling my eyes at him. 'It was a nice little daydream.'

'Why does it have to be a daydream? Why can't it be reality?'

'Because even if I was brave enough to up sticks and start over, I couldn't do that while I still have Dad. With any luck, he has years left in him.' My shoulders slumped. I knew that wasn't true. I'd devoured all the factsheets and guides I could get my hands on. I knew full well that late-stage dementia was the shortest of the three stages, typically lasting between one and two years. And that was before factoring in Dad's age. The sadness in Phil's eyes told me he was thinking the same. I cleared my throat and continued. 'By that time, they might have got in a beekeeper already and have all their shop suppliers sorted.'

'Why do you have to wait until your dad's gone?' Phil asked. 'Why not now?'

'It's too far from The Larks.'

'So move him out of The Larks. Your dream home and job could be right here. Mary's doing her house up to sell it so why don't you buy it? Why don't you be the beekeeper at Bumblebee Barn and get Honey Bee Hugs up and running again while Stanley is in a care home nearby?'

'What about my clients?'

'You wind up your business or, if that's too big a financial risk, you offer a virtual service. If they don't like that, that's their loss, but I reckon most of your clients would go for it.'

It was a long time since I'd felt positive about the future but what Phil had just described sounded like an absolute dream to me. Why hadn't I thought about moving Dad? The birds were the reason he loved The Larks so as long as I found somewhere he could sit and watch birds, he should be fine. Or would he? I'd need to get Marnie's advice on whether moving Dad could be detrimental to him.

'It does sound ideal, but I don't know if I can face starting over again where I don't know anyone.'

'But you do know people. Amber and Barney have invited you to their wedding, shown you round their farm, and you've spent an evening making wedding favours with some of Amber's bridesmaids who you said were all really welcoming and already felt like friends. So not only would you have a home and dream job on offer, you'd have the start of a new friendship group too.'

I appreciated him not pointing out that my only friends in Winchcote were my elderly neighbours and that, beyond that, my friendship circle was his family – wonderful people with whom I'd stay in touch no matter where I lived.

'You know what your mum always said,' he added, his tone teasing.

'I know, but this is huge. On a scary scale of one to ten, this is a twenty.'

'At least it's not a thirty,' he joked, but then his expression turned serious. 'I'm worried about you, Pops. I worry that you're lonely and that, when your dad's gone, you'll be even lonelier and I wish I lived closer so I could be there for you and help ease that pain.'

Tears pricked my eyes and I swallowed down the lump in my throat. 'That's not your job anymore.'

'Maybe not as your husband, but we started as and always will be friends, and friends are there for each other. You deserve to live a life that makes you happy, especially after you've spent seven years so far caring for your parents. And it sounds to me as though that life could be waiting for you right here in Yorkshire.'

As he spoke, a ball of excitement began building in my stomach. I didn't want to be lonely anymore and, as I'd said to Amber, despite being on my own at Whisperwood Farmhouse I hadn't felt lonely for a single minute. Could this be the place I was meant to be? Could this beautiful place be where I came to heal and start over with a new business, new friends, new life? I thought of Joel. New love?

17

JOEL

Cole's advice about acting had been great. Can't say it was a BAFTA-winning performance but playing a part – a slicker, more confident version of me – did the trick and my best man speech went down well. I was relieved when I could sit down and take a large gulp or two of alcohol to steady my nerves.

There was a traditional top table so I was at the end with Natasha next to me and Cole beside her. Cole shook my hand, congratulating me on a great speech and I thanked him for his helpful advice.

The food was delicious, and the conversation flowed but I felt a wave of despair every time I looked across to the table where Mum and Dad were sitting with Chez and Imogen. Imogen had been asked if she wanted to sit with me, her grandparents or the other bridesmaids and she'd chosen her grandparents because she didn't see them very often, which I thought was lovely of her and which had delighted Mum and Dad. Tim, Levi and their partners were also on the table, and everyone seemed to be having a good time except Chez who, from what I could see, was making minimal effort to join in the conversation and maximum effort to keep his wine topped up.

I decided I'd join them for coffee. Our table was first to be served so I excused myself, picked up my drink and slice of wedding cake and made my way across the room. Chez caught my eye as I approached, grabbed his glass of red wine and a bottle and walked off before I could reach the table. If he continued drinking at his current rate, he'd be steaming drunk by the time Lorna arrived this evening and I couldn't imagine her being impressed by that. I watched him leave the room, frustrated by his immaturity and rudeness.

I plonked myself down on Chez's vacated chair and Imogen clambered onto my lap for a cuddle.

'Did you enjoy your food?' I asked her.

'It was yummy.' She nuzzled into my neck, yawning.

'Are you tired?'

'Yes.'

'Do you want a sleep?'

'No. I don't want to miss anything.'

'There's nothing to miss now. We'll eat the cake then move into the bar so they can get the room ready for tonight. Then it's just chatting and drinking until the disco starts in two hours. So if you do want a nap, now's a good time. Cloud's in the room waiting for you.'

'I'm okay.'

'Say if you change your mind. You want to be fresh for your special dance.'

Coffees finished, Tim, Levi and their fiancées went through to the bar. Imogen was so quiet that I wondered if she'd fallen asleep on me but she perked up when Darcie joined us and asked if she wanted to get a drink of juice.

'Stay in one of the bars, please,' I told them. 'If you want to go anywhere else, can you message me?'

Darcie promised and left holding Imogen's hand.

'How was Chester?' I asked Mum and Dad once the girls had gone. 'He looked miserable each time I looked over.'

Mum slowly shook her head. 'He's not in a good place right now. We're worried he might be at the start of a decline.'

'I'm worried about that too. I wanted to talk to you about it after the wedding.'

'We suggested he come back to Portugal with us for a break,' Dad said, 'but he wants to be with Lorna.'

'Did he tell you they want to rent a place together?'

The surprised looks on both their faces answered that.

'Even before he lost his job, how did he think he'd manage to afford that?' Mum asked. 'And how would he cope next time they split up?'

'I said the same and got an earful as a result. He hates me at the moment.'

'Oh, I don't think he hates you, Joel. That's a very strong word.'

'Well, if he doesn't, he's giving a very good impression of someone who hates me.'

She took my hand in hers, tears pricking her eyes. 'We shouldn't have left you to deal with this. I'm so sorry.'

I squeezed her hand. 'Don't regret it. You did the right thing for you both, and you did it with our blessing. I don't actually think the big issue is Chez losing his job. I think falling out with Harry is what's killing him. Those two have been like brothers for years – just like me and Barney.'

Mum smiled at me. 'It was lovely what you said about Barney being like a brother to you in your speech. You two have always looked out for each other.'

'And so have Harry and Chez until now. Harry's stuck by him through all the difficult times and now, according to Chez, he's chosen his new girlfriend over Chez who Chez thinks is bad for Harry.'

'You don't think it's jealousy?' Dad asked.

'I wondered that at first, but he got on brilliantly with Fern and it only fell apart when Deana moved in.'

There weren't many guests left in the Rowan Room and I was conscious that the waiting staff were clearing round us so suggested we make a move. Mum wanted to have a rest before the evening do so she and Dad returned to their room and I went to check on Imogen and see whether she was flagging and would benefit from another prompt to relax for a bit.

Cole spotted me as soon as I entered the Juniper Lounge and whisked me away to introduce me to some of his showbiz pals. When Barney had shown me the guest list, I hadn't known who they all were so I'd gone online, not wanting to look like an idiot if I met them, but now most of those details had gone out of my head. Between introductions, I glanced round the room but there was no sign of Imogen and Darcie. Sophie appeared and whisked her dad away for a family photo which gave me the perfect excuse to slip out and see if Imogen was in the quieter bar, but there was no sign of her there either. I checked my phone but there weren't any messages so I returned to the Juniper Lounge thinking they might have gone in there via a different entrance and we'd missed each other, but there was no sign of them.

I knew I shouldn't worry – there were only wedding guests in the hotel and there was no way they'd have wandered off outside – but a feeling of panic was welling up inside me. I phoned Darcie but there was no answer. I phoned Fizz and then Phoebe but both their numbers went to voicemail.

I walked past the snug again, too busy searching for them to look where I was going, and I collided with someone.

'Oh God, I'm so sorry,' I said.

A brunette in an orange dress was crouched down retrieving the contents of her handbag which I must have knocked flying from her hands. Mortified, I knelt down and grabbed a lipstick which had rolled away. We both reached for her room key at the same time and our hands touched. I felt a spark of electricity and, as she looked up into my eyes, I gasped. It was the brunette from the garden centre.

'You were right about the teriyaki and the salmon,' she said, smiling widely, her eyes sparkling. 'Did your friend like her flowers?'

'Yes, she... Erm... They were...' I shook my head, bemused. 'I'm stunned to see you here, but you don't look surprised to see me.'

We both stood up, but didn't take our eyes from each other.

'I saw you earlier and recognised you. Joel, is it?'

I nodded, lost for words once more.

'I'm Poppy,' she said. 'And it's not just your fault we collided. I wasn't looking where I was going either.'

'I was looking for someone and I...' Why couldn't I seem to finish a sentence?

'Your daughter?' she asked.

'Yes, but how...?'

'I saw you together earlier. She's in the toilets with her friend. A guest knocked into them and spilt your daughter's blackcurrant drink down her dress. She was a bit upset but I took her into the loos and got the stain out. They're drying it under the hand dryer.'

I heaved a sigh of relief. 'I couldn't find her and I was starting to get worried. Thanks for sorting her out.'

'No bother. If you get to a stain quickly, it's so much easier to lift it. See you later.'

And she was gone and I realised that, although I knew her name, I still had no idea who she was and I badly wanted to know.

'Daddy!' Imogen ran down the corridor with Darcie. 'A man made me spill my drink, but a nice lady got the purple out. Look!' She pointed to her dress and I couldn't see any evidence of a blackcurrant juice disaster.

'Imogen's tired and the bars are noisy,' Darcie said. 'Can she come back to my room and watch telly for a bit? Phoebe says that's fine but I have to check it's okay with you first.'

'That's fine by me.'

Imogen beamed and hugged me. 'Thanks, Daddy. See you later.'

I waved them off and hesitated in the corridor, my thoughts turning back to Poppy now that I was reassured that Imogen was all right. I didn't recall there being a Poppy on the guest list. I knew all of Barney's friends and farming contacts and I'd met everyone on his side of the family at some point so she had to be one of Amber's guests. Was she here with someone? Suddenly I had to know so I sauntered casually into the Sycamore Snug. I spotted her immediately, sitting in a high-backed armchair with her legs crossed. On her own. Should I walk up to her? Offer her a drink? Bit naff when it was a free bar. I shook my head. I was overthinking this. She'd come to my daughter's rescue and all I needed to do was thank her for her kindness, apologise again for walking into her and, if she didn't look like she wanted to get rid of me, I could extend that conversation by asking her how she knew Amber. Surely a wedding had to be the easiest place to strike up a conversation because all the guests had one thing in common – the happy couple.

And if all else failed, I could give her another ready meal recommendation.

But my dithering lost me my chance. A man in a sharp suit and a tan that looked out of place in Yorkshire at this time of year joined her with a bottle of wine, two glasses and a packet of crisps which elicited a huge smile when he tossed them to her. She was obviously with him, and they looked happy together, lucky bloke.

My phone beeped and, thinking it might be a message from Darcie, I took it out of my pocket, my heart sinking when I saw who it was actually from.

FROM TILLY

Why are you ignoring my messages? I asked you if our daughter was wearing make-up and I think that deserves a response, don't you?

Feeling irritated at her for something so petty, I went back into the corridor and leaned against the wall as I tapped in a response.

TO TILLY

No, I don't. It's hardly a life-and-death situation. Yes, she is wearing make-up and it's a one-off treat on a special day which made our little girl very happy. I made the decision to let her wear make-up because I'm her dad and, shocking as you might find it, I have the right to make decisions from time to time. You make them all the time and I never question them so get over it and stop messaging me. As for ignoring your messages, I'm ignoring ALL messages. BECAUSE I'M AT MY BEST FRIEND'S WEDDING AND I HAVE BETTER THINGS TO DO. I'll have Imogen back with you by 11.30 as promised. Good night!

I couldn't believe Tilly was pestering me today about a tiny amount of make-up. I wished I hadn't sent her that photo now. Although if I hadn't done that, I'm sure she'd have found something else to message me about. She usually did when I had Imogen.

Feeling like I was neglecting my best man duties, I set off back to the main bar, but I took a quick peek in the snug as I passed. Poppy was laughing with the man who'd joined her, and I sighed. One day it would be my turn to make someone like her laugh like that, but today wasn't that day and it seemed she wasn't that person. She was obviously a friendly, smiley person and that moment I thought we'd shared in Bloomsberry's had been one-sided. How familiar!

18

JOEL

I was about to return to the Juniper Lounge and get back into the wedding spirit, but my teeth had that furry feeling, and my mouth had the dryness that came with afternoon drinking so I headed up to my room. My family suite came with a mini-bar so, after freshening up, I grabbed a bottle of cold water and took a couple of welcome glugs. I was going to sprawl out on the sofa but fatigue suddenly gripped me and I feared that, if I sat down, I might fall asleep. Instead, I wandered over to the window and opened it to let in some fresh air.

My room was at the front of Fennington Hall overlooking the gravel car park and the grounds beyond, including a second lake and an arboretum. A shout drew my attention towards the hotel entrance. Lorna was running down the steps with Chez racing after her. He grabbed the handle of her overnight bag, evidently trying to stop her leaving, but she snatched it from his grasp and he stumbled down the last couple of steps. I wasn't close enough to hear what they were saying but the volume of their voices, the gesticulating and the body language left me in no doubt that they were having a blazing row. She stormed a few paces across the car park, he caught her, there was more shouting and gesticulating and she set off once more. I felt guilty watching them, but they were arguing in a well-lit public place with evening guests arriving and having to dodge past them. I'd always thought that Lorna was the one with the fiery temper but it seemed my brother could give as good as he got, although the amount of alcohol he'd consumed across the afternoon was likely a contributory factor.

Lorna was striding along the middle of the car park, coming closer. Lights flashed on a blue hatchback – the car Lorna occasionally borrowed from her mum. Lorna tossed her bag onto the passenger seat, got in and slammed the door behind her, ignoring Chez banging on the window as she started the engine. Seconds later, she'd reversed with a wheelspin and sped out of the car park.

Chez cut such a sorrowful figure staring after her. I pushed the window open wider and shouted his name. He looked around him, clearly confused as to where the voice had come from.

'Up here! First floor.'

He looked up. 'Joel?'

'Are you okay?'

'Did you see that?'

'Yes.'

'Then why ask? Of course I'm not okay.'

'Wait there. I'll come down.'

'To give me another fatherly talk. No, thanks.' He took a couple of paces towards the hall then turned and gave me the finger. I closed the window and sank down onto one of the chairs with a heavy sigh. Sarcastic and snarky were Chester's default modes, but the aggression was new. I had enough hostility to deal with from Tilly and I'd put up with it so far because I wanted to see my daughter, but I wasn't prepared to take it from my brother too.

I took another glug of water and found Harry's number on my phone.

TO HARRY

> I know this is none of my business but Chez is in a really bad place right now and I think he could use a friend

I stopped typing and shook my head, deleting the message. My first few words said it all and I was fairly sure that sticking my nose in would backfire on me. It could also make things worse between Chez and Harry. After all, I didn't know the full story. All I had were my brother's moans that Harry sided with Deana over him but there'd be three sides to this story – Chez's, Harry's and the truth.

I sent Dad a message instead.

TO DAD

> Don't know if you'll pick this up but I've just seen Chez and Lorna have a big bust-up and she's gone. He refuses to speak to me, but he might listen to you. No idea where he is now and I'm not suggesting you go on a wild goose chase around the building but, if you do encounter him, can you see if you can get through to him?

FROM DAD

> We'll be coming back down in 10 mins so will watch out for him then. Enjoy your evening and don't worry about Chez. We'll sort it!

Dad was seemingly incapable of adding just one emoji to make a point and had gone crazy with the party-themed emojis adding people dancing, music notes, party poppers and all the drinks ones, which helped defuse the tension inside me. I hated passing the buck as they'd come a long way to be at the wedding and I wanted them to enjoy themselves, but they were Chez's parents and it felt like he needed them right now.

I finished my water and pushed the incident with Chez and the exchange of words with Tilly out of my head before going downstairs to join in the festivities. The laughter emanating from the Juniper Lounge immediately lifted my spirits.

The bar was busy and, despite an hour still to go until the evening do, I spotted several evening guests who were obviously keen to make the most of their night out. A large patio ran the full length of the bar and was illuminated with fairy lights, spotlights and the glow from several patio heaters so a number of guests had spilled outside.

I ordered a pint and worked my way round the room, joining in various conversations. I'd been down for about twenty minutes and there was no sign of my parents or Chez which either meant they'd found him and were having a chat or they hadn't found him and were relaxing in the snug.

Out of the corner of my eye, I spotted a streak of orange and turned to see Amber introducing Poppy to her dad. I had a clear view of her, and she looked exceptionally nervous which appeared to amuse her partner. Cole gave her a hug and Poppy's partner took several photos of them. After a brief chat during which Poppy appeared to relax, Jules, Sophie and her boyfriend, Devon, joined them, quickly followed by Brad and Tabs. Soon Poppy was having her photo taken with the whole of Amber's celebrity family. I couldn't take my eyes off her captivating smile. Her partner was taking all the photos. Why wouldn't he be in them too? Maybe he was camera shy.

I was aware of a presence beside me and looked down to see Zara grinning at me.

'She's very pretty,' she said.

'Who is?'

'Poppy. The woman in the orange dress who you can't take your eyes off.'

'I wasn't looking at her. I was just...' I shook my head. Why even bother to deny it? 'Yes, she's very pretty and, yes, I was looking at her. Who is she?'

'A guest at Whisperwood Farmhouse. Mary invited her and she's lovely. You should ask her to dance when the disco starts.'

'I can't do that. She's with someone.'

'They're not together. He's her ex-husband. Lives between London and Spain and is working in the area next week, so they're catching up.'

It was great news that they weren't an item, but could attending a wedding with her ex-husband be a sign of a reconciliation?

'Sounds like it might be complicated.'

Zara laughed and gave me a gentle punch on the arm. 'Far from it. They're just good friends. He's happily remarried with a new baby girl. And he's not staying late tonight so, if you like her, don't leave it too long. She barely knows anyone so, once he's gone, she might not want to stick around.'

My heart sank at the thought of her leaving.

'You know her. Can't you convince her to stay?'

She laughed again. 'I'll do my best. And it looks like Amber's family have adopted her so, if they have anything to do with it, she'll be on the dance floor until the very end.'

We both watched as Amber took Poppy off to meet some guests.

Zara nudged me. 'Shouldn't be me convincing her to stay anyway. It should be you. Do I need to remind you of a conversation we had a couple of years ago about missed opportunities?'

I rolled my eyes at her and she laughed.

'You said she's staying at Whisperwood? So she's not local.'

'Don't you dare let that put you off! Have you learned nothing?'

I hadn't acted on my attraction to Zara a few years back for that exact reason and she was right to challenge me not to make the same mistake again.

'If you're feeling something – and I can tell you are – then act on it. Talk to her, ask her to dance and take it from there. Please, Joel.'

Poppy glanced in our direction and, as her eyes met mine, her smile widened. My heart pounded as I smiled back and raised my hand in a small wave.

'I think she likes you too,' Zara said.

'What do you know about her?'

'Not much. She helped us make the favours the other night and she seems really lovely, but most of the talk was about weddings, which is how I know about her ex. Here's Mary. She might know more.'

Barney's grandma stopped. 'Did I hear my name?'

'We were trying to work out who all the guests were,' Zara said. 'Joel didn't know Poppy so I told him she's staying at Whisperwood.'

I smiled at Zara, appreciative of her quick-thinking and discretion. If Mary had a sniff of a suggestion that I was interested in Poppy, she'd have marched me straight over to her and blurted it out.

'Oh yes, such a sweet girl,' Mary said. 'She arrived on Monday for a week. Poor lass needed a break. Her dad's got late-stage Alzheimer's. Heartbroken she is. So sad.'

Natasha appeared, needing Zara's help to set up the photo booth and Mary excused herself, leaving me alone for a moment.

I glanced over at Poppy once more. She was with Samantha's family, crouching down beside Samantha and Josh's kids, laughing at something one of them had said. They passed her their bride and groom pigs and she moved them around. Whatever she was saying gave Thomas and Lyra the giggles. I couldn't take my eyes off her. It wasn't just her looks that captivated me, although I wasn't blind to how attractive she was. It was that she'd been kind to my daughter and now she was making Samantha's kids laugh. After what had happened with Marley, I couldn't even think about being with someone who didn't love kids. It had to be a dealbreaker if they didn't understand and accept that I came as a two-for-one package, accompanied by a whole lot of ex-shaped baggage.

I thought about what Mary had said about Poppy's dad and wondered whether the smiles and laughter were a mask or whether this was a rare moment to escape from the heartbreak for a few hours and let her hair down. Now that I knew about her dad, Poppy suddenly seemed vulnerable and my heart sank. If we did get talking and she opened up about him, I'd listen and empathise and very likely get pushed into the friend zone. *I met this really nice bloke at the wedding. Such a sweetie, but we're just friends.*

I sipped on my drink and reprimanded myself for the negative attitude. How about manifesting a different scenario? *I met this really nice bloke at the wedding. Such a sweetie and exactly what I've been looking for – someone who listens, cares, understands. He might be the one.* I liked that scenario a lot. I'd learn from my mistakes and take Zara's advice not to be put off by Poppy not being local. I wouldn't worry about the ex-husband either. We all had a past. I had an ex-fiancée and life would have been so much easier if we'd maintained the sort of friendship that Poppy and her ex clearly had. And I wouldn't place myself in the friend zone. I just needed to find the right moment to approach her.

19

POPPY

If Mum could see me now, she'd barely be able to believe it. Hobnobbing with Cole Crawford and his family, being introduced to their celebrity friends, and being welcomed as though I was a good friend. I was on an absolute high, but it wasn't just from meeting the Crawfords and friends – it was Joel. I'd caught his eye a few times and, when he smiled at me, butterflies went wild in my stomach. I wasn't planning to act on the feeling, but it was so nice to have that sensation again.

Just before 7 p.m. guests were invited to move into the Rowan Room where the bride and groom would be taking to the floor for their first dance. Phil and I followed the crowd and paused just inside the doorway, taking in the high ceiling, grand embellishments and the sparkling chandeliers catching the colourful lights. Surrounding the dance floor were plush chairs and round tables covered in fresh white linen with floral centrepieces and dried flower confetti on them. There was a couple of pretty sweetie carts in one corner and I could imagine them being a huge hit with children and adults alike, and there was a bar beside the entrance. We already had drinks so we made our way to the edge of the dance floor where the guests had gathered to watch the first dance.

'Good evening!' announced the DJ. 'For the guests who've just joined us this evening, your bride and groom bid you a warm welcome and for those who've been here a little longer, they hope you're enjoying yourselves. We'll be welcoming the newlyweds for their first dance very soon, after which the bride and bridesmaids have something special lined up. They've asked me to invite you to join in partway through, so watch those moves carefully. The third song will be for absolutely everyone. I'm excited for tonight, I'm open to requests and I wish you all a fantastic evening. Without further ado, please welcome Mr and Mrs Kinsella for their first dance as a married couple!'

To applause, cheers and some wolf whistles, Amber and Barney walked to the centre of the dance floor, holding hands and beaming at each other. They'd chosen 'My Universe' by Coldplay featuring K-pop sensations BTS. I hadn't listened closely to the lyrics before but the chorus was so uplifting and apt for a first wedding song. From the way they were looking at each other, Amber and Barney clearly were each other's universe. I remembered feeling that way about Phil. Would I feel that way again? I glanced up at Phil and he smiled at me, giving me a warm glow of friendship. Moments later, my eyes locked with Joel's across the other side of the dance floor and the butterflies in my stomach soared as he smiled back at me.

'My Universe' came to a close with the happy couple kissing. Barney left the dance floor, but Amber stayed and was joined by her bridesmaids. They organised themselves into a formation of four at the front and five at the back.

'Do we have any Swifties in the room?' the DJ asked.

There were several loud cheers, and I laughed as Imogen

bounced up and down, clapping her hands. I put my hand in the air and so did Phil.

'That's a relief,' he said, 'because it's over to Taylor for the next one. I'm told this was Imogen's idea, that she and Sophie choreographed it together via Zoom and this is the first time all nine have been in the same room at the same time, so what could possibly go wrong? I give you your bride and bridesmaids with Taylor Swift's "Paper Rings". Enjoy!'

I adored Taylor Swift's music and was full of admiration for everything she'd achieved in her career so far. The routine Imogen and Sophie had prepared was delightful and a great mix of different dance styles. I found myself copying the moves as I became familiar with them. Looking round the edge of the dance floor, I smiled at the other guests doing the same.

'Are you going to join in?' I asked Phil.

'Have I ever mastered a dance routine?' he replied, raising his eyebrows at me.

As a musician, Phil had great rhythm but, in all the years I'd known him, had remained incapable of committing any sort of dance routine to memory, no matter how simple. He couldn't even master 'Y.M.C.A.' despite being repeatedly told it was just a case of forming the appropriate letter with his arms. He'd manage the 'Y' and it would descend into chaos from there.

'You go,' he encouraged. 'I'll film it for your dad.'

I smiled at him gratefully. Dad used to love dancing and had always been the first on the floor at any parties, often leading the moves.

When the DJ announced that it was time to join in, Amber and her bridesmaids shuffled forwards into one long row so the guests could stand behind them for guidance, not that that helped when the direction changed. Joel took his position behind Imogen and, in a moment of bravery, I stood next to him and was rewarded with another of his dazzling smiles. He wasn't the best, bless him, turning the wrong way and colliding with me a couple of times, but he scored full marks for trying. It was so lovely laughing together.

The track changed to Olly Murs's 'Marry Me' and the DJ invited everyone on to the dance floor to throw whatever shapes they wanted. My heart melted as Joel picked Imogen up and hugged her tightly.

'That was brilliant,' he told her. 'I'm so proud of you, my little Swiftie.'

'Great song choice,' I said. 'I love Taylor Swift too.'

Imogen beamed at me. 'She's the best! My dress is all better now, too.'

'So I see. You'd never have known it was purple a couple of hours ago.'

'Thanks again for helping her,' Joel said.

'You're welcome. And thanks for helping me with my ready meal dilemma.' I inwardly cringed. Could I not have thought of something better to say? But what else could I say when his daughter was with us?

Imogen announced that she was thirsty and pulled Joel towards the bar. He gave me an apologetic look. 'You're sticking around all night?'

I hadn't been planning to but the word, 'Yes,' popped out, sending my butterflies flapping once more.

'Good. I'll see you later, then.'

I nodded, smiling. *Can't wait!*

'I was thinking about our first dance,' Phil said when I re-joined him and we found a table away from the dance floor. 'I still can't believe I stood on your dress.'

'Several times, I recall, although you weren't the only one. It was covered in footprints by the end of the night.'

'We had a good marriage, didn't we?' The tone and expression were a little uncertain, as though he was worried that I might be hurt that it was over and he'd met someone new, but that had never been the case. It was sad that we hadn't made it, but ending it had been right for us both and I still loved him, but only as a friend.

I gave him a reassuring smile. 'We absolutely did. You know how they talk about happy ever afters in books and films? I think we were that other variation – the happy for now – but you've found your happy ever after since then with Reina and Eliana.'

'I'd like you to find your happy ever after too.'

'Me too, but finding someone is so difficult. My two attempts after you weren't exactly resounding successes.'

'You can't let Mr-Coffee-Is-Code-For-Sex-Tosspot put you off.'

I laughed at the nickname. 'I know there are good men out there, but timing's everything and my life has been an emotional mess for quite some time. It's a lot to put on someone new, so it's easier not to try to. And, of course, now I've been so long out of the game that it feels a bit too scary to play again.'

'I completely get that, but what about doing something each day that scares you?'

I rolled my eyes at him. 'That phrase is haunting me at the moment. I'm still trying to live by it, but it's not easy.'

'You deserve a good man and good friends, Pops, because you're one of the loveliest people I've ever met.'

'Thank you. Right back at ya.'

'And, actually, timing might be everything, but sometimes what can seem the worst possible timing can turn out to be the best. Life's chaotic. I say embrace the chaos!'

Embrace the chaos! I liked that a lot. I spotted Joel near the bar. Timing really was terrible right now, but could it turn out to be spot on? The butterflies soared at the thought.

Fizz and Samantha appeared and pulled Phil and me onto the dance floor. My eyes keep getting drawn to Joel, who was now dancing with Imogen. He was clearly a doting dad and he looked so adorable. Every so often, he looked across and smiled at me, setting my heart pounding. I was fairly sure he was interested in me and he had to have found out that Phil and I weren't a couple because surely he wouldn't keep smiling at me if he thought we were together. Also, he'd specifically asked me if I'd be around all night and why ask that unless he knew that Phil wasn't my partner and would be leaving early? Perhaps he was biding his time until Phil left before asking me to dance or offering me a drink. The thought made me feel warm and fuzzy inside.

Phil and I took a break from dancing to visit the photo booth. I'd never seen so many props and I took several selfies of us wearing hats, feather boas and colourful sunglasses. We were about to leave when Amber appeared, so Phil took a photo of the pair of us together in a heart-shaped frame. She soon enlisted the rest of the bridesmaids and it would have been so easy to feel like the odd one out but they all made me feel like part of their tribe, shuffling places so that they could each stand next to me at some point. Fizz rounded up Barney and the groomsmen too and I could hardly believe I was being included in such special photos as though I was a lifelong friend. The whole evening was completely surreal – first meeting Cole Crawford and now this!

We'd pretty much exhausted the props when the official photographer came over to take more photos of Amber and Barney. He asked if the wedding party could stick around so he could get fun ones of them too. I placed the feather boa, sparkly cowboy hat and heart-shaped sunglasses I'd been wearing for the last photo back in the correct boxes and stood back to watch.

A call came through for Phil and he excused himself, telling me he'd be back as soon as possible. I was enjoying watching so I stayed where I was. As the photographer snapped a photo of the newlyweds with the best man and chief bridesmaid, Imogen joined me.

'Are you having fun?' I asked her.

She nodded enthusiastically.

'Have you been to a wedding before?'

'I went to Mummy's when she married Greg but I was only three and I don't remember it. Mummy was going to marry Daddy, but she told him she didn't want to marry him two weeks before their wedding and Grandma Ivy says that'll have cost Daddy a lot of money and it was mean of her to leave it so late but better late than on the day. Grandma Ivy doesn't like Mummy very much.'

'Grandma Ivy is your daddy's mum?' I asked, thinking she'd be quite justified in thinking ill of Imogen's mum if she really had left Joel a fortnight before their wedding.

'No. She's Mummy's mum. They don't like each other. Daddy's mum is that lady in the blue flowery dress.' She pointed to a woman in a pretty calf-length dress, dancing to ABBA's 'Super Trouper' with a man in a light-coloured suit. 'She's my Grandma Audrey and she's really nice but she can't live in this country because the weather's too cold and her Arthurs hurt her.'

I stifled a smile at the visual which popped into my head of several tiny Arthurian knights jabbing her with their swords. Presumably Imogen meant arthritis, but I wasn't going to correct her.

'She lives in Portugal with Granddad Trevor,' Imogen continued. 'He's the man dancing with her and he's nice too. Daddy wants to take me to visit them but Mummy won't let him because she says it's not fair on Leighton, Ezra and Delphine but Leighton's mummy takes him on an aeroplane every summer so I don't see why I can't go on one but Daddy doesn't like to make

Mummy angry so I can only see Grandma Audrey and Granddad Trevor when they fly to this country.'

That was an enormous information dump, and I had no idea who Leighton, Ezra and Delphine were, but I nodded as though I understood and didn't proffer any sort of opinion, not wishing for my ill-informed comments to be used as evidence in what sounded like a complicated family set-up. Thankfully Imogen changed the subject.

'I like your dress. I don't have any orange clothes. It's a very happy colour.'

'Thank you. Amber gave me it which was super kind of her. It's the first orange clothing I've ever owned and I really like it, but do you know what my favourite colour is? Sage green like on your dress.'

She spun round, fanning out the skirt as Joel joined us.

'Are you showing off your twirly dress again?' he asked her.

'Poppy says it's her favourite colour. My favourite colour is yellow because it's like the sunshine, but I like orange too like Poppy's dress, and I like my dress.'

'Imogen has declared she's never going to take her dress off,' Joel told me. 'I said she might need to when she has a bath.'

'I've never been a bridesmaid, but I once had a party dress I loved so much. It was pink and sparkly with lots of sequins on the top like yours, Imogen. I never wanted to take it off either so, when I went to bed that night, I kept it on. My mum came in to check on me, and she had to take it off and put me in a nightie. When she woke me up in the morning, I had my party dress on again so I must have got up in the night and changed. But it's not a good idea to do that because I had little scratches all down my arms from where I'd been lying on the sequins. Best not to wear pretty dresses in bed.'

Imogen was called to join the other bridesmaids for some final photos, leaving Joel and me together.

'Thanks for warning her about the sequins,' he said, smiling at me. 'I think I might have had to wrestle her out of it otherwise.'

'You're welcome. As soon as I started telling the story, I realised I might be encouraging some mischief, but at least it came with a warning.'

'I hear you're—' he began but Phil returned at that point, apologising for abandoning me. He looked from me to Joel and back to me and I realised too late that he was looking for an introduction.

'You must be the best man,' he said, putting out his hand and smiling at Joel. 'I'm Phil, Poppy's friend.'

'Joel. Good to meet you.'

There was an awkward pause, and I hoped Phil wouldn't fill it with an attempt to matchmake because that would be too embarrassing, but he stuck to a safe subject.

'You're a friend of the groom's or a relative?'

'Best mate since secondary school. We bonded over a shared hatred of PE lessons.'

Phil laughed. 'I can relate to that. I hated PE. You did too, didn't you, Pops?'

I nodded. 'The PE teacher was terrifying. Instilled a lifelong fear of sports in me.'

'Must be part of the job description,' Joel said. 'Mine was terrifying too. Never took up any sports because of him.'

'You don't play rugby?' I asked, instantly blushing because it was those broad shoulders of his which had made me think about the sport.

'I often get told I look like a rugby player, but I was small and skinny back then and each time I was in a scrum, I feared for my life.'

Phil had been small and skinny at school too and shared that he'd broken his arm getting tackled in rugby, but that it gave him a lifetime pass out of the game which he saw as a massive bonus. By the time he'd relayed that tale, the photographer was finished, the DJ put on the biggest song of the moment, and we were pulled onto the dance floor with the bridal party.

A couple of songs later, Avicii's 'Wake Me Up' started playing and Phil announced his lift had arrived and he'd have to go. I looked around to catch Joel's eye but he'd been dragged into some sort of bouncing scrum with Barney and two of the ushers and wasn't looking my way. I left to walk Phil out to the car park.

'I've had a great time today,' Phil said. 'Who knew being a last-minute plus one at a wedding could be so much fun?'

'Next time I wangle an invite to a showbiz wedding, I'll make sure I give you a shout.'

'They're a good bunch. I hope you're going to return to that dance floor when I'm gone.'

They'd made me feel so welcome that I had been planning to, but the cold breeze blew my confidence away. 'I'll probably go to bed now as it'll be strange being there on my own.'

'You're not on your own! You've got a room full of new friends and I bet they'll miss you if you don't return. Big girl pants again!'

'Still got them on from before,' I said, laughing. 'This whole wedding thing has been one long doing something today that scares me.'

'But you've kept facing that fear and you've had a great time so why walk away now?'

I glanced in the direction of the function room. I wasn't tired yet and, if I went to bed now, I'd regret it. It had been a long time since I let my hair down so why end the evening prematurely?

'Okay.'

'Good. But I have another challenge for you. I know it'll scare you, but I want you to dance with the best man and if that leads to a lot more than dancing, run with it.'

'Phil! You think I should have a one-night stand?' My cheeks flushed, but my body fizzed with delight at the thought of it.

'It might be fun.'

'But I've... well, I... It's just that...'

'There's a first time for everything,' he said, connecting the dots for me. 'A bit of no-strings fun might do you the world of good. Look at what you've already achieved in just one week. You've come on holiday on your own and you've had an amazing time. You've accepted an invite to a wedding from people you don't know. You've made some new friends including the one and only Cole Crawford. Last week, could you have imagined doing any of those things?'

'No, but—'

'But you did them and you loved them. So why not add in another new experience?'

I held my hands up to my burning cheeks. 'This is a surreal conversation to be having with my ex-husband.'

He laughed. 'It is a bit. Let's say goodnight and leave it there.'

We hugged each other and he kissed me on the cheek. 'I've loved seeing the brave new Poppy this evening.'

He got into his Uber and waved as they pulled away and I watched the car disappear down the long driveway. I did feel brave today, but I wasn't sure I was anywhere brave enough to do what Phil had suggested. A dance with Joel would be amazing and if that led to a drink together and maybe a kiss, that would be pretty special too. A zip of electricity raced through me as I imagined his hands in my hair, his lips on mine.

I returned to the hotel lobby, the warmth giving me a welcome hug. The sounds of laughter and music called to me but suddenly it all felt a little overwhelming. I'd socialised a lot today and, for someone who spent most of their days working alone with only the occasional one-sided conversation with next door's dog, I was feeling a bit peopled-out. I needed a spot of me time to recharge my batteries and then I'd return to the party. If I went to my bedroom, there was a danger I'd get too comfortable and talk myself out of returning but if I went out onto the terrace Blaine had directed me to earlier, I'd still be able to hear the music and laughter and feel that party vibe without the pressure of socialising.

I grabbed my coat from my room and made my way to the terrace. As anticipated, it was empty but it didn't mean it'd stay that way so I tucked myself away at a table behind some large screened-off potted plants so nobody would spot me if they did come out for some fresh air.

Sitting back, I gazed into the darkness thinking about the conversation I'd just had with Phil. I hadn't said anything to him about being attracted to Joel, but it boded well that he'd picked it up from both of us. Could I do as he'd suggested? Tempting as it was, a one-night stand felt like a step too far for me. It wasn't just several years since I'd slept with a man, it was also several since I'd kissed one. One step at a time. Could I kiss a stranger at a wedding? When that stranger was Joel, it was a very appealing thought. And if that did lead to something else... Despite my voice of protest, that was also an appealing thought.

20

JOEL

'Wake Me Up' by Avicii took me back in time. It had been the soundtrack to the summer in my early twenties when Barney, Tim, Levi and I went to Ibiza on a lads' holiday before Barney took over the responsibility of running the farm. Barney had told us that he'd asked the DJ to play it tonight and we'd better be ready for it so, as soon as we heard those opening guitar strums, the four of us gravitated together on the dance floor, put our arms round each other and bounced about just like we'd done on that holiday.

When the track ended, I looked around for Poppy but there was no sign of her. Zara caught my eye and beckoned me over.

'Phil had to go. She's gone outside to say goodbye to him.'

'She's coming back?'

'She didn't say, but she didn't say goodbye so I'm guessing she will. And when she does, if you don't get your act together and get her a drink or dance just with her, I'm going to bang your heads together.'

I was parched after the over-exertions to Avicii and concerned that I hadn't seen Chez since his argument with Lorna so I left the dance floor in search of a drink and my brother. I found my parents in the Sycamore Snug. Dad was at the bar ordering them both a pot of tea. I'd been planning on another pint but joined them at their table for a refreshing cuppa instead.

'You're sure he hasn't been in the disco?' Mum asked after I'd expressed concern about Chez's whereabouts.

'I've been in there all evening, and he hasn't appeared.'

'That's strange,' Dad said. 'We saw him in the corridor after the bridesmaids did their routine and asked if everything was okay. He insisted it was and said he was going to get changed – you know he's never liked wearing a suit – and would be back down shortly for the disco, so we assumed that's what he'd done.'

Mum sipped on her tea looking thoughtful. 'Perhaps he decided to stay in his room. Do you think we should check on him?'

She'd only just poured herself a second cup of tea, so I offered to go and promised to report back. A few minutes later, I knocked on Chester's door but there was no answer.

'I know you don't want to speak to me,' I called, 'but Mum and Dad are worried about you. Can you at least confirm you're in there?'

No response.

I returned to my parents. 'He's not in his room.'

'We know,' Mum said. 'I've just spoken to him. He said he went up to his room to change and, with Lorna gone, didn't feel in much of a party mood so he stayed there, but now he's bored. He's discovered a roof terrace, is getting some fresh air and will be down shortly.'

Neither of them seemed unduly concerned, but they hadn't been around through the many Lorna bust-ups like I had. I knew that Chez would be really down and that he probably shouldn't be alone.

'I think I'll go and find him,' I said. 'If I don't see you both later, I'll see you at breakfast.'

I hadn't noticed a roof terrace, so I went via the reception desk to seek directions. Looking through the windows a little later, the terrace appeared to be deserted but there were lots of columns, screens and planters so Chez could easily be tucked behind one of them. I opened the door and stepped out into the cold night air.

'Chez?'

He didn't respond but he'd have known it was me and, as I clearly wasn't his favourite person right now, he was most likely ignoring me. I didn't have to venture far before I spotted him on a metal chair behind a pillar, drinking straight from a bottle of red wine. His hair was dishevelled and he still had his suit on – so much for telling our parents he was getting changed – and there was a wine stain down his shirt.

He scowled up at me. 'When a person doesn't answer to their name being called, most people would take that as a big clue that they don't want to be found.' His voice was loud and slurred.

'I wanted to make sure you're okay.'

'I'm okay. You can go now.'

'Can we talk?'

'You mean can you lecture me?'

'No. I mean can we talk? I know this past week or so hasn't been great, but I'm worried about you.'

Chez jumped up with such force that he staggered to one side. I thought he was about to keel over but he somehow managed to right himself.

'Well, stop it! I don't need you to worry about me. You're like a bloody helicopter parent, always hovering around me, always trying to protect me by telling me what to do and how to live my life.'

That was spectacularly unfair as well as being inaccurate. I was sick of Chez lashing out at me like this, as though I was a punchbag with no feelings. It hurt.

'I've *never* tried to parent you.'

'Oh, purlease! You're *always* trying to parent me but news-flash! You're *not* my parent and, breaking news, according to you, you're not my brother either. Cheers for that.'

'What?'

He adopted an even snarkier tone as he quoted part of my best man speech back at me. '*Barney's not just my best mate, he's like a brother to me.*'

How on earth had that upset him? Mum and Dad had mentioned earlier about how much they'd loved that part of the speech and I'd never imagined Chez – the person who'd often referred to Harry as *my brother from another mother* – could take it negatively.

'Well, he is! We've always been close and that's something you say about close friends.'

'Bet you wish he was your brother instead of me.'

'You're talking crazy now. That speech had nothing to do with you.'

'Sure it didn't.' He held the bottle of wine to his lips and took several glugs, making me wince.

'Don't you think you should take it easier on the wine?' As soon as I said it, I wished I could take the words back. Telling someone who was very drunk that they'd had too much to drink was pretty much the same as asking an angry person to calm down. Sure enough, it inflamed Chez further.

'See! I told you! Helicopter parent. Trying to control how much I drink now. Well, let me tell you this, big brother. I will drink as much as I want to because I've lost my job, my girlfriend has dumped me and told me it's for good this time, and my best mate has chosen his girlfriend over me, so I have nothing and no one and if I want to drink several bottles of free wine at your *real* brother's wedding, that's what I'll do.'

I really hoped he was exaggerating, and he hadn't drunk several bottles. There was so much in that rant to pick up on, but I decided to go for the most recent incident.

'I'm sure you and Lorna will get back together,' I said, trying to keep my voice gentle and reassuring. 'You always do.'

'Not this time and I bet you're delighted about that.'

'Why would I be delighted?' I'd done nothing but help my brother and the constant accusations that I'd take delight in his misfortune were bewildering, hurtful and incredibly frustrating.

'Cos it makes you right. You said we'd never get a place together and now we won't. Bet you're sooooo happy.'

'Of course I'm not! I like Lorna and I wish you two could find a way to make it work without all the break-ups but I can't help thinking that maybe a split for good is what you both need. Maybe you're not right for each other.'

'There you go!' he cried. 'Parenting again! Offering your opinion where it isn't wanted.'

And then he was off on one, all sorts of accusations being hurled at me, conversations thrown back at me which I couldn't even recall, and twisting the meaning of innocent comments. Every couple of sentences, he'd pause to take a gulp from his wine and each time he resumed, his voice was angrier, louder, more bitter. I tried to reach for the bottle several times but he snatched it away and then, out of nowhere, he started shoving at me. I was bigger and heavier set than him and, in his drunken stupor, he could barely move me, which made him shove harder.

'Fight back!' he goaded.

'I'm not going to fight you, Chez.'

'Scared I'll hurt you?'

'I'm *not* going to fight you,' I repeated, my voice firmer. 'Why don't you put the wine down, go to bed and sleep it off? This thing with Lorna will probably have blown over by the morning.'

He took a swing at me, but I ducked and he stumbled but, once more, managed to regain his balance.

'Stop telling me what to do!' he yelled. 'And what do you know about relationships anyway? You were dumped two weeks before your wedding. Dumped by a woman who didn't want kids and has now had another two, so it was obviously you she didn't want, not the kids. Probably couldn't put up with your nagging. And how successful have you been with women since then? You can't get beyond a first date cos they only ever want to be friends although God knows why cos you're such an arsehole.'

He might not have winded me with his shoves, but he had with his words and I stared at him, barely recognising the brother I loved, worried about, cared for in the angry young man in front of me.

'Please, Chez...' But I was too hurt to find any words. Had he really thrown my broken engagement back at me like that?

He barged past me and stormed towards the door, but he stopped and turned round. 'You want me to put the wine down? How's this?'

He launched the bottle in my direction, and it smashed by my feet, showering me with red wine. Heart pounding, stomach churning, I stared down at my soaked trousers and the broken glass and looked up at Chez, expecting him to be shocked by what he'd done and how close the bottle had been to hitting me, but his expression held no remorse.

'I hate you!' he yelled before running off the terrace and slamming the door behind him.

I was shaking as I crouched down to pick up the broken glass. I laid several pieces in my left hand but the intensity of my shakes caused my hand to tighten and I flinched as I felt the sting of a cut. Blood dripped onto my chinos, mixing with the darker wine. He hated me. My brother really hated me. What had I ever done but care for him? I pictured the expression on his face, heard the venom in his voice and it was too much for me. I sank down onto my backside, the chunks of glass slipping from my hand as sobs shook my body.

Moments later, I jumped as a piece of heavy material – a coat perhaps? – was placed over my heaving shoulders.

'Can you stand up?'

I looked up into Poppy's concerned eyes. Where had she sprung from? Had she heard all of that?

'I can help you,' she said, her voice gentle.

'I need to...'

I sniffed and tried to get control of my tears as I leaned forward to pick up the glass, but I was shaking really badly now.

'You've cut yourself,' she said. 'We need to get that seen to.'

'The glass.'

'Leave it. I'll let one of the bar staff know in a bit, but I need you to come with me so I can get your hand cleaned up and see whether it needs stitches.'

She helped ease me to my feet and pressed a tissue onto my palm. 'Hold this but don't press too hard in case there's some glass in the cut. You don't want to push it in any deeper.'

Placing her arm round my waist, she led me back inside and all I could think was thank goodness it had been Poppy who'd seen that and not Imogen because that had to be the worst thing I'd ever experienced. Why did my brother hate me so much? Why had he wanted to hurt me with his words like that? And had he meant to hurt me physically too? Because, if he had, I wasn't sure how we'd recover.

21

POPPY

I felt Joel trembling as I led him along the corridor to my bedroom. There were so many things I wanted to say to him to try to take the pain away, but I remained silent. I knew nothing about Joel's brother or their relationship so it wasn't right for me to speak when I could imagine his mind was working overtime trying to process what had just happened. How must it feel to have your brother declare out loud *I hate you* with so much venom injected into those three words? How must it feel to have him hurl a glass bottle at you, wondering if he'd been aiming at you?

I wished I hadn't witnessed it, but if I hadn't been there Joel would have been all alone and nobody should be on their own after something like that. The moment I heard voices, I'd pressed my back against my chair and willed them to have a quick conversation and leave. By the time it was obvious it was an argument – every word coming to me loud and clear – it was too late to alert them to my presence. I thought one of the voices sounded like Joel's and, when his brother – Chez, was it? – quoted from his speech, I knew it was definitely him. Noticing a gap between two planters, I'd peered through it and saw that Chez was much younger than Joel – a fifteen-year age gap at a guess – which could explain the parenting comments. Imogen had said Joel's parents lived in Portugal so perhaps Joel had needed to step into a parental role in their absence. From what I'd seen and heard, Chez needed it. What he'd said to Joel had been cruel and hurtful, each word shocking me. The way Joel had managed to keep his voice so calm and reassuring when those words must have wounded, then not responding to his brother's attempts at a physical fight, filled me with admiration for him and endeared him to me even more.

We reached my bedroom and Joel leaned against the wall as I removed the key from my clutch bag and unlocked the door. He looked at me questioningly as though only just registering where we were.

'I've got a first-aid kit in my room.'

He raised his eyebrows with an unspoken *why?*

'My mum was a nurse, and she always had one with her and now I never travel without one in case of emergencies. Habit.'

He looked down at his hand where blood had seeped through the tissue.

'We'd best get that seen to.' I pushed open the door and flicked on the light, relieved that I was a tidy person and the clothes I'd discarded earlier were neatly folded on a chair rather than strewn across the bed.

I took my first-aid kit into the bathroom and Joel sat on the edge of the bath as I held his left hand under cold running water. The amount of blood was deceptive as the cut wasn't actually very deep, but it was long, crossing his whole palm. There was no glass in it so I gently dried it and, when the bleeding stopped, wrapped it in a sterile dressing as the area was too big for a plaster.

The whole time I worked, I could feel him watching me. With

the combination of his eyes on me and the feel of his skin beneath my fingers, it was my turn to shake. I'd forgotten what it was like to be this close to a man, my heartbeat quickening, feelings of desire pulsing through me.

I stepped back and gave him a gentle smile. 'That should heal pretty quickly but do keep the dressing clean.'

'Are you a nurse too?' he asked, his voice husky.

'An accountant so I'm more used to fixing balance sheets than people.'

'You have a gentle touch. Thank you.'

'You're welcome.'

Tears were still glistening in his dark brown eyes, making him look so vulnerable. I glanced down at his mouth and longed to kiss him to take the pain away.

'Can I get you anything else? A cup of tea?'

'I'm okay. I don't suppose... Is there any way you didn't hear what my brother said?' It was obvious from his pained expression that he knew what the answer was going to be.

I sat down on the toilet lid. 'Sorry. I was tucked round a corner, hoping you'd argue and leave without ever knowing I was there.'

'I wish you hadn't heard that. You must think I'm awful.'

'You? Quite the opposite. I'm in awe of how calm you were.'

'I didn't feel very calm. I felt completely out of my depth. Said all the wrong things, did all the wrong things. Story of my life at the moment.'

'When someone's angry and hurt like your brother clearly is, I don't think there are any *right* things to say and do. It sounded to me as though he's been bottling some things up and the drink gave him the courage to lash out at the person he cares about the most.'

'It didn't feel much like he cared when that bottle came

hurtling towards me.' He took a deep, shaky breath. 'Chez is four-teen and a half years younger than me. With a big age gap like that and no other siblings, I'd say it's pretty impossible not to step into a caring role. I was his babysitter, the one who helped him with his homework, the one who drove him to after-school clubs and friends' houses. When our parents moved abroad three years ago he lived with me for a while and, when he moved out, I looked out for him. I was really conscious of not trying to be the parent and letting him live his life the way he wanted but it seems I messed up. Rubbish brother and pathetic attempt at parenting.'

'That's not true! I've seen you with your daughter and you're clearly an amazing dad to her which is how it should be because you *are* her dad. What I saw and heard from you on the terrace was a brother trying to be a brother. I think Chez rejected that because what he really needs right now *is* a parent and it's easier to lash out at you than go to your parents and admit that he might officially be a grown-up but he needs his mum and dad.'

Aware that my speech had become a little impassioned, I lowered my voice, cringing. 'Apologies if I overstepped just now. I don't know your parents or your brother and I've got no right to make an assessment based on what happened on the terrace.'

'You're sure you're not a psychologist?' he asked, giving me a weak smile. 'Because I think you might have summed it up perfectly.'

'Definitely an accountant. Good with numbers, not so good with people.'

'You seem pretty good with people to me.'

We'd both leaned in closer and our faces weren't far apart and that's when I noticed the dark red spots.

'You've got spatters of wine on your face.'

I wrung out a cloth and cupped his face as I gently dabbed the wine away. Our faces were so close and all I could think about was how easy it would be to kiss him. His expression was dreamy, as though he was thinking the same, but suddenly he pulled back and stood up.

'Imogen! I've been gone ages. I'd better check she's okay.'

He looked in the mirror above the sink and raked his fingers through his hair before releasing a huge sigh, shoulders slumping.

'I've got wine on my shirt.' He glanced down and groaned. 'And my trousers are ruined.'

I'd been so concerned about the cut on his hand that I hadn't even looked at his trousers but they were covered in red wine and spots of blood.

'Why don't you get changed into something else before you look for Imogen? You wouldn't want her to think it's all blood on your trousers. I'll take your clothes to housekeeping. They should be able to clean them for you.'

Joel thanked me and we headed down one flight to his bedroom. His was a suite with a sofa and a couple of armchairs by the window so I perched on the edge of a chair while he changed in the bathroom.

I'd really liked how he looked in his wedding attire but, when he emerged from the bathroom a little later in his jeans and a pale blue shirt, that look did it for me too.

He glanced down at the neatly folded stained clothes in his hands with a frown. 'It doesn't feel right giving you my laundry to do, especially when you've already got a stain out of my daughter's dress.'

'Poppy's the name, stain removal's the game,' I quipped, immediately wishing I hadn't blurted out something so stupid, but it made Joel laugh and it was good to hear that after what he'd been through this evening.

'What are you going to do about your brother?' I asked as we made our way back along the corridor.

'I'll have to tell my parents what kicked off because I've no idea how to handle it from here. Chez'll go mad with me for involving them but, as he already claims he hates me, it can hardly make things worse. Right now, Imogen's my top priority. I'll find my parents later.'

It was clear to me that he loved his brother and was really worried about him. It must be hard to accept that he was out of his depth and needed reinforcements. He just kept going up in my estimation all the time. He was going through a crisis but his daughter – who had nothing to do with it – was at the forefront of his mind as his number one priority. What a kind and sensitive man Joel was.

'I can't thank you enough for all your help,' he said when we arrived in the lobby. 'Can I buy you a drink later – if there's such a thing when it's a free bar?'

I nodded. 'You can find me on the terrace.'

His eyes widened.

'Too soon?' I asked, feeling relieved when he laughed. 'I'll probably be in the snug so come and find me when you've tracked down Imogen and spoken to your parents.'

'I'm sorry you got caught up in what happened,' he said, his voice soft. 'But if anyone had to, I'm glad it was you.'

'Me too.'

Electricity crackled between us and he leaned closer. Was he going to kiss me? He was! I closed my eyes but he kissed me on the cheek. I caught the faint aroma of his aftershave – a woody scent which sent ripples of pleasure through me.

'See you later,' he said, smiling at me warmly.

I watched him cross the lobby and head towards the Juniper Lounge, a strong urge in me to run after him and hug him tightly and tell him everything would be okay, but I didn't know enough about his family to give those assurances, and I didn't want to keep him from Imogen any longer.

The little fantasy I'd had when I first walked into my room about tumbling onto my bed with a stranger rushed back into my mind. I'd vaguely pictured Joel back then but now the vision was so strong. I wanted to be with Joel and I was fairly sure the feeling was mutual. Flushing from head to toe, I drew in a deep breath. I couldn't stand here all night. I needed to alert the reception team to the broken glass and ask if someone could help with Joel's clothes. But after that, all I needed to do was wait in the Sycamore Snug for Joel and prepare myself to be brave.

22

JOEL

I left Poppy and crossed the lobby in a daze, feeling as though I'd woken from a really bad dream in which my brother proclaimed he hated me and threw a bottle of wine at me. If only it had been a dream. I wasn't sure where we could go from here. Chester needed help and I couldn't give him any because it seemed I was part of the problem. If he hated me that much, he couldn't possibly want to live with me, but with no job, no income, no girl-friend and no other close friends, what other options did he have? The thought of him remaining under my roof radiating hatred towards me made me feel sick. I couldn't bear the thought of getting home from work each day to his mess everywhere, to bare cupboards and an empty fridge, and being unable to say anything in case it kicked off again. Plus, with my own job situa-tion precarious, why should I be financially supporting someone who so clearly wanted nothing to do with me?

I was vaguely aware of someone coming towards me along the corridor but I didn't notice who it was. My head was too mashed from trying to find the words to tell my parents that they were going to have to step up and do something about Chez because I had enough of my own problems to deal with right now.

'Are you all right, Joel?'

It took me a moment to register that Fizz had stopped beside me.

'Yeah, I'm, er... Have you seen Imogen?'

'She's dancing with Darcie and Phoebe. Oh my God! What have you done to your hand?'

I didn't have the energy to cover for my brother. 'A run-in with Chez. He threw a bottle of wine at me, and I cut my hand picking up the glass.'

Fizz's mouth dropped open. 'He threw a bottle of wine at you?'

'It missed. I don't know if it was meant to or not.'

'The ungrateful little...' Fizz swallowed down whatever she'd been about to call him, but I filled in a few blanks in my head. 'I'm so sorry, Joel. What was he thinking? You've done *everything* for that lad. I know Chez has issues with his mental health and I really feel for him because depression is horrendous, but throwing a bottle at you is *not* depression. That's mindless violence and he shouldn't be allowed to get away with it.'

'What the hell's it got to do with you?'

I jumped at Chez's loud voice. Presumably he'd heard everything Fizz had just said.

'I'm concerned about your brother,' Fizz declared, her voice strong and confident.

'Of course you are. Why wouldn't you be? Everyone's on Joel's side.'

'Nobody's taking sides,' I said gently, hoping to defuse the situation.

'She is!' He jabbed his finger in Fizz's direction.

'Yes, I am. And do you know why? Because your actions have

injured Joel and if your aim had been better, it could have been a heck of a lot worse than a cut hand. Stop blaming everyone else for *your* issues. You did something wrong and here's your chance to act like a grown-up for once, own your actions and make amends.'

My stomach churned as I looked between Chez and Fizz, locked in a staring match. Fizz was right to call him out on his behaviour and I wondered if it would have made a difference if I'd stood up to him much earlier on. Fizz had made a great point – that there was a world of difference between depression affecting your behaviour and choosing to be aggressive. I'd allowed the lines to become so blurred that Chez had managed to get away with far too much.

Chez sighed and I wondered for a moment whether he was going to see sense but he shook his head and curled up his lip.

'Backstabbing bitch!' he snarled as he barged past us both, heading for the lobby.

'Chez! Get back here now!' I set off after him, determined he would apologise to Fizz for his disgusting language, but Fizz grabbed my arm.

'I've been called worse than that,' she said, smiling ruefully. 'He's being an arse but confronting him with it while he's this hammered isn't going to work. Let it go for tonight but, when he's sober, you can tell him I expect an apology. A sincere one.'

'You can have one from me for starters. I'm so sorry, Fizz. I shouldn't have spilled my guts.'

'Yes, you should. We're friends and friends open up about their problems. Do your parents know what he's done?'

'No, but I am going to tell them. I'd already been thinking I can't do this on my own anymore and tonight's just proved it. I was going to check on Imogen then find them. Hopefully they can get through to him.'

'Good. And once you've spoken to them, I want to see you back on the dance floor. Don't let Chester's strop ruin today for you.'

'I'll try not to. You said Imogen's in the disco?'

'Yes, and I was actually looking for you because I've got a special request. Darcie wants to know if Imogen can have a sleep-over in her room tonight. It adjoins ours and has twin beds so she'll be perfectly safe. I've asked Darcie not to mention it to Imogen as I wanted to make sure you were okay with it first.'

'It's fine by me, and probably for the best in case anything more kicks off with Chez. Last thing I need is him banging on my door in the early hours and scaring the life out of her.'

We found Imogen on the dance floor and ran Darcie's sugges-tion by her. As expected, she loved the idea, so I gave Fizz my room key and she disappeared with the girls to move Imogen's belongings and get Cloud settled on her new bed. Phoebe told me she'd seen my parents in the snug earlier, so I went to find them, noting that Poppy wasn't in there. I hoped she'd been waylaid and hadn't decided to call it a night, although I could hardly blame her if she had.

Mum spotted my clothes immediately. 'I didn't think you were planning to change,' she said.

'I wasn't.' I removed my hands from my pockets, revealing my bandage. 'Long story.'

I pulled up a chair and made sure I had one eye on the door, partly to watch out for Poppy but mainly to make sure Chez didn't walk in on me mid-conversation and accuse us all of conspiring against him or some other such nonsense. Keeping my voice low enough so that no nearby guests could hear, I filled them in on everything that had happened since Chez fell out with Harry, culminating in the ugly scene on the roof terrace. Mum pressed her fingers to her lips, eyes wide, cheeks pale as she took it all in and Dad kept his head bowed. I knew they'd both be blaming themselves for leaving and I wanted to nip that in the bud.

'You mustn't blame yourselves for any of this. You did the right thing for both of you leaving when you did and you'd have stayed if Chez had needed you, but he was in a good place and didn't back then. That's changed recently and I think he does need you now.'

Dad looked up, his eyes red, his brow furrowed. 'I'm sorry about tonight and what you've been through with your brother this past week. We'll book a room for him at our B&B from tomorrow night and spend some quality time with him this week.'

'It would be a weight off me if you could.'

'It's the least we can do,' Mum said. 'We're so grateful for everything you've done for your brother, but this ends now. What he's put you through this week isn't acceptable and don't even get me started on tonight.'

'I keep thinking I've failed him.'

They were both quick to reassure me that I'd done nothing wrong.

'I'll speak to him again about coming back to Portugal with us,' Dad said. 'He needs a break from everything that's making him angry and bringing him down.'

'What if he refuses again?'

'I'll make him see sense.'

If anyone could, Dad could. Seeing that Mum was flagging, I bid them goodnight so they could get to bed. A quick look round the bar confirmed that Poppy hadn't slipped by without me noticing. I checked out the Juniper Lounge. She wasn't in there either, but I spotted Zara and Snowy at the bar.

'She was on the dance floor a few minutes ago,' Zara said.

'Have you two had a drink yet or is it time for me to bang your heads together?'

'No drink, but she administered first aid to me.' I held up my hand.

'What happened?'

'You don't want to know. Dance floor, you say?'

'Yes. Go get her, tiger.'

My spirits lifted as I neared the function room and, when I spotted Poppy dancing with Imogen, my heart leapt. Suddenly the issues with Chez and work faded away and all I wanted to do was dance with the little girl who'd stolen my heart the moment she'd arrived in the world and the woman who was in danger of doing the same thing.

23

POPPY

I danced with Joel and his friends to several great tracks but by half ten it was obvious that Imogen was spent and needed sleep. Darcie admitted she was tired too and happy to go to bed. Joel scooped his daughter up – so adorable – and said he'd be back soon. I told him I'd be in the snug when he was ready.

I ordered a soft drink, parked myself at a table with two squidgy armchairs and took my phone out, spotting a message from Phil.

FROM PHIL

Great night tonight! Sorry I had to leave you early but hope it's going well with Joel and you're being brave

TO PHIL

Loved seeing you tonight. We've talked a bit and danced a lot. He's just taking his daughter back to the room and then we're having a drink. I want to do this but I don't think I'm brave enough

FROM PHIL

You're the bravest woman I know and the only
one stopping you taking the next step is you.
And, despite what I said earlier, the next step
doesn't have to be a big one. It just has to be
forwards

TO PHIL

I can do forwards. Thank you. Hopefully see you
again really soon x

Forwards. I could definitely do that. Bit of flirting? Maybe a
kiss? I crossed my legs, the split in the dress revealing a fair bit of
leg. Seductive. I could do that... I uncrossed my legs with a sigh.
No, I definitely couldn't do that. This wasn't me. I wasn't the sort
of person who flirted with a stranger, and I certainly wasn't the
sort to take anything further. It was time for bed. My bed. Alone. I
picked up my clutch bag and hastily left, but I hadn't made it far
along the corridor when Joel appeared.

'You were leaving.'

I wasn't sure if it was a statement or a question.

'Yes.'

'I'm sorry I was a while. Imogen wanted me to wait until she'd
fallen asleep and—'

'It's not that. I'd never dream of rushing you with your daughter. It's just that...'

'I can take it,' he said, his voice soft, his eyes warm.

'It's me. This. I really like you. In fact, you're the first person
I've been attracted to in a scary number of years, but it's all got a
bit overwhelming – place I don't know, guest at a wedding of
people I don't really know, trying to flirt with a stranger and
thinking all sorts of thoughts about that person which I shouldn't
be thinking, especially when he's at a wedding with his daughter
and, although I've heard rumours there isn't a wife or girlfriend

in the picture, I haven't categorically confirmed that and...' I'd run out of steam and shrugged apologetically.

Joel smiled. 'There's no wife or girlfriend and, as you've been honest, I will be too. I'm attracted to you – *very* attracted – and have also been thinking all sorts of things, but I have no expectations for any of them. What I'd love to do is have a drink and a chat and hopefully scratch off that stranger thing. But if you don't want that, I understand, and we can say goodnight with my thanks for your first aid and stain removal expertise.'

That made me smile and diminished the nerves a little.

'If it helps, it's scary for me too. I'm crap at this sort of thing which is why I've been single for more years than I care to say. Women usually friend zone me immediately and I don't know how to stop that happening so there's no need to worry about *after* because I can pretty much guarantee there won't be an after.'

The words and the tone were flippant but the sincerity in his eyes suggested that being labelled as a friend had caused some pain in the past. I could see beyond the joke and feel the vulnerability.

'What do you say?' he prompted.

'I say okay, let's scratch off that stranger thing.'

We returned to the bar but, in the short time we'd been talking, it had filled up and was the busiest I'd seen it all night. The volume of chatter and laughter wasn't going to be conducive to a getting-to-know-you conversation.

Joel must have had the same thoughts as me. 'Where did this lot spring from?'

'I'm guessing the DJ made an unpopular track choice.'

'What if I get a bottle of wine and we find somewhere quieter?'

'There were some alcoves with chairs in them near the room where Amber and Barney got married,' I suggested.

'Perfect. Why don't you grab an alcove while I go to the bar? And if you do want to leave but were uncomfortable saying it to my face just now, that's your embarrassment-free escape route.'

'I'm not going to run, but I'm still nervous.'

'Me too. But I think that's a good thing. It shows we both care. See you shortly.' He held up his crossed fingers and the hopeful smile he gave me melted my heart. Yes, I *did* care and that was surprising after such a short time. Something in my gut was telling me that Joel was going to be a very important person in my life, and I had no idea why. I was the practical accountant – not someone who believed in fate, destiny or gut feelings. But everything about my trip to Yorkshire so far felt very much like destiny at play. I loved it here and felt more like me than I had in a very long time. And the thought of leaving on Monday made me feel a little tearful.

24

JOEL

My heart was pounding as I returned to the snug to order a bottle of wine. Levi spotted me and called me over to join him, Tim and their fiancées.

'I can't. I'm meeting someone.'

'Orange dress?' Tim asked.

'Is it that obvious?'

'Yes!' they chorused followed by all four of them speaking at once. I didn't need to ask them to repeat themselves as I'd got the gist – *good choice*, *about time*, *be yourself* and *good luck*.

I needed more than luck, especially as I might have unintentionally friend zoned myself by raising the subject. What was wrong with me? Why had I planted that idea?

The first alcove I found had a couple of solid-looking chairs separated by a table on which there was the most enormous floral arrangement. She wasn't there but I wouldn't have chosen those chairs either. A bit further along, there was a squishy sofa and there she was.

'You stayed.'

'That thing you said about nerves and caring really resonated.'

I poured two glasses of wine and passed her one before sitting down at the other end of the sofa.

'Before I forget, Housekeeping are sorting out your clothes,' she said. 'They'll be at reception when you check out tomorrow.'

'Thanks so much for doing that for me. I really appreciate it.' After Chez had done nothing but take from me, it was touching to have someone willing to give instead.

'Have you seen your brother since?'

I told her about the confrontation with Fizz and the subsequent conversation with my parents. Poppy asked whether things had always been difficult between us and I found myself fully opening up about Chester's depression, his on-off relationship with Lorna, the falling out with Harry and how I'd tried to shield my parents from each of his dark moments.

'I didn't want them to worry with being so far away and Chez was adamant he didn't want me telling tales but I think that, in trying to protect them all, I might have made it worse.'

'Sounds like you were stuck between a rock and a hard place,' Poppy said. 'If you'd told your parents, you'd have broken Chez's confidence so you tried to support him yourself and ended up getting the brunt of his frustration. In your shoes, I don't think I'd have done anything different.'

'Do you have any brothers or sisters?'

'No. My parents never wanted children, but they took my birth mum in when she was four months pregnant with me and they never got rid of me.'

Poppy said it flippantly but the accompanying smile didn't reach her eyes. So many questions sprang to mind from that one statement, and I hesitated, wondering if it was too soon and too intrusive to ask them.

'So, how old is Imogen?' Poppy asked. 'She mentioned some other children earlier who I think are maybe siblings but not yours?'

'She's eight, she has a stepbrother, half-brother, half-sister and twin half-brothers on the way. And you've just changed the subject.' I couldn't not acknowledge what she'd said.

Poppy stared into her drink. 'I don't normally talk about me.'

'Why not?'

'Because I'm not very interesting.'

'Why would you think that?'

'Because the last two people I dated told me. I haven't dared inflict myself on anyone else since then.'

I reeled back, stunned that anyone would say that about her or that she'd believe it. 'Whoever they were, they couldn't have been more wrong. I find you fascinating.'

'You probably won't if you get to know me.'

She lifted her head, and my throat tightened as I noticed the tears glistening in her eyes. She'd been deeply hurt by the people who'd told her that and it was clear to me that *I'm not very interesting* was her version of me repeatedly being friend zoned. No wonder she was so nervous. No wonder she'd wanted to escape.

'Let me be the judge of that,' I said, gently. 'We don't have to talk about your family if you don't feel comfortable with that. Let's start simple. Favourite TV programme.'

She smiled. 'That's easy. *Darrington Detects.* Serious fangirl moment earlier when I met Cole Crawford. I still can't believe that happened. What about you?'

'Oh, I fangirl over him all the time too. That's one sexy vicar.'

Poppy laughed at that – a proper belly laugh – and I felt her melancholy lifting.

'I had another fangirl moment the first time I met Amber's sister, Sophie,' I told her. 'Fizz used to obsessively watch *Mercury's*

Rising and Barney and I would take the mickey out of it but it was secretly our guilty pleasure. Never dreamed my best mate would end up marrying Mercury Addison's big sister.'

'I loved *Mercury's Rising* too. Wasn't Sophie's boyfriend in that too?'

'Devon? Yes. They were together for several years but Sophie had a horrific experience on a reality TV show when she was eighteen and they split up. Then last year, they were cast in a period drama together, realised they were still deeply in love and they've been inseparable ever since.'

'Aw, that's so sweet. The whole family seem lovely.'

'They are. Barney's parents and sister have always been like a second family to me and now Amber's clan have adopted me too. So, another question. If you weren't an accountant, what would you like to be?'

'A full-time beekeeper. I already look after twenty hives and it would be a dream to expand it and make it into a proper business...'

I listened, fascinated, as she told me how she'd got into beekeeping and how her plans for skincare products hadn't progressed when her mum received a terminal illness diagnosis. With my assurance that I was genuinely interested in hearing more, she told me about her mum's demise, the double-whammy of her dad being diagnosed with Alzheimer's shortly afterwards and how the break at Whisperwood Farmhouse had been an attempt to stave off burnout.

She asked me about my relationship with Tilly, why she'd called off the engagement and about the sort of relationship we had now, and she told me about Phil and how wanting very different things out of life had ended their marriage but not their friendship. It sounded as though his family meant the same to her as Barney's meant to me and I was glad for her that she had such caring people around her.

Poppy was so easy to talk to and I felt like I could tell her anything. We bounced from topic to topic but, despite talking a lot about her parents, she didn't expand on her original statement about them, and I didn't push. She'd open up on that one when she was ready. Whoever the two men were who'd told her she wasn't interesting couldn't have been further from the truth. She had to be the most fascinating woman I'd ever met and I was hanging off every word, eager to learn more.

Noticing her empty glass sometime later, I went to top it up but, amazingly, we'd managed to finish the bottle.

'Would you like anything else to drink?' I asked.

'I don't think I can manage any more wine but I'd love a Baileys on ice.'

'Back in a few minutes.'

'Joel!' she called as I set off. 'I'm glad I didn't escape. This has been great. You're such a lovely man.'

I smiled and thanked her but, as I made my way to the bar, my stomach sank. *Such a lovely man.* I'd heard that comment so many times – the classic precursor to a request just to be friends. I did this every time – had a conversation with a woman in which I asked questions, listened, showed understanding and empathy and shared my own experiences where appropriate and where did it get me? Right in the middle of the friend zone.

In the bar, I spotted Amber across the room talking to her mum and smiled to myself, imagining Amber waving the manifesting book in front of my face and saying *Did the negative thoughts get you the job? No! So, are they going to get you the girl? Of course not!* It had felt different talking to Poppy, as though there'd been a deeper, stronger connection between us. I'd certainly opened up way more than I usually did, and I felt like she had too. *It's going well and it's going to continue to go well.*

I fancied a Baileys too but, when I returned from the bar with the two glasses, Poppy had gone. Of course she had! My shoulders slumped, my earlier positivity slinking away down the corridor. I placed the drinks down on the table, sank onto the sofa with a sigh and slumped forward with my head in my hands. Another one bites the dust. What should I have done instead? Moved straight in for a kiss without conversation? Taken her back to my room and tried to seduce her? It wasn't me. I couldn't show such a lack of respect so if that meant I was going to stay single, so be it. At least my integrity would remain intact.

'Are you okay, Joel?'

My head shot up and there was Poppy standing over me, looking concerned.

'I thought you'd gone.'

'I'd just nipped to the loo. Why would I leave?'

'Because you said I was lovely and that's usually followed by a request just to be friends, and I assumed that's what you meant and you'd maybe decided it would be easier to slope off rather than have that awkward conversation.' The minute I'd blurted that out, I felt stupid. I'd massively overreacted and, while I hadn't put her off earlier, I might well have done now.

Poppy sat down beside me. 'Why do you see being friends as such a bad thing?'

'It isn't. I'm glad I spent the evening with you. It's actually the best evening I've had for a long time which is quite a turnaround given what happened on the terrace, but I completely understand why you'd only want friendship. I was the one who said I had no expectations and I meant it. It's not your fault I desperately want to kiss you.'

Her brow knitted slightly. 'Do you?'

'God, yes! But I'm not going to throw myself at you so don't panic.'

She cocked her head to one side, a smile playing on her lips. 'Does it have to be a choice – friendship or passion?'

'In my experience, yes. And it's usually friendship.'

'Can't it be both? Phil and I started off as friends and that became so much more and it was an amazing relationship because we had friendship *and* passion. Yes, it ended and we reverted to being friends, but it only ended because we got together so young, before we knew who we were and what we really wanted out of life. We could have emerged from the other side battle scarred and resentful. Instead, we chose to let go and preserve the friendship. But those years where we had the friendship *and* the passion were perfect and it's my dream to find that again with someone else.'

Could that someone else be me? The words were in my head, but I couldn't seem to spit them out.

'I'm older now,' Poppy said. 'Hopefully wiser too and I know what I want.'

'What's that?' I asked, my heart pounding as she moved a little closer, her leg pressing against mine.

'You.'

She ran her fingers into my hair and pressed her lips against mine in the most incredible gentle kiss which left me wanting more.

'I'm still nervous,' she whispered, her eyes searching mine.

'Me too, but we both know what that means.'

I cupped her face and lowered my lips to hers, melting into a deeply passionate kiss which had my heart pounding. I'd wanted to do that all night. Heck, I'd wanted to do it when I saw her in the garden centre, and it was better than anything I'd imagined.

25

POPPY

I opened my eyes and experienced a moment of discombobulation from waking up somewhere unfamiliar. As my eyes rested on my dress draped over the dressing table chair, I smiled as the memories from last night flooded back to me. What a night! As our kisses intensified, Joel had taken my hand and led me back to his room. I loved the way he'd paused by the door, emphasising that this was about privacy and comfort and there was still no pressure or expectation. Maybe not from him but I was expecting great things after the way he kissed, taking my breath away.

I'm not sure how far we'd have taken things if his phone hadn't rung. He'd already told me he'd need to keep it switched on in case there was a problem with Imogen and I'd said I was the same because of Dad but, as soon as he told me it was Fizz calling, I knew our evening was over. As disappointing as that was, it made me like him even more that he was always there for his daughter.

As he spoke to Fizz in hushed tones, I rolled myself off the bed, adjusting my dress back into place. Sure enough, as I slipped my feet back into Fizz's sandals, I caught the end of the conversation.

'Tell her I'll be there in five minutes.' He disconnected and turned to me with a sigh. 'I'm so sorry. Imogen's crying. She feels sick.'

'Probably from all the excitement,' I said. 'I just need to track down my bag and I'll be gone.'

'I think you dropped it by the door.' He retrieved it for me and a wave of heat passed through me as I recalled tossing it there the moment we tumbled into his room, locked in a kiss.

His arm slipped round my waist as I took the bag from him and he pulled me closer, kissing me tenderly.

'I don't want to say goodbye,' he murmured.

'Then don't. Say *see you later*.'

'When do you go home?'

'First thing on Monday. I wish I could stay longer but I've got a client meeting on Tuesday and I really need to see my dad.'

'Do you have any plans for tomorrow night?'

'Just packing.'

'Can I come to the farmhouse? I could cook for you if you like. I'm pretty useful in the kitchen.'

'I'd love that, but I know things are tricky with your brother so, if you find you can't come, I'll understand.' There was a notepad and pen on the desk so I scribbled my number down.

'I'll be there. I promise.'

He kissed me with longing and pulled away with reluctance and I sensed that, even if he couldn't find the time, he'd call me to let me know. There was something so honest and honourable about Joel Grainger.

Light was streaming through a gap in the curtains where I hadn't properly closed them last night, creating a stripe on the pillow beside me. I was staring at it, thinking I should really get up and showered for breakfast when my phone rang. The number wasn't registered. Hopefully it was Joel but there was a possibility it was Damon using a different phone, so I answered with caution.

'Hello?'

'Poppy? It's Joel. Have I woken you up?'

'No. I'm still in bed but I was awake. How's Imogen?'

'She came back to my room, had a glass of milk and was okay after that. Do you mind if I put her on?'

'Erm, no, that's fine.'

The next voice I heard was Imogen's. 'Hi, Poppy, do you want to come to breakfast with us?' My heart melted. How sweet was that?

'I'd love to, thank you, but I'm not dressed yet. Are you going down now?'

'No. I need a bath so Daddy says half an hour. We can call for you.'

'Sounds good. I'll see you then. Can you put your daddy back on?'

'Okay. Bye.'

'Imogen says it's a yes,' Joel said, coming onto the phone shortly after.

'It is, but that means that the next time I see you, you'll be together. It's probably not a good idea for us to have a repeat performance of last night in front of your daughter but I wouldn't want you to think I'm giving you the cold shoulder.'

'I should have thought about that. Yeah, probably best to stick to friendship vibes around her for the moment, but only because of Tilly. I know how her mind works. She'd accuse me of abandoning Imogen so I could pick up strange women. Not that you're strange.'

'Don't worry. I know what you mean. It's so unfair on you that she's like that.'

'I swear it's Greg's influence, although maybe it was always simmering under the surface and I either didn't notice or didn't want to notice. So we'd best keep it under the radar although Imogen would be ecstatic if she thought something was going on.'

'She would?'

'Definitely! She thinks you're amazing and she was quizzing me about you this morning and whether you had a boyfriend. I get the impression she and Darcie were doing a spot of match-making last night. It was Imogen's idea to invite you to breakfast.'

'She's a gorgeous girl and I'm glad I'd have her seal of approval but I completely understand the Tilly situation so I'll be discreet.' I bit my lip and added in a sultry tone, 'It won't be easy though.' It was daring for me, but I couldn't help myself. In a very short space of time, Joel had really got under my skin and I wanted him to know that.

I could hear the smile in his voice. 'Same here. I'll see you soon. Can't wait.'

We said goodbye and hung up. I now had twenty-five minutes to get myself showered and looking presentable. No pressure.

* * *

Joel and Imogen turned up at my bedroom door bang on time.

'Are you hungry?' Imogen asked as soon as I opened the door. 'Because I am, and Daddy says I can have pancakes which are my favourites.'

'I'm very hungry and I love pancakes too, especially if they come with bacon and maple syrup.'

Her eyes widened. 'I've never had them like that before. They sound yummy.'

As we set off along the corridor, Imogen surprised me by slipping her hand into mine. My heart leapt and I felt quite emotional as I caught Joel's eye and he smiled and mouthed, 'She likes you.'

Fizz, Phoebe and Darcie were at the entrance to the dining room about to be seated so they changed their request to a table for six. I was glad of the company, thinking it would be easier to keep up the subterfuge of being friends if we were part of a group, although the knowing smiles Fizz and Phoebe exchanged suggested that turning up together had already given the game away.

'Good night last night?' Fizz asked me, a big grin on her face.

I glanced up at Joel and he shook his head, chuckling.

'The best,' I admitted.

We were led to a rectangular table and Imogen plonked herself down opposite me at one end, with Joel beside me opposite Darcie.

'Who was that man with you last night?' Imogen asked after we'd given our food and drink orders. 'How do you know him?'

It made me laugh when children blurted out direct questions like that.

'That was Phil and he used to be my husband but we split up several years ago and now we're just good friends.'

She frowned. 'Mummy and Daddy split up but they're not friends.'

'That's probably more common than staying friends with your ex.'

'Oh. Okay. So would you like to be my daddy's girlfriend?'

I burst out laughing. No filter whatsoever!

'Imogen!' Joel cried. 'You can't just come out with something like that.'

'Why not? You like Poppy. You were dancing with her last night, and you told me you think she's beautiful.'

My cheeks flushed and my stomach tingled as I caught Joel's eye.

'Well, she is,' he said, his voice tender, 'but I think it's time we changed the subject, young lady. We're embarrassing Poppy.'

'It's fine,' I said, not wanting her to think she'd done something wrong. 'Imogen, I hear you're learning to ride...'

All too soon, breakfast was over and I knew I was going to have to say goodbye. I wished I could stay here forever, encased in this bubble of happiness with these wonderful people. We were about to leave when Joel's parents appeared and paused by our table to say hello. Joel introduced me which prompted Imogen to make another matchmaking attempt.

'Daddy really likes Poppy and so do I. I think they should go out.'

Ten out of ten for persistence and it gave me a warm glow to think that I already had Imogen's seal of approval which would make things so much easier if Joel wanted to see me again after I went home. I already knew I wanted to see him. Distance was going to be an issue, but it wasn't like we lived at other ends of the country to each other.

'I think that's your daddy and Poppy's decision,' Joel's mum said, smiling at us both. 'Nice to meet you, Poppy.'

Imogen asked if she could stay with her grandparents while Joel packed up the room so I said goodbye to her and was rewarded with an unexpected hug. I swear she took a little piece of my heart with her when she ran off to join Joel's parents.

I thanked Fizz and Phoebe for making me feel so welcome which triggered more hugs and hopes that I'd visit the area again.

Then, as we left the restaurant, we passed Amber and Barney, so I had a chance to thank them too. Amber made me promise to stay in touch and said I was welcome to visit any time. By the time I'd hugged them both, I was on the verge of tears. They'd all been so friendly and welcoming and I hated having to say goodbye.

Joel said he'd walk me back to my room so we stopped off at reception to pick up his clothes which thankfully bore no evidence of last night's disaster.

'Sorry about Imogen's interrogation,' he said we approached my bedroom. 'If I'd known she was going to do that, I'd have plonked her down at the other end of the table.'

'It was fine. It made me laugh and it was nice to be wanted.'

We paused by the door and Joel took my hand in his. 'I'm conscious we were interrupted last night and we haven't been able to talk about what happens next. And I'm conscious that *next* is complicated because you don't live here, you've got a business to run, bees to attend to and the heartbreaking situation with your dad, but I can't help thinking there's something special between us. I hope we can spend some time this evening exploring whether there's any way to uncomplicate things. If that's something you'd like to do, and I haven't been friend zoned.'

'Believe me, you're nowhere near being friend zoned. I don't do what we were doing last night with any of my friends.'

'Pleased to hear it,' he said, laughing.

I smiled at him and squeezed his hand. 'It *is* complicated and it's not going to be easy but I'm feeling like it isn't impossible, so let's talk later and see what we can come up with.'

He released my hand and slipped his arm round my waist, pulling me into a tender, heart-melting kiss.

'I don't know what time I'll make it over yet – depends on what's going on with Chez.'

'I'm not going anywhere, so message me when you know your plans.'

He held me tight and, at that moment, I knew that no matter how difficult or complicated it was for both of us, I was going to pull out all the stops to make it work. I'd already broken the cycle of the everyday visits to Dad and felt better in myself for doing so. Maybe Joel and I could meet up every so often at a halfway point. I was willing to give anything a try because I could already feel myself falling for him and I wasn't prepared to let him slip through my fingers. What had Phil said last night about timing? *Timing might be everything, but sometimes what can seem the worst possible timing can turn out to be the best. Life's chaotic. I say embrace the chaos!* This was me well and truly embracing the chaos.

26

JOEL

I hated saying goodbye to Poppy, even though I was going to see her again later. As she closed her door after another incredible kiss, I felt like I was leaving part of my heart behind and the intensity of the emotion took my breath away. I leaned against the wall for a couple of moments before returning to my room to pack.

As I placed Cloud in Imogen's case, I replayed her interrogation over breakfast in my head. Poppy had responded to it so well and hadn't given anything away about us. There was a big risk that Imogen would tell Tilly about Poppy anyway. I had never and would never ask Imogen to cover anything up for me – not fair on her and likely to backfire on me at a later date. If Imogen did mention Poppy, Tilly would jump to the conclusion that Poppy was my long-term secret girlfriend who'd attended as my plus one and she'd be fuming that I'd introduced her to Imogen without Tilly's approval. I'd cross that bridge if I came to it.

I loved how Poppy had skilfully steered the conversation away from her love life by asking Imogen about riding. She couldn't have picked a better subject as Imogen told her all about the lessons Barney had given her on Munchie and how she'd been scrapbooking her progress. That led to her telling Poppy about how Zara had introduced her to the world of scrapbooking after presenting her with a scrapbook and box full of tape, ribbons and stickers for Christmas two years ago. I'd bought her a Polaroid camera for the following birthday which she used only for special photos to go in the book. She'd taken a few at the wedding across the afternoon and was planning on a special section in her scrapbook devoted to the big day. The pair of them had discussed ideas for those pages and Poppy had said she'd love to see it when it was finished, as though that was their normal. And the strange thing was that, despite knowing her for less than twenty-four hours, it really felt like it was.

It took ages to say goodbye to everyone, but I was still ahead of schedule for dropping Imogen back at Tilly's. Despite that, she'd already sent three texts and left a voicemail making sure I'd have her back well before lunch. I'd ignored them all. I understood that she was eager to have Imogen home, especially when I'd had her two weekends in a row, but both weekends had only involved one overnight stay, so it wasn't like Tilly hadn't seen Imogen at all. It would be great if that insight into my world – missing Imogen constantly – would make Tilly more understanding of my situation and willing to do something about it, but I doubted it.

When the car was loaded and Imogen was settled, I sent Tilly a text to confirm we were leaving. My phone beeped with a reply as I started the ignition but I didn't bother opening it.

'Have you had a good time?' I asked Imogen as I set off down the drive.

'It was awesome. I love weddings. I can't wait for Fizz and

Phoebe's wedding and I don't mind not being a bridesmaid. Can I still wear a pretty dress that twirls?'

'Next time I see you on a weekend, we'll go shopping for one.'

For the next half an hour, she barely drew a breath, chattering about all the things she'd loved about the wedding – doing the Taylor Swift routine, the photo booth, the sweetie cart, seeing her grandparents and having a sleepover with Darcie, if only for a few hours.

'Leighton will be so jealous when I tell him about the sweetie cart,' she said.

'You got a bag of sweets for him, though, didn't you?'

'Yes, but I ate them all.'

I bit back a smile. That might explain her feeling sick last night.

'I hear you're going to have two more half-brothers in the summer. Are you excited about that?'

'No. I don't need any more brothers and it's not fair that we have to move to fit them in.'

My stomach lurched. Tilly hadn't mentioned anything about moving. They were already short on space but I'd been led to believe that money was tight, so I couldn't imagine how they were going to afford a bigger house.

'You're moving?' I asked.

'Yes. How far away is Scotland?'

I felt the colour draining from my face as I gripped tightly onto the steering wheel. Scotland? *Scotland?* What the hell?

* * *

I was seething by the time I pulled up outside Tilly's house. Scotland? Seriously? Even if they were planning on only just going over the border, we were still talking three and a half hours away. How dare she even think about taking my daughter so far away without breathing a word to me about it?

The front door opened and Tilly stepped out, wrapping her cardigan around her stomach. As Imogen ran up the garden path to hug her mum, I removed her suitcase, coat and dress carrier from the boot, my jaw clenching.

Tilly had stepped into the hall and pushed the door to, presumably to keep out the cold. Or unwanted fathers. I could hear her inside gushing about how much she'd missed Imogen and how she hated it when she was away which just added fuel to the fire burning inside me.

I pushed open the door and placed Imogen's belongings just inside.

'I need to go, sweetie,' I said. 'Goodbye hug?'

Imogen released Tilly and raced to me, hugging me tightly and thanking me for taking her.

'Why don't you go in and tell Greg and the others all about it?' I suggested. 'I need a word with your mummy outside.'

Tilly glared at me. 'It's cold out.'

'Then put a coat on,' I muttered, my voice cold as I glared at her. Then I smiled and said in a brighter tone, 'Bye, Imogen. See you later in the week for tea with Grandma Audrey and Granddad Trevor.'

'I hadn't agreed to that,' Tilly protested when Imogen disappeared into the lounge.

'It's not your decision to make. Put your coat on. We need to talk.'

She grabbed her coat and followed me outside. 'She's already spent the weekend with them,' she said, her voice thick with the whiny tone she always used when trying to stop me from spending time with Imogen.

'She was at a wedding with a couple of hundred guests. She barely saw them.'

'That's not my fault.'

'Fine. We won't have tea with them this week. I'll book a week in Portugal over Easter instead. Which would you prefer?'

She reeled back, surprise in her eyes that I'd challenged her.

'I'll take that as a yes to tea this week.'

'Okay, but there's no need to be so arsey about it.'

'You think this is arsey? I haven't even started being arsey. What should we talk about next? Ooh, how about you planning on moving to Scotland with our daughter?'

She tutted loudly. 'She wasn't meant to say anything.'

'Don't blame Imogen. What the hell, Tilly? When were you going to tell me?'

'Ssh! She'll hear you! It's not definitely happening. We've seen a camping and glamping site for sale so the reason we're hoping to go to Scotland over Easter is to check it out.'

It all fell into place – that guilty look last weekend when I'd broached the issue of Greg wanting Imogen to call him Daddy but Tilly thinking Imogen had let something else slip. She'd covered her tracks by mentioning the holiday, but she'd clearly thought Imogen had told me about the move.

'Where in Scotland?' It came out gruff, but I didn't care.

'Does it matter?'

'Of course it matters! It's four and a half hours to Edinburgh which is bad enough but somewhere like Inverness is probably another three hours on top of that.'

The flinch followed by an averted gaze when I said Inverness confirmed we were talking the Highlands rather than the borders. Absolutely unbelievable.

'How could you keep something like this from me? How could

you ask our daughter to keep it quiet? And how the hell could you think it's okay to even consider it?'

'It might not happen.'

'There's no *might* about it. It's *not* happening. She's my daughter and there's no way on earth I'm letting you take her to Scotland.'

She straightened up and fixed me with a hard stare. 'It's not your decision to make,' she said, repeating my words from moments ago. 'I have full custody of our daughter. I think you'll find that I can do whatever I like.'

She slammed the door and locked it. I stood on the path, feet rooted to the spot, my stomach in knots. She couldn't take Imogen to Scotland. She just couldn't. But Tilly had always done whatever the hell she liked and if she decided that campsite was for her, she'd get it.

Out of the corner of my eye, I spotted the lounge blinds twitching. I had to get out of there, away from prying eyes. I ran to my car and pulled away but I only made it down their street and round the corner before I had to slam on the brakes and yank on the handbrake, thinking I was going to throw up. I wound the window down and took in several deep gulps of air until the nausea subsided and I sank back into my seat, shaking. I felt like my heart had been ripped out of my chest. I couldn't live without Imogen. Every goodbye was painful when she lived in the same town as me. I could not have her living hours away and I knew she wouldn't want it either. And I wasn't going to let it happen.

27

POPPY

I pulled onto the drive at Whisperwood Farmhouse shortly after
11 a.m. and had the strongest sensation of coming home. I
couldn't remember the last time I'd experienced that feeling of
contentment at Dove Cottage. If anything, pulling onto the drive
there made me feel anxious and lonely.

It didn't take long to unpack my bag and I was soon settled at
the kitchen table with my laptop open and a coffee to give me a
burst of energy. I was so engrossed in my work that my phone
ringing made me jump and I was surprised to see it was already
one o'clock. Joel's name flashed up on the screen.

'I think I'm going to have to cancel tonight,' he blurted out as
soon as I answered, making my heart sink. 'I'm so sorry. I really
want to come but my head is a mess right now and I'm not going
to be good company.'

The words were garbled and he sounded really distressed.

'Is it Chez?'

'No. It's Tilly. I've just found out that she and Greg want to buy
a campsite in the Scottish Highlands.'

'Oh, Joel. But that's hours away.'

'I know! I've told her she can't take Imogen away from me, but she says she can. I don't know if that's true. I've been online and I can't find a definitive answer.'

'One of my clients is a former solicitor and I'm pretty sure she specialised in family law. I don't know if she'll pick up her emails on a Sunday but I can put some feelers out if you like.'

'Would you? I'm going to email my solicitor but I'm on shift for the next two days so I'm not going to be able to get an appointment until Wednesday at the earliest.'

Joel ran through some of the details I'd need around the custody arrangements he had and added that, while it was something they were only exploring at the moment, Tilly never wasted time with frivolous dreams. If she was willing to go to Scotland over Easter to check out the campsite, it meant it was happening and the only thing that would stop her forging ahead would be the discovery of a major problem with the site.

He sounded so much calmer now that he'd offloaded. 'I know you said you don't think you'll be good company, but why don't you come round tonight anyway? We can get a takeaway and I can be your sounding board about what to do next if the worst happens and you can't stop the move.'

'You really want to spend your last night here listening to me moaning?'

'I really want to spend my last night here with *you*. You know what I said yesterday about being able to have friendship *and* passion? This is the friendship part. Being with someone means being there for the good stuff and the tough times. I know ours is a new friendship and I'm sure you'd normally talk something like this through with Barney...'

'But he's off on his honeymoon,' he finished. 'How does seven sound? I'll pick up a Chinese takeaway on the way but the best one's on the other side of Reddfield so it'll need heating up.'

Arrangements confirmed, I prepared an email to my client about Joel's situation but, moments after I sent it, an out-of-office message came back announcing she was away for a fortnight. It looked like my only contact wasn't going to be helpful. I didn't want Joel to get his hopes up so I messaged him straightaway to let him know, then settled down to work.

* * *

My heart leapt when I spotted headlights in the lane just before seven o'clock. Rain had been battering the back windows for the past half an hour, but I had it all warm and cosy inside with the log burner lit and a couple of candles. Joel got out of his car, clutching a paper bag, and ran towards the house.

'That's seriously heavy rain,' he said.

I took the soggy bag from him before it fell apart, and took it through to the kitchen. He followed me, his hair wet and dripping down his face. I grabbed a hand towel and gently dabbed it against his cheeks and forehead. It felt unexpectedly intimate and my heart raced as I rubbed the towel over his hair, my face so close to his. Joel was obviously feeling it too as he drew me into a slow, tender kiss before hugging me tightly and holding on for ages. I could feel how much he was hurting and wished I could ease the pain.

The takeaway smelled delicious and my tummy was rumbling, but dishing it up and whacking it in the microwave didn't feel like the top priority right now.

'How are you feeling?' I asked.

'Better for seeing you. It's been a tough day. As if the Scotland thing wasn't bad enough, Chez went AWOL. He checked out of Fennington Hall this morning and he wasn't answering his phone. I spent the afternoon driving round the area trying to find him – Harry's, Lorna's mum's house, work, his favourite pubs, even the playground he used to go to as a kid but there was no sign of him and none of them had heard from him.'

'Oh, Joel, that's the last thing you all need.'

'Mum was frantic. She left him a teary voicemail begging him not to do anything stupid and to get in touch to let us know he's okay because, if anything happened to him, it would kill her. Talk about harrowing. Fortunately, it did the trick. He messaged her to say that, other than having the mother of all hangovers, he was fine and she wasn't to worry as he wouldn't do anything stupid. He was embarrassed and angry – not sure if that was at himself or me – so he needed some space away from people.'

'Where is he now?'

'I'm not sure but I've had it up to here today.' He raised his hand way above his head. 'I've left it with Mum and Dad. I think they're going to pick him up in York or something. I can't even...' He shook his head, and I hugged him once more. I knew that feeling well, when it seemed like one thing after another kept going wrong without any respite and it all became too much.

* * *

I'd once read an article about first dates, listing all the *safe* subjects such as friends, work and hobbies and the topics to avoid – a long list which included religion, politics, exes, difficult family situations and health issues. At the time, I'd thought it was a pile of crap and now I knew that for certain. Over the two evenings I'd spent with Joel so far, we'd explored several of those no-go topics because they were the things that had shaped us into the people we were today and were important to us. To pussyfoot around them would be to deny everything that was affecting us both right now. Curled up on either end of the large two-seater sofa, we talked a lot more about the obstacles Tilly repeatedly put in Joel's way and how carefully he had to pick his battles, fearful that she'd reduce his already limited access to Imogen. It all sounded so unfair, and I found myself disliking her intensely.

Mid-conversation, Joel's mum rang to say that Chester was back. He put her on speakerphone so he didn't have to repeat it. They'd picked him up in York, had been to Joel's to get some fresh clothes, and he was booked into a room at their B&B in Reddfield for the rest of their stay. He was showering now and would be dining with them shortly.

'How was he?' Joel asked.

'Quiet. Subdued. Freezing cold – daft lad didn't have a coat with him – so we're going to tread carefully this evening.'

'You are going to discuss Portugal, though?'

Joel's dad answered. 'Yes, and we'll be quite insistent about it but there's no point raising it until we think he's going to be more receptive to the idea. You know what he's like for digging his heels in.'

When the call ended, Joel released a heavy sigh of relief. I asked if he wanted to talk some more about his brother but he declined, saying he longed for an evening without worrying about Chez.

It seemed a suitable time for food so we broke off to heat up the takeaway and had a lighter conversation while we ate about what it had been like for Joel growing up in the area. The more he spoke about it, the more drawn I felt towards it. It wasn't just that the surroundings were beautiful – Winchcote and Saltersbeck Farm were too. It was the people I'd met and the freshness of it – a place that held no connection to the sadness of the past seven years where I could truly relax. As he spoke about spending time at Bumblebee Barn, I pictured that field Amber had shown me and once more imagined being the beekeeper, the sights, sounds and smells so strong, so engaging.

After eating, we returned to the lounge and resumed our conversation about Tilly. Joel shared his current work situation and how he hoped he'd finally get confirmation tomorrow as to whether or not his job was at risk.

'You have so much going on right now,' I said, stroking my hand lightly down his arm. 'I bet you'll be glad to see the back of this month.'

'Yes and no. I've had plenty of crap thrown at me but there's been a shedload of good stuff too. My best mate got married yesterday and Amber's amazing. I had a proud dad moment seeing my daughter as their bridesmaid and again with that dance routine. My parents are over for a week and it's always good to see them. And, unexpected bonus, I met someone who should never have been accused of being boring because, to me, she's fascinating, inspiring, caring, intelligent and, even though I'd only spent one evening in her company, I felt like part of me was missing when she wasn't by my side today.'

Nobody had ever said anything quite so romantic to me and I felt myself welling up – not just because the sentiment was so beautiful but because I felt the same way too. There was something about this place, the people and particularly the man right next to me that was so familiar to me, as though it had always been part of my life but just out of reach until now. It wasn't a dream. This was reality and I wanted to savour every single moment of it.

I leaned over and kissed Joel, my heart racing as the kiss became increasingly passionate. *Do one thing every day that scares you.* I slowly pulled back, rolled off the sofa, took Joel's hand in mine and gave it a gentle tug. 'I missed you too and I haven't been able to stop thinking about you or about last night when we got interrupted just as things were getting really interesting…'

'You're sure?'

'Never been more so.'

* * *

We lay side by side in the bed a little later, smiling contentedly at each other. I was glad we'd been interrupted last night as I couldn't have imagined anything better than tonight, without any alcohol inside us but a day of deepening feelings creating an even stronger connection.

'I wish you didn't have to leave tomorrow,' Joel said, stroking my hair back from my face.

'I wish I *never* had to go back. I love it here.'

'Then stay.'

'If only I could. I'd buy this place from Mary in a heartbeat.'

'What's stopping you?'

'Dad. Even though he has no idea who I am, I need to visit him for my own peace of mind. I'd never forgive myself if I stopped. I've been thinking about whether he could move to a different care home, but I'm worried it might be too stressful for him.'

'But if it wasn't too stressful for him, you'd consider it?'

'I would, which is not what I was expecting when I came here. I was only meant to be recharging my batteries, and I never expected to fall in love with this place and want to stay. Selling Dove Cottage – where I live now – is something I've only just accepted that I need to do. I mentioned it to Phil and said I was thinking about buying somewhere near Dad's care home, but he suggested I hold off on buying because that would tie me to the area when the sad truth is my dad won't be around much longer.'

My voice caught on the last few words and I swallowed hard.

'That must be so hard to deal with,' Joel said, gently.

'It is. They say that when a loved one has dementia, you lose them twice – the day they actually pass away and the day they lose their connection to you.' I closed my eyes for a moment, not wanting to shroud our special evening with sadness. When I opened them again, Joel was looking at me, his eyes full of concern.

'I'm all right,' I said, stroking my hand across his cheek. 'Just a lot going on up here right now.' I tapped the side of my head. 'Coming here was meant to clear my head, not add more to it, but they're good thoughts. I feel as though my future's here, but my present has to be near Dad and I'm a little scared that the future I want might slip away from me because I can't commit to moving here. Not yet.'

'Then we need to find a way for your present and your future to work together so you can have both.'

'I'd like both,' I whispered, snuggling closer to him.

'I'd like you to have both.'

28

JOEL

I groaned as my phone alarm sounded at 4.45 a.m. the next morning, allowing me time to get home and changed into my work gear before my shift started at six.

'I wish you didn't have to go,' Poppy murmured, her hand seeking mine.

'Me too. I've never thrown a sickie in my life but it's so tempting right now.'

I nipped to the bathroom and, when I returned, Poppy was sitting up in bed, her arms wrapped round her knees, tears in her eyes.

'Are you okay?' I asked, rushing over to her, worried that she might have had a phone call with some bad news about her dad.

She sniffed. 'I don't like goodbyes.'

I sat down beside her and gathered her into my arms. 'Neither do I. But it's not a goodbye – it's a *see you later*, remember? We'll sort something out. I'll come to you or we'll meet halfway.'

She nodded into my chest. I wished we could have put a definite date in the diary last night but there was too much uncertainty at my end to do that. I needed to know about my job, secure an appointment with my solicitor, find out if Tilly was definitely taking Imogen to Scotland over the Easter holidays and work out when I was next seeing her as Tilly hadn't committed to any dates.

I released Poppy reluctantly and pulled on last night's clothes.

'What if I stayed one more night?' Poppy asked.

'I thought you had a meeting tomorrow morning.'

'I do, but I'm sure she'll be okay to move it and I can see my dad as soon as I get back on Tuesday. I'm desperate to see him but...' She broke off with a shrug. 'What do you say?'

'I'd love it. If I come straight from work, I can be here for quarter to seven. I'd have to leave early in the morning. Assuming it's okay to stay, that is.'

'What do you think?' she said, smiling shyly. 'It's a deal, then. I'll ring Mary but she's said all along that I'm okay until Friday. I wish I could stay that long.'

'One more night is an unexpected bonus so I'll happily take that.' I understood what a big thing it was for her to stay one extra day and wouldn't dream of putting any pressure on her to stay any longer.

'Do you want to get another takeaway?' she asked.

'No. I was going to cook last night so I'll do it tonight instead. Don't worry about getting any ingredients. Leave it with me. It'll all be sorted.'

I kissed her goodbye, thanking my lucky stars that I'd have one more night with her.

* * *

I arrived at work to chaos. There'd been a power outage during the night and we were massively behind on production so it was all hands on deck for the first few hours but at least it meant the time flew. When I returned to the office, Sal was there looking stony-faced. I didn't need to ask what was up as she thrust an envelope into my hand with my name on, marked private and confidential. I clocked a matching envelope on her desk with her name on and a screwed-up letter next to it.

'I'm not going to say anything,' she said, her voice brittle. 'I'll let you read it first.'

With a sigh, I ripped open the envelope and scanned down the contents of the letter.

'They can't be serious,' I cried.

'Makes you feel really valued, doesn't it?'

I sank down onto my chair, shaking my head. It was the news we'd finally been waiting for – an announcement of the restructure plans. I'd expected my job to be at risk in that they might reduce the number of shift managers, but I hadn't expected them to eliminate the role altogether. They were getting rid of all the shift manager and engineering manager positions and introducing a team of supervisors who'd report to a new assistant production manager. Existing shift and engineering managers would each have a consultation meeting over the next couple of weeks after which they'd be invited to apply for the supervisor roles.

'Less money for the same responsibilities,' Sal snapped as I scanned down the enclosed job description. 'Can you believe the nerve of it? Oh, and don't get excited about the assistant production manager role. Somebody from Bramblecote already has that.'

I flicked the letter over but there was nothing on the back. 'How do you know that?'

'Eloise told me when she delivered these. She stuck around while I opened it and poor lass got the brunt of my reaction, although she knew it wasn't directed at her. She's out of a job too.

They'll be running HR from their head office but she's welcome to apply for an HR assistant role if she wants. As if! The woman's the flaming HR Director!'

I scanned down the letter again, shaking my head in disbelief. 'That's made my next decision really easy.'

'Jumping ship?' she asked.

'Yep. No way am I taking a demotion *and* a pay cut to do exactly the same role. I'll take the redundancy money and run, thank you very much. You?'

'I've got an interview lined up on Thursday so, with any luck, I can take my dinky redundancy cheque and run straight into another job. Cuppa?'

'No. I think I'll pay Eloise a visit and see how she's doing. She's been really good to me.'

'She's been good to all of us and they've shafted her.'

They'd shafted us all yet, strangely, I felt really calm about it. Instead of being a disaster, this might be the best thing that could have happened. Like Barney suggested, I could take the summer off to spend with Imogen while Tilly had her hands full with her new twins, I'd have more time to see Poppy, and I could take that time for a major rethink. I knew for sure that I didn't want to work in a factory again. No more twelve-hour shifts. No more nights. It was an exciting thought.

But as I headed to Eloise's office, my heart sank. What about Scotland? I'd said last night that Poppy and I would find a way to make her present and future work together, but what if my future meant moving to Scotland because that was the only way I could see Imogen? I was going to have to do one hell of a lot of manifesting to stop that happening because I wanted my present and my future to include my daughter *and* Poppy. And I wanted it to be right here in Yorkshire.

29

POPPY

After Joel left, I struggled to drift back off to sleep so I got up and started working. I was used to rising early and found that, as long as I had a strong coffee to hand, I could race through tasks first thing. I'd therefore accomplished stacks before 9 a.m. at which point it felt reasonable to start making phone calls. My priority was to ring Marnie because, if Dad had taken a turn for the worse, staying an extra night wasn't an option. She assured me there was no need for me to rush back, especially when the break was doing exactly as intended – recharging my batteries. My next call was to Mary to confirm staying one more night, which was no problem. I rescheduled my client meeting for Wednesday and then FaceTimed Sharon.

'You look and sound a lot brighter than you have in a long time,' she said.

'I feel it. You were so right to push me to get away. I think I was close to breaking point. I love it here, I've made some friends and I got to see Phil.'

'I've spoken to him, and he said you were on good form. He said I was to ask you about the best man.'

My cheeks flushed as I told her about Joel and admitted that he was the reason for staying one more night.

'I'm so pleased for you,' she said, smiling. 'But why don't you stay until the end of the week?'

I shook my head. 'I'll fret too much about Dad and end up undoing all the good this past week has done me. I need to see him myself. I miss him and I need a hug.'

'I can understand that. I had a couple of lovely visits with him. He showed me his Poppy bear.'

He might not remember me but the love he clearly had for the bear I'd given him swelled my heart.

'I've made a big decision,' I told Sharon. 'I'm going to sell Dove Cottage. I know you and Ian have always loved it so, if you could see yourselves living there, you'd have first refusal. No offence taken if you're not interested.'

'Oh, gosh, honey. Selling up is huge.'

'I know, but it's the right thing to do. I need a fresh start and Dove Cottage needs somebody to love it again. Someone like you.'

'It would be perfect for us. I'll have a word with Ian and we can talk about it when you get back.'

When Sharon and I had finished catching up, I messaged Wilf to tell him I'd be back tomorrow. An hour later, a response came through and my stomach churned as I read it.

FROM WILF

Damon was at your house again this morning. I went out and he demanded to know where you were. He was more wound up than I've seen him. I don't like it. I think it's time to call the police

TO WILF

I'm so sorry he keeps turning up. Do you really think I need to involve the police? You don't think it's worth me trying to speak to him tomorrow?

FROM WILF

I have no problem telling him to clear off so no need to apologise. And yes to the police. If you think it's worth one more try to get through to him, that's your choice but it seems like you've given him plenty of chances already. Enjoy your last day and see you tomorrow. Benji says woof

I put my phone down with a sigh, wondering if Wilf was right. Damon hadn't crossed my mind for days, which had been lovely, but now I felt a heaviness in my stomach knowing I was going to have to face him tomorrow. Was the situation serious enough to involve the police? If an ex-police officer was suggesting it, perhaps it was, but I still preferred the idea I'd discussed with Phil of getting his mum to have a word first.

Feeling restless after Wilf's text, I drove to Bloomsberry's to get something for lunch and some small gifts to thank Amber, Fizz, Natasha and Samantha for helping me with my wedding attire.

As I wandered through the extensive gift section, my eyes were drawn to a flash of something yellow in a clear plastic bag with a sale sticker on it. I looked closer and saw that it was a felt blue tit in a bag with felt versions of several other common garden birds – a great tit, goldfinch, chaffinch, bullfinch, house sparrow and robin. It seemed they were part of a mobile, but the hanging part was broken and the starling was missing so it had been reduced. I thought about Dad's disappointment on wet days when he couldn't see as many birds. If I bought some of those removable hanging strips, we could hang the felt birds in his bedroom and he could see garden birds every single day. I popped it in my basket and continued my search.

I found some scented candles for Fizz, Samantha and Natasha, and a wooden heart sculpture with tealights around the base for Amber. In the wedding section, I spotted some washi tape, sequins and stickers which I thought Imogen might like for the pages in her scrapbook so I couldn't resist buying them for Joel to pass on to her. I wished I could see her one more time before I left. She was such a delight to be around, but it was time to return to Winchcote and put plans into place to get my life back on track.

My final stop was the food section for lunch. I paused by the fridge, smiling. Was it really only six days since I first saw Joel right here? So much had happened since then. Who knew that I'd meet the man of my dreams by a fridge full of ready meals?

* * *

I heard a car pull up outside around mid-afternoon and was surprised to see Fizz approaching the house with shopping bags in her hands.

'Food delivery,' she said when I opened the door.

'For me?'

'Courtesy of Chef Joel. I understand he's making you a meal tonight.'

'He sent you shopping?'

She laughed. 'I offered. I was going anyway.'

I led her through to the kitchen.

'You're in for such a treat,' she said as she placed several items in the fridge. 'Joel's an amazing chef. Such a shame he didn't make a career of it after all.'

'I thought he'd worked in the factory straight from college.'

'Oh, he did, but he studied catering at college and...' She shook her head. 'Not my story to tell. Ask him about it later. When Grandma said you were staying an extra night, I wondered if he might have had something to do with it.'

'He had *everything* to do with it,' I admitted. 'And if it wasn't for my dad, I'd stay even longer. I don't know what's come over me, Fizz. I'm not the sort of person who throws her plans out the window for a man she's only just met.'

Fizz smiled at me. 'That's because you hadn't met someone worth doing that for and now you have. I'm so thrilled for you both. Joel's a great bloke and I've never understood why he hasn't been snapped up, but I do now. He was waiting for you to come along.'

It was such a lovely thought, and it gave me a warm glow inside.

'Joel has had such a nightmare with women dismissing him as too nice and just wanting to be friends,' Fizz said as we sat down in the lounge with mugs of tea. 'How can someone be *too nice*? I've never understood that. It's as though nice equates to boring and Joel is *not* boring. He's great fun.'

We discussed the friendship aspect of relationships and Fizz agreed that, for her, friendship was fundamental for making a relationship work.

'Phoebe and I were friends first for a long time and we're both convinced it's why our relationship is so strong. You're absolutely right that you can have passion *and* friendship.'

'I think Joel's lovely and I feel like a little schoolgirl going all gooey over him!'

'It's super cute to see and I know Joel will pull out all the stops to make the distance work for you both. I can tell you mean the world to him.'

'It's mutual.'

'Good. Because I have something for you.' She dipped into her bag and handed me an envelope. 'An invitation to our wedding. It's the last Saturday in May at Hedgehog Hollow.'

My throat tightened with emotion, a sense of belonging enveloping me. 'Thank you so much! I'd love to come.'

'Whatever happens with you and Joel, Phoebe and I want you there. But I don't think we have anything to worry about with you two. I think this is it, isn't it?'

Tears pricked my eyes and I nodded. 'It feels like it.'

She clapped her hands together, squealing. 'I'm so happy for you both. I wish I could find out more, but I've got to love you and leave you. Phoebe's meeting me at Bumblebee Barn in ten minutes to finalise a few things with Natasha and Zara, our awesome wedding planners.'

I presented Fizz with a gift bag containing her sandals and the thank-you candle and asked her if she wouldn't mind being delivery woman for the others. I'd also bought another bouquet of flowers for Mary and she said she'd deliver them too as her next stop after Bumblebee Barn was her grandma's house. I followed her out to her car and placed the flowers across the back seat.

'It's been an absolute joy meeting you,' she said. 'Phoebe and I have both sent you friend requests on Facebook and followed you on Instagram. Our phone numbers and emails are on the invitation so there's no escaping us. You're one of us now, like it or not.'

'I like it,' I said, laughing. 'Very much.'

She hugged me tightly and I had that sensation once more of having found something very special in Yorkshire. When she'd gone, I stood on the drive looking at the house for several minutes. It was so beautiful. I could definitely see myself living here and, more than that, I could imagine myself living here with Joel. Was it really possible to meet somebody and know within forty-eight hours that they were the person you wanted to spend the rest of your life with? Because that's how I felt about Joel and I couldn't wait to see him tonight.

* * *

My early start this morning had put me ahead with my work and I was able to stop at five but my excitement at seeing Joel meant I was quicker getting ready than usual, leaving way too much time before he arrived. I decided to distract myself with an episode of *Darrington Detects* but hadn't got far into it before Wilf rang and my stomach lurched. Wilf texted – he *never* rang.

'I'm so sorry to interrupt your holiday but Damon has just been to my house demanding to know what you're doing in York and who all the people you're with are.'

'What? Where's he got that from?'

'I don't know. Obviously I didn't correct him about the location but wasn't that wedding near York? Have you put something on social media?'

'Nothing! I've been really careful not to...' I closed my eyes and groaned. 'My new friends connected with me on the socials. They might have tagged me in some photos.'

'That's probably it, then. You might want to check there's nothing connecting you to the holiday cottage. I'm guessing there isn't with it being York he mentioned.'

'Thanks for the heads up and I'm so sorry he turned up at your house. I never wanted you to get involved.'

'I can hold my own with him so don't you worry. I'll let you go so you can do whatever you need to do to make sure he has no access to your information. But please, Poppy, call the police. This isn't normal.'

The second I disconnected, I opened up Facebook. As

suspected, I'd been tagged in several photos but they were all wedding-related with no mention of Whisperwood Farmhouse. The privacy settings on them were for friends and family only so Damon could only have seen them if we were friends and we weren't... were we? My stomach lurched again. Maybe we were! I had a vague recollection of him sending me a friend request when I first moved back home but he never posted anything himself and had never engaged with the few posts I shared so I'd forgotten about it. Sure enough, he was there on my friends list. I removed and blocked him before double checking that my privacy settings were for friends only, which they were. Fennington Hall being tagged wasn't going to lead Damon to me even if he had been poking around on my socials to see where I was and what I was doing. He knew I was in Yorkshire, but it was an enormous area and there was no way he could track me down to Whisperwood Farmhouse. I could relax. For now. Returning to Dove Cottage tomorrow would be an entirely different matter.

When Joel arrived, I was so grateful to have his strong arms around me as I told him all about Damon.

'He doesn't sound stable,' he said. 'I agree with your neighbour. I think you should let the police know he's stalking you.'

'Stalking? But he's never threatened me.'

'I'm not sure he has to. Hang on.'

Joel tapped something into his phone and brought up a page from the police website and scrolled down to the definition of stalking. The words *obsession* and *aggressive* jumped out at me. Examples were given and several of them applied to Damon's recent behaviour which Joel was quick to point out.

'He's repeatedly turned up at your home uninvited and he went to your dad's care home knowing you'd be there. That's not normal behaviour.'

Hearing him repeat Damon's behaviour back to me made me

view it differently. If a friend told me that someone had been doing all that to them, I'd have immediately called out stalking and urged them to go to the police. Why hadn't I realised this before now?

Joel pointed to a section listing with the acronym *FOUR* for the four warning signs of stalking behaviour: *Fixated*, *Obsessive*, *Unwanted*, *Repeated*. Yes to all! I'd made excuses for Damon so far, heaping the blame on myself for not being clear enough with him, but how clear did I need to be? I'd said no more times than I cared to remember. I'd asked him to leave, I'd told him not to come to The Larks. Yes, he'd helped me and shown me kindness on one of the worst days of my life, but I didn't owe him my life as a result.

'I'll call the police when I get back.' I sighed heavily. 'Stalking. I never thought... Or maybe deep down I did and I just didn't have the headspace to deal with it.'

Joel hugged me. 'You've got me and you've got Wilf. We'll get it sorted.'

We moved into the kitchen to prepare the meal, but Joel said he had something to show me first. He handed me a letter he'd been given at work about the restructure.

I winced as I scanned down it. 'That sounds harsh. I'm so sorry.'

'Don't be, because I'm not. I've already told Eloise that I want to take the redundancy package and leave as soon as possible. It might take a while before she can get that confirmed, but I feel a whole lot lighter knowing I'm leaving.'

'You sound really positive.'

'I feel it. I'm thinking now that it's the best thing that could have happened. It's time for a change. I stayed way too long in something that was only ever meant to be a summer job while I decided what I wanted to do with my life.'

'When Fizz dropped the food off, she mentioned that you were going to be a chef but she wouldn't say anything more – said it was your tale to tell.'

Joel laughed. 'That makes it sound exciting and it really wasn't.'

He told me about studying catering at college and the intention to go into the family business but how working for his dad and uncle caused tension, so he ducked out to avoid a family rift.

'Why didn't you look for a job in a different restaurant?'

'Looking back, it's a stupid reason. The part that gave me a buzz and still does is experimenting. If my own dad was struggling to let me have free rein over dishes, what hope was there for me anywhere else? I'd have had to start right at the bottom and I couldn't face it, so I ditched that career completely.'

'Do you regret it?'

'Occasionally.' He smiled and shook his head. 'Regularly. Every so often, I thought about it but the reality was that working in a restaurant would be no better for Imogen than working shifts. In fact, it would be worse because at least shifts gave me some time off on evenings and weekends. In a restaurant, they're the hours I'd have been needed so I'd have never got to see her.'

While our meal was in the oven, we moved into the lounge and I showed him the felt birds I'd bought at Bloomsberry's and how the staff must have thought I was a little mad when I'd stood by the fridge for a while, smiling at the ready meals.

'Special place,' he said. 'Where dreams come true.'

My heart melted as he tenderly kissed me.

'Look what Fizz gave me today.' I reached for her wedding invite and waved it at Joel. 'Looks like you're stuck with me until at least the end of May.'

Joel frowned and counted on his fingers. 'Oh, I dunno,' he

said, his voice teasing. 'That's a whole ten weeks away. It's a lot to ask.'

'Cheeky!' I cried, playfully whacking him with a cushion.

He cupped my face between his hands and gently kissed me. 'There's another four weddings after that and I'd like you to be with me at all of them. And for any weddings, anniversaries and births that come along after that.'

'Sounds perfect,' I whispered.

* * *

'Oh, my God! Joel! This is delicious!' I forked in another mouthful, releasing a moan of pleasure. 'If this is indicative of your skills in the kitchen, I'm *never* letting you go.'

'It's a deal,' he said with a grin. 'With my cooking and your first aid and stain removal abilities, we might achieve domestic perfection.'

Every mouthful was a delight with the flavours working so perfectly together. It was criminal that he'd never been able to showcase his abilities. I dropped my fork with a clatter as an idea struck me.

'Everything okay?' Joel asked looking concerned.

'I've just had a thought. When Amber gave me a tour of the farm, she showed me the barn for the farm shop and there was another empty barn. I asked her what it was going to be and she said they didn't know. What if you opened your own bistro there?'

'On Barney's farm?'

'Yes! There's a farm shop near where I live and it has a bistro next door where the chef makes meals using the local produce the shop sells. Most of the business is day trade with just two or three nights a week and it does brilliantly. You could do something like that. You'd need to work weekends at the start, but you could take on a weekend chef once it was up and running.'

Joel's eyes lit up. 'I know the barn you mean. It would be a good size for it.'

'What do you think? Would something like that interest you?'

'I'd love it.'

I could tell from his wide smile that he was already imagining what it might look like.

'Do you think Amber and Barney would be interested?'

'I think they'd love it too. We'd need to get planning permission, but it's a working farm and it's an existing building...'

We moved back into the lounge and spent the rest of the evening talking about how a bistro at Bumblebee Barn might work. I shared my little fantasy about opening an apiary on Barney's farm, and supplying honey to the shop alongside my Honey Bee Hugs skincare range. The future sounded so idyllic. But a dose of reality suddenly hit me.

'A shadow just crossed your face,' Joel said. 'What is it?'

'What if Tilly does move to Scotland? I'm assuming you'd go too.'

He sighed heavily. 'I can't imagine moving away from this area and all my friends but, if that's the only way I can see Imogen regularly, I won't have a choice.'

'When are you seeing your solicitor?'

'Thursday morning.'

'Let's hope it's good news and she can't move Imogen without your agreement. If she can and you have to relocate, we'll find a way to make it work. Not sure what, but...'

I tried to imagine me living here without him and it felt so wrong. I wanted this farmhouse but I wanted it to be *ours* rather than *mine*. I imagined dropping off honey at the Bumblebee Barn farm shop and seeing an empty barn instead of Joel waving at me from his bistro and it was so clear to me that, while I wanted my future to be here in this place with these people, I didn't want it without Joel. I could find another house if Mary had already sold Whisperwood Farmhouse before I was ready to move, I could find somewhere else for my hives if Amber and Barney had already found a beekeeper, but being here without Joel was a dealbreaker. If he announced that he was moving to Australia, I'd be booking my ticket.

I took his hand in mine. This didn't even feel brave – it felt right. 'They have honey bees in the Highlands, right?'

'Aren't there bees everywhere?' he asked, looking momentarily confused. And then a smile spread across his face as he evidently registered what I meant. 'You'd come with me?'

I nodded. 'I never thought I'd find someone like you and, now that I have, I don't want to let you go. If your home needs to be in Scotland, then so does mine.'

30

JOEL

I stared at Poppy, my heart racing. 'You mean that?'

'Every word.'

'But you love it here.'

'I do, but there are other places, other houses, other farms. Are there other Joels? Other Imogens?' She shook her head. 'I think the pair of you are unique.'

She'd included Imogen. She'd unconditionally accepted that we came as a two-for-one deal and that my future had to be where my daughter was. I already knew I was falling in love with Poppy, but those feelings switched up a gear.

'You're pretty unique yourself,' I said, drawing her into a kiss.

How amazing was she to be willing to give up on her dreams to be with me? I didn't want her to have to do that. I wanted her to have Whisperwood Farmhouse, to be the Bumblebee Barn beekeeper, to spend time with my friends who'd welcomed her into the fold. It gave me renewed strength for my solicitor's appointment. For Poppy and for Imogen, I was going to fight Tilly so hard. Imogen *would* get to stay with her friends and Poppy *would* fulfil her dreams.

We lay cuddled up on the sofa for a while. I gazed into the flames flickering in the log burner thinking how homely Whisperwood Farmhouse felt. I'd had my place decorated after Tilly moved in but hadn't done anything with it since. She'd made it all cosy with pictures, candles, cushions and throws which she'd taken with her and I'd never replaced. Nineteen Conifer Close was a house but it wasn't a home, and I hadn't realised that until now. It wasn't right that a holiday cottage could feel more like a home than my own place. No wonder Poppy had fallen in love with the farmhouse.

'Any update on Chez?' Poppy asked after a while.

'Not yet. I tried ringing Mum on the way here but there was no answer.'

'Why don't you call her now for a quick check-in? I bought some hot chocolate in Bloomsberry's earlier. I can make us some while you're doing that.'

Mum answered this time and said they'd spent most of the day with Chez and he was embarrassed by the way he'd spoken to me and extremely sorry about throwing the bottle.

'He doesn't know what possessed him and he promises he wasn't aiming at you.'

I wasn't going to contradict her. The more I replayed it in my head, the more convinced I was that he *had* meant for the bottle to hit me. I put that down to his drunken state as I couldn't imagine him doing that sober, no matter how angry he was, but I wasn't going to make an issue of it. I also wasn't going to make an issue of the fact that he could have phoned or messaged me to say sorry himself. Sending a message via Mum hardly smacked of sincerity – it was simply another sign of how immature my brother really was.

Mum said they looked forward to spending the day with me on Wednesday. Chez had agreed to join us and they'd mediate if necessary. If he didn't take the opportunity to apologise to me in person then, the mediation would definitely be needed as I wasn't going to let him get away with it. Drunk or not, his behaviour had been completely unacceptable, and I was sick of people walking all over me just because I was the nice bloke. It didn't mean I was also a pushover. I wasn't accepting any more crap from him, and I wasn't accepting it from Tilly either.

'Your dad's spoken to him about Portugal but it's still a no,' Mum said. 'He's convinced he'll get back with Lorna once she calms down and accepts his apology.'

'Seriously? I know I keep saying this, but how many times can you keep breaking up before you accept it doesn't work?'

'We've said the same thing, but he's convinced he knows best.'

'Didn't she say it was for good this time?' I vividly remembered him hurling that at me as though it was my fault.

'Apparently she's said that before.' Mum sighed. 'We'll just have to see what happens.'

As we finished the call, Poppy appeared with the drinks and I filled her in on the conversation with Mum.

'It sounds like you get on well with your parents,' she said. 'The problems from the restaurant didn't cause any lasting damage?'

'I left before they could. There were a couple of tricky months but then it was back to normal. They're both great and I really miss them, but we speak regularly and have lots of video calls.' I sipped on my hot chocolate and smiled approvingly. 'You said something about your parents at the wedding – about them not wanting children – but then you changed the subject. If you want to talk about it…'

She held my gaze for a few moments before nodding. 'You know what? I think I do. The woman I call Mum – Joy Wells – was really my great-aunt. The woman who gave birth to me was called

Evie Miller and she was Mum's niece, daughter of her older brother. Evie discovered she was pregnant when she was sixteen but she'd already split up with my birth dad by then. She was an only child and her parents were incredibly protective and strict with her. Despite that, they had a good relationship but she knew they'd hit the roof when they found out. She tried to keep it secret, but horrendous sickness put paid to that and, as predicted, they went berserk. They forced her to tell them who the father was and marched her round to his house demanding he *do the right thing* and marry her. His parents were really strict too so they were of the same mind, but Evie refused to marry someone she didn't love. Her parents gave her an ultimatum – marry him before I was born and they might play a small role in her life, or leave home and never see them again. Evie couldn't believe they were so prehistoric in their attitudes or that they'd be so willing to cut her out of their lives, so she packed a bag and ran away. My parents were disgusted when they heard what had happened and they managed to find Evie and take her in.

'A couple of weeks sleeping rough had taken its toll on her. Mum said she'd always been a vivacious child, full of fire, and it was as though somebody had blown out her spark. After I was born, Evie had severe post-natal depression. She'd managed to convince herself that her parents would forgive her and want to see their only grandchild and she asked Mum and Dad to invite them round, but they wanted nothing to do with her or me.'

'That's awful. She must have been devastated.'

'She was. She slid further into depression and overdosed on her meds three times. Mum and Dad had made a choice not to have children but they became parents to her and to me.'

'Was there a reason they didn't want kids?' I asked when she paused.

'They loved their careers and each other and felt no strong

desire to have a family. They had big plans to retire early to travel the world and had been saving for years, but they gave all that up for Evie and me.'

'What happened to her?'

'Mum bought my first school uniform and Evie cried when she saw me in it. Mum told me it was as though she suddenly realised that four years had passed and she'd missed every milestone. Mum suggested she come to school with me on my first day, so she did, and that very afternoon she contacted her doctor and asked for help. Across that year, she made great progress. She got a part-time job in a pub and took on a lot more responsibility for me and then, shortly after I turned five, she was on her way home from work when a drunk driver travelling the wrong way down the dual carriageway ploughed into her.'

My stomach plummeted. 'Oh, Poppy. No!'

'He didn't even have his lights on, so she stood no chance. He'd been out for his work Christmas do, took advantage of the free bar and was too stingy to pay for a taxi home. He walked away with a few bruises, a broken wrist and a two-year suspended sentence. Don't even get me started on the injustice of that.' She took a deep breath. 'After that, my parents officially adopted me, and they were the best parents I could ever have dreamed of.'

'I'm so sorry about Evie. Do you remember her?'

'I have vague recollections of there being a woman in the house who had long, dark hair, but nothing concrete.'

'What about your birth father?'

Poppy shook her head. 'Dad went to see him and his parents after I was born, but he wasn't interested. They told him there was an open door if he ever changed his mind but he never came and I've never wanted to find him. Joy and Stanley Wells are my parents and I don't want or need a relationship with the man who was effectively a sperm donor. But sometimes...' She sighed heavily.

'Sometimes...?' I prompted as she stared off into the distance.

Her eyes met mine. 'I've never told anyone this before. Sometimes I feel guilty for entering their lives when they'd made a decision not to have children. It's my issue. They never made me feel like that and my logical mind is telling me that they're the ones who found Evie, invited her in, insisted she stay and chose to adopt me. I wasn't the one influencing it all. But I think about how different their lives could have been without me. Mum loved the quote *do one thing every day that scares you* and told me the scariest thing they ever did was become parents when they weren't prepared for it. I worry that they'd have preferred not to face that particular fear and I guess that's why I've devoted the past seven years to caring for them both. I love them and I'd have done it regardless, but I think I've taken it to the near-burnout extreme because I want to prove how grateful I am to them for throwing away their dreams to look after me.'

'I see it differently. I don't think they threw away their dreams. I think they found a different dream.'

Tears welled in her eyes and I noticed her swallowing hard. I raised her hand to my lips and kissed it, keeping my eyes on hers.

'As for that quote, doing the things that scare us can bring great rewards. From what you've told me about your parents, that's what raising you was – something scary and unexpected which changed their lives for the better.'

'You really think that?'

'I'm sure of it. When Tilly announced she was pregnant, I felt that fear. We hadn't planned on a baby until after we were married. We both felt too young and unprepared and, while the situation with Tilly now is far from ideal, I've never regretted for even a second that Imogen came along. It terrified me, but

Imogen changed my life for the better and I'm sure your parents felt the same about you.'

We talked some more about Poppy's childhood and I assured her it sounded idyllic with parents who loved her wholeheartedly and unconditionally.

As we were getting ready for bed a little later, I noticed a frame on the dressing table with that quote embroidered inside it. Poppy told me that her mum had made it and why.

'Have you done anything lately that's scared you?' I asked as we settled under the duvet.

'Everything about this trip has scared me, but it's all turned out to be amazing. What about you?'

She'd been honest with me earlier about wanting to follow me to Scotland and I didn't want her to have any doubts about my strength of feelings for her so I needed to be honest in return – more honest than I'd ever been with anyone.

'Being with you scares me because I already know I can't bear to be without you and my heart is going to break into a million pieces when I have to leave you in the morning.'

Tears glistened in her eyes as she cupped my face in her hands and drew me into a kiss.

31

POPPY

I pushed open the door to Dove Cottage on Tuesday afternoon and stepped over the threshold with a heavy heart. My eyes were itchy from shedding so many tears over the last half an hour. I'd left a piece of my heart behind in Whisperwood Farmhouse and the rest of it at The Larks where I'd just visited Dad.

Picturing his face when I gave him the felt birds set me off again as I closed and locked the door behind me. He'd insisted we go to his room, where he'd carefully hung each bird on the removable hanging strips I'd stuck to his wall. He was particularly captivated by the robin.

'People think robins only come out at Christmas but you can see them all year round,' he said, stroking the robin's colourful breast. 'The person who made this got the colour right. They're orange rather than red.'

'So they are,' I said, as though I hadn't realised. Dad always liked it when he could teach me something and I had no problem hearing his lessons hundreds of times because the joy in his eyes was worth the repetition.

He sat down on his bed, and I sat beside him.

'Do you know why people associate them with Christmas?' he asked.

I did, but I pleaded ignorance.

'There are two main stories. The first is from the Victorian days. The postmen wore red-breasted uniforms and, because of that, they were nicknamed robins. The robin birds started appearing on Christmas cards to represent the robin postmen and, because of that, people associate robins with Christmas and notice them more at that time of year.'

He bobbed the robin across the bed, as though it was hopping around a garden.

'The other story is that, when Jesus was on the cross, a robin appeared and sat on His shoulder, singing a song to distract Him from the pain. The blood dripped from Jesus's crown of thorns onto the robin and stained his chest and, after that, all the robins were born with a red – or orange – breast. Which story do you like best?'

'Impossible to choose,' I said. 'They're both lovely, just like that little chap.'

He bobbed the robin again. 'I think so.'

The hug he gave me without prompt nearly broke me. I bit my lip as I held on tight, hoping he couldn't feel the silent tears dripping from my cheeks and soaking into his blazer.

He looked tired so I left him to have a nap, clutching the robin in his hand, and sought out Marnie, who admitted that she had noticed a decline across the week but nothing significant enough to have bothered me, knowing I'd need to regain my strength for what was to come. I asked what she thought about moving him to another home.

'It's not beyond the realms of possibility but I personally wouldn't recommend it and...' She sighed heavily. 'Completely transparent as always. I don't think it'll be long.'

They were the words I'd been dreading. 'Months? Weeks? Days?' I asked, the words barely audible.

'Impossible to predict, but I'd suggest you prepare yourself for weeks.'

'But he was really lucid today.'

Marnie didn't say anything and I guessed what the words would be if she had. *Yes, but yesterday he could barely string a sentence together.* My heart shattered.

* * *

By the time I'd unpacked and set a load of washing away, my eyes were a little less red and my face not so blotchy. I nipped next door with a box of Wilf's favourite shortbread biscuits to both apologise and thank him for getting involved in the Damon situation.

'Have you reconsidered going to the police?' he asked. 'There's something not right about him.'

'I will. I just can't face it today. I've been to see Dad and it's not good. We could be talking weeks.'

'Oh, Poppy. I'm so sorry.'

'It's a lot to go through the Damon stuff after that.'

'Understandable. Hopefully he won't turn up but you might want to get CCTV or one of those doorbell cameras installed for when he does. Video evidence might be helpful.'

When I returned home, I went straight online and ordered a doorbell camera for next-day delivery, after which I made appointments for two estate agents to come round to value Dove Cottage later in the week. As soon as I told the estate agents which house it was, they said they had people on their lists desperate to buy a property like mine in Winchcote and I'd likely have an offer before a *for sale* board even went up. If Ian and

Sharon weren't interested, it was good to know I wouldn't struggle to sell. Booking the valuations wasn't a kneejerk reaction to what Marnie had said because I'd already made the firm decision. It was more of a practical thing – if Dad didn't have long, I wouldn't have the time or inclination to organise it later, so it was best to get the ball rolling now.

Next, I rang Sharon to say that I was back and had scheduled a couple of estate agents to value the house. She'd spoken to Ian and they were both very interested in making Dove Cottage their home, but it had been years since they'd visited so would need a good look around before they confirmed that for definite.

'On to less positive news...' I said, filling her in on my visit to Dad and what Marnie had said.

I felt strangely detached as I talked to Sharon about Dad. Marnie had warned me that the emotions I felt as Dad approached end of life might not be what I expected and I remembered reading about that in a booklet. Because I'd started to lose Dad when the Alzheimer's took hold, and properly lost him when he no longer remembered me, I'd done so much of my grieving already and might find that I felt numb and possibly even relieved. That made sense to me – after all, who'd want to see someone they loved go through all of that suffering?

But when Joel FaceTimed me in the evening and asked me how my visit to Dad had been and whether he'd liked the felt birds, I broke down in tears.

'I wish I could be there for you,' he said, looking tearful himself.

'I know you would be if you could, but you've got an important couple of days ahead of you and then you're back at work. Besides, she said weeks, not days. And even then I know you might not be able to be here with me.'

Feeling the tears again, I asked if we could change the subject.

'No problem,' Joel said. 'Tilly messaged me to say they're definitely going to Scotland on holiday – away for ten days from this Saturday. I said I wanted to see Imogen before they go but she ignored that so I sent her another message suggesting that Imogen didn't go to Scotland with them at all and she spend the ten days with me instead.'

'I'm guessing that got a reply?'

'Yep. Cue enormous rant about precious family time and me being ridiculous for demanding to have so much time with Imogen. I don't know how she could type it without seeing the double standards. The upshot is that I've got a great example of how unreasonable she is to show to my solicitor.'

'Did you say your parents are seeing her this week?'

'Yes, all confirmed for Thursday. I'm picking her up from school and we're meeting Mum and Dad for tea.'

'Glad you've got that sorted. Give her my love.'

'I will, and I'll give her that bag of crafts. She's going to love them.'

I updated Joel on the rest of my day and told him that there'd been no sign of Damon so far but, on Wilf's advice, I'd ordered a doorbell camera.

I yawned and apologised. 'I don't want to say goodbye but I can barely keep my eyes open.'

'I'm not surprised. You've had a long drive and a tough day. You get some sleep and I'll speak to you tomorrow night.'

I wished him luck with Chez tomorrow and blew him a kiss. Today had been tough but having Joel to talk to was a great comfort. Even though he hadn't been here in person, I'd felt his hugs. I was going to need a lot of those over the next few weeks.

32

JOEL

I met Mum and Dad at their B&B the following day. There was a small residents' lounge which the landlady had told them was almost never used during the day – more conducive for a serious talk than going to a busy café.

'Chester went for a run this morning,' Mum said after I'd hugged her and Dad. 'He got lost and was out longer than expected so he's just having a shower. He sends his apologies and says being late wasn't intentional.'

I wasn't surprised at the tardiness – punctuality wasn't my brother's strongest point – but I was shocked at the run. Chez had been known to lift the occasional dumbbell or do a few crunches but he detested most forms of exercise, especially running.

Mum was pouring tea from a pot when Chez appeared, his hair still damp from the shower.

'All right?' he asked.

'All right. You?'

'Yeah. Getting by.'

It wasn't the finest start to a conversation, but it had at least involved some eye contact. Mum offered him a tea, but he produced an energy drink from his pocket and opened that before sitting down.

Silence.

I could have kicked things off but I couldn't help thinking I'd be accused of parenting again if I took control, so I picked up my cup and saucer and sat back in my chair, waiting for someone else to make a start. I wasn't expecting that person to be Chez.

'I'm sorry about what I said on Saturday and I'm really sorry about the bottle. I don't know why I did that. I shouldn't... I mean, I could have... Erm... I know I was a twat at the wedding and before that with the mess and eating your food and what me and Lorna did in...' He glanced at Mum and Dad, whose expressions were blank. It was the only part I'd missed out. They didn't need to know what their teenage son and his girlfriend had been doing on their granddaughter's bed.

'Yeah, erm, all of it. Sorry, bro.'

It wasn't particularly eloquent but it was an apology, it sounded genuine enough, and he'd acknowledged that the issue was bigger than the wedding incident. I wondered how much he actually recalled of what he'd said that night so I wasn't going to brush it straight under the carpet like I usually did. He needed to know how badly his behaviour had affected me.

'You do realise that what you said really hurt me? Or was that the intention?'

He shrugged. 'I'm struggling at the minute and I guess I do need help but you can't seem to stop being a parent and it kills me. All I want is for you to be my brother! Why's that so hard for you?'

I bit back a sigh as his voice got higher and louder. What had been the point in the apology when he clearly still thought I was the one in the wrong?

'Let's explore what that means,' Dad said, his voice calm.

'Imagine we're living round the corner from you and you're struggling. What would you want or need from us as parents?'

Chez shrugged once more. 'For you to listen, to care, not to judge, to be patient with me.'

'All fair points. And what would you want or need from Joel as your brother?'

'I'd want him to listen, to be there for me, to get me, not to get arsey or impatient.'

Dad nodded. 'What's different about those two lists?'

I looked towards Dad with admiration. Well played that man.

'Chez?' he prompted.

'Nowt, I guess,' Chez muttered.

'Exactly. What I'm hearing is that you've lashed out at your brother for being exactly what you wanted and needed him to be – a caring brother displaying exactly the same behaviours a caring parent would demonstrate.'

'But he's always having a go at me about being messy.'

'It's *his* house,' Mum said, 'so he has every right to be annoyed. It's about showing respect for the person putting a roof over your head, especially when they have no obligation to do it.'

Chez sipped on his drink, seemingly mulling this over.

'He had a go at me for eating all his food,' he said eventually.

'Did you pay for any of the food?' Dad asked.

'No.'

'Did you ask him if it was okay to eat it?'

'No.'

'Then please explain what makes you think you're the one who's right to be angry in this situation.'

God, Dad was good.

Chez shrugged again. 'I don't have the right.'

Over the next couple of hours, we explored everything that had been building up inside Chez until he finally admitted that he was angry with them for abandoning him when he needed them. Mum cried at that point, and I was upset for her but I was glad Chez had finally admitted it. I'd long suspected it and had even questioned him but he'd told me *Don't be so pathetic – I'm not a kid who needs Mummy and Daddy to look after me and tuck me in at night.*

We paused the conversation while we went out for lunch in a nearby café, making small talk. There was so much I wanted to tell my parents about my job and Imogen and Poppy, but I didn't want to take the attention away from Chez and onto me. Towards the end of lunch, the subject of going to Portugal arose again and I threw in my own encouragement for him to take a break, but he remained adamant he wasn't going. His mission was to get a job and win Lorna back and I wondered if the run this morning was something to do with that. He'd told me before that she'd joked about him developing a beer belly prematurely and that the closest thing he was ever going to get to a six-pack was a trip to the fridge.

After lunch, Chez said he needed some space. I personally thought there was more to discuss but, in his shoes, I'd have wanted a timeout so we wished him a relaxing afternoon and said we'd see him for tea. He messaged a few hours later to say he needed longer to clear his head and wouldn't be joining us for tea. It was disappointing and it felt like a cop-out, but we'd made a good start and not having Chez around gave me a chance to update Mum and Dad on everything that was going on with me.

We'd settled the bill after our pub tea that evening and were heading back to the B&B when my phone rang.

'It's Harry,' I said, surprised to see his number on the screen.

'Hi, Joel,' he said when I answered. 'Can you come to my flat? Chez is here and he's in a right state. I don't think he's drunk, but he's not making any sense. I don't know what to do.'

My stomach lurched. 'Stay with him and try to calm him down. I'll be there really soon.'

We were only a few minutes from the B&B, so we walked Mum back then Dad and I power-walked across the town centre to Harry's flat. I wanted to tell Dad not to worry but how could I reassure him when I was worried about my brother? If only he'd come out for tea with us as planned!

A woman answered the door who I presumed was Deana. After everything I'd heard about her from Chez, I'd expected her to look hard as nails but she was pretty and petite and immediately made me think of a nursery school teacher.

'Thank God you're here,' she said, her tone anxious. 'He's in the lounge. We don't understand what he's saying. We're so worried.'

Chez was sitting in the middle of the lounge floor, arms wrapped round his crossed legs, head down, rocking back and forth and muttering.

'Chester?' Dad crouched beside him. 'Chester? It's Dad. Can you hear me?'

Dad gave his shoulder a gentle nudge and repeated what he'd just said, but Chester carried on mumbling incoherently.

'How long's he been here?' I asked.

'Ten, maybe fifteen minutes before I called you,' Harry said, his face pale.

'I found him,' Deana said, her eyes filling with tears. 'I went out to get some chips and he was on the bench outside the flat, rocking like that. I rang Harry and we managed to get him up the stairs together. We catch the occasional word but nothing makes sense.'

'He says Lorna a lot,' Harry added, putting his arm round Deana and kissing the top of her head.

I was only getting a snapshot of Deana in unusual circumstances but my initial impression was that she was far from the monster that Chez had made her out to be. I could see that the flat was immaculate and I suspected their clashes had been over Chester's immaturity and mess.

Dad tried to move Chester's arms, and something fell out of his hand onto the wooden floor.

'A ring box,' I said, reaching for it. 'Don't say...'

'She said no,' Chez murmured. 'No, no, no, no, no.'

I flicked it open, grimacing at the diamond ring inside. I turned it round for Dad to see and he released a heavy sigh. I closed the box and zipped it safely inside my jacket pocket.

'We need to get you back to the B&B,' Dad said. 'Come on, Chester, you've got to help us here. We can talk about this later.'

'I can drive you,' Deana offered. 'It'll take you ages to walk him like this.'

* * *

'Drink this.' Mum held a glass of water against Chester's cracked lips in his room at the B&B.

It had been a struggle, but we'd managed to bundle him out to Deana's car and into his bedroom at this end. The odd sentence tumbled out, but he was mostly incoherent. I'd messaged Poppy from the car with the briefest explanation and apologies that I might not be able to call her. She'd messaged back to suggest we check his pupils in case he'd taken something he shouldn't have, but his pupils were thankfully normal.

It took about an hour of constant questions and sips of water to finally get the story from Chester. He'd gone for a walk after lunch to clear his head, and his shoelace came undone, so he bent down to fasten it. When he stood up, he realised he was outside a jeweller's and there was a ring in the window which caught his eye. Suddenly that seemed like the answer to winning Lorna back so he asked her to meet him to talk. She agreed but, instead of talking, he proposed. She hadn't just said no to his proposal – she'd given him a list of reasons why he was unsuitable husband material ranging from messy to immature, selfish to moody. Every accusation had stung Chester all the more because they'd been the things that we'd talked about this afternoon which, deep down, he knew to be true about himself. Lorna had told him that they brought out the worst in each other and the best thing for both of them was to never see each other again. Seeing her walking away, knowing it truly was over for good this time, had broken something in him. None of us were experts, but it sounded like he'd had some sort of breakdown and had been trying to get to Harry for help, but he hadn't quite made it. It was lucky that Deana had found him.

There were twin beds in Chez's room so we all agreed that Mum would stay with him for the night. He objected but not for long. In my mind, what he really needed right now was his mum.

'I think I'd better come back to Portugal with you,' Chez said as Dad and I prepared to leave. 'I need to get my shit together and I might as well do that somewhere warm.'

'I think that's a very good idea,' Dad said. 'We can sort out a ticket in the morning.'

'If I change my mind, make me change it back. Lorna wants me out of her life and I'm not sure I can stay away when we're in the same town. We need to be in different countries.'

I didn't want my brother to be heartbroken like he so clearly was, but I couldn't help feeling relieved that Lorna had reached this conclusion about their relationship. Love shouldn't be this hard and I hoped some space far away from Lorna would help Chez realise that himself.

* * *

I stayed with Dad in his room for a while, conscious that tonight would have been a shock for him and keen to make sure he was okay. By the time I made it back to my place, it was after 1 a.m. and I was shattered. Poppy had messaged to say I was welcome to call her, no matter how late it was, but she'd understand if I was too drained and needed my bed.

TO POPPY

> Much as I long to hear your voice, I've only just got back and it's stupid o'clock so I'd better let us both get some sleep. I'll tell you all about it tomorrow. Thanks for being here for me x

FROM POPPY

I'll always be here for you. Sleep well x

As I settled under the duvet, I didn't just want to hear Poppy's voice – I wanted to see her. I recalled our conversation on Monday morning when I'd joked I was tempted to throw a sickie so I didn't have to leave her. I'd never taken a day off sick in the whole time I'd worked at the factory. But what if I didn't go in for my three night shifts across the weekend? What could they do? Sack me? When I'd told Eloise that I wanted to take the redundancy package, she said she'd expected me to say that and was sorry for all the stress. She'd then added, *I think this is going to be stressful for all the managers. I wouldn't be surprised if some of them phone in sick.* I'd rolled my eyes and agreed with her but now that I replayed that conversation in my head, her tone of voice had been unusual, exaggerating the words. Had she been dropping a hint? The more I thought about it, the more I was convinced she had been. If Bramblecote Country Foods could eliminate my job without ever meeting me or any of my colleagues, I clearly wasn't important to them, so why should they be important to me?

I leaned over to the bedside cabinet and grabbed my phone.

TO POPPY

> I'm sick of being a pushover. If my new bosses don't care, neither do I. Can I drive down to see you after I've had tea with Imogen? I'll be phoning in sick and giving the night shifts a miss x

FROM POPPY

> You rebel! But I don't blame you at all. Can't wait to see you x

I plumped my pillows and settled down to sleep, feeling better than I had in a long time. The episode with Chez tonight had been hard but it had led him to what I believed was the best decision he could possibly have made for his emotional well-being – to go to Portugal with my parents. It was also a weight off my mind that he wouldn't be my responsibility for the foreseeable future, meaning I could focus on my fight to keep Imogen in Yorkshire as well as continuing to build my relationship with Poppy.

33

POPPY

It was nearly midnight when Joel pulled onto the drive of Dove Cottage and I rushed out to see him, the strength of my feelings towards him needing a release. Evidently, he felt the same as he dropped his car keys onto the ground as he kissed me with passion, leaving us both breathless.

'Best welcome ever,' he said, smiling at me.

'Best arrival ever,' I quipped. 'But it's freezing out here. Grab your stuff and let's get inside.'

I was going to offer him a tea and give him a tour but, the moment the door closed, he took me in his arms again and those things didn't seem so important anymore as I led him upstairs to my bedroom.

The following morning, we had a lazy start with breakfast in bed while he told me about his appointment with his solicitor.

'There are two issues – access to Imogen and the move to Scotland. For the access, Tilly keeps banging on about having sole custody, but she doesn't have that. We both have parental responsibility but, because of my shifts, there's no set pattern for when I have Imogen which has always been the sticking point in the past – Tilly pretends to be reasonable by suggesting days I can have Imogen each week, knowing full well I can't commit to that, so it's gone back and forth between our solicitors with no resolution. My solicitor recognises that she's just being awkward, which is common in situations like this. Inevitably, it's the child who suffers so the goal is to find a way forward that works for all three of us and, if I was still working shifts, it's not unusual to have an agreement to plan visits around a shift pattern.

'As for moving to Scotland, I have rights to stop her. We operate within the legal jurisdiction of England and Wales and Tilly cannot move Imogen to Scotland – outside the legal jurisdiction – without my consent.'

I grasped Joel's arm. 'That's fantastic news. So, what happens next?'

'I can make an application for something called a prohibited steps order to stop her but Tilly can contest that. However, any decisions the courts make would have Imogen's welfare at the heart as well as the principle that she has a right to have a relationship with both parents so that would help my case.'

'It sounds a lot more positive than we were expecting.'

'It does. Apparently there's stacks of case law and it's really complicated but Tilly choosing Scotland rather than, say, Cornwall, does work in my favour with my consent being needed. My solicitor asked me what the rationale was for moving to Scotland – why not open a campsite in Yorkshire if that's what they really want to do? I'll put that challenge to her after their holiday. I'm hoping Tilly will get up there, realise how ridiculously far it is, and drop the whole idea.'

'And if she doesn't?'

'When she's back, I'll tell her we need to go somewhere for a proper grown-up discussion – a five-minute conversation on her doorstep won't cut it – and I'll lay it on the line.'

'Sounds sensible. Are you feeling more positive about it now?'

'Much more. I really hope we don't have to drag it through the courts. That's not parenting Imogen – that's just fighting.'

I loved the way Joel put his daughter first in everything. It sounded to me as though Tilly put herself first instead, although I appreciated that was perhaps a little unfair when I'd never met her.

We took the breakfast dishes down to the kitchen and I gave Joel a tour of the house, telling him the garden could wait until we were dressed.

'It's a great house,' he said as we returned to my bedroom, 'but I can tell it belongs to your parents. The only room that feels like you is this one.'

'It's the only room I've changed. I did it after Mum's diagnosis when I knew I'd be here for quite some time.'

He looked around him. 'This reminds me of Whisperwood Farmhouse.'

'Which is one of many reasons why I loved it there so much. It's 100 per cent my taste and I'm already missing it. What's weird is that Dove Cottage feels more like a holiday home I'm staying in temporarily and Whisperwood feels like my real home.'

'Whisperwood *will* be your real home. Scotland's not going to happen because I'm not going to let it. It's not right for you, me or Imogen. I think you should let Mary know you'd like to buy it but you have this place to sell first and things are a little complicated with your dad. She'll understand. She'll give you time.'

I smiled at him. 'You're right. I'll get in touch. I've started the ball rolling with this place so there's no reason not to make that next step.'

* * *

I wanted Joel to meet Dad. Even though Dad wouldn't understand the importance of the introduction, it would mean the world to me. Joel wouldn't see the dad I knew and loved, but at least he'd have physically met him. I could bring my *real* dad alive through photographs, videos and memories.

Marnie was in the reception when we arrived, so I introduced her to Joel and she shook his hand with enthusiasm.

'Good to meet you, Joel. You take care of this one. She's an absolute gem.'

'How is he today?' I asked. I'd visited again on Wednesday afternoon after setting up my doorbell camera, but I'd given yesterday a miss.

'Not so good. He's still in bed. He's developed a cough so we're keeping a close eye on him.'

I knocked on Dad's door and pushed it open. He was facing the window, but he turned his head slowly when I greeted him. He looked exhausted, dark patches below his pale, watery eyes.

'How are you this morning, Stanley?' I asked.

His lips moved but nothing coherent came out.

'I'm Poppy,' I said, 'and this is my boyfriend, Joel. Is it okay if we sit with you for a while?'

The movement of his head was imperceptible, but his eyes flicked towards the chair beside his bed. I sat down and Joel perched on the arm.

Dad unfurled his hand and the felt robin was resting in his palm.

'That's a beautiful bird,' Joel said. 'What sort is it, Stanley?'

'Robin,' he whispered before coughing.

There was a jug of water next to his bed, so we helped prop him up on his pillows and I sat beside him with a glass, holding it to his lips as he sipped. How many times had I done this for Mum when her muscles had been so wasted that she'd been unable to do it herself?

We only stayed twenty minutes as it was clear Dad needed his sleep, but that was enough time to see why Marnie had said weeks instead of months. Whatever had brought him to life on Tuesday – and even to some extent for my Wednesday visit – had gone and the frail man in the bed today was the reality of what this disease had done to him.

'That was hard to see,' Joel said, hugging me tightly by the van a little later. 'I can't even begin to imagine what you're going through.'

I couldn't speak for my tears so I just held on to him, so grateful to him for being here with me.

I'd brought the van with me so I could drive us straight over to Saltersbeck Farm to introduce Joel to Sharon, Ian and Bertie, who all gave him a warm welcome. As we returned to the van to drive to Honey Bee Croft, Sharon hugged me and whispered in my ear, 'He's wonderful, honey. I'm so happy for you.' It meant the world to me to have her stamp of approval.

'Are you ready to get kitted up and meet the bees?' I asked Joel as I parked the van at the entrance to Honey Bee Croft.

'I think so.'

Joel was taller and broader than Dad but beesuits weren't exactly a snug fit and he'd tried on one of Dad's this morning, which had enough space for him to move easily.

'Tomorrow's the first day of spring but the weather's still too cold for any major external activity so it'll be my usual checks of hefting and removing the dead bodies.'

I'd talked Joel through the anatomy of a hive using the colourful images in one of my favourite textbooks but the best learning always took place by an actual hive. As I explained to Joel what I was doing and why, it struck me that I'd never taught anyone before. I'd never needed to. Dad had taught Sharon and Ian the basics years ago so they could take over when he was on holiday, but I'd never passed on my knowledge and it was really exciting. Joel was a quick learner and he asked me a stack of questions, giving me a glimpse into what it must have been like when Dad taught me.

'I loved that,' Joel said, stepping out of his beesuit back at the van.

'You sound surprised.'

'I am. It's fascinating and I love how knowledgeable and passionate you are. I can't wait to see one of the hives open.'

'I can't wait to show you.'

Driving back to Dove Cottage, I shared with Joel some of my most special memories of being at Honey Bee Croft with my parents, how excited Dad and I got identifying the different worker bees and the thrill of opening a healthy hive. From Joel's initial reaction, I could see him getting hooked just like Dad and me.

* * *

We hadn't been home for long when the doorbell rang. It felt cool inside the house so Joel had gone upstairs to get a hoodie.

'That'll be Wilf with Benji,' I shouted up to him.

But it wasn't them. My heart started pounding.

'Whose car's that?' Damon demanded.

'None of your business.'

'It's him, isn't it? The guy from the photos in York? Who is he?'

His shouts brought Joel running downstairs. He put his arm round my shoulders protectively.

'Get off her!' Damon yelled. 'She's *my* girlfriend.'

'Stop it, Damon!' I cried. 'I am *not* your girlfriend. I've *never* been your girlfriend and I *never* will be. Whatever you think there is between us is in your head only.'

'You need to go,' Joel said, his voice calm but firm.

'I'm not taking orders from you.'

'Then take them from me,' I said, mirroring Joel's tone. 'I want you to leave and I don't want you to come back. Ever. If you don't go now, I'll call the police.'

Damon shook his head. 'You wouldn't do that. You love me and you know it. I don't know why you kid yourself that you don't.'

'I'm not in love with you. You're the one who needs to stop kidding yourself.'

'Go! Now!' Joel said, still calm but so commanding.

Damon curled his lip up. 'You've got to stop wasting your time on idiots like him, Poppy, and you need to pack it in with those damn bees too. I'm all you need.'

I removed my phone from my pocket and dialled 999. I held it up so he could see and poised my thumb over the green button. 'Do I need to press this?'

'This isn't over,' Damon muttered. He glared at Joel. 'I'm watching you.'

'If you come back here to watch either of us, I'll be the one calling the police.' Joel stepped out onto the doorstep and sized up to Damon. I knew he wouldn't hit Damon, but his physical presence – significantly taller and broader than Damon – should be enough to intimidate. Sure enough, Damon stepped back onto the drive.

'Do yourself a favour and actually listen to Poppy for once,'

Joel continued. 'She doesn't love you and never has. She isn't yours. She's a person, not a possession, and she doesn't *belong* to anyone. This is her property and you're not welcome on it or in her life and you need to go now before you end up in serious trouble. Do I make myself clear?'

'What the hell are you doing here?' Wilf sounded furious as he crossed the drive with a yapping Benji.

Damon looked up at Joel on the doorstep and Wilf closing in from his side and fled.

Joel put his arms out and I sank against his chest, shaking. He led me inside and Wilf followed with Benji.

'I thought you were going to call the police,' Wilf said.

'I was, but I got distracted with work and Dad and...' I shook my head. 'He didn't come back so I thought he'd got the message.'

'He obviously hasn't. You need to call them, Poppy.'

Joel nodded. 'I agree.'

'You're right. I need to report him and I will, but let me call his mum first and give her a heads up.' I raised my hands up to silence them both as they voiced their objections. 'Jenny was a friend of my mum's and she's a lovely woman. I want to let her know what's happening – warn her in case he's aggressive with her. I'll ring the police immediately after. I promise.'

Alerting Jenny felt like the right thing to do. I'd have preferred to do it face to face but, as Damon lived with his mum, there was a risk he'd be there if I visited and no way did I want to see him again.

Wilf took Benji back home and I dug out Mum's old address book. There was a landline number for Jenny but no mobile, so I hoped it was still connected. It rang for so long that I was on the verge of hanging up and calling the police, fearful that Damon might have arrived home by now in a foul mood and taken it out on Jenny, when she finally answered.

'Hi, Jenny, it's Poppy Wells – Joy's daughter.'

'Oh, my goodness! How lovely to hear from you.'

'Is Damon there?' I asked, thinking that if my call was on speakerphone and he was listening, he'd be livid.

'No. I thought he was with you.'

'He was here, but he left and he wasn't...' I winced. This was not an easy conversation to have. 'He was pretty angry with me.'

'Aw, Poppy, please don't tell me the engagement's off.'

My stomach lurched. 'Engagement? You think Damon and I are engaged?'

I felt sick as I discovered how far Damon's obsession with me had gone. He'd told Jenny that we'd got together last October and engaged at Christmas but we hadn't set a wedding date just yet because I'd had a breakdown after Dad's diagnosis and barely left the house. He'd given that as the reason why I hadn't seen Jenny to celebrate and she'd been unable to visit me instead because various health and mobility issues had her housebound. Telling her it was all lies and explaining what had really happened was one of the hardest conversations I'd ever had. I wished I'd been able to do it in person as she sounded broken and I longed to hug her.

'I feel so stupid,' she said, her voice strained, as though she was fighting through tears. 'So many things have just clicked into place. Questions I didn't even realise were questions have been answered. I'm a nurse, for goodness' sake! How can I not have seen this?'

'It sounds like you've had a lot to deal with,' I said, gently.

'Even so... Oh my gosh, Poppy. I'm so sorry. The photos. They're all of you and I never questioned it but, if you'd really been a couple, of course there'd have been photos of you together.'

My stomach lurched again and I shuddered. He had photos of

me? He must have taken them without me knowing, or helped himself to them from my socials. That was so creepy.

'Sometimes you can be too close to a person to see what's really going on.' I was anxious to get off the phone and call the police, but I didn't want Jenny to blame herself.

'It's kind of you to say that, but I should have noticed something. I'm so sorry, Poppy. He's really scared you, hasn't he?'

'He has and it has to stop. I wanted to warn you that—'

'You're going to the police,' she interrupted, her voice resigned. 'I'm so sorry he's put you through all this. He clearly needs help, and I'll make sure he gets it.'

'Will you be all right? He won't hurt you or anything?'

'He might be an obsessive liar but my son's not a violent man. You call the police. I'll be fine.'

We said goodbye and I disconnected the call, my heart heavy for Jenny. What a shock that must have been for her. I looked up at Joel. Out of respect for Jenny, I hadn't put my phone on speaker but Joel would have got the gist of it. His comforting hug gave me the strength I needed to make my next call.

* * *

It had been a long and emotional day, so Joel and I went to bed early. I was drifting off when my phone rang. I grasped at it in a panic, my immediate thought being that it would be someone from The Larks telling me to get there quickly. But it wasn't The Larks. It was Sharon.

'Poppy! The hives are on fire.'

My breath caught in my throat. 'Fire?'

Beside me, Joel flicked on the light.

'The fire brigade's on their way,' she said, sounding tearful, 'but they're going to be too late. I'm so sorry.'

34

JOEL

'On my way,' Poppy said, her voice coming out all strangled before she hung up the phone. She turned to me, her face deathly white. 'The bees. The hives are on fire.'

'Oh, my God!'

In silence, we moved at speed around the room, pulling on clothes. Down the stairs, grabbing coats, Poppy locking up the house as I unlocked my car. Off the drive, through the village, towards the farm.

'I can smell the smoke,' she said as we pulled onto the farm track, her voice cracking into a sob.

I wanted to reassure her, tell her everything would be all right, but they'd just be words. Lies. If it had been a dry day and the fire had started by accident, there might have been some hope that it hadn't reached all the hives, although that probably wouldn't have saved the bees from the smoke. But it had been wet recently and, even though neither of us voiced it, I knew that Poppy would be of the same mind as me. This was arson and there was only one person who'd do such a thing. The one who hadn't been home when the police visited. The one who'd told her earlier to *pack it in with those damn bees.* Looked like he'd decided to make that happen himself.

We crossed the farmyard and followed the track towards the blue lights – an eerie sight in the darkness. No flames. Only smoke.

There were two fire engines and two police cars and I parked the car just past them. Sharon and Ian were talking to a police officer. As Poppy and I made our way over to them, I felt her shaking as she clung to my arm.

Introductions were made and the officer gave us the devastating news – the fire was out but the hives were gone and nothing could be salvaged. Poppy sagged against me and I wrapped my arms round her as she sobbed. I pushed down the lump in my throat, distraught for her. As if the destruction of the bees wasn't devastating enough, this was also her dad's legacy, wiped out at a time when he was close to going too. How could she begin to even deal with all that pain?

Sharon was hovering nearby, tears streaming down her smoke-blackened face, clearly eager to comfort Poppy, so I stepped back and allowed the women to hug. Ian joined them and I turned my head away for a moment, wiping away my own tears.

One of the firefighters was heading in our direction with another police officer and I hoped neither of them would utter the obvious words – *at least nobody was hurt* – because they were. Poppy was hurt. Her family were hurt. And those bees had perished for nothing.

'It was definitely arson,' the firefighter said, holding up a can of fuel and some rags. 'We found these.'

'Can you think of anyone who'd want to do something like that?' the police officer asked.

Poppy turned in Sharon's arms. 'Damon Speight. He's been

stalking me. I reported him earlier but I should have done it sooner. They told me to, but I didn't imagine...' She took a deep shuddery breath before rattling off his address. 'His mum isn't well. Please tell her I'm sorry.'

* * *

'It's my fault,' Poppy said when we pulled onto the drive at Dove Cottage a couple of hours later, acknowledging the police officer stationed in a car by the verge outside.

'It's not your fault,' I said, twisting in my seat to face her. 'You didn't start the fire. This is all on Damon, and you're not in any way responsible for the fantasy world he's created. You're a kind person who occasionally passed the time of day with someone you recognised from school. *He* turned that into something it wasn't.'

'You and Wilf were right about involving the police sooner. I knew he was obsessed. Not to this extent, but I knew it wasn't right.'

'But you could never have predicted this and you can't take any of the blame. He's a sick man who wouldn't take no for an answer. That's nothing to do with you. You have to believe that. Come on, let's go inside.'

Poppy was exhausted and soon drifted off to sleep, cuddled up to my side. I kissed her forehead, the smell of smoke in her hair transporting me back to Sharon and Ian's farm. What a night! There'd been some more questions before the fire brigade and police left, leaving the four of us standing in a line, the only light coming from the headlights of my car, illuminating the police cordon blowing in the wind. Sharon and Ian insisted we went back to the farmhouse for a drink and to warm up. We were offered a room for the night but Poppy wanted her own bed, comforted in the knowledge that there'd be a police officer keeping watch in case Damon turned up at the house. I hoped the police had got him. I hoped they'd throw the book at him. And, more than anything, I hoped Poppy would be able to accept that none of this was her fault.

35

POPPY

I was fresh from the shower the following morning when a couple of police officers arrived with the news that they'd arrested Damon and charged him with offences relating to arson and stalking. I'd need to go to the police station to give a formal statement about the stalking but I was surprised to hear that Jenny had already given her own statement which backed up what I'd said. A further surprise was that the police had been on their way to Jenny's house after I'd named Damon as the likely arsonist when a call came through from Jenny reporting him. They weren't able to give me any further details but I was concerned about Jenny so I rang her after they'd left.

She was relieved to hear from me and full of apologies for what Damon had done.

'A couple of hours after you rang, he arrived home and I asked him if there was anything he'd like to tell me about you. I wanted to give him the opportunity to come clean but he spun me a pack of lies again about how excited you were about the wedding. I asked if he could invite you for dinner so I could be part of the wedding plans and out came the excuses about you not being well and not up to visitors. *That's funny,* I said to him, *because Poppy sounded fine when she rang earlier*. His face fell and he tried to make out that the pair of you were going through a rough patch because you had so many distractions in your life, but he was going to sort it out. I told him that the only thing he was going to do was get an appointment to speak to a mental health professional and he wasn't to bother you again or I'd call the police myself. He stormed out, so he wasn't here when the police called. I was up late watching telly when he returned, dirty and reeking of smoke. *What have you done?* I asked and he just stood there all calm and serene. *What I said I'd do. Eliminated one of Poppy's distractions. She'll be able to focus on me now.'*

I pressed my hand across my mouth, picturing Damon's face as he uttered those disturbing words.

'I phoned the police, Poppy. I didn't know exactly what he'd done, but I knew it was something bad.'

I thanked her, knowing that making the call had to be a tough thing for a mother to do.

'Wrong is wrong,' she said. 'He's my son and I'll always love him but I don't have to like him or anything he's done. I'm sorry I didn't pick up on anything sooner. It all seems so implausible now that I know the truth, but I had no reason at the time to think he was lying. I can say sorry a million times, but it'll never be enough.'

'None of this is your fault, Jenny. It really isn't.'

'I hope you're hearing those words and applying them to yourself. You always were a sensitive little soul so I can imagine you're absorbing a stack of blame.'

'I am.'

'Then let it go. Shovel a bit of it in my direction and heap the rest on my son and then put this whole sorry episode behind you. Get on with your life and be happy.'

I felt so much better after that conversation, especially as Jenny had shared that she had a younger sister in Wales who'd been pestering Jenny to move in with her ever since her health began deteriorating. She'd decided to accept that offer and have her own fresh start and the support she needed.

We said we'd stay in touch, but I knew we wouldn't. We both needed to let go and move on.

Joel and I went to see Dad that afternoon. His cough had worsened and the doctor had been called. I voiced my fears to Marnie that it could be a chest infection which might develop into pneumonia.

'It's possible. Let's wait and see what the doctor says.'

I'd read the information. I'd always known that, at Dad's age, something else could take him before dementia did. And if it did, perhaps it would be a blessing. I knew the end-of-life symptoms for a person with dementia and nearly all of them snatched their dignity away, causing pain and distress. I didn't want that for my beloved dad. Who would? If he had to go, I wanted it to be quickly and quietly.

I returned to his bedroom on my own and kissed his forehead, smiling at the robin lying in his open palm.

'Try not to go without me,' I whispered. 'But if it hurts, it's okay to let go. Mum's waiting for you.'

I did feel how Marnie had warned I might – a sense of resignation tinged with relief. With my dreams for a future with Joel in Yorkshire and with the bees here gone, did Dad somehow know that it was time for me to start afresh and this was his way of giving me his blessing? I held his hand, the robin pressed between us.

'I love you, Dad. Thanks for everything you and Mum did for me. Missing you always and forever.'

36

JOEL

I phoned in sick again on Sunday, feeling like such a fraud but equally not caring about it because, right now, I was where I needed and wanted to be.

While Poppy caught up on some work in her office, I sat in the lounge and FaceTimed my parents who'd flown back to Portugal with Chez on Friday. My brother was having a swim so I couldn't speak to him but Mum and Dad both said he already seemed a lot more relaxed. They hadn't booked him a return flight, the hope being that he'd ultimately find work locally and stay.

When we said goodbye, I was about to find Poppy to update her on the conversation, but my phone rang again, this time with a FaceTime request from Tilly. She *never* FaceTimed me and to do so while she was on holiday couldn't be a good thing.

'Everything okay?' I asked when I answered.

'Imogen wants to speak to you.'

'Okay. That's fine.'

'No, it's not fine. She's been nagging me to FaceTime you since she woke up and she refused to get ready for our day out until I let her.'

'So why didn't you let her call me sooner and why are you being all angry with me?'

'I'm not angry with you. I'm just frustrated. I said she could speak to you tonight, but she got herself into such a state about wanting to speak to you now that she threw up in the tent.'

'Oh, my God! Is she all right?'

'*She* is. The tent isn't. It stinks in there. I've never seen her like this before so I've said she can speak to you, but I wanted to give you a heads up that she's upset before she comes on the phone. Are you okay to talk to her now?'

'Of course. Put her on.'

'Hey, sweetie,' I said gently when Imogen's face appeared on the screen a couple of minutes later. She was pale and tearful, clutching Cloud against her face and I longed to hug her. 'I hear you've been sick.'

'You have to come and get me, Daddy! I hate it here!'

'You love camping.'

'Not here! There isn't a playground and Mummy and Greg say we might live here, and I don't want to. It took forever to get here and Ezra and Delphine were both sick in the car and I don't want to go to a new school without all my friends. I want to see Darcie and ride Munchie and see you all the time. I want to live with you. If they make me move here, I'll run away.'

Her rant was punctuated by sobs.

'Ssh,' I soothed. 'Look at me, sweetie. I'm right here.'

'I want you, Daddy. Come and get me.'

'I can't do that. I'm not just down the road.'

'But I *hate* it here.' She shouted the word *hate*.

'Take a deep breath with me. And another. You're scaring Cloud.'

She sniffed and wiped her tears on her sleeve as she cuddled her sheep closer.

'I wish I could come and get you, but I'm at Poppy's house right now because her dad's very poorly. You've got Mummy and Greg and your brother and sister to look after you, but Poppy doesn't have anyone so I need to be here with her. Can you understand that?'

She nodded, wide-eyed.

'I wish I could be with you, but this is your special time with your family and you usually love holidays. I bet you'd love this one if you let yourself. We'll get together when you're home and do something special then, okay?'

She nodded but the sadness in her eyes broke my heart.

'I don't want to move here, Daddy.'

'I don't want you to either and Mummy and I need to talk about that.' I didn't want to dwell on that with her and have her worrying about it. 'So they don't have a playground, eh? I reckon you could still have some great adventures with Cloud. There must be lots of grass if it's a campsite. Is there?'

'Yes.'

'Show me.'

She turned the phone round and filmed round her. It was a bit fast and made my eyes boggle but, as far as I could tell, there was plenty of open space.

'When I was younger, I used to love playing tig and hide and seek with my friends or just running around pretending we were superheroes. Can't you do that with Ezra and Delphine? I'm sure they'd love their big sister to play with them.'

'I could teach them tig.'

'I think they'll love that. Are you okay now? No more talk about running away?'

She nodded and smiled at me. 'I'm okay. Thank you, Daddy.'

'You're welcome, sweetie. I love you.'

'I love you too.' She blew me a kiss before handing the phone back to Tilly who'd been hovering in the background.

'I've been trying to calm her down for ages,' she said, looking and sounding relieved. 'Thanks for doing that for me.'

'I didn't do it for you,' I said, a hard edge to my voice which I hated but which she needed to hear. 'I did it for Imogen and if I didn't think it would do more harm than good, I'd be jumping on a plane right now and bringing her back with me.'

'You can't do that!'

'I just said I'm not going to! Did you hear everything I said to her?'

She nodded.

'Then you heard me saying we need to talk. A heads up on that is I'm not standing for any more of this nonsense. I've seen my solicitor and you do *not* have sole custody of our daughter. Also, you can *not* move her to the other end of the country on a whim and you certainly can't move her to Scotland without my permission.'

'It's not a whim. This is our dream. You know we love camping.'

'Loving camping and running a campsite in Scotland are two completely different things. I think you need to seriously ask yourself whether you're wearing rose-tinted glasses here. Being the owner rather than the camper will be exceptionally hard work. Do you really want to take that on with newborn twins and four more kids to look after? And what does Leighton's mum think about it?'

Tilly shrugged. 'She doesn't know yet.'

'Because you know she'll say no. So what's Greg going to do? Is he really prepared to lose his son for a dream that could turn out to be the hardest job he's ever had?'

She bit her lip and looked down. The lack of arguing back

filled me with hope that she might be having doubts herself, so I forged on.

'Honestly, Tilly, can't you see how crazy this is? Open a campsite if you must but do it in Yorkshire. You still get your dream, but you don't rip three families apart in the process.'

'We haven't made any firm decisions yet,' she said, but the hostility I was so used to was absent from her tone. She looked worn out. She looked like she wanted to run away too.

'Imogen can call me any time she wants and I'm happy to talk her down if this happens again but, when you get back, you and I need to have a long talk. I've let you get away with too much and I'm not standing for it anymore. Imogen's my daughter and I have rights. Okay?'

There was silence and I raised my eyebrows at her.

'Okay,' she said, with a sigh. 'I'll see you when we get back.'

She disconnected the call, and I ran my fingers through my hair with a sigh. That was the most compliant I'd ever seen her. Perhaps Imogen wasn't the only one who hated the campsite. Perhaps it wasn't Tilly's dream either.

37

POPPY

As I feared, Dad did have a chest infection. He was placed on antibiotics and I was told the next twenty-four hours would be critical. Nobody needed to expand on what that could mean. Across the weekend, I don't know what I'd have done without the practical or emotional support from Joel. Even though he had a lot to deal with himself, he'd shopped, cooked, listened to me, hugged me, reassured me and made me laugh. With my permission, he'd been in touch with my new friends in Yorkshire to let them know what had happened with the bees and the news about my dad. I'd been touched by all the messages of love and support. I'd never felt such a part of something and realised that, ever since Mum passed away and Dad was diagnosed, I'd been looking for my tribe and now I felt as though I'd found them.

Joel made a delicious Sunday roast and invited Wilf to join us. He brought Benji with him and left the Yorkshire terrier with us for the afternoon while he went to visit his friend. We'd planned on a long walk but the temperature had dropped and there was slow and steady rain, so we made it a quick walk through the village before returning to Dove Cottage for hot chocolate. Benji snuggled between us on the sofa and I had the central heating on, but it wasn't the same as lighting the log burner in Whisperwood Farmhouse.

'You know what I'd like to do?' Joel asked when we were partway through our drinks. 'I'd like to see photos of you when you were little. I'd love to see what your parents looked like too, unless you'd find that too hard just now.'

I thought it was a great suggestion so I dug out a pile of photo albums and we sat at the dining table going through them with Benji curled up on my knee. It was a lovely trip down memory lane, giving me an opportunity to laugh as I shared various anecdotes. Joel threw in stories about his family, and I was glad that the rain had kept us indoors as it had been the perfect way to spend the afternoon, remembering my dad how he used to be. Afterwards, Joel helped me carry the albums back to the spare bedroom and return them to the shelving units.

'What's all that?' he asked, pointing to a pile of crates beside the shelves.

'All the equipment for my Honey Bee Hugs range.' I grabbed a dusty folder from the top and opened it to show him the branding I'd developed.

'This is amazing.'

I talked Joel through my product range and showed him my equipment, feeling the excitement bubbling inside me as the passion I'd felt for my products and the ideas I'd had for taking it forward came flooding back.

'You have to move to Whisperwood, get some hives on Bumblebee Barn and get this business up and running,' Joel said as we put the crates back. 'It's your calling.'

'And you have to look into opening that bistro. That's your calling.'

I picked Benji up and cuddled him as we returned to the

lounge to indulge in a fantasy world where both businesses were up and running and incredibly successful and, in the darkness, it felt like there was light at the end of the tunnel. All I needed to do now was arrange for Sharon and Ian to look round Dove Cottage and put in that call to Mary about Whisperwood Farmhouse. It had been at the back of my mind all weekend but, with everything going on with Dad, the police and Damon, it had taken a back seat. But next week I'd do it and turn my dreams into reality.

38

JOEL

Having called in sick for all three of my night shifts, I had to be back at work on Thursday for the start of my day shifts. I felt terrible about leaving Poppy when her dad was in hospital, but Stanley was clearly made of strong stuff because he did seem to be fighting his chest infection. Poppy had been going to hospital for the morning and afternoon visiting hours so, after a tearful goodbye on both our parts, I set off back to Yorkshire before she left on Wednesday morning.

Arriving home early in the afternoon, I leaned against the kitchen worktop eating a prepacked sandwich I'd bought from a service station. The house felt empty without Chez, even though we'd barely seen each other during his recent stay and it felt soulless without Poppy, even though she'd never even visited. I missed her so much, I felt a physical ache inside of me. The worst thing was not knowing when I'd be able to see her again. I could have driven to Winchcote after my Saturday shift ended to spend Easter Sunday and Monday with her, but I could see how anxious she was becoming about her rising work levels so we'd agreed not to commit to anything and to play it by ear depending on what happened with her dad.

While I'd been at Dove Cottage, the estate agents had visited and both came up with the same proposed asking price. Sharon and Ian had then stopped by so Poppy and I took Benji for a walk round the village while they had a good look round. When we returned and they gave her an asking price offer, Poppy burst into tears. It meant so much to her that the house – and particularly the garden – would be loved once more. Knowing she had a firm sale, she rang Mary and told her that she'd love to have first refusal on Whisperwood Farmhouse and Mary had confirmed that nothing would give her greater pleasure than to sell it to someone who so clearly loved it.

* * *

After my shift on Friday evening, I spoke to Poppy and we made the difficult decision that I wouldn't drive down on Saturday night. She was snowed under with work after squeezing in a solicitor appointment for the sale of Dove Cottage and spending time choosing paint colours for Whisperwood Farmhouse. Mary had suggested it made more sense for Poppy to liaise with the decorators so that Whisperwood would be done up to her taste. She ran the colour choices by me, wanting to make sure they were to my taste too. When she'd still been in Yorkshire and we'd spent that evening fantasising about her buying the house, being Bumblebee Barn's beekeeper and me opening a bistro, we'd talked about us both living at Whisperwood, but she hadn't mentioned that since. I wondered if my approval of the colour scheme was because she imagined me moving in with her at some point down the line. I wasn't going to ask because I appreciated that moving to Yorkshire was an enormous step for her and I personally didn't need that reassurance. I had no doubt that living together would be in our future, but it would happen when the time was right.

Early on Easter Sunday evening, I was sitting on the sofa and flicking through the TV channels, enjoying the smells drifting from the kitchen as a couple of casseroles cooked in the oven ready for my meals next week. My mind kept drifting to Imogen. Only two more days and she'd be back from Scotland. It felt like she'd been away for months. We'd had a couple of FaceTime conversations since that distraught one. She'd decided that the campsite wasn't that bad after all, but was still adamant that she wasn't moving to Scotland, although there was thankfully no further talk about running away. After the most recent call, I'd spoken to a very pale and subdued-looking Tilly who, without any prompt from me, had suggested Wednesday for a proper conversation. I hoped Imogen's reaction to moving had made her think twice about it as I really didn't want to have to go down the legal route to stop her.

I heard a car pull up outside and, in the glow from the street lamp, I recognised it as Tilly's. She wasn't due back until Tuesday. If there was something wrong with Imogen, she'd have phoned rather than turned up.

I opened the door before she had a chance to ring the bell. 'I thought you were still in Scotland.'

'Urgh, don't! Can we talk?'

I stood back to let her in.

'We got back this afternoon,' she said, plonking herself down on the sofa with a sigh. 'Worst holiday we've ever had. The kids hated it. Why am I telling you that? You already know. Truth is, I wasn't too impressed either. The campsite needs a lot of work and you were right about the reality of doing that with newborn twins. The nearest school is miles away. Actually, it isn't but the roads are so bad that it takes forever to get there. It's just not practical for a young family.'

I genuinely felt sorry for her. It hurt when your dreams were crushed.

'Greg and I hardly ever argue but it was all we seemed to do while we were away. At one point, I was this close to jumping in the car and abandoning him there. I told him he was being stubborn – that it might be a long-held dream, it might remind him of the happy camping trips he had in Scotland as a kid, but it wasn't going to be a happy place for our family.'

'So you're not moving?'

'We're not moving. Imogen's meltdown broke my heart. They go on about how resilient kids are and Imogen has proved that over and over, so the fact that she got so upset was a massive wake-up call about how wrong this move was for her.'

I could hardly believe what I was hearing and had to double-check it. 'Moving's *definitely* off the cards?'

'Yes.'

'And Greg's accepted this?'

'He doesn't have a choice.'

Her voice cracked and tears pooled in her eyes. Despite the hell she'd put me through, I wasn't heartless. 'Are you two okay?'

'Bet it'd make you really happy if I said no.'

I'd had enough of her sarcastic quips and suggestions that I wanted their relationship to fall apart. 'Why do you say things like that? Of course I wouldn't be happy! What sort of person do you think I am?'

She shook her head and sighed. 'Sorry. I can't seem to help myself. I know you're not like that. I'm just...' She sighed again. 'Forget it.' She started to push herself up.

'Cup of tea?' I asked. 'And a chance to offload?'

She sank back down, a tear escaping down her cheek. 'Yes, please, to both.'

'Well, that was certainly a turn-up for the books,' I muttered as I waved Tilly off and closed the front door an hour later.

We still had a lot more to talk about but we'd managed to get a lot out in the open. I was sorry to hear that things were rough right now between her and Greg – didn't like the bloke but Tilly clearly loved him so I hoped they could get past this quickly – but I was so relieved to hear that she'd woken up to the impact of the move on Imogen. She'd been devastated by Imogen's emotional reaction to the move. Ezra and Delphine had understandably been upset at seeing their big sister so distraught and they'd had several fraught days.

Tilly admitted that what I'd said about her looking at the move with rose-tinted glasses had been an eye-opener too.

'Greg had painted a vision of us living the dream in beautiful surroundings and, after what you said, I wondered if he'd even considered how we'd manage routine maintenance or things going wrong. I put a few scenarios to him – a blocked toilet, a leak in a glamping pod, a herd of Highland cows getting through a broken fence – and do you know what his answer was to all of them? *I'd get a bloke in to sort it.* And at that moment I realised we were living in cloud cuckoo land. As if we could afford *a bloke* every time something went wrong. So not only is Scotland off the cards – running a campsite anywhere is.'

'Obviously I'm relieved, but I'm sorry your dream's over. What'll you do instead?'

'Don't know and, right now, I'm too exhausted to care. I

thought being pregnant with one baby was bad, but it was a walk in the park compared to twins.'

It was too good an opportunity to miss, so I mooted the idea of Imogen staying with me more as Tilly progressed with her pregnancy, which was met with a tut and a roll of the eyes.

'And how are you going to manage that when you work shifts?'

'I won't be working shifts. I'm taking redundancy.'

I half-expected her to challenge me on how I was going to keep up my maintenance payments, but she surprised me by saying she was sorry to hear that and asking if I was all right. When she asked what I was going to do instead, I told her I was taking some time out to consider my options. I didn't mention anything about the bistro. It wasn't right to say anything to Tilly before I'd even spoken to Barney and Amber and, even if they approved, there were so many hurdles to jump over that it might not even happen – although I'd been doing a lot of manifesting about it.

'That's how I can help more with Imogen,' I said. 'I know it's a struggle for you to let go, but it's hard for me to be without her and it's tough on her too. What Imogen wants has to be our priority and I know she wants to spend more time with me because she constantly tells me that.'

Tilly didn't respond and I wondered if she somehow saw Imogen wanting to spend more time with me as a rejection of her when it was far from that.

'I'm not suggesting she leaves home and moves in with me permanently,' I said. 'But you've already admitted how exhausted you are and it's only going to get harder. And that's before the twins even arrive. Let me help by having Imogen more so that you can focus on them and, when you're settled in a routine with them and I know what my future career looks like, we can talk about a more balanced custody arrangement.'

'I'll think about it,' she said, an edge to her voice. 'I need to go before they send out a search party for me.'

I followed her to the door and it struck me that, as I'd been transparent about my work situation, there was something else I needed to be honest about.

'You heard that first FaceTime with Imogen so you'll have heard me mention Poppy,' I blurted out, feeling nervous about her reaction. 'I met her at the wedding and we've been seeing each other.'

Tilly completely threw me by smiling. 'I asked Imogen who Poppy was and she told me how you met at the wedding. She said you were just friends, but she thought you should be more. I'm pleased for you, Joel. I told you before that I only ever wanted you to be happy.'

'You're not angry that Imogen has met her already?'

'How could I be? It's not like you planned it. Sounds like destiny to me. I hope it works out for you both. I really do.'

She set off along the path, then turned. 'I'm glad you're leaving that factory. It was never right for you. I think you should do something with your cooking. I always thought you had a gift for it.'

And then she was gone, leaving me standing in the doorway, mouth open, wondering what had just happened. That was the Tilly I recognised – the woman I'd loved. I hadn't expected that trip to Scotland to be the best thing that could have ever happened but it looked like it might have been.

39

POPPY

'Goodbye, sweet pea,' I said, hugging Imogen tightly on the platform at Cheltenham Spa train station on the last Sunday of the Easter holidays. 'It's been so lovely to see you.'

She kissed my cheek and stepped back as Joel embraced me and gently kissed my lips. *No tears. Not in front of Imogen.*

We reluctantly let go as the train pulled in. Joel picked up their bag in one hand and took Imogen's hand in his other and boarded the train, waving from their seats as it pulled out minutes later.

I'd just had the loveliest weekend. Joel had FaceTimed me last Sunday, reeling from Tilly turning up at his house with a major about-turn on Scotland and a mostly reasonable attitude. They'd met up again as originally planned a few days ago and had not only had an extremely healthy and effective discussion about him seeing Imogen more, but she'd studied his rota and suggested that, as he had this weekend off, he should book a couple of train tickets and bring Imogen down to Winchcote to see me, joking that Imogen would kill her if she suggested the journey by car after the mammoth Scotland drive.

Joel had already been planning to visit and assured me it was okay to say no to Imogen joining him, especially considering my dad was still in hospital and I'd want to visit him each day, but I loved the idea. I'd missed Imogen, and had a feeling her sunshine personality would be the perfect tonic to those difficult visits where all I could do was sit beside Dad's bed, holding his hand as he slept, cringing at the rattle in his chest.

Joel and Imogen had arrived on Friday evening but, as they were leaving before hospital visiting time on Sunday morning, we'd only had one full day together. Despite the quick visit, we'd packed a lot in with a takeaway on Friday night, a visit to Pittville Park in Cheltenham yesterday where Imogen had played on the playground and the three of us had taken a boat out on the lake, and a meal in a local pub last night. She'd brought her Polaroid camera with her and took a few photos, telling me she was going to create another special section in her scrapbook for her weekend away.

Returning to Dove Cottage after the hospital, the house felt far too quiet. I tried to relax in front of the television but was too restless so I went into my office. I managed a couple of hours working, but was fidgety the whole time. I'd decided to call it a day when Mary rang to check that the decorators had let me know they'd be starting at Whisperwood a week tomorrow. We had a lovely chat about my weekend with Joel and Imogen and she shared that she'd had Amber and Barney round to her house to tell her all about their honeymoon. When we finished talking, I noticed a missed call and dialled into the voicemail, my heart sinking at the message asking me to get to the hospital as soon as possible. That could only mean one thing. I grabbed my bag and coat and dashed out of the house, calling Sharon on the way who said she'd meet me there.

After Dad's diagnosis, we'd had several difficult but necessary conversations about the end. Dove Cottage was already in my name, but he wanted to talk about his will, pensions, investments, funeral arrangements.

'When the time comes, I don't want to be resuscitated, sweet pea,' he'd said. 'If my heart stops beating, that's because it's flown to the beautiful woman who stole it when I was twenty-one. I know I'll probably have no control over it but, if I have any sway at all, I'll slip away quietly when you're not there because I don't want you to see that.'

And he got his wish. By the time I got to the hospital, I was too late. Sharon and Ian arrived moments after I heard the news, and they only needed to glance at me to know. We huddled together in the waiting room, mourning the departure of a wonderful father and friend.

I was asked if I wanted to go in and say goodbye, which I did. Dad somehow looked younger, perhaps because he was finally at peace. His felt birds were arranged on the bedside table but my throat tightened at the sight of the robin perched on the sheet above his heart. Presumably it had been in his hand and one of the nurses had placed it there. My feelings were in turmoil because, although I was sad, I was definitely relieved for him.

Lowering myself onto the chair beside the bed, I told him about my amazing couple of days with Joel and Imogen – exactly what I'd have said to him at visiting hour a little later.

'You'd have loved Imogen,' I told him. 'I found myself calling her sweet pea, just like you used to call me. She likes it.' I imagined him smiling at that.

A nurse came in to check I was okay. I didn't want to leave Dad alone, but I had to, and that's when the tears began.

'I'll be okay,' I said, trying to smile to reassure him. 'Don't you worry about me. I've found love again and I've got some genuine friends. About time, eh?'

I took his hand in mine and squeezed the lifeless fingers. 'Send my love to Mum and to Evie. Watch out for the bees and tell them I'm sorry I couldn't save them.'

Releasing his hand, I gathered the birds from the cabinet and placed them carefully inside my bag. I leaned over and kissed Dad's cold cheek, whispering goodbye for one last time, then curled my fingers around the robin.

'You got what you wanted – slipping away quietly without me. But know that you'll never really be without me. You've got a piece of my heart forever.'

* * *

Ian drove my car home and Sharon took me in theirs. I felt numb as I looked down at the felt robin in my hand, unable to form any words, no more tears left to cry.

While Sharon busied herself in the kitchen making drinks, I wandered over to the mantelpiece and placed the robin between the black and white framed photo of my parents on their wedding day and the gold-plated carriage clock Dad had bought Mum for their golden wedding anniversary.

'Can we do anything? Call anyone?' Ian asked when Sharon joined us with mugs of tea.

'Can you let Phil and Bertie know? Tell Phil I'll speak to him soon – just not today.'

'We can do that,' Sharon said. 'Do you want to call Joel?'

I glanced at the clock. 'He'll still be on his way home. I'd rather not tell him while he's with Imogen.'

'Do you want anything to eat?' Sharon asked.

I shook my head. A dog barking outside drew my attention to the window. 'That sounds like Benji. I should let Wilf know. I won't be long.' I took a sip from my tea and placed it down on the coaster. 'You don't have to stay. I'm all right.'

'We'll wait,' Ian said. 'You take as long as you need.'

When Wilf opened the door, he took one look at my face and sighed heavily. 'When?'

'A couple of hours ago.'

'Come in. Benji's eating, but I'm sure he'll oblige you with a cuddle when he's done.'

Benji ran through to the lounge moments later with his pet pig and jumped up onto the sofa, dropping it into my lap before curling up against me. I sank my fingers into his fur, grateful for his warmth.

When I returned next door, the house was silent and I found Sharon and Ian outside, huddled together on the bench below the kitchen window.

'Aren't you cold?' I asked, noting that neither of them were wearing coats.

'A bit,' Sharon said, 'but we got chatting about your dad and it felt right to continue that in his favourite place.'

'We've put some food out for the hedgehogs too,' Ian said. 'Saves you a job later.'

I lowered myself onto the doorstep and gazed out over the garden. Darkness had fallen but solar lights dotted between the shrubs and along the fence took the edge off. A rustle drew my eyes to a hedgehog heading for one of the many feeding stations Dad had placed around the garden. I pointed it out to Sharon and Ian and smiled as their delighted expressions mirrored the one I'd seen on Dad's face every time he spotted a hedgehog, rabbit or fox in the garden. I was so glad they were going to buy Dove Cottage and, even though I knew they'd completely refurbish the inside, the garden was my parents' true legacy and they'd care for it and love it just as Mum and Dad had.

'We'll take good care of it,' Sharon said, as though reading my thoughts. 'I was thinking I could take some cuttings and you could plant them in your new garden so you'll have a part of Dove Cottage – a happy part – with you always.'

I smiled at her and nodded, tears pricking my eyes. That sounded wonderful.

40

JOEL

Two months later

'Wow!' I said as Poppy entered the lounge. 'And here was me thinking nothing could beat that orange dress from Amber and Barney's wedding.'

She gave me a twirl in her stunning red floral dress.

Imogen appeared moments later in a pale yellow party dress with a layered skirt which fanned out when she twirled.

'You look beautiful, sweetie,' I said. 'Are you both ready for our second wedding of the year?'

Driving to Hedgehog Hollow for Fizz and Phoebe's wedding, it was amazing to think how much life had changed for all of us since Barney and Amber's wedding just under three months ago. Who'd have guessed that, when I was psyching myself up to attend six weddings without a plus one, I'd meet the woman of my dreams at the first one and ours would become the seventh. It wasn't official yet. Poppy knew I was going to ask her to marry me and she'd told me already it would be a yes when I did but we'd agreed that me actually asking would be a surprise moment after things had settled a little.

Sharon and Ian would be completing on the purchase of Dove Cottage next week, and a young couple with their first child on the way were buying my place. Poppy had moved in with me a couple of weeks after her dad's funeral and we agreed that it made no sense for her to move into Whisperwood Farmhouse on her own when we knew we never wanted to be apart again. So, we were buying our forever home together and were renaming it Honey Bee Croft in remembrance of her parents.

Our first month or so together had been less than conventional so it had been great to spend time during the second month doing the things that might be a more usual start to a relationship – nights out at the pub, visits to the cinema, day trips as she explored her new home and I saw my local area through fresh eyes.

Imogen adored Poppy and the feeling was mutual. Poppy had met Tilly who amazed us both by hugging her and thanking her for making me happy. Even Greg had shaken her hand and told her that I was a good bloke and she was lucky to have me. I really hadn't seen that one coming!

Tilly and I were currently taking it in turns to have Imogen for weekends and I had her a couple of nights a week too, which worked around her attending riding lessons and going to Snowy's Gymnastics Club where she was loving trampolining. I could tell Tilly was struggling with seeing Imogen less but it was obvious how happy our daughter was to have more of a balance, so she kept quiet about it – most of the time!

I'd finished at the factory a month ago and had felt like a weight had been lifted as I walked out after my final shift. Eloise had been a star in making it possible for me to leave with a full redundancy payout but without having to work my full notice.

Sal had also managed to negotiate an early release and had walked straight into another job as she'd hoped. She'd stayed in touch and told me she liked the work better, although she missed me – or more specifically missed my food.

When Barney and Amber returned from their honeymoon, tanned and glowing, I gave them some time to settle back into their routine before inviting myself round for a takeaway and an enormous catch-up on everything they'd missed and the ideas Poppy and I had for our future at Bumblebee Barn. They'd loved the proposals and we were now working on ideas for the bistro. We wanted to be certain about our offering before we submitted a plan to the council for developing the barn. In the meantime, I'd been in my element spending time in the large kitchen at Bumblebee Barn experimenting with meals, creating sample menus and working out costings. I finally felt like I was heading towards the place I was always meant to be, but had taken the scenic route to get to.

* * *

We arrived at Hedgehog Hollow and parked in the yard. The wedding was taking place outside by the gazebo overlooking the wildflower meadow. Samantha and Josh had been the first to get married there and Fizz and Phoebe had told me they could never have considered anywhere else for their nuptials when Hedgehog Hollow had been the place they'd met and fallen in love.

'Such a gorgeous day,' Poppy said as we exited my car. The day had dawned with grey skies and light drizzle but the forecast had promised blue sky and sunshine by late morning and that's what had been delivered. 'And what a setting. I love it here.'

In place of chairs, there were haybales laid out for the guests with pastel-coloured fleecy blankets draped across them. Instead of one aisle down the middle, there were two, allowing Fizz and Phoebe to walk in at the same time.

We were welcomed by Fizz's long-term best friend, Robbie. 'You can sit wherever you like,' he said before crouching down and telling Imogen in a lower voice, 'but I'd pick a bale with a blanket so the hay doesn't poke you in the bum.'

That made Imogen giggle. As we set off down the furthest aisle, she spotted my parents and ran up to them. There were hugs all round and Mum held on extra tightly to Poppy, expressing her sorrow about Stanley's passing.

Chez shook my hand then gave me a hug. To everyone's relief, he'd decided to stay in Portugal, had picked up the language already and secured himself a job in a garage. He looked like a different man – tanned, toned and with an air of maturity about him.

'Before you ask, I haven't told Lorna I'm here,' he said. 'And I won't be getting in touch.'

'I'm pleased to hear it. Fresh start, eh?'

'Fresh start.'

Shortly after we'd taken our seats, a string quartet began playing and I frowned for a moment as I realised it wasn't a classical piece but couldn't quite place it.

'"Halo",' Poppy whispered. As soon as she said that, I could hear the lyrics to the Beyoncé track in my head.

The first to walk down the aisle were the mothers of the brides – Natasha for Fizz and long-term family friend Rosemary in Phoebe's case, accompanied by her guide dog. Beside me, Imogen excitedly pointed out the flowers decorating the dog's harness. Next were the best men – Barney for Fizz with Phoebe having her friend and colleague Leo. They were followed by bridesmaids Amber, Samantha, Darcie and Zara, all dressed in shades of purple. Finally came Samantha's two little ones – Thomas and Lyra – holding soft toy bride hedgehogs.

Fizz and Phoebe looked absolutely stunning as they walked down the aisles at the same time, smiling across at each other. They were both wearing traditional-style wedding dresses but Fizz's had touches of her favourite colour pink and Phoebe's included some lilac. Phoebe was holding onto Josh's arm and Fizz onto her dad's, and they met at the front of the middle section of guests where Leo and Barney were waiting to take them on to the wedding gazebo.

'Friends, family, a very warm welcome to you on this most special of occasions,' announced the celebrant. 'I'm delighted today to join together in marriage these two beautiful women, Felicity Jade Kinsella and Phoebe Annabelle Corbyn...'

I glanced at Poppy and she smiled back at me, entwining her fingers in mine. At some point next year, this would be us. At Barney and Amber's wedding, Poppy had asked me, *Does it have to be a choice – friendship or passion?* No, it didn't. It was possible to have both. This incredible woman sitting next to me was my best friend and so much more. Our short time together so far had been extraordinary and I couldn't wait to see what was next for us. Although I might have sent a few ideas into the universe. It had served me pretty well so far.

41

POPPY

As Joel smiled at me and squeezed my hand, I knew he was thinking exactly the same as I was – it would be us soon. I'd have expected the idea of getting engaged to a man who'd been a stranger to me only a few months ago would have scared me but it felt so right, as though those stars were always meant to align and bring us together.

Since I'd met Joel, I'd done so many things that had scared me, but every single one had turned out to bring so much joy. I'd therefore decided it was time to stop being afraid and throw myself into life. When Joel had asked me if I wanted to ride a quad bike at Bumblebee Barn, I'd strapped that helmet on and driven my bike through the mud at top speed, squealing and laughing at the same time. I'd bounced on the trampoline at Snowy's gym club. I'd asked Joel if he'd like to sell his place and buy Whisperwood Farmhouse with me. And tonight at the disco in Wildflower Byre, I was going to dance like nobody was watching. I'd admired how Joel had danced at Amber and Barney's wedding with absolute abandon and twirled with his daughter without a care in the world and had thought I could never be like that. Well, I could be and I was. Joel and Imogen had helped me to see that.

The ceremony was beautiful and, as the bridesmaids followed the happy couple up the aisle afterwards, I found my eyes drawn to Samantha and Amber in particular. Their dresses had full skirts but I could just make out Samantha's small pregnancy bump. She'd announced a few weeks ago that she and Josh were expecting their third baby, due in early November. Amber wasn't showing yet but she wasn't far behind Samantha – something which only the family and closest friends of the newlyweds knew. Baby Kinsella was due the first week in December and would be the first baby on both sides of the family.

Many of the guests had risen to follow the bridal party down to Wildflower Byre for the drinks reception and wedding breakfast.

Snowy passed with his grandfather, Eddie, and his twelve-year-old son, Harrison. A talented trampolinist, Harrison had taken Imogen under his wing at his dad's gymnastics club. He smiled and waved at Imogen.

'Can I go with Harrison?' she asked Joel.

'That's fine. See you down there in a bit.'

'Can we hang back until everyone's gone?' Joel said when Imogen left. 'I want to give you something.'

When my eyes widened, he laughed. 'Not that sort of something. I wouldn't be so crass as to propose at someone else's wedding, but it is related.'

Once everyone had gone, he led me onto the wedding gazebo and reached into the pocket inside his suit, producing a small jewellery pouch.

'When we met, I was scared I'd talked myself into the friend zone with you. You challenged me as to why it had to be friendship or passion and showed me how it's possible to have both and be happier than I could ever have imagined. So this is for you.'

He handed me the pouch and I removed the contents, laughing. It was a friendship bracelet with intertwined silver hearts in the middle.

'Friendship and passion,' I said, putting my wrist out so he could fasten it in place. 'I love it.'

'And I love you. I'll make it official one day soon and this'll be us saying *I do* next year.'

'I was thinking why wait when you know you've found what you've always been looking for? What if, when you do propose, the plan is to marry this year?'

'This year?' His smile widened. 'I'm liking the sound of that. Better make sure that proposal is really soon.'

He drew me into a slow and tender kiss then led me down the track in the direction of the music and laughter.

'So, Poppy Wells, have you done anything lately that's scared you?' he asked.

'Just the one thing.'

'What's that?'

I looked around me. There was nobody in sight so I opened my clutch bag. 'I've got something for you too. Close your eyes for a moment.'

He closed them and I took a deep breath as I removed the item and held it out in front of me. 'You can open them now.'

He stared at the item then at me. 'Is that…? You're…'

'There must be something in the water round here,' I said, smiling at him. 'First Samantha, then Amber, and now me.'

He pressed his steepled hands to his lips, blinking back tears. 'I wasn't expecting that.'

'Me neither. Scary, right?'

'Scary, but absolutely bloody fantastic. Oh, my God! Poppy!

We're having a baby!' He looked up at the sky. 'Did you hear that, Stanley and Joy? Your first grandchild. Pretty amazing, eh?'

He wrapped his arms around me and kissed me as though nobody was watching. I'd found my tribe the day I said yes to a much-needed break in East Yorkshire and my new friends weren't the only ones expanding that tribe. I was too. This year had been a sad one but, my goodness, had it been a happy one too and every day just got better and better.

EPILOGUE
JOEL

One year later

'Good evening, everyone!' Cole Crawford called, smiling at the gathering of friends, family and influential locals. 'It's wonderful to see so many of you here tonight to celebrate with us. The past fourteen months have been an incredible time for my family. Last March, my amazing daughter Amber married my wonderful son-in-law Barney and in December they welcomed their first child and mine and Jules's first grandchild, Hayden.'

Everyone looked towards Amber, Barney and Hayden – now five months old – who wriggled in Amber's arms as though aware that all eyes were on him. I glanced down at Imogen standing beside me. Since the arrival of her twin half-brothers – Caleb and Heath – she'd become infatuated with babies, which was just as well because she was surrounded by them. Imogen had been dying to meet Samantha and Josh's son Brody and, later, Hayden, but was a little put out that all four babies were boys. Poppy and I had chosen not to find out the gender of our baby and we'd both been extra delighted to announce to Imogen that she'd got her wish with the arrival of Martha Joy Grainger on 6 February.

'As well as a new addition to their family,' Cole continued, 'Amber and Barney have been busy working on a new addition to their business. Tonight might well be a sneak preview before we open to the public tomorrow but the tills are operational and our team are poised to use them, so feel very welcome to spend, spend, spend!'

Cole paused for laughter and raised a pair of shiny scissors. 'I'm delighted to declare Bumblebee Farm Shop open!'

To applause and cheers, he cut the bright yellow ribbon across the open door and the guests made their way inside. Imogen hung back with me to wait for Poppy.

'I recorded it for you,' I said holding up my phone as Poppy wheeled a sleeping Martha towards us in her pram a few minutes later. She'd been due a feed around ribbon-cutting time and we'd been hoping she'd hold out, but no such luck, so Poppy had taken her into the farmhouse.

'You sweetheart,' she said, kissing me lightly before turning to Imogen. 'Isn't your dad the best?'

Imogen grinned at her, nodding enthusiastically, before peering into the pram and lightly stroking Martha's cheek. Poppy and I smiled at each other and I felt immense gratitude that, despite my troubled history with Tilly, between us we'd somehow managed to raise a kind girl who was so eager to help with her siblings.

Darcie and Harrison appeared at the doorway, spotted Imogen, and beckoned her to join them. She hugged us both and ran towards the farm shop.

'Are you ready to go in?' I asked.

'Let's stay out here for a moment and drink it all in.'

Together we turned towards the next barn over and I slipped

my arm round her waist as she rested her head against my shoulder.

'It's looking great,' she said.

The building work on Bumblebee Bistro had started a couple of months ago and we were aiming for an early autumn opening. Behind the bistro was an enormous vegetable garden and it gave me such a buzz to know that I'd be preparing meals using produce I'd grown on my best mate's land. When I'd been scrabbling around last year wondering what the hell to do with my life if I left the factory, I'd never have imagined I'd end up coming full circle and cooking again. Poppy's genius idea and Tilly's surprising comment that I had a gift for cooking had led me here and I couldn't imagine a role more perfect. I got to work outdoors, I got to experiment with food and, when the bistro opened, I'd have most evenings free to spend with Poppy, Imogen and Martha.

In his speech just now, Cole had described fourteen incredible months for his family but it had also been fourteen incredible months for mine. Chez was still in Portugal and thriving. He was fluent in the language, loved his job and for the past eight months had been dating a Portuguese nurse called Calista. He'd been back to the UK a few times, visiting Harry and Deana the first time to apologise to them for giving them a scare last March and for being so hostile towards Deana when she moved in. Their friendship had gradually got back on track and Harry had asked Chez to be his best man next year after proposing to Deana.

Mum and Dad were still living the dream in Portugal. They'd stayed with us in Honey Bee Croft after Poppy and I had settled in and had visited again after Martha was born, although they'd booked themselves into one of the holiday cottages at Hedgehog Hollow, wanting to give us time and space on our own with our newborn. We'd also visited them in

Portugal and had even had Tilly's approval to take Imogen with us. What an amazing moment it had been to see her board her first aeroplane, take off for the first time, and arrive in a foreign country.

My relationship with Tilly was barely recognisable these days and I put that down to a combination of two things – Poppy's soothing influence and Tilly being run ragged with so many children. It was rare now that Tilly objected to Imogen staying an extra night if she wanted to.

And, of course, I'd been to seven rather than six weddings in the past fourteen months and one of them had been my own – something I'd thought would never happen until Amber got me into thinking positively and manifesting.

Poppy had loved my proposal. The weekend before Fizz and Phoebe's wedding, we'd been looking into getting a kitten but, when we'd visited a rescue centre just outside Whitsborough Bay, we'd both fallen in love with a beautiful black four-year-old moggy called Moby whose owner had passed away suddenly. He'd been wearing a turquoise collar and we'd been told that he identified more as a dog than a cat as he mewed to be let out the house to do his business and loved going for walks on a lead.

We collected him the Saturday after the wedding and, as neither of us had ever walked a cat, I suggested we take Moby for a walk early that evening. It was warm and sunny as we wandered along the track between Honey Bee Croft and Barney's farm with Moby trotting alongside us. As we approached a gate into what Barney called Spring Field, I stopped, frowning.

'I think there's something snagged on Moby's lead.'

Poppy picked Moby up to take a look and, as her fingers touched the engagement ring hooked onto his collar, I got down on bended knee and asked her to marry me. The simple approach had been perfect for us.

* * *

Poppy

The preview opening of Bumblebee Farm Shop was a wonderful evening. I'd helped Zara create my Honey Bee Hugs display but nothing beat going into the farm shop and seeing people around the stand reading the leaflets, smelling and trying the samples, and adding the products to their baskets – especially people I didn't know.

'I'm so proud of you,' Joel said, squeezing my hand as we watched a couple of customers add the full range to their baskets.

I'd cut back on my clients to the point where I only needed to devote a maximum of two days a week to being an accountant, dividing the rest of my days between the bees and Martha and I couldn't wait to fulfil my dream of leaving accountancy behind completely.

We'd been invited back to the farmhouse for a barbeque after the shop closed, but there was somewhere I wanted to visit first. Amber took Imogen and Martha with her while Joel and I rode one of the quad bikes up to the apiary in what we'd called Top Bee in keeping with Barney's field names. Before taking delivery of my new hives, I'd scattered Mum's and Dad's ashes across Top Bee so that my parents would always be with me and the bees. I wanted to share the news of my successful Honey Bee Hugs launch with them.

Joel sat on Mum's bench – which had avoided fire and smoke damage with being at the entrance to the original Honey Bee Croft – and I wandered towards the hives, standing a safe distance away and watching the bees flying in and out for several minutes.

'The farm shop opened this evening,' I said. 'Lots of people were buying my products. It was amazing to see. I re-designed my logo. There's a queen and a worker bee on it now and guess what I've called them? Joy and Stanley. We're going to get stationery and textiles made with them on. Bet you never thought you'd be immortalised as a couple of honey bees!'

They'd never have imagined it, but they'd have absolutely loved it.

'That's it for now. I'll speak to you again soon.'

I blew a kiss into the air and stood there for a couple more minutes before returning to Joel.

'Good chat?' he asked.

'Always.'

I cuddled up to him on the bench, feeling so relaxed. I'd come here on the morning of our wedding last September and sat on the bench on my own, my hands clasped across my expanding stomach, and I'd felt their presence so strongly, wholeheartedly supporting the man I'd found for my happy ever after.

I'd hesitated over who to ask to give me away on our wedding day but had decided on Phil. The ex-husband might be an unusual choice but he was the one who'd given me the confidence to go for it with Joel, pushing me each time I wobbled. I had so many new friends I could have asked to be my bridesmaid but I decided to just have Imogen. Beautiful and attentive, she couldn't have been a more ideal choice.

Pinned to the underside of the lace panels on my wedding dress were Mum's embroidered quote and Dad's robin, so I could have them both with me in spirit.

We'd returned to Bumblebee Barn after the ceremony for a hog roast and barbeque in a marquee. Our guest list had been nothing like the size of Amber and Barney's but the small wedding had been absolutely perfect because we were surrounded by all the important people in our lives – my new tribe.

I FaceTimed Sharon and Ian every couple of weeks and we'd visited each other. Bertie and Cheryl's baby boy was thriving and Phil and Reina were expecting their second baby – another girl – in August. Wilf and Benji were both doing well. They'd been to our wedding and had visited last month to meet Martha, during which time an immediate friendship had formed between Benji and Moby who followed each other everywhere.

'I suppose we'd better head back and see what the girls are up to,' I said to Joel. 'But I'm glad we came and shared it with Mum and Dad.'

He took my hand and we slowly walked towards the quad bike.

'So, Poppy Grainger,' Joel said, 'have you done anything lately that's scared you?'

I laughed, remembering that the last time he'd posed that question, I'd whipped out my positive pregnancy test.

'Other than going into labour?' I teased. 'Actually, no. Because with you by my side, nothing does anymore. What about you?'

'Same answer.'

Reaching the quad bike, we fastened our helmets and Joel got on. I took one last look towards Top Bee and imagined Mum and Dad sitting on the bench. No, they'd be dancing by the bench. They were in this place, in my heart and one day I'd be able to tell their granddaughter all about the journalist and the nurse who'd given up their dreams of travelling the world to focus on a new dream of being exceptional parents to a lost and lonely young woman, her baby daughter and, in time, twenty hives of bees. And hopefully I'd be telling that same story to Martha's brother too. After all, Joel and I had been doing some manifesting and the universe hadn't let us down so far.

As we set off down the farm, I gazed across the fields at the beautiful white farmhouse in the distance and smiled contentedly. I'd never forget that day over a year ago when Joel and I sat in the lounge and fantasised about a future that seemed unattainable. Now we had it all and so much more – our dream businesses, each other, our perfect little family and our forever home at Honey Bee Croft.

ACKNOWLEDGEMENTS

I hope you've enjoyed the third and final trip to Bumblebee Barn. It's always a bit strange when I end a series and say goodbye to the characters who've lived in my head and heart for such a long time. It's especially strange this time as it isn't just a goodbye to the characters from Bumblebee Barn – it's goodbye to those from Hedgehog Hollow too. While writing The Bumblebee Barn Collection, it's been so lovely revisiting the rescue centre team and having a glimpse into their lives beyond the final Hedgehog Hollow book. I particularly loved being able to give Fizz and Phoebe their wedding day at last. I say *at last* because I originally had it in the first book in this series and then the second before it finally felt like the right fit with the story being told in *A Forever Home at Honey Bee Croft*.

As well as this book being the end of the series, it has also been the end of an era for me as this was the final book I worked on with my wonderful editor, Nia Beynon, who left on maternity leave (waves to Nia, her husband and their new baby girl!). Nia left me in the more than capable hands of the wonderful Emily Ruston. They were able to work on the first edits together before Nia left so a huge thank you to them both for helping to shape Joel's and Poppy's emotional journeys into a positive future together and thank you specifically to Emily for being kind with her comments and passionate about my couple.

I knew early on that Joel would be the hero of this story and that he'd find love with a beekeeper, but it took quite some time before Poppy showed up in my head and shared her back story, so there were a few fraught moments writing this book when I wasn't really sure who my heroine was or how I was going to bring the couple together!

I'd originally envisaged a lot more detail about beekeeping and I bought the most stunning book called *The Bee Book* published by DK, authored by Chadwick, Alton, Tennant, Fitz-maurice and Earl. Packed full of pictures, graphics and fabulous detail, it was a wonderful read but the more I learned about beekeeping, the more complicated I realised it was. I love that readers often learn things from my books but there was a definite danger of overwhelming readers with terminology and detail, taking them away from the story I wanted to tell. Therefore, although my heroine is a beekeeper, I've made the beekeeping elements more about the connection Poppy has to her dad, how the bees make her feel and her dreams of a future business rather than the technicalities of beekeeping. It helped that the time of year I chose to set this book was out of season for bees. Thank you to Maria who works for a company who manufacture beehives and who kindly sent me a catalogue and offered me a tour of the factory – very much appreciated.

Thank you to Cindy, a paralegal, for some advice on family law, and Georgiana Harding, an associate solicitor, who connected me to a colleague specialising in family law to look at Joel's situation. Every family matter will be different. The way I've explored Joel's issues with Tilly is representative of the current UK law although I may have described it in a more simplistic way for ease of reading.

According to the NHS at the time of writing, one in eleven people in the UK over the age of sixty-five have dementia. There are several forms and, as with all medical issues, each patient's experience of dementia will be different, and how their loved ones feel and react will be different. If you have experience of this cruel disease, I send you my love and empathy. This story covers Stanley's symptoms and Poppy's reactions. They are fictional people whose experiences may not exactly reflect your own, but what they go through is based on extensive research with huge thanks to the information provided by the NHS and many extremely helpful factsheets and booklets from the Alzheimer's Society. Equally, depression can present itself in various ways and be dealt with differently by each person it touches. If your life has been touched by depression, Chester's experiences might not mirror your own or those of a loved one.

Another issue covered in the book is stalking, with Damon's behaviour escalating until his final act of destruction. As an onlooker, it might be easy to shout at Poppy and tell her that she should have realised that Damon was unstable and turned to the police much sooner, but Poppy's situation is representative of how real people can feel – that, because it's not violent, it can't possibly be stalking or, because they know the person, there's no real threat. But there is. Thank you to www.police.uk and various helpful websites for the FOUR warning signs.

Thank you to a couple of members of my Facebook group, Redland's Readers, for their help in coming up with the names of the rooms and bars in Fennington Hall. My mind had turned to mush and, as always, I knew I could rely on my group – in this case, Lesley Pay and Karen Jackson – for some inspiration. Please feel welcome to join us in Redland's Readers if you haven't done so already.

This book is dedicated to my daughter, Ashleigh, who turned eighteen a month before publication. It therefore felt right to dedicate it to her as she officially turned into an adult. She is a massive Swiftie – a trait which I gave to Imogen. While I was writing this book, Taylor Swift was astounding audiences world-wide with her Eras Tour. I love gigs but I find huge stadiums a little intimidating and was delighted for Ashleigh that she had the opportunity to see Taylor with a friend. I've loved seeing concertgoers raving about her incredible performances but it has disappointed me to see how many people there are who are willing to tear her down and dismiss her songs when they're probably only familiar with a couple of the biggest widely played hits and have never listened to any of her other songs – hits or album tracks – which are full of thoughtful lyrics and beautiful melodies. We can't all like the same music but does that make it right to vehemently slate something that's not to your personal taste? The hate for Taylor Swift is off the scale and it has struck me more than ever that, the more successful a woman becomes, the more hate they're subjected to. It's so incredibly unfair and unjustified, especially in Swift's case. She is such a talented singer, songwriter and performer. I wish my daughter could have entered into adulthood in a world where people aren't quite so cruel. Kindness costs nothing. And breathe!

As always, there are so many people to thank for helping produce the various formats of this book. As these acknowledgements are quite long, I'm just going to list everyone – Cecily Blench, Susan Sugden, Lizzie Gardiner, Claire Fenby, Issy Flynn, Ben Wilson and the rest of the Boldwood Books production team. Thanks to Rebecca Norfolk and Luke R. Francis for their voice narration talents, Rachel Gilbey and the wonderful reviewers on the blog tour, my amazing husband Mark, my fabulous parents, my bestie Sharon Booth, and all the amazing authors within and beyond Boldwood Books who support what I do. Special thanks to the Facebook group 'The Friendly Book Community' who've always been so supportive of my books.

My final thanks are to you, my readers, for loving my worlds and sharing that love with others. Without you, I couldn't keep telling the stories that burn inside me and I'm so grateful every day that your support and encouragement allows me to live my dream, even if putting fingers to keyboard each day with no idea where the story's going can be pretty scary. But you have to *do one thing every day that scares you*, don't you?

Big hugs, Jessica xx

ABOUT THE AUTHOR

Jessica Redland is a million-copy bestseller, writing uplifting stories of love, friendship, family and community. Her Escape to the Lakes books transport readers to the stunning Lake District and her Hedgehog Hollow series takes them to the beautiful countryside of the Yorkshire Wolds.

Sign up to Jessica Redland's mailing list here for news, competitions and updates on future books.

Visit Jessica's website: www.jessicaredland.com

Follow Jessica on social media:

facebook.com/JessicaRedlandAuthor

x.com/JessicaRedland

instagram.com/JessicaRedlandAuthor

bookbub.com/authors/jessica-redland

ALSO BY JESSICA REDLAND

YORKSHIRE WOLDS

Hedgehog Hollow

Finding Love at Hedgehog Hollow New
Arrivals at Hedgehog Hollow Family
Secrets at Hedgehog Hollow
A Wedding at Hedgehog Hollow Chasing
Dreams at Hedgehog Hollow Christmas
Miracles at Hedgehog Hollow

The Bumblebee Barn Collection Healing
Hearts at Bumblebee Barn
A New Dawn at Owl's Lodge
A Forever Home at Honey Bee Croft

THE LAKE DISTRICT

Escape to the Lakes

The Start of Something Wonderful
A Breath of Fresh Air
The Best is Yet to Come

Boldw⊙⊙d

Boldwood Books is an award-winning fiction
publishing company seeking out the best
stories from around the world.

Find out more at www.boldwoodbooks.com

Join our reader community for brilliant books,
competitions and offers!

Follow us
@BoldwoodBooks
@TheBoldBookClub

Sign up to our weekly
deals newsletter

https://bit.ly/BoldwoodBNewsletter

Printed in Great Britain
by Amazon

57015536R00205